Stolen

A Prairie Heritage, Book 5

by
Vikki Kestell

Faith-Filled Fiction™

A Division of Growing Up in God
www.faith-filledfiction.com | www.vikkikestell.com

A Prairie Heritage

Prequel: *Land of Dust and Tears* (free Kindle download)
Book 1: *A Rose Blooms Twice*
Book 2: *Wild Heart on the Prairie*
Book 3: *Joy on This Mountain*
Book 4: *The Captive Within*
Book 5: *Stolen*
Book 6: *Lost Are Found*

Scripture quotations taken from
The King James Version (KJV), Public Domain.

New Living Translation (NLT)
Scripture quotations marked NLT are taken from the
Holy Bible, New Living Translation, copyright 1996, 2004.
Used by permission of Tyndale House Publishers, Inc.,
Wheaton, Illinois 60189

Stolen
Vikki Kestell

Available in Kindle and Print Format
>**Denver, 1910:** *Stolen* returns to Denver and Palmer House—a most extraordinary refuge for young women rescued from prostitution—and to the lives of Rose Thoresen, Joy Thoresen Michaels, and their unorthodox "family."
>
>Taking up where *The Captive Within* leaves off, *Stolen* finds Mei-Xing safe, but after six harrowing months of captivity, Mei-Xing stuns those who love her when she returns to Palmer House *with child*.
>
>If Su-Chong's mother, Fang-Hua Chen, discovers that her son, now dead, has left behind a child, will she allow Mei-Xing to keep him—or will she set in motion plans to steal him away? Will O'Dell, Martha Palmer, Minister Liáng, and others concerned for the safety of Mei-Xing and her child be forced to face off with those who would see Mei-Xing and the work of Palmer House destroyed?

A Rose Blooms Twice
Vikki Kestell

Available in Kindle and Print Format
>Rose Brownlee has suffered more loss than most people can endure. Now she must find a purpose and a way to move on with her life.
>
>Will she bow to conventional wisdom or will she, like Abraham of old, choose to follow where God leads her . . . even to a wild and strange land she does not know?
>
>Set in the American prairie of the late 1800s, this story of loss, disillusionment, rebirth, and love will inspire, challenge, and encourage you.

Wild Heart on the Prairie
Vikki Kestell

Available in Kindle and Print Format

Brothers Jan (Yahn) and Karl Thoresen have left their native land of Norway and braved many perils and hardships to bring their families to America—the land of freedom and hope. Like thousands of others, Jan and his wife Elli long for the opportunity of a better life and future for their children.

After enduring an ocean crossing and the arduous journey west, they encounter a land so vast and wide that it defies mastery. Jan finds that his struggles are not only with the land, but with a restless and unmanageable heart. Will Jan find a way to overcome this wild land or will the prairie master him?

Wild Heart on the Prairie is chronologically both the prequel and the companion to *A Rose Blooms Twice*.

Joy on This Mountain
Vikki Kestell

—Finalist in the 2014 Selah Christian Book Awards—

Available in Kindle and Print Format

Joy on This Mountain is the blazing sequel to the breakthrough historical novels, *A Rose Blooms Twice* and *Wild Heart on the Prairie*.

The year is 1908: The little town of Corinth, Colorado, lies in the gateway to the majestic Rocky Mountains just west of Denver . . . just far enough from the city to avoid close scrutiny, but close enough to be accessible. Few know of the wickedness hidden in the small town, so picturesquely set in the foothills of the mighty mountains.

The legacy of Jan and Rose has far-reaching and unexpected consequences.

The Captive Within
Vikki Kestell

Available in Kindle and Print Format

The Captive Within opens the day after *Joy on This Mountain* ends. The two infamous houses of Corinth, Colorado, are closed and the young women who had been imprisoned there have been released. Soon after, Rose and Joy leave Corinth to establish a home and a haven for "their" girls in Denver.

Before long, Rose and Joy face a heartrending challenge: What does it take to unlock and free the soul of a defiled woman? And as they wrestle for a foothold in Denver, Rose discovers that the long abandoned house given to them hides a dark secret of its own.

Lost Are Found
Vikki Kestell

Available in Kindle and Print Format

Joy Thoresen Michaels has lost the two most precious people in her life: her husband and her only child. She cannot receive her husband back from the dead, but she has hope for her son—hope that he will be recovered:

> "I spoke a moment ago about my prairie heritage—the enduring faith my papa and mama lived as an example for me. It is because of their faith that I have such hope for Edmund even though he is, today, lost to us.
>
> "You see, what is lost to us is not—*is not*—lost to God! I remember Papa saying this very thing: *In God, the lost are found.* Our Lord sees the entire world—and nothing in all of his creation is hidden to him! I am comforted to know that wherever Edmund is, *God is there with him.*"

Four families bind themselves in a solemn pledge: They vow to never stop searching for Edmund and to never stop trusting that God *will* restore him to them, whether in this life or the next.

Lost Are Found, the conclusion of this spiritually rich series, chronicles how God answers those who utterly trust in him, no matter the circumstances—*and no matter how long the wait.*

Forward

The God who made us is concerned with all that happens in this life—but his purposes span eternity, and his purposes are great.

When we live without God's infinite perspective, the disappointments and losses we encounter in this life will defeat us; but when our hearts steadfastly focus on God's eternal purposes, every transient pain or sorrow glows with the sure promises of tomorrow.

—Vikki Kestell

Acknowledgements

Many thanks to my esteemed proofreaders, **Cheryl Adkins, Greg McCann,** and **Jan England**, who share in the work of this ministry and who will share in its eternal rewards.

To My Readers

This book is a work of fiction, what I term "faith-filled fiction," intended to demonstrate how people of God should and can respond to difficult and dangerous situations with courage and conviction. The characters and events that appear in this book are not based on any known persons or historical facts; the challenges described are, however, very real, both historically and contemporarily.

I give God all the glory.

Chapter 1

These all died in faith,
not having received the promises,
but having seen them afar off,
and were persuaded of them,
and embraced them,
and confessed that they were
strangers and pilgrims
on the earth.
(Hebrews 11:13)

(Journal Entry, May 10, 1910)

O Father, Mei-Xing is safe! How I thank you! Through great struggles, Mr. O'Dell found where Su-Chong Chen had kept her a prisoner since November and brought her home to us at Palmer House. We are so grateful, Lord, for you guiding him.

I shudder when I think of Mei-Xing locked inside an airless, windowless room for six months. I grieve to think of the hardships and fear she experienced—and yet you sustained her, Lord. Thank you.

With all that has happened these past four days, I have had scarce time or energy to chronicle in my journal, so I must begin now or I shall soon be too far behind. We are still celebrating Mei-Xing's return and making adjustments—chief of which is preparing for a new baby in the house.

Doctor Murphy has been to see Mei-Xing. Her dry, cracked lips, so painful to her, are healing, and he declares her to be in relatively good health. This is remarkable given the great ordeal she suffered.

After speaking to her and examining her, the doctor believes her baby will arrive in the fall, likely late September or early October. Mei-Xing is such a tiny thing; I would have judged her pregnancy to be near term if the doctor had not said differently!

Mei-Xing requires clothing for her pregnancy. Her only dress at present is the great, oversized thing she arrived in—stolen, she says, by Su-Chong. She tells us that he often burgled homes and stores in the night, stealing food and whatever else they needed.

Of course, her clothing and other possessions from before her disappearance are in her room here at Palmer House, but none of those clothes fit her—she must have maternity garments until the baby is born. Mrs. Palmer pressed a more-than-generous gift on us to address this need.

Because Mei-Xing was confined indoors for so many months, the doctor has advised a regimen of regular exercise: careful walking out-of-doors in the fresh air and sunshine and plenty of wholesome food. He speaks of her bodily well-being, but I must also consider her emotional well-being.

Mei-Xing declined to attend church Sunday. She is, understandably, still weak from her ordeal, but it is likely that she fears censure. Perhaps Pastor Carmichael can encourage her on that point.

Breona confides to me a related matter: Mei-Xing is often terrified. Breona stays close by her, for although Mei-Xing knows that Su-Chong is dead and can no longer harm her, she suffers from nervousness during the day and bad dreams and wakefulness at night.

Breona believes Mei-Xing worries that Su-Chong's mother, if she were to ever have knowledge of her son's baby, would come for him. It is of grave concern to Mei-Xing and, I confess, to me also.

Lord, please give us your wisdom.

Four days after Mei-Xing's return, Palmer House—a most extraordinary refuge for young women rescued from prostitution—remained in a happy uproar.

I cannot stop smiling, Rose mused. *Thank you forever, Lord, for bringing Mei-Xing, the daughter of my heart, safely home!* She looked around the breakfast table. *And thank you for our girls, who are content and growing in you, Lord.*

Tabitha and Breona, once at sharp odds with each other, had their heads together, discussing household duties and plans. Sara and Mei-Xing were speaking in low voices with Corrine listening and nodding.

Jenny, who was relatively new to the house, sat between Flora and Maria, spellbound as Mr. Wheatley regaled them with yet another tall tale. Across from Mr. Wheatley, Alice and Marion— who had only arrived at Palmer House that week—scarcely touched their food as the old gent spun his tale.

Marit and Nancy shuttled between the kitchen and dining room, bringing out platters and pitchers and depositing them on the table. Marit and Billy's young son, Will, bounced on Billy's knee. Spying his mother and the steaming platters of food, Will shrieked his joyous readiness for the morning meal.

When all were seated, they thanked God for his bounty. Will hollered an unabashed "Amen" and the meal began. Rose glanced around the table, a bit disappointed that Joy and Grant, her daughter and son-in-law, were absent. They now took their breakfasts in their cottage behind Palmer House.

Since the day Grant had been diagnosed with a heart condition, Joy had been safeguarding Grant's energy, sparing him from situations or tasks that overtaxed his body. Grant had reduced his work schedule at their fine furnishings store to two days a week— and for a mere two hours those days. It was the walk to and from the trolley that was most fatiguing for him.

But there was something else . . . *something about Joy*. Rose's brow puckered as she tried to put her finger on it.

"I thank ye for coming to see me, Mr. O'Dell." Martha Palmer was ensconced in a chair set upon a low dais in the corner of her parlor. The elderly woman's frail body was bent over, nearly in half. Even seated, she leaned forward upon a cane for support.

Mrs. Palmer could not lift her head to look up; she was forced to turn her head to the side to see visitors. The inches added by the dais meant that she did not have to twist her neck quite so far.

Edmund O'Dell, Pinkerton agent, was seated in a chair to the side of the dais, placing him eye-to-eye with his hostess. He, too, used a cane these days. It rested against the arm of his overstuffed chair, near his stylish derby.

"I came as soon as I received your message."

The old woman nodded, her shock of white hair waving a little as she did. "Quite so. Quite so. And I thank ye. Can you guess why I have asked to speak with you?"

O'Dell cast his mind over the events of the last week. They had not been far from his thoughts. "It must concern Mei-Xing."

"Yes. The girl has come to mean a great deal to me. A great deal."

She nodded again and her thin hands trembled upon the head of her cane. "You saved her, Mr. O'Dell," she whispered. "You saved her and brought her home. For that you have my undying gratitude."

O'Dell did not respond immediately and the room dropped into quiet. The ticking of the mantel clock and the intermittent drone of a fly in the parlor window were the only sounds for long moments.

He sighed. "Thank you, but I must give credit where it is due."

O'Dell shifted in his seat. His hip was troubling him. The fact was, he was worn, physically. A few months back he'd taken a beating he hoped never to repeat in his lifetime. He had nearly died and still felt the damage deep in his body.

But inside? In his soul? That was a different story.

It is well with my soul, O'Dell rejoiced.

"I would never have found Mei-Xing if God had not intervened," he admitted. "If he had not directed . . . so many things."

"Oh?" Martha leaned toward him a bit. "Would you indulge an old woman and tell me about it?"

O'Dell shrugged and smiled. "It would take . . . time."

"I have nothing else more important, Mr. O'Dell. And I love to hear what God has done."

His smile broadened a little. "Perhaps a pot of tea to carry us through?"

"An excellent idea, Mr. O'Dell!" Mrs. Palmer rang the little bell on the side table. "Sadie will be here with it directly. Why don't you begin?"

He did, but his thoughts wandered as he recited the events of the last six months.

So much evil—and so much more of God's grace! O'Dell mused. *Dean Morgan and Su-Chong Chen's escape from the justice they were due. Mei-Xing taken and missing for half a year. Both events set in motion by Su-Chong's vindictive mother, Fang-Hua.*

Long nights in a Seattle hospital and longer nights recovering in a secret house on the outskirts of the city. Minister Liáng . . . telling me of the God of Grace. Bao Shin Xang, Su-Chong's treacherous cousin—repentant and forgiven. Misdirection from Morgan's shifty uncle, Freddy Fetch. And ministering angels dressed in black habits and white wimples.

When O'Dell finished, his recounting had taken two hours and two pots of tea, with Mrs. Palmer only interrupting to ask clarifying questions. The room was quiet again as Mrs. Palmer mulled over what she had heard.

"Extraordinary, Mr. O'Dell. Almost unbelievable." She thought a minute more. "So now we know who Mei-Xing's parents are—and who is responsible for sending her to *that place* . . . up the mountain."

O'Dell nodded. "I will be leaving for Chicago shortly"—he cracked a wry smile—"to prove to my boss and his superiors that I'm still alive. Then I must return to Seattle and meet with Minister Liáng. He and Bao are anxious to hear the details of Mei-Xing's rescue."

"Will you also meet with Mei-Xing's parents, Mr. and Mrs. Li, now that she has been found? Will you be the one bearing the news to them that she is alive?"

O'Dell rubbed his chin. "Sadly, no. It is Mei-Xing's decision. I have stayed in Denver these last few days, hoping I could persuade her to go home or at least allow Minister Liáng to speak to her father and mother but . . ."

"But?"

"Her parents have believed their daughter to be dead for more than two years. As much as I have tried to convince Mei-Xing otherwise, she has chosen to let them continue in that belief."

"Why ever so?" Mrs. Palmer demanded, growing agitated.

O'Dell's laugh was sardonic. "While I was recovering in Seattle, I learned something of the politics of these two powerful clans, the Li and Chen families, Mrs. Palmer. Mei-Xing would rather let sleeping dogs lie—or, perhaps more aptly, *let sleeping dragons lie*—than to arouse them."

He bent a resigned look on the old woman. "Mei-Xing has a child on the way. She will do nothing to jeopardize his safety and future—particularly where it concerns *Fang-Hua Chen*."

Martha Palmer frowned and her wrinkled face folded into deeper lines. "I don't agree with allowing sleeping dogs to lie, Mr. O'Dell, proverbial or otherwise. In my experience sleeping dogs tend to wake up and bite when least expected."

O'Dell stared back at her with perfect understanding. "I couldn't agree more."

"Well? What are we to do, then?"

O'Dell shifted and rose to his feet, wincing as his hip complained. He leaned the weight of the throbbing leg on his cane.

"As I mentioned, I will be leaving for Chicago soon, possibly tomorrow." He nodded, as though confirming the departure date to himself. "When I finish there and return to Seattle, Minister Liáng and I will talk further on this. More importantly, we will pray. God will guide us."

He reached for the derby that was perched on the arm of his chair. "I know you care for Mei-Xing. I know you care about the women of Palmer House and the important work they do. In them we share a common bond and a common concern."

Martha Palmer nodded.

O'Dell's eyes were serious. "I also know you have the resources to protect them, whereas I . . ."

She nodded again, once. "I take your point. I will make arrangements immediately. However, the few men the Pinkerton Agency provided last fall proved insufficient. Will you advise me?"

"Thank you," O'Dell answered quietly. "I would be happy to recommend a reliable party, someone whose experience and character I trust. He will employ a number of men sufficient for the job."

"That would be most welcome. Please keep in touch, Mr. O'Dell."

Martha Palmer did not stand but she offered him her hand. As he took it, she grasped hold and would not let go until he leaned close to her.

"That girl's well-being is of utmost importance to me, Mr. O'Dell." Her voice caught. "If, when you return to Seattle, you hear anything concerning her safety, I would be much obliged if you would act in her interests. I promise you, *I will spare no expense.*"

O'Dell squeezed her hand. "Then I will count on you to watch over her and Palmer House here, and you may depend on me to act when needed."

As O'Dell maneuvered his painful hip down Mrs. Palmer's front steps, he thought on the other reason he needed to leave Denver soon: *Cal Judd.* Judd had served half of his meager one-year sentence and O'Dell was already hearing rumors of an early release from Groves, Denver's police chief.

I must plan to be far from Denver when Judd walks out of prison, O'Dell warned himself, not for the first time. As he limped to the car Mrs. Palmer had called for him, he added, *Judd has had months to plan how he will make me pay for interfering with his business—and worse, for helping Esther to escape from him.*

He scowled. *If my body weren't so deucedly weak I would stay and settle with the scoundrel once and for all.*

O'Dell wasn't accustomed to running for cover—and he didn't much like it. It smacked of cowardice and, just as Martha Palmer had said, sleeping dogs left to their own devices usually did awake and bite when least expected.

He reached into his breast pocket for a cigar, but his pocket was empty. O'Dell chuckled at the power of habit. For some reason, he hadn't felt right about replenishing his cigar supply; the need for them had started to fall away, even if his old habits still occasionally surprised him.

O'Dell frowned as his thoughts again turned to Cal Judd. *I would rather finish this business with Judd and never again worry about leading him to those living at Palmer House*, he fretted.

Then his thoughts turned toward the little house on the outskirts of Seattle where Bao Shin Xang still hid from Fang-Hua Chen. O'Dell didn't blame Bao for hiding—Fang-Hua, rich, powerful, and without conscience, was actively seeking to destroy him. Bao had once been Fang-Hua's trusted instrument but, since his defection, he was a hunted man.

At least I need no longer worry about Dean Morgan. Bao's sources inside Fang-Hua's house had assured them that Morgan had fled Seattle for parts unknown. Morgan hoped to never encounter Fang-Hua Chen again.

O'Dell had his own experience with Fang-Hua to reflect on. It was she who had ordered her thugs to thrash O'Dell and leave him to die.

I should have died, O'Dell vividly recalled, *I would have died, but for God himself sparing my life.*

O'Dell had spent weeks in the hospital and weeks recovering in the little house Minister Liáng had rented to hide O'Dell from Fang-Hua. Now it was Bao who hid there from Fang-Hua, but he was not alone: The same nurse who had cared for O'Dell when he was released from the hospital was Bao's companion.

Darla.

When O'Dell had left Seattle two weeks ago, Darla had asked if he would write to her. He had agreed—but he had not done so as yet. He had sent only a short and cryptic wire to Minister Liáng: *Luke 15:6.* O'Dell knew Liáng would understand when he looked for and read the verse,

And when he cometh home,
he calleth together his friends and neighbours,
saying unto them, Rejoice with me;
for I have found my sheep which was lost.

The newspapers were carrying the news that Su-Chong, an escapee from the Denver jail, was dead as the result of being shot during the commission of a burglary—but the papers carried nothing of Mei-Xing.

O'Dell's influence with Chief Groves had seen to that: Mei-Xing had been removed from the apartment where Su-Chong had hidden her—and where he had bled to death—without local reporters being the wiser. Liáng would read the wire and work out that O'Dell had found Mei-Xing and that she was safe.

However, Liáng would *not* know the whole story until O'Dell provided him with it. *He would not know that Mei-Xing was carrying Fang-Hua's grandchild until O'Dell returned to Seattle.*

O'Dell shivered. Minister Liáng, Bao, and Miss Greenbow deserved to know the details—details that could not be trusted to a letter. But first O'Dell had orders to report to the Chicago Pinkerton office. He would wire Liáng again to say his return to Seattle would be delayed.

O'Dell stepped into his hotel room, scrawled the contents of the wire to Liáng, and began to pack his bag.

Two uniformed policemen delivered the news of Su-Chong's death to his parents. Su-Chong's father, Wei Lin Chen, displayed no emotion as the officers described where Su-Chong's body had been discovered and how he had died. Fang-Hua also remained silent and implacable, but the strength left her legs and she sank to the floor.

Servants rushed to assist her; Wei Lin gave little attention to her distress.

Su-Chong had died a bad death.

He was unmarried. He had no children to prepare the funeral for him. He was worthy of no respect—and the manner of his death was a further disgrace to his family.

His body would not be brought into the Chen's house or courtyard. No white cloth would hang over the front doorway to the Chen's home proclaiming their loss. No gong would stand to the left of their doorway. Friends and relatives would not visit or gather to mourn.

His body would be kept at a funeral home and his parents would not publicly grieve him. The funeral would be short, small, and silent.

Fang-Hua twisted her face into a mask that betrayed no emotion, and yet the emotions roiled within. *My son! My son is dead!* Her pain slammed inside her chest with each thudding beat of her heart.

Later, Fang-Hua and Wei Lin read the newspaper reports of Su-Chong's death without speaking. They read how he had been shot *while stealing.*

A bad death indeed.

Anger flared in Fang-Hua's breast—anger toward the chit of a girl who had cast off Su-Chong's affections, causing him to leave his home and family in the first place. Anger toward the man she called *Reggie* for taking Su-Chong into his service, making Su-Chong vulnerable to arrest. Even anger toward her son for forsaking his familial duty, for his obsession with a woman—an inconsequential *girl*—not worthy of him.

The newspapers made no mention of Mei-Xing Li, and Fang-Hua's eyes narrowed. To where had the little whore disappeared? Fang-Hua's men had searched all of Denver for months and had discovered no trace of Mei-Xing.

She toyed with the possibility that Su-Chong had killed Mei-Xing and hidden her body where it would never be found. The idea did not sit right with her. No, *somehow* the girl had escaped—and that thought only served to incense Fang-Hua more.

Where has the little chit hidden herself all this time? she raged. *Why were my men unable to find her?*

The days after Su-Chong's body was delivered to the funeral home were no different from any ordinary days. His burial was accomplished with no fanfare, no publicity, no ceremonial respect. Afterward, Wei Lin went to his office and Fang-Hua attended to her duties.

Outwardly Fang-Hua was cool and composed, but inwardly she screamed in pain and frustration. And unease.

She watched Wei Lin warily. Her husband had to be considering the deeper implications of Su-Chong's death on his own lineage and the Chen family line. Those implications terrified Fang-Hua.

The fact was, Wei Lin required another son, and Fang-Hua could not give him one.

The one son Fang-Hua had borne and the financial power she wielded in her own right had been all that had kept Wei Lin attached to her. *But now Su-Chong was gone.* Wei Lin could—would likely—divorce Fang-Hua and marry a young woman capable of giving him many sons.

A servant interrupted to announce unexpected visitors: Jinhai and Ting-Xiu Li.

What? The little whore's parents? The rage burning within Fang-Hua tore at her belly. With great self-control she tamped it down.

I can give nothing away, she whispered to herself. *I must speak and show nothing to make them or Wei Lin suspicious of me.*

She no longer had to fear her son exposing her secrets to her husband. That danger, at least, was past. Only Bao Shin Xang and Mei-Xing Li—*a living Mei-Xing who should be dead!*—posed threats.

Prudence required Fang-Hua to remain unperturbed and gracious to the Lis, thanking them for their visit, though it was unwarranted—even inappropriate!—given the circumstances of Su-Chong's death.

The servant ushered Jinhai and Ting-Xiu Li into the room. They were dressed in formal black, the only color suitable for an unmarried son's death. Jinhai bowed and his wife followed suit.

How I hate them! Fang-Hua sneered within herself. *Oh, if only Jinhai knew what I know, how I have defiled their daughter,* she gloated. But, of course, she and Wei Lin were "close family friends" with the Lis. Fang-Hua would be forced to accept their condolences—uncalled for as they were—most graciously.

What was this? She had not been following the conversation and now Jinhai was babbling about something . . . something unsuitably sincere for the occasion.

". . . and so we grieved as you must be grieving, behind closed doors, not even able to mourn her publicly," Jinhai murmured, his eyes downcast. "We were cut to our cores, and nothing could console us. Until we met with a Christian minister. He showed us from the Christian Bible how to have a relationship with the living God, the Creator of all things.

"Such peace we now have in our souls!" he exclaimed. "Such happiness in our hearts. And so we have come, humbly, to offer our sympathy and to also offer to share what we have found in Jesus, the Christian Savior. We—"

"*Thank* you . . ." Fang-Hua interrupted, drawling her words, "for your *concern* for us. Your friendship with our family has always been and will always remain a great . . . *honor*."

Although her words were spoken in a soft and silky voice and her face remained placid, her eyes sought out Jinhai's and hardened.

You should know that I hate you and yours, Fang-Hua told him with her eyes. *With my words I honor you, but look into my soul, Jinhai Li. Look deeply and see how I despise you.*

Jinhai stammered to a stop, the hairs on the back of his neck pricking and rising. Fang-Hua's gleaming eyes belied the sweet words she mouthed. The ill will emanating from her was palpable.

Disturbed and shaken, Jinhai bowed deeply; his wife, although confused, followed suit. "Please call on us if we can assist you in any way," Jinhai murmured, his words soft. He backed away, pulling his wife with him, and left the Chen home.

Chapter 2

O'Dell stepped off the train in Chicago's Union Station. The late afternoon air was thick with steam and smoke, the platforms bustling and crowded. O'Dell wound his way through the throng until he reached the street entrance on Canal. There he caught a cab to the Pinkerton offices.

With a flourish, O'Dell tossed his derby onto the hat rack in Parson's office and grinned. Parsons scowled in return.

"Took your time reporting in, O'Dell," Parsons growled. He eyed the cane O'Dell used to maneuver himself into the single chair before Parson's desk.

"Don't mind the cane; my mind is functioning at full throttle," O'Dell remarked. He looked about Parson's office. Not much had changed in O'Dell's absence—except O'Dell. He wondered if Parsons could see that change in him.

"Well. Good work on tracking Su-Chong Chen and recovering Miss Li. The Denver powers-that-be have sung your praises to the heavens."

O'Dell shrugged.

"Yeah, well I regret to tell you, we have had no *paying* clients sing your praises in months," Parsons growled. "Management, while happy for Pinkerton to garner recognition and glory, breaks out in a rash when its top missing-persons detective continues to draw a salary but hasn't brought in a dime—in how long?"

Parsons made a show of consulting papers on his desk. "Oh. Yes. More than six months!"

"Reporting for duty, sir," O'Dell smiled. *Perhaps now is not the best time to bring up my return to Seattle.*

Parsons studied him. "Jackson is leaving."

O'Dell understood at once. Management of the Denver office was on the table. Again.

"Jackson wasn't in charge long. He get a better offer somewhere?"

"His wife is ill. He's taking her to drier climates. Arizona, I heard."

O'Dell nodded but said nothing.

"Chief Groves and Marshal Pounder have both petitioned Pinkerton management to assign you there. They say you work well with law enforcement. They trust you, and trust is in short supply in Colorado."

O'Dell snorted. "Denver is not, shall we say, a hospitable environment for me at present."

"Cal Judd?"

"Uh-huh." O'Dell studied his fingernails.

Parsons knew the offer was declined. "I want all of your reports regarding Su-Chong Chen and Miss Li written and filed in two days." He handed O'Dell a sizable folder. "We'll meet again then. Familiarize yourself with the details of the three cases in this folder. Since you've demonstrated an oversized penchant for *pro bono* work, management insists that I assign your next cases and oversee them."

So I won't be returning to Seattle right away after all—I will have to send further regrets to Liáng. O'Dell sighed but kept the frustration off his face.

"No problem. I'll get started on the reports. Same desk?"

Mr. Wheatley shuffled down the hall to answer the ringing of the front doorbell of Palmer House. "Good morning, Mrs. Palmer!" He greeted the old woman with real affection. She leaned heavily on the arm of her driver, Benton, and on her cane.

"Good morn' t' ye, Mr. Wheatley! I would see Mrs. Thoresen if she is at home." Without waiting for an answer, Martha Palmer tottered over the threshold and hobbled into the parlor off the left hand side of the hallway.

"Yes, ma'am; I will let her know you are here." But Mr. Wheatley did not move away from the door—away from the sight of nine sturdy men lingering on the porch. "I, uh—" He left the door open and hastened after Mrs. Palmer.

"Mrs. Palmer, shall I ask the, uh, gentlemen on the porch to join you?"

"Not just yet, if you please."

He shuffled back to the entry. "I beg your pardon," he muttered. He closed the door on the men and went in search of Miss Rose. He found her in the kitchen near the back of the house going over the menus with Marit.

"Miss Rose, Mrs. Palmer to see you. She is waiting in the parlor."

"Goodness!" Rose jumped up, straightened her skirt and collar, and patted her hair. She walked briskly to the front of the house and into the parlor.

"Good morning, Mrs. Palmer! It is a pleasure to see you this morning."

"Good day t' ye, Mrs. Thoresen. Do you have a few minutes to spare for me?"

"Certainly. Would you care for tea? Perhaps one of Marit's baked treats?"

"I would indeed," Martha Palmer replied, her eyes gleaming.

"Would you like Mei-Xing to join us?"

But Mrs. Palmer pressed her lips together and slowly shook her head. "No, thank you. Not at present, if you please."

"I see." Rose didn't see, but knew Mrs. Palmer would have a reason behind her visit and would soon tell it to her. "Let me just speak to Marit. I believe she has a nice almond cake this morning."

When they were settled and Rose had passed a steaming cup to Mrs. Palmer, the elderly woman began. "I asked Mr. O'Dell to visit me before he left."

"Yes?"

"He and I agree on a topic of some importance."

Rose set her cup on the little table near her chair and waited.

"I will be quite frank with you, Mrs. Thoresen. Even though she has come back to us, Mei-Xing is not safe, and neither is her child. Our Mr. O'Dell has told me a great deal about the man who abducted her *and his mother*—that witch-woman in Seattle.

"Mr. O'Dell says that all the while Mei-Xing was held prisoner by Su-Chong, his mother was seeking to find and destroy her! Now that Mei-Xing has been recovered, Mr. O'Dell fears this *woman* will again look for Mei-Xing both to do away with her and possibly to take her child."

Rose sighed and looked down at her hands folded in her lap. "I have reason to believe that Mei-Xing herself is worried on the same account—that Su-Chong's mother will hear she has a grandchild and attempt to take him."

"We must not allow that, Mrs. Thoresen. So I have taken it upon myself to provide the security and protection she and the child will need—and better than last time, I might add."

"Oh?"

Martha Palmer's head wagged over her cane. "Yes. Nine men stand on your porch at this very moment. Mr. O'Dell recommended their leader, who hand-picked each of them. They are now in my employ. Two of them will be on guard at all times. An automobile is at their disposal for Mei-Xing's needs. When she leaves the house, they will accompany her. When she sleeps, they will watch over her and this house."

As Mrs. Palmer spoke Rose's brows lifted. "How long will they guard her and the baby?"

Martha Palmer's eyes narrowed. "As long as there is a threat, Mrs. Thoresen. As long as there is a threat."

Her voice roughened. "I am an old woman. I have no family other than a nephew I have not seen in years. You may not realize this, but you and the girls in this house are very dear to me—as dear as family can be. And Mei-Xing . . ."

Her voice trembling as she spoke, Martha Palmer declared, "I will not allow anyone to lay a finger on her."

Rose nodded, grateful. "I thank you, Mrs. Palmer. Your protection will be very welcome to Mei-Xing. To all of us."

"Good. Then I would like a few words with Mei-Xing—alone, if you please—after which I will introduce the men in my employ. They will assume their duties today."

"I will send her to you."

Rose left the room and went in search of Mei-Xing. She found her at the kitchen table with Breona. "Mei-Xing, Mrs. Palmer would like a word in private with you."

"Yes, ma'am. Thank you."

Mei-Xing entered the parlor and closed the door behind her. "You wished to see me, Mrs. Palmer?"

"Yes, my dear. Come sit by me so I may speak to you." When Mei-Xing had settled in a chair near Mrs. Palmer, the old woman laid a fragile hand upon Mei-Xing's.

"Do you wish to continue with me in your previous position?"

Mei-Xing was surprised and at a loss for words. "I-I did not think it would be possible . . . at this time . . . in my condition." She looked down, shamed.

"My dear, I go out less and less these days. It will not be necessary for you to go into public while you are expecting."

Mei-Xing thought and then said, "But . . . in a few months, when the . . . baby comes?"

Mrs. Palmer nodded. "When you came to work for me I offered you two options. One of them was to live in my home. I would like you to consider moving to my home again."

Mei-Xing cocked her head, just a little, a familiar indication that she was thinking. "I thank you for your generous proposal," she replied quietly, "I am sincerely grateful but . . . but this is my home. I regret that I cannot accept your offer."

Mrs. Palmer cleared her throat. "I thought as much, but I wanted to see if you might change your mind."

"I shall be sorry to leave your employ," Mei-Xing whispered.

"Nonsense. You are not leaving my employ! You will continue living here and I see no reason why you cannot bring the babe to work with you. When he is a little older, one of the maids will watch him when necessary. Let me make myself perfectly clear: I require your services and will make whatever accommodations are needed."

Mei-Xing drew a shaky breath. "I cannot believe you are being so kind to me. But I . . . will not my having a baby outside of marriage reflect poorly on you?"

Martha Palmer made a noise that held more than a hint of derision. "I stopped concerning myself with what people thought of me a long time ago. I care only for my Savior's opinion and that of those he has given me to" —her voice caught for just a second— "to love."

She cleared her throat. "So. You will assume your duties as soon as it is practical. When your laying in comes, you will take as much time as you need to regain your strength. When you come back to work, the child will come with you. Are we agreed?"

Mei-Xing nodded. "Yes, ma'am. You are more than considerate!"

"Posh! Now that is settled, we have but one more piece of business to conclude."

Mei-Xing looked confused. "I beg your pardon?"

Martha patted Mei-Xing's hand once more. "I spent some time with Mr. O'Dell before he left for Chicago. You have been a very private person about your past, my dear, but some of that must give way now for the safety of your child, hey?"

Mei-Xing's head jerked up and her face paled with alarm.

"Yes," Martha insisted. "I now know about this baby's father and his unscrupulous mother. We must take precautions, you and I, to ensure your continued safety and that of your child. To that end, I have made certain arrangements.

"Please tell Mrs. Thoresen that I would see her and you in the great room. And ask Mr. Wheatley to show the gentlemen on the porch to the same room."

A few minutes later Rose, Mei-Xing, Breona, Mr. Wheatley, Mrs. Palmer, and nine strangers faced each other in the house's great room. Mrs. Palmer introduced one of the strangers, a tall man with dark brown hair.

"This is Mr. Gresham and his associates. Mr. O'Dell recommended Mr. Gresham, and I have hired him to oversee the safety and security of Mei-Xing, her baby, and this house. Mr. Gresham, will you please outline the details you and I agreed upon?"

"Yes, ma'am, Mrs. Palmer. I am Samuel Gresham. I am an old friend of Mr. O'Dell's, with whom I believe you are well acquainted?"

When he received nods in the affirmative, Gresham continued. "Mr. O'Dell can vouch for my experience and professionalism in the field of personal security. My men and I, at Mrs. Palmer's direction, will work in armed, two-man shifts to provide protective services to Miss Li at all times and on all days."

He addressed himself to Mei-Xing. "Miss Li, once you are acquainted with us, we hope you will feel comfortable with our presence. We will provide automobile service for you to travel from here to Mrs. Palmer's home and back each day; we will accompany you—discreetly, of course—on any outings; and we will mount a guard on this house at the end of each day.

"While we were waiting outside, we did a surveillance of the house and grounds. You have, I believe, two cottages in the back of the property?" Gresham looked to Rose for the answer to his query.

"Yes," Rose replied. "Mr. and Mrs. Evans live in one cottage; my daughter and her husband, Mr. and Mrs. Michaels, live in the other."

"Very good, ma'am. We will include them in our rounds."

He turned and introduced his men. "Please meet my crew, Misters Donaldson, Morrow, Cluney, Betts, Goldstein, Jeffers, Hicks, and Rawley." Each man, as his name was called, nodded.

Gresham turned again to Mei-Xing. "Do you have any questions, miss?"

Mei-Xing ducked her head and shook it.

"Does anyone else have questions? No?"

"Thank you, Mr. Gresham," Martha Palmer signaled the end of the meeting. "Please assume your posts."

"Thank you, ma'am. Morrow and Jeffers will be on duty until four o'clock today." Gresham gestured with his chin; his men nodded and filed out.

Minister Liáng stared at the wire on his desk. He smoothed the paper and read it again. *Mr. O'Dell would not be returning to Seattle any time soon.*

Liáng was frustrated.

Yes, O'Dell's first wire had confirmed (covertly) that Mei-Xing was safe, yet Liáng, along with Bao, knew little more! They had no details regarding Mei-Xing's rescue and still had many questions: Who had taken her from the porch of Palmer House last November? Where had she been held all those months and where was she found? Was she in good health? More importantly to Liáng, would he be able to facilitate a reunion between Mei-Xing and her parents?

Aside from these issues, Liáng grew more concerned for Bao each day: Fang-Hua's men were actively scouring the city for him.

He would be much safer—and I would breathe easier—if I could remove him from Seattle, Liáng mused. *Denver is a good distance away.*

Liáng sighed, studied his busy calendar, and came to a decision. His elders would chafe at another absence—had he not taken leave less than six months ago? But Liáng was resolute: He must go to Denver and see Mei-Xing for himself.

I will take Bao with me, he decided. *He is in too much danger here. Perhaps the Lord will open a door of refuge for him there.*

Joy forced herself to swallow a bite of toast and waited. No, it was not going to stay down. Even as she was losing the little she had put in her stomach, Joy laughed.

Blackie, curled under their little table, whined and watched her with anxious eyes. "I am fine, Blackie," she reassured him. "More than fine!"

I am truly pregnant! she rejoiced. She could scarcely believe it! Although she was mere weeks along, she knew exactly when she had conceived—the night they had received the news concerning Grant's health.

A miracle, Lord, she breathed. *You have given us a great gift, a miracle.*

As soon as words "given *us*" crossed through her thoughts, her heart twisted. Grant would be overjoyed, just as she was, but their delight would be bittersweet, tempered by the doctor's prognosis: Grant would likely not live to see his child grow up.

Joy wiped her mouth and took a sip of water. Grant had left their little cottage several minutes before to fetch the morning paper from the front porch of Palmer House. That daily task left him fatigued, but he would not give it up.

She sat down and, while Blackie rested his head on her leg, Joy nibbled again on the slice of toast. This time it seemed to settle in her queasy stomach. She turned to dressing for the day.

She had just finished brushing and braiding her hair when Grant returned with the paper under his arm. He sat down on their little sofa and lowered his head to catch his breath. Joy sat down next to him and waited.

"Grant."

He nodded but had not yet become comfortable in his breathing. A few minutes later he looked up, his face still pale. "Sorry."

"There's no call to be sorry, darling," Joy replied. "But perhaps we should follow Dr. Peabody's recommendation?"

"You mean for the breathing apparatus?"

Joy nodded. "He declares it will make you more comfortable. I do not like to see you like this."

Grant thought for a moment. "All right."

"I will call his office for you," Joy offered, glad that he had agreed. "But first . . . first, I have something to tell you. Something . . . wonderful."

"Oh?" Grant teased. Joy grinned, so glad to see his normally cheerful disposition reassert itself. He reached for her and she slid into his arms. "What wonderful news do you have for me, eh?"

"Weeell," Joy let the word drag until he squeezed her.

"Come on, you little tease!" he laughed. "Just tell me."

"All right. But I must watch your face as I do."

She drew away so that they were face to face. She stared into his hazel eyes, the beautiful eyes of the man she fallen in love with. "Grant."

"Yes, Love?"

"I'm going to have a baby."

Grant's face paled further. He stilled, and Joy read the many conflicting thoughts and emotions as they raced across his face.

"Truly?"

Joy nodded. "Yes, truly."

"We have wanted a baby for a long time, haven't we?"

Joy nodded again. So many of his memories were still gone; he often had to call on her to validate his spotty recollections. "For years. Are you happy?"

"I . . . I am overjoyed . . . but . . . ."

"I know, my darling." Tears tickled down Joy's face. "But, please, let us embrace this gift from God and not think of later on! As long as we can, let us enjoy the love and blessings we have."

"Yes, you are right." Grant held her and turned her news over in his mind. "Why, I'm going to be a father! Oh, Joy. This is the most wonderful news."

"Oh, it is, Grant! And I would like to hold this wonderful news just between us, at least for a few weeks. Is that all right?"

Grant kissed Joy's forehead, then her eyes, her nose, and finally her mouth. "I may not be able to keep it to myself but, as you wish, I will try."

Later that morning Joy called Dr. Peabody's office and ordered the breathing machine he had recommended.

"Dr. Peabody requests that you and Mr. Michaels come to the office and receive training on the use of the machine," his nurse instructed. "Then we will have it delivered. Replacement tanks will be delivered each week."

Joy wondered how much such a machine and its parts would cost and how they would afford them. She steadfastly pushed those thoughts from her mind.

Dear Miss Greenbow,

O'Dell stared at the paper. *Now what should I write?* O'Dell had spent two days scribing a thick stack of reports for Parsons, all the while knowing that *this* letter was overdue and feeling less and less inclined to write it.

And while O'Dell's reports withheld no detail, however small, regarding his search for Su-Chong Chen and Mei-Xing, his communications with Miss Greenbow—*Darla*—must be circumspect. Her safety—and Bao's—dictated that O'Dell not mention certain names or places.

Dear Miss Greenbow,

Although I had intended to return to Seattle as soon as my business in D. was complete, I was summoned back to my home office and could not refuse. You know how many months I have been away from my employer. Management seems bent on exercising its will over my time and pursuits in an effort to recoup a portion of my services lost during my convalescence.

O'Dell's lip curled. *Not much of a start to a love letter, Ed, old man,* he scoffed. O'Dell set his pen on the desk to finally examine his feelings for the woman to whom he wrote.

Darla Greenbow. Calm, competent, strong. A true friend.

A lover and follower of God, O'Dell added. She had withstood O'Dell in his most cantankerous moods and modeled her faith before him with tenacity and humor.

That he *liked* Miss Greenbow was evident. A smile touched his mouth just thinking about her. He liked and admired her. And he saw something in her that they shared: They were both "getting on" and were desirous of finding a suitable match and building a family. She would love him faithfully and be an exceptional mother—of that he had no doubt.

Is that all I want? O'Dell queried himself. *A suitable wife and a family?* That was where his heart was stuck.

I don't know if I will ever love Miss Greenbow as . . .

O'Dell did not dare complete the sentence. He did not dare fill in the name.

That avenue is closed. Forever, he reminded himself. *I must move on and Darla is a wonderful, godly woman.*

O'Dell was new to his faith, but not so new that he did not recognize the sweet, soft Voice that pricked at his conscience.

Then she deserves someone who will love her unreservedly.

He sighed. Picked up his pen and reread, *Management seems bent on exercising its will over my time and location in an effort to recoup a portion of my services lost during my convalescence.* Added, *Therefore, I do not know when I will be returning to Seattle.*

He hesitated.

I must beg your pardon and ask that you forgive me. Your friendship has been a blessing to my new life in Christ but, given our distance, I feel I should not write again and encourage hopes to which I cannot give myself wholeheartedly.

He ground his fingers into his eyes. *I don't want to hurt her, Lord!*

You must speak the truth in love. It is better to hurt than to harm.

Shaking his head, O'Dell penned the final words.

Cordially,

Edmund O'Dell

He stuffed the letter into an envelope and addressed it before his courage deserted him.

Chapter 3

Breona sat on the edge of her bed watching Mei-Xing sleep in the bed just across the room they shared. Four weeks had passed since Mei-Xing's return to Palmer House.

Lord, 'tis bein' ever so grateful I am t' have my dearest friend back! Breona prayed. *Sure an' she has suffered much, boot I'm thankin' you for givin' her back t' us! We will keep 'er an' 'er wee un safe an' loved.* Smiling, she headed downstairs to begin the day's chores.

Later that day Mr. Wheatley answered the front doorbell. "Minister Liáng! Come in, come in! You must have heard our good news!"

"Yes, Mr. O'Dell was kind enough to send me a wire so I would know she had been found. However, he has been delayed in his return to Seattle. With no details about Mei-Xing's well-being and after reading the accounts of Su-Chong's death in the newspapers, the lack of information preyed on my mind. I felt I needed to come and see with my own eyes how she is."

Mr. Wheatley showed Liáng to the parlor. The young minister seated himself but waited far longer than he had expected for Mei-Xing to appear. After half an hour, Rose Thoresen greeted him instead.

"Minister Liáng, it is a pleasure to see you in Denver again. I apologize for making you wait—Breona will bring tea shortly." They exchanged pleasantries for another quarter of an hour until Liáng, anxious to meet Mei-Xing, spoke candidly.

"Mrs. Thoresen, is Miss Li here? I would like to meet her at last and speak with her."

"She is here, but it was . . . important that we talk first."

That was when Liáng noticed Rose's hesitancy and became alarmed. "Is she all right? Mr. O'Dell gave me no information regarding her ordeal or her well-being!"

Breona entered carrying a tea tray just then. Liáng did not miss the suspicious glare the dark-eyed young woman turned on him. Rose waited until Breona left the room to answer Liáng's question.

"Mei-Xing is well, Mr. Liáng . . . but before she will meet with you I must have your assurance as a gentleman that you will comply with her wishes."

"Her wishes?"

Rose nodded and remained silent.

Liáng looked at Rose. "I read the newspapers. They reported that the police found Su-Chong Chen's body and that he had apparently been hiding in an apartment in downtown Denver all these months since his escape from jail. They reported that he had been shot. The papers made no mention of anyone else."

Rose sipped her tea. "Mr. O'Dell convinced them to leave Mei-Xing out of the official reports. He took her away before the reporters came."

Liáng frowned. "So Mei-Xing was with Su-Chong in this apartment?"

"Again, I must have your assurances before I say anything further."

Liáng sat back and studied Rose. He sighed at last and nodded. "You have my word as a gentleman and as a Christian, Mrs. Thoresen. I will respect Miss Li's wishes."

"Thank you." Rose took another sip of tea. "To answer your question, yes. Mei-Xing was with Su-Chong, but not of her own free will. He kidnapped her from the front porch of this house," Rose hesitated before adding, "and kept her locked in a room—a prisoner, Mr. Liáng—for nearly six months."

Liáng grew sorrowful, fearful of what she would say next, but there was no easy way to break the news to him.

"Mei-Xing returned to us expecting a child."

Liáng's mouth tightened. "A child! When?"

"The doctor believes late September . . . even though she appears further along." Neither of them spoke as Rose poured Liáng a second cup of tea.

"You must have questions," Rose murmured.

Liáng rubbed a hand over his eyes. "Indeed, this complicates matters. Who knows?"

"Only a few trusted individuals outside this house. And you."

"You may trust me, Mrs. Thoresen," Liáng replied, "But I was hoping . . ." His voice dropped to a wistful whisper. "We were hoping to reunite her with her parents."

"I understand, but this is where your trust is required, Minister Liáng. Sadly, Mei-Xing does not wish to return to her parents."

The look Liáng turned on Rose twisted her heart. "Not ever?"

Rose inclined her head, silent.

"Then they are never to know she is alive? They are to be left grieving?"

Rose nodded again. "Those are Mei-Xing's wishes. I must tell you that I have seen it before. These girls are not as their families remember them and so . . . they choose not to return."

Liáng lapsed into silence for several minutes before he uttered, "That is not all, is it? It *must* be Fang-Hua! Mei-Xing is afraid for the child!"

Rose said nothing but her eyes told him it was true.

"I cannot blame Mei-Xing," Liáng exclaimed, "but I also cannot help but think it is a mistake to hide."

He looked up at Rose. "You remember how the last time I was here I told you of Su-Chong's cousin Bao and his role in sending Mei-Xing to . . . Corinth."

Rose nodded.

"Now Bao, too, is hiding from Fang-Hua." Liáng withdrew a clean, pressed handkerchief from his breast pocket and pressed it to his brow. "You see, after Su-Chong escaped from the jail here in Denver, Fang-Hua somehow learned that Su-Chong had *seen* Mei-Xing the night he was arrested—and so he knew she had not died by suicide as the newspapers reported. Fang-Hua became concerned that her son would look too closely at the details of Mei-Xing's 'death' and discover his mother's role in sending the girl to Corinth.

"Fang-Hua sent more men to Denver to find Su-Chong and to . . . do away with Mei-Xing, but they failed to find either of them. This caused Fang-Hua to panic. A living Mei-Xing was a threat to her! She ordered Su-Chong's cousin Bao to lead yet another group of men here to Denver to find and kill Mei-Xing. Bao knew if he refused his aunt, she would have him done away with on the spot— *so he ran.*

"Now that Fang-Hua can no longer trust Bao, he is as much a threat to her as Mei-Xing is. Fang-Hua has placed a price on Bao's head. She cannot chance him bearing witness to what she ordered him to do to Mei-Xing."

Liáng hurried to add, "You see, as long as the truth is *hidden*, as long as Fang-Hua is not exposed and called to account, Bao will never be safe—and Mei-Xing and her baby will never be safe! This is why bearing witness to her deeds is of the utmost importance."

His words troubled Rose. "Be that as it may, I cannot force Mei-Xing to expose herself and her child to the danger such a revelation would create, Mr. Liáng, nor would I ever try."

"I see." Liáng nodded and thought for a long moment.

Rose watched as he wrestled with his thoughts. She saw when he came to a decision.

"I must also tell you, Mrs. Thoresen, that I did not come to Denver alone." Liáng paused. "You see, Bao is with me. He has given his life to Christ. Now he wishes to confess his sin to Mei-Xing and ask her forgiveness."

Rose began shaking her head. "I don't know. I don't know if that is wise."

He studied his hands. "Will you allow me to ask her?"

Rose still shook her head. "I don't know. She is so fragile still. You will not pressure her?"

"No."

"If I agree to what you ask, I will be present when you meet with her," Rose warned.

"I understand."

Rose's mouth tightened. "And it will be her decision."

He readily agreed but still Rose hesitated. "Minister Liáng, she does not yet know who you are, only that you know her parents and can give some news of them to her. We have not had opportunity to tell her all that Mr. O'Dell found when he was in Seattle."

"I will be careful," Liáng promised. "And I will be kind. You have my word."

Rose left the parlor. When she returned, Liáng stood to his feet. Trailing behind Rose was the girl Liáng knew only from photographs that did her no justice.

She is exquisite! was Liáng's first impression. Her skin was flawless, the shape of her face perfect, her hair a gleaming ebony. In that moment, Liáng felt he understood Su-Chong's obsession with her.

Mei-Xing nodded to him. "Sir?"

He bowed formally. "Yaochuan Min Liáng, at your service, Miss Li."

She bowed in return, graceful despite her pregnancy.

As they settled into chairs, she asked, "You have news of my parents?" Her voice trembled just a little.

"Yes. I believe I bring good news to you. I understand from Mrs. Thoresen that you have come to know Christ?"

Before she answered, she tipped her head on its side, just a little, as though she were listening—a gesture that, in an odd way, touched Liáng's heart.

"Yes, I have," she replied. "I came to Miss Rose and Miss Joy broken in heart and body. They showed me the love of God and shared with me the message of salvation." She looked down. "I would not be here today if it were not for God's love and grace toward me."

Liáng nodded, a smile tugging at his mouth. "Then I believe you will be happy to hear my news, dear lady. In their grief after your, er, *death*, your parents were distraught. They reached out to God for help. They, too, have given their lives to the Savior."

Mei-Xing blinked against sudden moisture. "Truly?" She looked into his face for confirmation.

Liáng swallowed, caught in the mirror of her dark eyes. "Truly, Miss Li. I am their pastor."

"Their pastor!"

He nodded. "They have been members of my congregation for more than a year now." He gentled his voice further. "May I tell you a story? A true story?"

Mei-Xing looked to Rose and back. "About them?"

"It begins with them but it is more a story of how the God of Grace is able to turn great evil to eternal good."

She studied him for another minute, and then nodded.

"Very well," Liáng began. "Then let me say that some months ago I called upon your parents. They have become cherished friends, and I value my fellowship with them. While we were visiting that day, a servant came into the room and whispered in your father's ear. He arose and went to a window and looked out across the street below."

Mei-Xing nodded, picturing her parents' home and its view across the street.

"*Come, Minister Liáng, if you would*, he asked. I, too, looked from the window and saw a man standing across the street. This man paced to the corner and back in obvious agitation.

"*Who is he?* I asked.

"*The cousin of our daughter's former fiancé,* he answered. *Bao Shin Xang.*"

Mei-Xing started from her chair, exclaiming, "Bao!"

"Yes." Liáng's eyes narrowed. "*Bao.* The very man you trusted; the man who betrayed you."

Mei-Xing's eyes were wide and she hovered near Rose's chair, trembling. "How do you know this?" Rose placed a hand on her arm to steady her.

"Please," Liáng encouraged. "Please sit, Miss Li. I do not wish to disturb you. All is well, I promise."

Mei-Xing watched him and, after a few moments, resumed her seat.

"Where was I? Ah, yes. Even from your father's window, it was clear to see that Bao was in great agitation. Your father, knowing nothing of Bao's perfidy, asked if I would go down and see if I could help him. This I did."

He looked at Mei-Xing. "You will perhaps not know this, but Bao was in love with your servant, Ling-Ling. He was promised he could marry her . . . if he carried out a certain person's instructions concerning you."

Anxious, Mei-Xing twisted the skirt of her dress. "*Fang-Hua!* She arranged a marriage between Bao and Ling-Ling?"

"Yes. But just as the fruit of sin is often bitter, Bao's marriage to Ling-Ling was not a happy one." Liáng shook his head. "And then Ling-Ling died in childbirth this past December."

Mei-Xing said nothing and kept her expression carefully blank but Liáng could sense sorrow warring with deep anger, not far beneath the surface.

"Bao grew a conscience after this, Miss Li. He recounts how his days and nights were haunted by your face."

"My face? *My face!*" Mei-Xing struggled to remain calm. "After what he did?"

"Yes. He could not live with the guilt of what he had done . . . to you. The day he stood outside your parents' house, he planned to tell them everything—that you had *not* killed yourself, but that he had sent you to a living hell and planted evidence of your suicide." Liáng's voice grew rough as he spoke. "Then he intended to kill himself."

Mei-Xing's mouth formed a little "o" and her breath caught in her throat.

"I dragged him to a nearby tea house that day, and he confessed to me what he had done." Liáng and Mei-Xing could have been the only ones in the room now. He leaned forward in his chair and their eyes locked.

"You must understand—his story was so fantastic, I could not believe it! But I was determined to find out the truth. I left Seattle a few days later. When I arrived in Denver, I boarded the next train to the little town Bao had told me of: Corinth. There, not far from the siding, I met a man."

Another smile touched Liáng's mouth. "He asked me to call him Flinty."

"Oh!" Mei-Xing's voice caught in a sob. "Flinty!"

Liáng looked from Mei-Xing to Rose, confused and then alarmed at their sadness.

"We lost Flinty to influenza only a few months ago," Rose whispered.

Liáng was stunned. "I had no idea. I-I am truly saddened." He shook his head. "Flinty told me that our meeting was God's appointment! What precious fellowship we shared that night in Corinth. I shall miss him!"

Liáng paused, remembering. "That night I learned from Flinty that you had recently been abducted, Miss Li, and that Mr. O'Dell had gone to Seattle to look for your family or Su-Chong's family in an effort to find who had taken you. The next morning Flinty and I came down the mountain together and to this house where I met Mrs. Thoresen."

Mei-Xing looked to Rose for confirmation. She nodded to Mei-Xing, and Liáng continued his narrative.

"Mrs. Thoresen suggested I return to Seattle and aid Mr. O'Dell with the information I could provide. However, I could not find him.

"Mr. O'Dell is very good at his job, Miss Li, but he had not been in Seattle long before Fang-Hua's men discovered that he was asking many questions about Chen affairs. Fang-Hua had her men beat O'Dell and leave him to die near the docks."

Mei-Xing gasped and tears trickled down her face. "Mr. O'Dell has been a good and faithful friend! It grieves me to hear he suffered on my account. He did not tell me."

Liáng nodded. "Of course. He loves the family in this house and would not burden you with this knowledge. Because of his injuries, when I returned to Seattle as Mrs. Thoresen suggested, I could find no trace of him—his belongings remained in his hotel room but no one had seen him for days!"

Liáng held up a finger. "And God again intervened! Mr. O'Dell had been found alive and taken to a hospital. The Lord led me to that same hospital, where he and I grew to know each other over the weeks he was recovering."

Liáng knew he had Mei-Xing and Rose's rapt attention, but he experienced a strange impulse to tease Mei-Xing a little. "How is my story so far, Miss Li? Is it of any interest to you?"

When she looked into his eyes, he was smiling, and she had to smile back through her tears. "Of great interest, Mr. Liáng. Please! Continue."

He glanced at Rose, who had relaxed. She smiled and bent her head. Liáng returned to his tale. "I cannot, for the sake of time, share every nuance and detail of the weeks that followed. Today I will relate only what I believe is most important.

"It was while Mr. O'Dell was in the hospital that Fang-Hua again grew nervous. Her son had escaped from jail, and her men had failed to bring him home. I believe she grew concerned that he was still obsessed with finding you and that you would reveal her role in what had been done to you. So she sent her thugs to Denver to make you disappear forever."

Mei-Xing's mouth dropped open and Rose stirred in her chair.

"But they could not find you, Miss Li! You see, don't you? You see how the God of Grace was working? *They* could not find and kill you because *Su-Chong* had already hidden you away! Only Su-Chong could have possibly hidden you so effectively from them."

Mei-Xing uttered a soft exclamation and Liáng continued. "About the same time, I rented a small house in which Mr. O'Dell could recuperate—taking care that the house was safely distant from prying eyes. But when Fang-Hua's thugs returned from Denver empty-handed, she was not satisfied. She commanded Bao to take other men to Denver and do a better job.

"Bao, by this time, had repented of his evil deeds. However, he knew that if he refused Fang-Hua, she would not hesitate to summarily do away with him. So! So I hid him in the same house Mr. O'Dell was in."

Liáng laughed. "Let us just say that the atmosphere in that tiny house was quite tense for a while. But then God moved and changed Mr. O'Dell's heart *and* Bao's heart. Now he and Bao are brothers in Christ."

"They are? They have both found the Lord Jesus? We have prayed for Mr. O'Dell for a long while!"

"Yes, indeed they are. Is this not amazing, Miss Li? Since the terrible night Bao put you on the train, no less than five individuals have come to a saving knowledge of Jesus Christ—you, your parents, Bao, and Mr. O'Dell."

He watched her with grave eyes. "God has turned the most unspeakable wrong done to you into a most precious and eternal good. One thing remains today that I would ask you. A very large thing, Miss Li."

He paused and then whispered, "I must ask, Miss Li: Are you willing to do this difficult thing?"

She blinked in surprise. "What is this thing, Mr. Liáng?"

Quite naturally, he reached across and took her hands. "Will you receive Bao and let him confess what he did to you?"

Mei-Xing swallowed and she withdrew her hands from his. "He . . . he is here?"

"He is. I left him waiting where the cab dropped us off. Just out on the curb."

Mei-Xing looked ill, and Liáng prepared for her refusal—until he heard her murmuring under her breath.

"O God, please help me! His sin is no greater than my own! Please give me the strength to fully and freely forgive him just as you have fully and freely forgiven me. Please!"

Yes, Lord God! he prayed with her. *Please help this dear sister. Give her the courage to do what her heart and your word are asking.*

Liáng stood and Mei-Xing stared with trust into his face. "Will you be here with me?"

The faith she placed in him humbled Liáng. He reached out his hand and she took it. "I will be right here," he promised. "I will not leave your side."

With a gentle squeeze to her hand, he released her and looked to Rose. "May I have your permission to bring Bao into your home?"

Rose looked at Mei-Xing and back. "Yes."

He nodded, bowed, and left the room.

Several minutes later he returned with Bao. Mei-Xing had retreated to the other side of the parlor, instinctively placing space between herself and the man who had betrayed her. Liáng nodded to her and stepped aside so Bao could enter.

Rose did not know what she had expected to see, but certainly not *this* man whose physical appearance was as one not far from death. His clothes hung on his body and his face was drawn and stricken.

"Oh!" Mei-Xing uttered the exclamation and burst into tears. "Bao! My friend! What has happened to you?" she cried.

Bao took one look at Mei-Xing and fell to his knees sobbing. "Please forgive me, Mei-Xing! I beg you! Please forgive me!"

Mei-Xing dropped beside him on the floor. She placed her hand on his head. "I forgive you, Bao, just as God in Christ forgave me." Then she cradled Bao's head against her lap as he wept.

Chapter 4
(Journal Entry, June 4, 1910)

Lord, since Minister Liáng's visit yesterday, bringing Bao with him, I have seen with my own eyes a depth of forgiveness and reconciliation I was not entirely sure was possible. What a work you perform in the hearts of men and women! Is there any greater demonstration of Christ's redemption? You are so much greater than we can ever know.

I must also bring before you something puzzling, something I do not yet understand. While we at Palmer House are all grateful that Mei-Xing has come home to us, a certain reticence, a drawing back from Mei-Xing, has fallen upon some of the girls. I notice it most in Tabitha even as she struggles to hide it. I do not understand it and do not like to see it, Lord, for it could very well produce disunity in our home.

Father, I ask for your wisdom and insight to help me grasp the meaning of this reticence—this drawing back—and how to address it.

Rose invited Liáng and Bao to dine with them the next evening. Liáng, anxious to see at first hand more of the ministry Rose and Joy had founded, accepted the invitation with alacrity.

But as they arrived that afternoon, he also cautioned Rose, "Surely everyone living here knows of Bao's role in Mei-Xing's life? How will they respond to him?"

"Ah." Rose nodded, thinking on the situation. She turned to Bao and offered a sincere smile. "Bao, you did well yesterday with Mei-Xing. It is possible, though, that others living at Palmer House will question why you are here. Perhaps, if the subject arises, you could simply ask for the forgiveness of any who love Mei-Xing and have grieved with her?"

"I will do so gladly," Bao returned. The young man's eyes were not quite so haunted, but Rose could not help being concerned for his health.

Rose seated Liáng and Bao in deep chairs in the great room to wait until dinner was announced. As the afternoon drew toward dinner time, the young women of the house began returning from their various places of employment.

Liáng and Bao sprang to their feet in respect and watched as Rose greeted each one with an embrace and a kindly spoken, "How was your day, my dear?"

The modestly dressed women nodded at Liáng and Bao and chattered together, happy to be home.

"Oh, Miss Rose! I began reading a new book to my little grandmother," one girl exclaimed. "It is called *The Pilgrim's Progress*. Have you read it? My little lady and I are enthralled."

Liáng, who speculated that the girl likely worked as a companion to an elderly woman, listened with interest to the conversations around him.

"Sara, I received the enrollment materials from nursing school." A fiery redhead beckoned to a young woman who had come through the door with several others.

"Oh, Tabs! I cannot believe it—in only two years you will be a real nurse!" the attractive brunette replied.

Another girl chimed in, "Marit must be making gingerbread for dessert! Do you smell that heavenly aroma?"

"Aye, 'tis causin' m' mouth t' water!" the dark-haired, black-eyed woman Liáng knew as Breona responded. "Jenny, there's a good girl, will ye be whippin' th' cream for Marit?"

"Yes, Breona!" Jenny, the reader of *The Pilgrim's Progress*, ran off to the kitchen to help the as-yet-unseen Marit.

A tall, slender woman, her white-blonde hair braided and pinned up stylishly, recognized Liáng. She had only entered the house a moment before.

"Minister Liáng!" she smiled. Liáng and Bao both bowed.

"It is good to see you again, Mrs. Michaels," Liáng smiled in reply. "May I introduce my companion, Bao Shin Xang?"

Joy hesitated, and it was apparent that she recognized Bao's name.

"As you have likely heard, Bao and I met with Miss Li yesterday," Liáng offered. He turned and nodded to Bao.

"Yes," the young man murmured. He did not flinch under Joy's inspection but his chin dropped toward his chest. "I asked for her forgiveness and she was gracious enough to grant it." Bao swallowed. "I would also ask forgiveness of you, Mrs. Michaels. My actions have affected you and all who live here. I am sincerely repentant." Bao's chin dropped even lower.

Joy nodded slowly. "I accept your apology and forgive you for Christ's sake, Mr. Xang." As he looked up, Joy held out her hand.

Before Liáng and Bao returned to their hotel for the evening, another visitor called at Palmer House. Rose introduced him to Liáng and Bao.

"Minister Liáng, Mr. Xang, may I introduce our pastor, Isaac Carmichael?"

Liáng studied the young preacher even as Carmichael studied them.

"I came to speak with Miss Li, if she would be willing to see me," Pastor Carmichael explained to Rose. She nodded and left to ask Mei-Xing, so Carmichael turned back to Liáng. "Tomorrow is Sunday, Mr. Liáng. Will you worship with us?"

"Yes, with pleasure! I have heard a great deal about your ministry; I would count my visit deficient were I to miss it." Liáng had heard so many of the girls talk about the church that he was truly curious.

Mei-Xing came downstairs to the foyer where they stood. She nodded at Liáng and spoke to Pastor Carmichael. "You wished to see me, sir?"

"Yes. I, um, perhaps we could speak privately for a moment? Perhaps in the parlor?"

Mei-Xing glanced at the floor, clearly reluctant.

"Would you feel more comfortable if someone stayed in the room with us?" Pastor Carmichael asked, sensitive to Mei-Xing's reticence.

Liáng was surprised when Mei-Xing cut her eyes toward him. Carmichael noticed it also.

"Do you wish Minister Liáng to remain while we talk?" Liáng appreciated how gentle Carmichael's tone was.

Mei-Xing nodded. She led the way into the parlor, seated herself in one of the parlor's chairs, and glanced toward Liáng. He came and stood just behind the corner of her chair and she looked up at him with gratitude.

"Miss Li," Pastor Carmichael began, "I have asked to speak with you because I would like you to know how happy your church family is that you have returned to us. I hope you understand that we know you were taken from this house against your will. What happened while you were being held captive is between you and God. We do not judge you."

Mei-Xing fiddled with the fold of her dress. Liáng from where he stood watched her carefully.

Carmichael continued. "You have been back now for two weeks and we did not see you at service Sunday."

Color rose into Mei-Xing's face.

"I know you are in a . . . delicate condition, Miss Li, and I know that your condition may generate uncomfortable questions, but I would have you know that you are still welcome at Calvary Temple. We will stand by you, Miss Li."

Mei-Xing stared at her hands. "I thank you, Pastor Carmichael, but . . ."

The silence dragged on for a minute until she added, "I have confessed to God and to Miss Rose and Miss Joy that I am to blame for my . . . condition. Yes, I was taken and held against my will but . . . in a moment of weakness I gave myself to Su-Chong."

Pastor Carmichael nodded, his face grave. "I see." He thought a few moments longer. "But as you said, you have confessed that indiscretion to the Lord? You have sought him earnestly and repented of your acts?"

"Yes, sir, I have."

"And has God forgiven you?"

"I—yes, sir. He has."

"Then are you forgiven?"

Mei-Xing looked up. "Yes, sir. I believe I am."

"If you have truly repented and God has forgiven you, then how should we, your church family, view you?"

Liáng's mouth twitched in a small smile. He appreciated the sensitivity with which Carmichael was leading Mei-Xing toward the truth.

"I—" Mei-Xing glanced a question at Liáng. He bent his head in assurance.

"I . . . would hope they would forgive me also," Mei-Xing replied.

"Yes, they most certainly will. All that remains to be done is for you to show yourself unafraid to worship with us." Pastor Carmichael smiled at Mei-Xing. "So shall we expect you tomorrow?"

Mei-Xing swallowed but nodded. Liáng patted her shoulder once, to signal his approval. She looked up to him again. "Will you be there tomorrow?"

"I will, indeed," he murmured. "As will your entire Palmer House family, I believe. We will all be with you, Miss Li."

Liáng and Bao were staying at a hotel not far from Palmer House. They arrived back at the house Sunday morning a few minutes before the household set out for church. The guards would come in an automobile to drive Mei-Xing, Joy, and Grant to church; the remainder of the house would walk to service and meet them there.

While it was not too far to walk, the distance was still significant. The group went two abreast down the sidewalks, and Liáng, near the back of the long line, looked ahead and chuckled. Their lines resembled something like a gaggle of geese with Mrs. Thoresen and Breona setting a brisk pace at the head of the two columns. Mr. Wheatley, Marit, and Billy—with young Will astride Billy's broad shoulders—were just ahead of Liáng and Bao, who brought up the rear of the lines.

The young women chattered amicably as they walked, but Liáng now knew that the atmosphere in the house had not always been harmonious.

Mrs. Thoresen had shared that the first months in the house had been, as she put it, "tumultuous and messy." She confided, "We were struggling to live together in unity under the same roof with our many human failings. It was a difficult time." Liáng listened closely and deduced that Rose Thoresen's firm hand had kept the house from falling into chaos.

When they arrived where church was held and filed through the doors, Liáng's mouth parted and he stared. It was like no house of worship he had ever visited! The building was immense—a brick warehouse, high-ceilinged, cavernous, and *old*. Even as his eyes adjusted to the dim interior light, his head turned this way and that to take in as many details as he could.

Apparently, the cadre from Palmer House was recognized and expected. Two grinning ushers, dressed in clean but everyday wear, showed them to a block of seats off the middle aisle where Mei-Xing, Joy, and Grant already waited. Four or five to a row, four rows deep, they seated themselves—on every kind of seat Liáng could imagine!

He and Bao found themselves side-by-side with Mr. Wheatley on a backless wooden bench that could have seen many years of previous service in a school, police station, or even saloon. Palmer House girls sat in the rows ahead of them on mismatched dining chairs.

Mei-Xing, from a few rows ahead, turned and smiled a tentative welcome to him. He bowed his head and smiled back.

What Liáng really wanted to do was to stand in the back of the building where he could watch and observe the proceedings from a better advantage. "Bao, please keep my seat. I will return shortly."

As he walked toward the back he realized that the cavernous room was filling fast—and more attendees flowed through the street-side doors. He found himself a niche against the back wall where he could watch . . . and be amazed.

The diversity of the crowd was staggering. White and black. Mexican and Asian. Poor and wealthy. The well-heeled were seated alongside those whose clothes were patched and faded. A Chinese couple, shepherding their three young children, passed near Liáng. He smiled and bowed—and then he began to notice many Chinese in the crowd.

When the singing commenced Liáng was again surprised. An organist began to play and the congregation to sing, but no one led the singing; neither were there any hymnbooks in evidence.

But what astounded Liáng and produced a lump in his throat was the passion with which the familiar hymns were sung. Compared to the swell of ardent praise that climbed to the rafters of the warehouse, his own congregation's worship was bland, even insipid.

Liáng began to hum along. As he opened his mouth to sing, a longing to touch God—for God to reach down and pull him close— took hold of him. But, he realized, he did not need to pull the Divine down from on high, for as the worship continued, the very presence of God swelled in Liáng's breast, filling him with awe, reverence, and joy.

Liáng found himself singing for One and only One. He did not realize he was weeping—he only knew he was experiencing the communion that Jesus promised his followers: *Those who worship the Father must worship him in spirit and in truth.*

When Isaac Carmichael strode onto the platform, Liáng's hunger for more of God was intense. He and the crowd of many hundreds stilled.

"I wish to speak this morning on the Name of Jesus," Pastor Carmichael began, his voice echoing to every corner of the warehouse. "The *Name of Jesus*—the name by which he will save *to the uttermost* all those who come to him!

"I say again, the Bible proclaims that the Name of Jesus saves *to the uttermost!* What is the uttermost? What can the Name of Jesus perform? Let me say that the God of the Bible, the God of all creation, is infinite, all-powerful, and all-knowing.

"Because God is infinite, all-powerful, and all-knowing, his *uttermost* knows no bounds, has no limits, and cannot be constrained!

"We have all fallen short of the glory and standards of God. Each of us has made a great hash of our lives and opportunities. Many of us here this morning are in deep distress—some of us are in terrible, even dire, straits.

"What do we do when we are in trouble or distress? We call for help! We may call on mother, father, husband, wife, friend, and sometimes strangers. And while they may lend their help or assistance, in our souls we cry out for help that they *cannot* give, for are they not human even as we are human? Are they not fallible, made of the same flawed humanity as are we?

"Neither mother, father, husband, wife, friend, nor stranger can save *to the uttermost!* How can they save us from destruction when they are as weak and helpless to save as we? But here is what our great God tells us:

> *For the eyes of the Lord*
> *run to and fro*
> *throughout the whole earth,*
> ***to shew himself strong***
> *in the behalf of them*
> *whose heart is perfect toward him.*

"God is strong! He is not weak as we are weak! And he is looking, nay, *searching,* running to and fro throughout the whole earth to show himself strong on behalf of them whose hearts are perfect toward him— those who are seeking him with their entire heart.

"And this great God, the Father of our Lord Jesus, has given all power *in heaven and on earth* to his Son, that at the Name of Jesus every knee shall bow and every tongue confess that he is Lord of all—to the glory of his name.

"He has given *all power* in heaven and on earth to Jesus that he might save us *to the uttermost*—that is, save us from any and every situation, redeem us from every guilt and shame, and purchase us from all horrible and debasing experiences!

"So I say to you this morning—call upon the Name of Jesus, the name that is able to save you *to the uttermost*."

Carmichael paused and was silent a long, potent minute before he asked, "Shall I tell you about the Name of Jesus?" Carmichael began to pace and a great roar of assent followed him.

As he strode across the platform he cried out, "The Name of Jesus and *only* the Name of Jesus looses the oppressed from *every* bondage!"

A shout rose from the congregation.

"The Name of Jesus and *only* the Name of Jesus heals the brokenhearted of *every* pain."

Amen! and *Yes, Lord!* they answered him.

"The Name of Jesus and *only* the Name of Jesus pours soothing oil upon *every* wound!

"The Name of Jesus and *only* the Name of Jesus forgives the most unconscionable sinner of *every* sin!"

Praise and sobs rolled across the hall.

"The Name of Jesus and *only* the Name of Jesus sets the captive free of *every* chain!

"The Name of Jesus and *only* the Name of Jesus remakes the ashes of *every* life into his glorious image.

"The Name of Jesus and *only* the Name of Jesus, will mend the willing husband and wife whose marriage has gone badly wrong."

Liáng closed his eyes as his spirit called a great *Yes, amen!* to each of Carmichael's utterances.

Then Carmichael stepped to the center of the platform and near its edge. His voice softened and the congregation leaned toward him so as not to miss him say, "By the Name of Jesus and *only* by the Name of Jesus are we reborn, shed of our past, ushered into the Kingdom of God, made right before God, and promised eternal life.

"Come," he said quietly. "Come to the altar and confess your sins to the Lamb who takes them away. Come. Come to the altar and bow your knee before the King of Kings and Lord of Lords.

"Come to the altar and surrender your poor, sinful lives for robes of righteousness. Come to the altar and receive forgiveness of sin and help in time of need. Come and call upon the most precious name of all—the Name of Jesus! *Come.*"

He bowed his head and waited. A great, soft sigh floated over the crowd and a restless shuffling and shifting grew. Liáng's head snapped up—across the expanse of the warehouse many men and women left their seats and pressed toward the aisles—center, right, and left.

Some wept. Some ran. Some staggered. Others dropped to their knees before they could reach the altars, confessing their sins where they were and calling out to Jesus for forgiveness. At the same time a great babble of prayer and thanksgiving ascended from the congregation.

Thunderstruck, Liáng watched as a hundred—perhaps two hundred!—souls reached the altars calling on the Name of Jesus. Rich and poor knelt together. Liáng was shaken to his core by the might, *the raw, untainted power*, of the Gospel.

Lord! his heart wept. *What am I to do? How shallow is my life and ministry when compared to this!*

Pastor Carmichael stepped off the platform and began praying with those who had come. Other believers discreetly came forward to pray with those at the altar, and Liáng realized that Rose, Joy, and Breona were among those ministering to the women.

And then he saw . . . Bao kneeling and weeping before the Lord. Carmichael had placed a gentle hand on Bao's shoulder and was praying for him.

The organ's tune was so soft that Liáng did not notice it until whispered voices took up the melody it played. In the quiet of the holy moment, the congregation sang a hymn that, while unfamiliar to Liáng, spoke to his spirit.

> *At the cross of Jesus bowing,*
> *Here I find a safe retreat*
> *From a world of care and trouble,*
> *In His presence calm and sweet.*

> *Sweet stillness of heaven around me I feel,*
> *While low at the cross of my Jesus I kneel.*

> *At the cross of Jesus bowing,*
> *Here I count my blessings o'er;*
> *Here I drink from life's pure fountain,*
> *Drink until I thirst no more.*

> *Sweet stillness of heaven around me I feel,*
> *While low at the cross of my Jesus I kneel.*

Liáng fell to his knees.

O God, you have brought me here today to revive my soul and to advance your great purposes. Speak to me, Lord, and I will obey. Reveal your plan, O Lord, and I will follow.

Chapter 5

The church emptied slowly after the service ended. Some of those who had come to the altar were still praying, and many in the congregation were reluctant to leave the sweet time of fellowship. Liáng introduced himself to a few of the Chinese families milling about and heard glowing testimonies about the move of God in their lives.

Eventually the Palmer House residents assembled for the walk back home. Mei-Xing, Joy, and Grant had already made their way outside to their waiting automobile. Liáng motioned Rose aside for a word.

"Madam Thoresen, if you do not mind, Bao and I would like to speak to Pastor Carmichael when he is available. We will find our way back to our hotel afterward."

They both glanced toward the front of the church where Carmichael was praying for a few latecomers to the altar. Bao still knelt there.

Liáng paused. He noticed Breona was at the front also, engaged in earnest conversation with a young woman.

"Breona has a tremendous heart for women bound in prostitution," Rose murmured. "We will not leave until she is ready."

Liáng nodded. The young woman Breona spoke to dabbed at her eyes with a hanky. Breona said something and the woman nodded. They bowed their heads together and prayed.

Liáng felt like he was invading their privacy but could not tear his eyes away. Eventually they finished and, to his surprise, Breona led the woman toward them.

Breona nodded at him before saying, "Miss Rose, this is Edith. Miss Edith, please t' be meetin' Miss Rose, what runs our home."

The girl, perhaps fifteen or sixteen years old, had curling brown hair and dark eyes. Haunted eyes.

Breona said carefully, "Edith be livin' at th' *Silver Spurs*, Miss Rose."

Liáng noticed as a tiny shudder ran through Rose Thoresen, and he saw a flash of communication pass from Breona to Rose and back.

"Yes, I understand," Rose whispered. "Dear Edith, will you tell me what you experienced this morning?"

Edith opened her mouth but had to wipe her eyes again before she could speak. "I-I am not sure how to say it, ma'am. I hate my life and hate . . . what I do. I cried out to Jesus to help me and it feels like he has touched me. Oh! I never want to go back! But where else can I go?"

The young woman trembled from head to toe so violently that Liáng feared she would collapse. Rose must have thought the same thing for she placed her arms around the woman and held her.

"God has heard your prayers, Edith. Are you willing to forsake everything, even leave behind all possessions you may have at the *Silver Spurs*? Are you willing to leave Denver, if necessary, to make a new start?"

"Oh, yes! Please don't make me go back there! I will gladly leave behind the few things I have to get away from there."

Liáng did not quite understand what was being negotiated between the two women or the concern that passed between Mrs. Thoresen and Breona. He felt a soft tap on his arm and turned. Isaac Carmichael gestured him away.

"I am glad you stayed, my friend," Carmichael said.

"Thank you, but I was waiting for you! Would you be available to take a meal with us, Bao and I?"

Carmichael looked toward the altar where Bao still knelt. "God is doing a deep work in that young man."

"I am glad," Liáng confessed. "He has done terrible things but he has also suffered greatly. Just a few months ago he lost his wife and son in childbirth. The guilt and condemnation that hell pours on sinners has been his constant, tormenting companion."

"He is the one then? The one who betrayed Mei-Xing?" When Liáng nodded, Carmichael again looked to where Bao knelt praying, "Then God is indeed doing a deep work—a glorious thing."

Liáng looked at Carmichael. "When we arrived two days ago, I shared with Mei-Xing how God has used Bao's evil deed to bring five people to the Savior—her, her parents, Mr. O'Dell, and now Bao himself.

"You see, the day I met Bao, he was ready to confess all to her parents and, afterwards, kill himself. But now that he is reborn in Christ, he is in fear that his new life will be taken from him, for Su-Chong Chen's mother, Fang-Hua, has ordered his death."

Carmichael's eyes widened. "That is a lot to take in."

"It is—and I must tell you, I cannot, in good conscience, take Bao back to Seattle. I am hoping to find a place for him to start over—far from Seattle and from the eyes and ears that report to Fang-Hua."

One corner of Carmichael's mouth turned up and he clasped Liáng's arm. "Well! Then we have much to talk of over our dinner. I believe in a God who arranges people's comings and goings to fit his plans—as you do, I think."

Liáng saw the Palmer House folk ready themselves to leave. It looked as though Edith would be going with them.

Liáng turned to say something to Carmichael—who was also watching the Palmer House women. Or one of them, anyway.

Just then Breona slanted her eyes toward Liáng and Carmichael. Liáng offered a half bow, but Carmichael grinned foolishly at the feisty Irish girl. She jerked her gaze away, but not before Liáng saw a red stain flooding up her neck to her cheeks.

Carmichael chuckled and tipped back on his heels.

"So! You favor the one called Breona?" Liáng queried.

"That I do. That I do," Carmichael responded, still smiling. "She is brave and strong and loves the Lord." He shook his head. "But I have little to offer her at present."

"That will change, I am sure!" Liáng encouraged.

They watched Bao rise and look about himself, surprised, it seemed, to see that the warehouse was nearly empty.

"Let us find a good, hot meal, shall we?" Liáng asked. "I have so much to ask you!"

The three men walked to a small, nondescript diner Carmichael frequented, one of only a few in Denver open on Sundays.

"I am a terrible cook," Carmichael laughed, "so Miss Betty sees me often! We have become friends in this last year."

"Miss Betty," it turned out, was a stern, hatchet-faced woman Liáng judged to be in her sixties. She gave them a gruff greeting and plopped menus in front of them.

"Don't let her bark discourage you," Carmichael whispered. "Her cooking is excellent and she has a very tender heart."

As they waited for their food, Carmichael and Liáng spoke nonstop on many topics. It was during dinner that Liáng began to pepper Carmichael with the questions to which his heart demanded answers.

"How is it possible that such diverse people can worship together as one? I have never seen such a thing! And to see people of the street coming to the Lord Jesus in such numbers!"

Carmichael shook his head. "I do not know how it has come to be, other than I commit myself to bring the word to those I know who need it. Even the well-off are being touched and transformed."

"But Pastor Carmichael, when I compare the move of God I saw this morning to my church and ministry I am in awe and, to be truthful, ashamed. The worship! The effectiveness of the preaching! I tell you sincerely, my church is tepid and apathetic and my preaching without power in comparison."

Carmichael lowered his head. "You cannot attribute any of that to me, my friend. We are experiencing a sovereign move of God. I confess to *you*, that I can scarcely keep up with what the Lord is doing. The work is . . . daunting."

He turned to Bao, who was listening intently to their exchange. "Will you share with us what God accomplished in your heart this morning, friend?"

Bao grew quiet and it was a long moment before he answered. "Minister Liáng can tell you of the horrible things I have done, sir. He will attest that I sincerely repented of my past life several weeks ago. But . . . but I could not escape the shame of my deeds . . . until this morning. I think—no, I *know*—that this day I encountered the Lord Jesus in the very core of my being, and he washed me in places where I had been terrified to even look."

Bao sighed softly. "I acknowledge now that, just as you said, nothing in all creation is hidden from him. He led me to relinquish even those parts of me I could not face, and he helped me to confront them and watch as he cleansed away all guilt. He asked me to surrender *everything*. Everything."

Carmichael grasped Bao's shoulder. "Yes! To surrender all—the good and the ill—is the point where God through Christ meets us and confirms his work in us."

"To surrender all," Liáng murmured. "How I long to do so!"

"What would prevent that?" Carmichael inquired.

"Sadly, my wealthy congregation would not tolerate a minister whose soul was *entirely* surrendered to the Lord." Even as he spoke, Liáng realized that he was rapidly approaching a point of decision.

"I must leave them," he gasped. Wonder, regret, and relief intermingled in his words.

Carmichael leaned toward Liáng. "Do you know, my friend, how many Chinese attend our services?" he whispered. "So many of them have been beaten down by life. They have no wealth, only a wealth of sorrow and pain.

"Very few speak English; those who do have many, many family members who would come to Christ if someone could speak their tongue—if one such as yourself would bring God's word to them and shepherd them after their conversion."

Tears formed in Liáng's eyes. "I would give my life to such a commission."

"Will you join with me then? Will you pray for the Lord's leading to come to Denver and join me?"

The power of the moment was not lost on any of them, and Bao looked between the two men, his expression eager. "Is there a place for me here? Minister Liáng has not said as much, but I know—for my safety—he wishes to see me away from Seattle permanently.

"I have nothing left in that city—I cannot claim my home, my money, or my goods without drawing danger—so I relinquish them gladly. Is there some work I can do here? I will give myself to whatever the Lord requires, however common or lowly."

The three men had finished their dinner and spoke in excited whispers long after Miss Betty had removed their dishes. They planned and they prayed until Miss Betty cleared her throat.

As Carmichael had warned, the restaurant's gruff proprietor did have a bark, but she also showed that she had a soft spot for Pastor Carmichael. The three men had not ordered dessert, but Miss Betty plopped dishes of warm bread pudding, swimming in cream, in front of them.

"Eat up," she commanded. "Won't have good food goin' t' waste."

Bao breathed in the aroma and clenched his spoon as if it might jump from his hands. He surprised Carmichael and Liáng by climbing to his feet and bowing to Miss Betty.

"Lovely lady, I thank you for your generosity," he told her in earnest. "I have not had bread pudding such as this since I was a child. The Lord bless you!"

Miss Betty, flummoxed and speechless, shifted her weight from foot to foot, and finally muttered a feeble, "Well!" and fled to her kitchen.

Liáng stared at Bao. He was devouring the pudding—just as he'd devoured his dinner, even extra dinner rolls.

"My friend, it seems your appetite has returned," Liáng observed. Carmichael stared, too, as Bao scraped clean his empty dish.

"I cannot tell you how good this food is," Bao replied. He eyed Liáng's pudding and, when Liáng pushed it toward him, grinned and tucked into the warm, sweet confection.

Liáng turned to Carmichael. "God *has* done a marvelous work today." He tipped his head toward Bao, his friend who had not eaten with appetite in the many months Liáng had known him.

While Carmichael, Liáng, and Bao were sharing their Sunday meal, so were those who lived at Palmer House. "Girls, this is Edith," Rose announced.

Edith blushed and looked down, even though most of the girls at Palmer House had already introduced themselves to the new arrival. Rose, however, wished to formalize Edith's introduction and, at the same time, make plain to the girl the challenges she—and all of them—faced.

"Edith may not be able to stay with us long," Rose continued. "We will look to be sending her where we sent Esther and the others who came to us via the *Silver Spurs*."

At the mention of *Silver Spurs*, the table drew a collective breath, and all eyes again shifted to Edith. The owner of the *Silver Spurs*, Cal Judd, was a threat no one at Palmer House took lightly—least of all Tabitha.

Tabitha sent a look of commiseration toward Edith. The girl appeared to be no more than sixteen, while Tabitha was in her late twenties. Tabitha and Edith's paths at the *Silver Spurs* had not crossed; Tabitha had been rescued from the brothel more than a year ago. Nevertheless, Tabitha recognized a kindred wounded spirit in Edith.

"Miss Rose, since Corrine and Jenny are sharing a room and I have a room to myself at present, I would be happy to have Edith as a roommate."

Rose smiled her appreciation. "Just what I was hoping to hear, Tabitha. Thank you. Would you please help her get settled after dinner? In the meantime, why don't we have a discussion at the table about Palmer House and what our expectations are here?"

Everyone was surprised when Jenny, herself new to Palmer House, eagerly spoke up. "Edith, we have Bible study at breakfast every morning! It is my favorite thing in the world."

After that, all the girls shared their understanding of their chores and responsibilities, the conditions of being part of Palmer House. Edith appeared a bit overwhelmed by it all, so Rose concluded, "That is probably enough for Edith at the moment, ladies.

"I only wish to add that we operate our home as a family. We work as a family, take care of and respect each other, and treat each other with kindness—even when we have squabbles. And, yes, we do have our occasional squabbles. We also are not afraid to confess our faults to each other."

She turned to Edith and added, "What we haven't yet mentioned is that the owner of the *Silver Spurs* is someone whose attention we wish to avoid. He is still in prison, but we understand it may not be long before he is released."

At these words, Edith grew still, in much the way a hunted animal freezes under the searching eyes of a predator.

"That is why, my dear," Rose finished in a quiet voice, "we may ask your permission to send you to friends who live at a distance from us. We do not wish that man to *ever* find you again, nor do we wish to draw his attention to our home."

Edith nodded, her brown curls bouncing a little as she did. When the table was excused, Tabitha asked Edith to follow her. "I know you came directly from church and left your belongings behind at the *Silver Spurs*, so we will find you some clothes you may call your own."

Rose could not help smiling as they walked away and she heard Tabitha say, "You may not believe this, but when *I* left the *Silver Spurs* I was wearing nothing but a peignoir! Not another stitch! Not even shoes. I can just imagine how the men who were there that night are still talking about *that*."

Tabitha has grown so much in you since then, Lord, Rose pondered, *but I sense such a conflict in her heart lately. It causes me to wonder what is worrying her . . . even what she might be hiding.*

During the next week, Liáng and Bao met with Isaac Carmichael daily to pray and seek the Lord for his direction. As they assembled in Carmichael's small house each morning, Liáng studied the tiny two-bedroom dwelling and prayed for the Lord to provide a safe place for Bao.

Each day when they finished their devotions, Carmichael took them on his rounds, visiting those in his congregation who were sick or who had requested a visit. They visited ten or more families each day, praying for the sick, lifting up their needs for work, food, clothing, education, and salvation. Every day they led unsaved family members to the Lord.

And then Carmichael took Liáng and Bao to visit the Chinese of his congregation. When they did so, Carmichael asked Liáng to take the lead, introducing him as a fellow minister. Liáng fell to ministering to the Chinese families with zeal, his satisfaction with the work he did with Carmichael growing daily.

When the three of them visited widows and the elderly, they brought along tools. While there, they made household repairs and took note of other needs.

Quite naturally, Carmichael began to task Bao with various errands: He gave Bao money to purchase and deliver medicines; he sent Bao with notes to other congregation members making mention of needs and asking for money, furnishings, food, or clothing for the widows and their children; he put Bao to work wherever a need presented itself.

He is testing Bao, Liáng surmised, *testing whether Bao would be a willing and apt fit as an assistant.*

Liáng and Bao even worked alongside Carmichael in the warehouse, sweeping the great auditorium and straightening the hundreds of chairs and benches.

"Bao," Carmichael said Friday morning. "You have seen and participated in the work of this church. I can offer you no more than a place here in my humble home, food to eat, and a part in the work I do. Will it be enough?"

Bao stood and bowed to Carmichael. "It is enough and more—it would be an honor to serve with you."

"Then, my friend, I welcome you," Carmichael replied. The two men embraced.

This house will not do for all three of us, Liáng mused, but he said nothing. He would be returning to Seattle tomorrow—without Bao. It was an answer to prayer!

As for Liáng, his congregation expected him to fill his pulpit on Sunday. He would return to his duties, even if temporarily. Then Liáng recalled the small house where he had hidden O'Dell and Bao, and he thought of Miss Greenbow.

I must vacate the house and release Miss Greenbow, he reflected, *and then I must prepare to leave my church.*

Chapter 6

Joy unlocked the back door to *Michaels' Fine Furnishings*. Billy, Sara, Corrine, and Blackie followed her inside. Joy and her employees readied themselves and the store for a new day of business. At nine o'clock sharp, Joy unlocked the front door and hung the "Open" sign in its place.

Joy's stomach roiled as she walked back toward the office. *Growing a baby is wonderful, Lord,* she reflected, *but I will be glad when this part passes!*

Abruptly, Joy bolted for the small water closet just off the office. When Joy stepped out of the wash room, Sara noticed her pasty face.

"Are you all right, Miss Joy?"

When Joy didn't answer, Sara ran to fetch her a glass of water. Before she could hand it over, Joy rushed back into the water closet. Sara heard the unmistakable sounds of stomach distress. Blackie sat down outside the water closet door and waited, attentive and anxious, for Joy to emerge.

Sara looked across the store to Corrine at the cash register. They both turned their attention to the bathroom door as a somewhat green Joy emerged. Sara glanced back at Corrine and gave her a slow, exaggerated wink. It took several moments before Corrine's mouth dropped open. Sara placed a warning finger to her lips.

"Here, Miss Joy." Sara smiled and offered the glass of water. Joy took it with a shaky hand.

Joy had taken a few sips before she noticed Sara's broad smile. "What is it, Sara?"

"I am so very happy for you and Mr. Grant," Sara answered.

Flustered, Joy tried to pretend she didn't know what Sara was implying but Sarah, still smiling, shook her head. "How far along are you?"

Joy managed a small, weak laugh. "I'm that transparent, am I?"

"It is hard to hide morning sickness."

Sara was still smiling and Joy could not resist her goodwill. "Hide it? I just want to survive it!" And then they were laughing together.

"We weren't going to tell anyone yet," Joy admitted. "Grant wanted to shout it to the world but I . . . I wanted to treasure and savor this wonderful secret just a little longer."

Sara leaned toward Joy and whispered, "Well, you might want to make sure your mother knows before everyone else figures it out."

"Oh! That would *never* do! I will tell her as soon as we are home this evening."

Corrine scuttled across the room and glanced between Sara and Joy. "You are whispering about something!" she accused them.

"Yes, I suppose we are," Joy laughed. "Please don't make me tell—just yet."

Corrine wagged her finger. "Then you had better out with it soon!"

Joy laughed again. Yes. All right. Tonight at dinner."

Corrine squeezed Sara's arm. "Just think! *Two* babies at Palmer House!"

"Tut-tut! No talking about it until after dinner," Joy admonished, grinning.

Joy peeped into the great room and found Rose as she had expected to: seated at her desk, wrestling with the house's books, a harried but determined look on her brow.

"Mama?"

Rose glanced up and the weight of the house's finances dropped away. "Joy! You are home early, aren't you?"

"Yes, a little. Sarah will lock up today. I left early . . . so I could visit with you. Do you have a minute?"

"Indeed, I do!" Rose laughed and then grimaced. "On days like today I so miss Flinty's knowledge and counsel."

She and Joy sank into two of the great room's overstuffed chairs. Rose rubbed her tired eyes. "We have patched and repaired the roof, but we must have a new one, you know, and so much of what I do—contacting roofers, asking for bids, deciding if they are honest—would be easier for . . . well, for a man to do."

Joy thought for a moment. "Grant is feeling quite without purpose because coming to the store is too much, Mama, but he would be pleased to offer any advice that doesn't require him to run up and down stairs."

"Of course! Why did I not think of him?" Rose sighed. "And do you think he would be willing to help me with the house's books?"

"He would be delighted, Mama. Please ask him?"

"Yes. Yes, I will. Now what did you want to talk about?"

Joy studied her mother knowing this moment would be etched in her heart forever. "Well . . . I wanted to talk about babies." She smiled and Rose smiled back.

"Oh, I know! I am so excited that we will have another baby in the house! Little Will is growing so quickly. He is not really a baby anymore."

"Yes, but I said *babies*, not *baby*, Mama." Joy was teasing her mama, drawing out the pleasure of announcing this miraculous surprise.

Rose blinked. "Babies? As in more than one baby?"

"Yes, Mama." Joy couldn't help it. The memory of her father's last words to her was etched into her soul: *I bless you. I bless your children. The Lord will give . . .* Tears began to prick her eyes.

"Why, Joy! Dear, what is the matter?"

"The matter? At this moment, I am a happy woman, Mama. A happy, happy mother-to-be."

Rose's eye widened. "Mother-to-be?"

Joy nodded. "I am expecting, Mama."

"You're going to have a baby?"

"Yes, Mama. Grant and I are having a baby! In January, I think. It is a miracle."

Rose gathered her daughter into her arms. "My daughter, a mother! O Lord Jesus! Thank you!"

Then Rose held Joy by the shoulders and stared into her eyes. "Why, that means I am going to be a grandmother! I'm going to be a *grandmother*!"

Their joyous laughter echoed around the high walls and ceiling of the great room.

That evening at dinner, a perplexed Breona studied Joy and Grant. *They be positively bubblin' wi' somethin',* she marveled, unable to ascertain *what*.

She pursed her lips and slanted a look toward Miss Rose. *Loike a cat in th' cream,* she muttered to herself. Rose's usually pale face was flushed with color and an irrepressible smile tugged at her mouth.

Sarah and Corrine stifled giggles and Joy, with a playful frown, hushed them. Breona set her fork on her plate and her eyes narrowed. Corrine glanced Breona's way, blushed, and casually— *much too casually!*—dabbed at her mouth with her napkin.

Breona folded her arms and frowned. *Why, they be hidin' somethin'!* she groused, put out that she was not in on the secret.

She did not have to wait long. As they neared the end of the meal, Grant spoke.

"Everyone," Grant opened, gaining the attention of those at the table, "Joy and I have something . . . to tell you." He glanced at Joy, who could scarcely keep from blurting the news herself. They exchanged a tender look.

"We are, Joy and I," Grant grinned, "going to have a little one."

The few seconds of silence after his announcement were followed by chaos and jubilation. Several women at the table left their chairs and ran to embrace Joy.

Breona was overcome. *Miss Joy is t' have a bairn! Oh, thank you, heavenly Father!*

Then she caught sight of Tabitha, two seats down from her. The old coldness—an angry, defiant stoniness—had fixed itself on Tabitha's face. Without a word, she left the table and climbed the staircase.

Concerned, Breona's head swiveled toward Rose, but Rose, her mouth parted in apprehension, was already staring after Tabitha.

Liáng and Miss Greenbow gave the little house a final examination. They had worked all morning and it was now clean and ready to turn back to the landlord. However, as they had cleaned, Liáng sensed that the woman, their dear friend, was disturbed.

She has already said that she had a new assignment, Liáng worried, *so it could not be the loss of this job.*

"Miss Greenbow," he asked gently, "is something troubling you? May I be of any help?"

She twisted the rag in her hand and sighed. "Thank you, but I don't think you can be of help."

Liáng thought for a moment. "Is it because you have not heard from Mr. O'Dell?"

She looked away. "Well, I *have* heard from him, actually."

The flatness of her response told Liáng all he needed to know. "I am truly sorry. I had hoped . . ."

She sighed. "I suppose I had, too, but . . . truthfully, I am not entirely surprised."

Liáng looked a question to her.

"I think . . . I think his heart already is—and has been for some time—engaged elsewhere, Mr. Liáng. To someone he cannot have, I surmise."

"Oh, my dear!" Liáng took her hand. "I had no idea."

She sniffed and laughed a little but sniffed again. "I have prayed over it and the Lord has assured me that all is well. I know Mr. O'Dell is an honorable man. If he could not give me his whole heart . . ."

"Then he would not trifle with yours? Is that it?"

She nodded. "Yes. That is what I believe."

Liáng thought over Miss Greenbow's words as he drove back to the parsonage: *I think his heart already is—and has been for some time—engaged elsewhere.* As Liáng pondered those words, he frowned and listened to the whispers of his own heart. Part of him dreaded the coming Sunday morning, for he would be announcing his resignation during the morning service.

When his flock asked him where he would be going, he would find it difficult to explain that *his* heart, too, was engaged elsewhere—but not to a larger, well-heeled congregation, one that would pay him more and provide him with a nicer home and a newer automobile! No, his heart was pulled by a sovereign move of God happening in a crumbling warehouse. A move of God that thrilled and challenged Liáng to the depths of his soul.

How would he explain his choice to the people he had so faithfully served for eight years but who were, at best, moderate in their love for God?

I will say only that I am called to Denver to minister to the large Chinese population there, he decided. Yet he knew that good friends—including Jinhai Li—would press him for more details. To Jinhai, at least, he would feel free to speak of the move of God in downtown Denver, a mighty move of the Spirit that was calling drunks, prostitutes, and the destitute to the Savior and delivering them in miraculous ways.

However, and especially to Jinhai, Liáng would be careful to make no mention of another way in which his heart was becoming engaged. No, he could make no mention of that individual. He needed to keep that thought to himself, tucked deep inside, but carried with great care.

"Just so, Mr. Michaels. Place this over your mouth and nose and breathe normally." Dr. Peabody held a hard, ugly, rubber, cup-like device in his hands and demonstrated. From the outside of the cup emerged a fat hose. The hose, in turn, led to a cylindrical tank standing near the doctor. The tank had gauges on its top and a bag that expanded and deflated as Dr. Peabody breathed.

Joy's eyes went wide and she looked from the breathing apparatus to Grant and back. The noises it emitted made her skin crawl.

Grant, however, took the offered mask and, after studying it, placed it on his face as directed. He breathed in the extra oxygen for a minute and then sighed and relaxed.

"How do you feel?" Joy whispered.

"Better," he spoke through the mask. "I feel better."

Doctor Peabody lifted Grant's free hand and examined his nail beds. "Good," he muttered and scribbled something in Grant's record.

Grant removed the mask. "How often do I use it?"

The doctor stared at him and frowned. "My dear man, you are going to require its use day and night. Do not worry about becoming dependent upon it."

He looked away and murmured, "As the heart, er, declines, you will notice that your need for oxygen increases. You can adjust the flow of gas with this dial. The straps on the side of the mask will allow you to fasten it to your head so you can sleep with it."

The doctor turned to his desk and wrote some instructions. "You must schedule regular tank deliveries so that you do not run out—that would be quite unwise. I've listed the telephone number here. Oh, and someone must help you move the tank when you change rooms. The hose is long, providing a nice range of movement, but it has its limits."

He pointed at Grant. "You, sir, are never to attempt to move the tank yourself, nor are you, Mrs. Michaels, particularly in your condition. The tank is quite heavy and unwieldy."

Grant and Joy glanced at each other. This was far more than they had anticipated—and they would need to move the tank farther than merely from room-to-room! They would need to move it from the cottage to the main house and back again each day, at a minimum!

"Billy," Joy blurted. "Billy is as strong as a horse! I know he will be happy to do this for us, Grant."

Grant nodded, but the disquieting sensation of his world shrinking, contracting even further, was overwhelming. Sensing that he was short of breath, he raised the mask to his face and inhaled. Almost immediately, his anxiety eased. He pulled the cup away and stared at it.

"I believe it truly is helping me." He was both relieved and in awe.

Joy had perceived her husband's disquiet. She placed her hand upon his. "If it helps you, then it is worth its weight in gold, no matter the inconvenience."

❞ ❧ ❟

Chapter 7

(Journal Entry, July 15, 1910)

Grant's heart doctor has prescribed an apparatus to help with Grant's breathing. We are adjusting to the machine's unsightly presence and continual sounds, but the improvement Grant is experiencing is remarkable. All of us can see how much more comfortable he is, how well his complexion appears, and how great a difference the machine has made in his daily enthusiasm and energy.

Billy has proven himself a blessing of inestimable worth in this regard: Each morning when Grant is ready, he carries the tank into the house with Grant following along behind him. When Grant and Joy are ready to retire, Billy takes the machine back to their cottage. We did not foresee, however, the difficulties we would encounter during the day, after Billy has left for the shop.

It was Mr. Wheatley who recognized that Grant needed an easier means of conveying the tank and its gadgets through the house—particularly when needing to use the necessary. Calling on the memory of his friend, Mr. Wheatley said, "I figure Flinty would have taken one look at this contraption and built wheels for it. Since he is not here, I hope I can do half as good a job as he!"

Well, Mr. Wheatley and Grant put their heads together and, employing the wheels from an old baby buggy, they designed a little cart that Mr. Wheatley hammered and screwed together. Last evening, Billy strapped the "contraption," as Mr. Wheatley refers to it, onto the cart. Now even Grant can wheel it from room to room without overtaxing his strength.

The marvels of science can be such a blessing, Lord! We thank you for this machine. We all realize that it is keeping Grant with us longer, even if we do not speak of it.

Esther dabbed at the perspiration beading on her brow. Changing the window display in their tiny store was the highlight of the week—not only for her but for the women of RiverBend and its surrounds. The bright sunlight beating through the glass while she arranged colorful hats, dresses, and other accessories had, however, overheated her.

I do not think I will ever get over how such a simple presentation of pretty things can be the talk of the town, Esther mused, smiling.

"Here, Esther." Ava handed Esther a glass of cool water and then fanned herself. "It's going to be a scorcher today."

Of the six women who had fled Denver and the *Silver Spurs* on Christmas Eve last year, only Esther and Ava remained in RiverBend. *Six of us fled Denver, but mostly we all fled Cal Judd*, Esther reminded herself. Even as hot as the reflected sunlight had made her, Esther shivered.

With most of the community hearing "through the grapevine" why Esther and the other women had abandoned Denver for the unlikely haven of RiverBend, their stay had seemed temporary at best. After all, RiverBend was a small town that existed only to serve the farmers of the area—mostly simple, God-fearing, church-going families. The town did not have a drinking or "sporting" establishment, nor would its citizenry ever tolerate one.

Esther and the other girls had feared (and rightly so) that the community would shun them. For the first few weeks, their presence had created a firestorm of controversy and division.

Pastor Medford had personally visited the most vocal of the critics. He had shared with them what Joy Thoresen Michaels had found in Corinth, how God had moved to destroy the stronghold of evil in that town and how—one girl at a time—many damaged hearts were coming to repentance and salvation in Christ.

Joy and her mother, Rose Thoresen, were respected in RiverBend, as were Pastor Medford and his wife. Jacob and Vera Medford spent countless hours in the homes of their congregation's members and with other pastors and leaders of the farming community. With great conviction, the Medfords shared Joy and Rose's ministry in Denver and how God was blessing it with many redeemed hearts and lives.

Still, criticisms did arise. To each dissenting voice Jacob placed the question, "What should we, who profess to be followers of Christ, do to help those women who have been forced into such slavery and have now turned to Jesus?" Once confronted with such a decision, the critical voices had, with the exception of a few adamant individuals, trickled to a stop.

The girls still faced suspicious looks and scrutiny from some, but not all the folks had been insensible to the needs of Esther and her companions. Jacob Medford had spoken passionately to his church, reminding them that Jesus had not come to heal the well *but the sick*, and his people had responded from their hearts.

Enough of RiverBend's citizenry wanted the girls to succeed at leaving their old lives for new ones that, in their simple ways, they had welcomed and helped the six women while they got their bearings and began to make long-term plans.

It had not been easy on the girls or Pastor Medford's church. Esther could not recall how many times she had wanted to quit and leave, but where could she go?

That was when the girls learned that farmers are tenacious people who do not give up easily: They refused to give up on the girls when they inadvertently scandalized the town with colorful language or behavior, and they refused to give up on the girls as, with difficulty, they adjusted to the simple conventions of country life.

Fiona McKennie and Vera Medford, old friends of Rose Thoresen, had patiently taught the girls to work with their hands, earning their own way, learning new skills, and developing self-respect for an honest job done well. Perhaps more importantly, they had patiently shared the Good News with each young woman and had seen all but one of them surrender their lives to the Savior.

Three of the girls had, with help from Pastor and Mrs. Medford and their congregation, found employment in other towns where their past lives would remain anonymous. Jesse, however, had shocked them all—especially Esther!—by accepting a marriage proposal from a young farmer. He was a widower with two small children who lived far from town.

"He is good and kind," Jesse had mumbled when Esther gaped at her announcement, "and I already love his children. I might never have another chance for a respectable marriage and a family . . . what with my past and all."

As the Nebraska winter gave way, Esther and Ava continued in RiverBend, slowly slipping into the fabric of the town. Esther sold the jewelry Cal Judd had given her. With the money from the sale, she opened this shop. She and Ava ordered stylish but inexpensive, ready-made dresses and hats from a catalog and added their own fashionable touches to them to make them desirable.

In just two months they had established themselves and their little business in RiverBend, garnering enough income to make the rent and put a little food on the table. They were struggling to become financially independent and were slowly connecting to the lifeblood of the community, a bond so spiritually vital that Esther no longer thought of leaving.

And as the prairie greened that spring, Esther had surprised even herself: She fell in love with the land. Beautiful, elegant, sophisticated Esther, whom Cal Judd had clothed in the finest fashions and jewels, was finding peace in the simple beauty of low, undulating hillocks and open vistas.

It is enough for now, Esther smiled, admiring the window display from outside. *What is that verse Vera quoted to me? Something about godliness and contentment being great gain.*

"Good morning, Mrs. Bruntrüllsen!" Esther smiled and waved to the woman crossing the street and received a hearty greeting in return.

Contentment! It is great gain, Esther admitted, still smiling. *It is what I've been seeking for a long while.*

Liáng stepped from the train onto the platform of Union Station, Denver. *I am here, Lord,* he said in silent prayer. *It has taken me nearly two months, but I am here. Here to do your will.*

He had to chuckle to himself. In the eyes of his congregation, his Seattle friends, and even his oldest acquaintances from seminary, he was stepping down in life.

No, Lord, I am not, he breathed. *I am honored to answer the high calling you have placed upon my life.*

He laughed again. He had a little in his pocket and a little more in a savings account. He had sold many of his belongings, although all the furnishings of the parsonage belonged not to him, but to the church. Those furnishings would remain in the parsonage for the next pastor. The trunks Liáng had packed were laden with books, and clothes, and little else.

"Minister Liáng!"

Liáng rounded at the call. Isaac Carmichael and Bao Shin Xang waved to him and he waved back. For now the three bachelors would be crowded in the tiny two-bedroom house, with Liáng and Bao sharing the second bedroom.

The house would provide little of the privacy Liáng was accustomed to, yet he felt blessed that Carmichael had offered to share the house. It was Carmichael who was sacrificing *his* privacy to accommodate Bao and Liáng!

Bao and Carmichael soon joined him. Liáng embraced the two men, glad to see their faces again.

"I have borrowed a truck from one of our church members to haul your trunks," Carmichael pointed. "I don't know where we shall put your things when we get home, but the more the merrier. And great news—" he grinned here —"we are invited to dinner tonight at Palmer House!"

Liáng drew in a deep breath and exhaled, a vision of dark eyes dancing before him. *Thank you, Lord!*

"I can't think of a better welcome to Denver," he answered.

The heat of summer surged back in late August, far beyond its normal boundaries. The people of Denver longed for cooling rains to relieve their discomfort. Complaints about the above-average temperatures and prayers for late monsoon rains to quench the heat were heard upon lips universally.

Within Palmer House, windows were propped open wide in the hopes of catching breezes to freshen the house. Each night the women tossed upon their beds, too miserable to sleep well. Each day the girls avoided the upper reaches of the house where temperatures—and tempers—soared. Mei-Xing, in her last month of pregnancy, suffered terribly. Dark circles rimmed her eyes and advertised of sleepless nights.

"Tabitha," Rose called to the figure hurrying down the hallway.

The younger woman would be leaving them in a few short weeks for nursing school in Boulder. Rose had come to depend upon Tabitha's advice regarding health issues—for even as she prepared for her departure in late September, she had set her mind to learn all she could from Doctor Murphy and to devour whatever medical reading she could lay hands upon.

Tabitha turned and walked back to Rose's desk. "Yes, Miss Rose?"

"Tabitha, I am growing troubled about Mei-Xing and her baby in this heat," Rose began. "I don't like the way Mei-Xing is looking; she cannot be sleeping well. Can you recommend something to relieve her?"

At the mention of Mei-Xing's name, Tabitha averted her eyes.

Rose had seen—and been puzzled by—Tabitha's behavior more than once. Perhaps because of the heat, perhaps because she was weary herself, she snapped, "Tabitha! Is there a problem I should know of?"

Tabitha's face registered surprise: Miss Rose rarely lost her temper. "Why, what do you mean?"

Rose hrmphed. "I mentioned Mei-Xing and you turned down your mouth like you had bitten into a sour apple! I don't understand it, and I want to know what the problem is!"

"Oh . . ." That was all Tabitha said, but that single word was potent.

Rose, contrite, came out from behind her desk and placed a hand on Tabitha's arm. "I am sorry for snapping at you, Tabitha. It was wrong. Will you forgive me?"

"Of course! We are all so miserably hot, and I—" but Tabitha did not finish her sentence.

"Please." Rose took Tabitha by the arm. "You will be leaving us soon and, as incredibly *proud* of you as I am and as delighted as I am for you, I will miss you terribly! Please, let's sit and talk a bit, shall we?" She led Tabitha into the parlor and closed the door behind them.

"Tabitha," Rose began, "I confess that I need your help."

The red-haired woman glanced up. She was always eager to help!

"What I need help with is . . . understanding what is troubling you with regard to Mei-Xing."

Tabitha again dropped her eyes to the floor and Rose frowned, uneasy and perplexed.

"Can you not help me to understand? Can you not tell me what bothers you so?"

Rose had never seen Tabitha fidget as she did now—or be at a loss for words, either. Her face, bent toward the hands she folded in her lap, was flushed. What Tabitha said next confounded Rose.

"I shall be glad to be away to nursing school next month . . . perhaps *before* Mei-Xing's baby comes," Tabitha muttered.

Rose sighed and frowned, as mystified as ever. "You will be glad to be away when Mei-Xing's baby arrives?"

Tabitha's reply was even less audible. "Yes."

Rose blinked. And waited. Tabitha said nothing. "What are you not telling me, my dear girl?" Rose whispered. "Are you afraid for her?"

"No! That is," Tabitha exhaled, "No, I am not afraid for her; I am certain she will do fine. I-I love Mei-Xing, Miss Rose."

Rose sank to her knees in front of Tabitha and held Tabitha's hands in her own. "It has to do with Mei-Xing's baby then, not with Mei-Xing herself. Is that it? And so also with Joy's baby?"

Tabitha dipped her head lower. A great tear plopped onto their joined hands.

"Can you not tell me?" Rose implored.

A racking sob burst from Tabitha—the expression of a pain so deep that Rose did not try to fathom it. She only reached for Tabitha and wrapped her arms as tightly as she could about Tabitha's shaking shoulders.

Rose held Tabitha as the girl moaned and wept. As Rose's tears joined Tabitha's, the Holy Spirit whispered the truth to Rose's heart.

"O Jesus!" Rose gasped.

Many minutes later, Tabitha, with her head upon Rose's shoulder, confessed her pain aloud.

"When I became pregnant, I was so young—just fifteen. I didn't even realize I was expecting. No one ever told me . . . what to look for.

"I'd been traded to a low-class brothel in Kansas City. I didn't even get sick to my stomach! But I did have . . . other symptoms and my body started changing. A 'client' mentioned to the madam that I had complained that certain things pained me. The madam stripped me down, examined my body, and asked questions. I was shocked when she said I was with child."

Tabitha shook her head and looked at the wall as if seeing something else, far away. "I-I can't speak of it; it is so hard to think of those days, Miss Rose. It grieves me so much!"

Rose held Tabitha while she wept again. "You do not need to tell me. I understand what happened. I understand now why it pains you to see Mei-Xing and Joy both expecting babies."

But Tabitha kept talking. "The madam sent for a woman. Two men held me down while she pushed something sharp into me. It hurt. Oh, Miss Rose! It hurt so bad!"

"There, there," Rose muttered. Her heart was clenched so tight she could not breathe. "You can let it go, Tabitha. You can let it go." Rose did not want to hear any more. Her heart was already breaking.

Tabitha whispered. "I bled for two weeks and could not work. The madam was so angry. She finally sent for a doctor who examined me and shook his head.

"He and the madam had a great row in the next room. I heard him shout, *She will never be able to have children!* The madam cursed him and shouted back, *Good! This is a business, not an orphanage. We don't want our girls dropping their bastards here!*"

"O God," Rose moaned, leaning her forehead on Tabitha's shoulder.

Tabitha seemed unaware of Rose's distress. "The doctor was right. I never got pregnant again. I won't be able to have children. I will never grow a babe inside of me."

Tabitha's words petered out and they were both silent. Rose sighed, begging for wisdom, and Tabitha roused herself. "So, you see, it is good that I am going away to nursing school. Perhaps my life can be of some good use other than raising a family."

Rose placed her hands on Tabitha's cheeks and cupped her face with tender fingers. "Do not limit or underestimate our God, Tabitha," she implored. "I, too, believe nursing school is his path for you—but not because you are defective. He has gifted you to nurse, hasn't he? You will encounter many hurting souls in your chosen field. You will have opportunity to minister to their bodies *and* their hearts. Because of what you have suffered, you will have compassion for those who hurt."

Tabitha nodded her agreement and leaned into Rose's embrace. They both stirred when a crack of thunder heralded a much-desired rainfall.

That evening, after a good, soaking rain, the house was finally cool. Rose found herself nodding off before bedtime and realized that most of the girls had already given in to the allure of sweet, undisturbed sleep.

She was tempted to put off writing in her journal but, determined, turned to a fresh page and jotted the date.

(Journal Entry, August 29, 1910)

Lord, I want to thank you for Tabitha's courage today to confess what has been a great burden and torment to her soul. I thank you that your forgiveness knows no limits. We place limitations on your grace, but you do not.

Father God, surely she is not the only one of our girls who carries this sadness? Will you show me what I am to do?

Fiona McKennie, the aging but indomitable matriarch of a large family in the RiverBend community, took Esther and Ava under her wing as harvest set in.

"But what about our store?" Esther objected. It was Sunday after church, and Fiona was insisting that the girls come home with her to learn and take part in canning, pickling, and drying her garden's mountain of produce.

"And who will be coomin' t' town during harvest?" Fiona laughed. "Nae a woman wi' a garden, I am promisin' ye!"

Esther and Ava looked at each other. What Fiona said might be true—Esther and Ava had not seen a customer in the shop in two days.

When Fiona smiled, her cheeks rounded like ripe apples and her black eyes crinkled up in mirth. She grinned now and added, "Ye'll be puttin' up food for your ownsel's and thankin' me coom winter, little misses."

Esther was intrigued. "Well then! We are at your disposal, Fiona."

She and Ava packed a bag with aprons and a few changes of clothing—second-hand dresses women of the church had given them, dresses they wore when they cleaned the shop and their small quarters in at the back. Esther printed a note and pasted it to the "Closed" sign hanging on the shop door.

She paused before locking the door behind them to study the note. The words *Back After Harvest* stared at her and, for some reason, she chuckled.

"Are we becoming farmers, Ava?" she giggled.

Ava scowled and muttered something Esther could not make out as the two women climbed into the wagon behind Fiona and her husband Brian. The road was rutted and bumpy, but Esther hardly noticed. She was studying the land as they wound through the prairie toward Brian and Fiona's farm.

Her eyes ate up the scenery and the faraway views. *Such peace, Lord!* she prayed in wonder.

Just before they turned onto McKennie land, Fiona pointed east where the road rambled on. "Farther doon th' road be Thoresen land."

"Mrs. Thoresen has land here?" Esther was surprised.

"Aye! Her own homestead where she and Jan were livin' 'till he passed. 'Cross th' creek was bein' Jan's land, now b'longin' t' his son Søren, who is bein' married t' our Meg."

Esther and Ava knew Søren and Meg from church—and other Thoresens, many more than they could count or remember by name.

Fiona wasn't finished. "Søren and Meg's youngest, Jon, farms Rose's land now. An' b'side Søren and Meg is more Thoresen land, b'longin' t' Jan's nephews, Karl and Kjell Thoresen, an' their sons. Their brother, Arnie, chose th' lawyerin' life. He an' his family be livin' in Omaha."

Now Esther's head was spinning. "It seems as though everyone is related to everyone else around here," she frowned.

"Aye, 'tis bein' a bit loik that," Fiona laughed in response. "Ah, s'many years hev passed. If ye could have bin seein' th' land when first we coomed . . ."

Brian "hrmmed" and nodded.

Esther was surprised—and oddly touched—when Fiona laid her graying head on Brian's shoulder and they became quiet, caught up in their shared memories.

What would it be like to live your entire life where such continuity grew and multiplied year after year, generation upon generation?

Esther stared over the fields and felt an unfamiliar yearning stirring in her heart.

Chapter 8

September

Breona awakened in the dark to Mei-Xing's groans. She whipped the covers off and scuttled to Mei-Xing's bed.

"Whist?" she whispered. Mei-Xing did not answer; she lay curled on her side, very much asleep. Breona frowned as she padded back to her bed. Within seconds she dozed off.

Some time later, Mei-Xing groaned anew, again awakening Breona. This time Breona did not get up, but she began praying for her friend.

As dawn crept into the bedroom, Breona arose. She was always the first up in the house and relished her morning cup of coffee in the quiet kitchen before others began to stir. She dressed and went down the back stairs to the kitchen to put the coffee on.

Half an hour later, she was joined by Rose Thoresen. "Good morning, Breona." Rose mumbled the greeting and went directly to the large pot on the stove.

She sat down near Breona, took a sip, and sighed. "Another fine day!"

"Yis," Breona agreed. "And a foine day fer a babe t' be borned, I'm thinkin'!"

Rose's head snapped up. "You think so?"

"Aye. I'm b'laivin' Mei-Xing t' be in labor." Breona described Mei-Xing's moans as she slept.

After they finished their coffee, Rose and Breona climbed the stairs to the second floor. Breona quietly opened the door to her and Mei-Xing's bedroom. Mei-Xing sat on the edge of her bed, her arms wrapped protectively about her belly.

"How are you feeling, dear one?" Rose asked. She knelt beside the bed and looked into Mei-Xing's face.

"I-I'm not sure." She stifled a groan and arched her back. "My back hurts. The pain woke me."

Rose laid a hand on her stomach and felt its rigidity. "When this eases, let's have you walk about a bit, all right?"

Word of Mei-Xing's labor spread through the house. All during the day different girls stopped to offer encouragement and to say they were praying—including Tabitha, who would be leaving for nursing school in two days.

Breona stayed by Mei-Xing's side and prepared her bed for the delivery. About three o'clock in the afternoon, Rose used the house's telephone to call Doctor Murphy.

Mei-Xing's baby was born the following morning after a long and difficult labor. "Mei-Xing has a fine daughter," Doctor Murphy reported to those in the great room awaiting news. "Mother and child are both well." He smiled at the happy clamor his news created.

Rose sat upon the side of Mei-Xing's bed holding the tiny baby—and she *was* tiny. Like her mother, the infant's hair was black and full, her skin white with the faintest blush of pink. "She is so beautiful, Mei-Xing!" Rose exclaimed.

Joy sat beside Rose and leaned over her shoulder. "Oh! She has opened her eyes! Look, Mama!" Even as Joy leaned against her mother's side, her own baby kicked vigorously and Rose felt it.

Joy laughed. "Another baby heard from, eh, Mama?"

Mei-Xing smiled in the exhausted triumph only a woman who has labored to birth a child can know. The newborn blinked and stared, her black eyes searching but unable yet to see. Then she opened her mouth, yawned, and returned to sleep.

With a sigh of contentment, Rose relinquished the sleeping infant and stood. "I must see how the house is faring," she stated. "We have been so marvelously distracted for an entire day and a night! But I fear that the laundry may still be piled in baskets and that Marit has been abandoned to prepare the meals by herself." She excused herself and closed the door softly.

Joy held Mei-Xing's baby now, staring in wonder. "I find it so hard to believe that the little life growing in me will come out some day soon and that I will be holding him or her just like this." She opened the infant's fist and spread the tiny fingers, marveling at their perfection.

"Our babies will be like cousins, you know," Joy murmured. "They will play together, nap together, be doted upon by many surrogate aunts. They will even share the same grandmother."

Mei-Xing looked a question to Joy.

"I know you love my mother, Mei-Xing. And I know she loves you as a daughter," Joy answered, her voice soft. "All my life I have been her only child, but . . . before me she had other children. Did you know that?"

Mei-Xing's face wore her shock. "I had no idea."

Joy nodded. "She had a son and two daughters from her first marriage. It is almost too sad to speak of."

For many minutes they were companionably silent until Mei-Xing's baby stirred and began to fuss. Joy handed her to Mei-Xing. As the baby's fussing increased, Mei-Xing looked to Joy for help.

"You haven't fed her yet?"

Mei-Xing shook her head. "She was so wide awake at first and then she slept. I don't really know how to do it."

Joy laughed. "Don't look at me! I don't know how, either! But perhaps we can figure it out together? If you don't mind?"

"Please!" Mei-Xing laughed in return.

After a few awkward tries the baby latched on and Mei-Xing and Joy watched, fascinated, as the infant girl suckled.

"How does it feel?" Joy was in awe.

"Very strange," Mei-Xing replied, making a face. "As though a string were attached from my baby's mouth to my womb and each time she sucks, she pulls the string a little."

Joy's brows arched in surprised revelation. "Well!"

"Joy," Mei-Xing said carefully. "You were talking to me of your mother . . . and our babies earlier."

"Oh. Yes. I was thinking aloud, I guess, how Mama would have liked to have many grandchildren. But, she only has me, you know, and I despaired of ever making her a grandmother. My brother Søren has children—grandchildren, even! But Mama did not raise Søren. Their relationship has always been a deep friendship, but not like mother and son.

"Then the Lord gave us the lodge in Corinth and later this house, and while I feel I have a multitude of sisters, Mama feels that the Lord has given her a multitude of daughters. You especially."

Mei-Xing's voice was a bare whisper. "Truly?" She touched Joy's hand.

"Truly." Joy gathered Mei-Xing's fingers in her own and cleared her throat a bit. "That is why, Mei-Xing, I know that this little daughter of yours will have a grandmother in my mama."

"Nothing could make me happier," Mei-Xing confessed, tears standing in her eyes. "I thank you, Joy, for your generous heart. You have always been so good to me."

"We will always be good to each other, little sister," Joy whispered. "What God brings together, he bonds forever with his love."

Later, when just Rose and Mei-Xing were in the room, Rose asked, "Have you picked out a name for your daughter?"

Mei-Xing sighed. "I think so, but I confess I am glad she is a girl and not a boy. I am wondering . . . is that wrong?"

Rose examined Mei-Xing's face. "I think it depends. Why are you glad she is not a boy?" Rose thought she knew, but felt that Mei-Xing should confirm it.

"Because . . . because girls are not as important . . . not as desired as boys . . . to some." Mei-Xing fell silent.

"I don't agree with such thinking. I think this baby is *very* important and *very* desired," Rose probed. "I already love this baby girl, don't you?"

Mei-Xing was quick to answer. "Oh, yes! I love her as my life, Miss Rose! That is not . . . exactly what I meant." She cradled the swaddled bundle closer. "I love you as my life, little girl," she crooned.

"Then you mean that *someone else* might desire this little girl less than they might if . . . she were a little boy?"

Mei-Xing nodded. "Yes. You know what I am thinking, Miss Rose. In my culture, daughters are not valued as sons are. If Fang-Hua ever discovered I had a baby but found out my baby was a girl, she would not care as much. But if my baby—*her son's baby*—were a *boy* . . . I would never be able to rest. I would never be able to stop being vigilant. That is why . . . I am glad she is a girl."

Rose nodded. "I understand."

Breona slipped into the room. "I was thinkin' a cup of tea would be pleasin' t' ye."

"Yes! Thank you." Mei-Xing handed the baby to Rose and took the cup gratefully.

"Hev ye named the babe?" Breona asked, looking over Rose's shoulder.

"Why, we were just talking about that very thing!" Rose exclaimed.

Mei-Xing nodded. "This little one is a precious treasure to me! That is why I have decided her first name will be *Shan*—which means *precious coral*. It is only the second name I have . . . not quite decided on." Mei-Xing colored and looked down.

"I think Shan is beautiful!" Rose laughed.

"Aye, *Sean* is havin' a good sound t' it!" Breona concurred. "Almost bein' Irish, I'm thinkin'," she added under her breath.

"Would you like to tell us the other name you are thinking of? I'm sure it is just as lovely," Rose asked.

Mei-Xing colored again. "Rose?" she whispered.

"Yes, dear?" Rose leaned forward.

"I-I meant, for the second name . . . *Rose*." Mei-Xing licked her lips. "Her name would be Shan-Rose. Shan-Rose Li. That is, if it is all right with you."

Rose was stunned—and delighted. "I am honored, Mei-Xing."

A grin lit Breona's face. "*Sean Rose? A right* Irish name!"

Mei-Xing and Breona laughed.

The baby stirred, stretched, and began to fuss. Within seconds, her face reddening, she was screaming for nourishment.

"Aye, an' wit' a foine Irish temper, too!" Breona muttered.

The following morning Tabitha would leave for nursing school.

Weeks before, Mr. Wheatley had uncovered an old trunk on the third floor and had spent many evenings refurbishing it for Tabitha's use. He had rubbed and polished the old leather and brass fittings until they shone, repaired and oiled the hinges and, with Billy's help, had tacked a new lining of watered silk into the trunk's interior.

It was not a large trunk, but even after Tabitha placed all she owned into it, the space remaining only made obvious how meager her earthly possessions were. The evening before she was to leave was when the girls began visiting Tabitha, bearing small offerings to add to the little that the trunk contained.

Jenny folded a crocheted afghan of pale blue yarn into the trunk. "My little grandmother did most of it," she confessed. "She is teaching me but I had to pull out so many rows that if she hadn't helped me finish it, it would not have been done in time to give it to you."

Breona had purchased scented soaps and wrapped them in soft tissue. Their gentle perfume was already freshening the old trunk. "'Tis proud of ye I am," she murmured.

Sarah and Corrine added a matched dresser set—comb, brush, and hand mirror—purchased from Grant and Joy's fine furnishings shop with their wages.

Maria, Nancy, and Flora had pooled their little bit and, with shy smiles, placed a beautiful pair of slippers in Tabitha's hands. "Now we know your feet will be warm in the evenings," Flora whispered, "and you will not forget us."

Marit tucked a box of home-baked cookies into a corner of the trunk and hugged Tabitha, adding, "Ve love you. Don't forget us."

"Is there room for these?" Joy laid a set of linens and a down pillow in the trunk. "Mei-Xing sewed the pillow case and hemmed the sheets last month," Joy whispered. "May you always have sweet dreams as you lay your head upon this pillow."

Tabitha stood stock still as the girls trailed through her room, quietly bestowing their gifts, but she was powerless to stop the tears that ran unheeded down her cheeks.

Rose entered last. She placed an elegant boxed stationery set in Tabitha's hands. Rose laid her cheek against Tabitha's. "So you will always write home to us."

Early in the morning one of Mr. Gresham's men, Cluney, arrived in the automobile they used to transport Mei-Xing to and from Mrs. Palmer's house. Billy hauled Tabitha's trunk downstairs and to the car; Cluney waited to escort Tabitha to the automobile and drive her to the train.

Everyone in the house pressed their cheek to Tabitha's and whispered their goodbyes. "I will be back in June," she tried to answer, but she could not say the words without choking.

"We know," Rose comforted her. "And we will be right here, waiting for you to come home."

O'Dell rubbed his eyes and leaned far back in the chair he'd sat in for four hours. Then he massaged his hip. It was healing, no doubt about it, but O'Dell had found that either too much activity or too little caused it to ache.

I wasn't cut out for this sedentary life, he grumbled. He stood and winced as his hip protested.

It was a good thing that Parsons had assigned him another case. He'd be taking the train to Albany tomorrow. No more reports to write until he returned.

His thoughts turned to the letter in his coat pocket. Fishing it out, he unfolded it and read it again. He shook his head and grinned. Liáng had quit his church and moved to Denver! Reading between the lines without Liáng coming out and saying so, O'Dell deduced that Bao was with him.

This is exciting news, Lord, he mused. *I'm glad and relieved that Bao is away from Seattle, away from Fang-Hua Chen.* O'Dell shuddered and rubbed his hip again. *I have my own 'fond' memories of her.*

Liáng also, without writing her name, had indicated that Miss Greenbow had found another position. O'Dell wondered what she had thought when she'd read his letter. He had not received a response and had not expected to, but he was happy to receive this tidbit of news from Liáng.

Please bless Darla, dear Lord, and help her, O'Dell prayed. He sincerely wanted God's best for his friend, but . . .

But I know that your best for her does not include me, Lord. Thank you for giving me your guidance and peace in that regard.

Chapter 9

October

He didn't know how Fang-Hua's thugs had found him. Morgan had established himself with a new identity in faraway Sacramento, and yet, somehow, it had not been far enough! Fang-Hua's men had found and delivered him to her in one piece. More or less.

And now *Regis St. John*, AKA Shelby Franklin and Dean Morgan—lately known as Paul Westford—calculated his odds and did not find them to his liking. He really had but one card left up his sleeve, and to reveal it here, now, was to leave him with nothing in reserve.

On the other hand, the information would certainly do him no good if he were *dead*.

"Madam Chen," he opened, bowing low before the woman's chair. "I have important news for you."

She eyed him as a snake eyes a doomed mouse before it strikes.

"You can have no news that will be of significance to me," she hissed. With a flick of her hand, the four men in the room were on him. Two of them pushed him to his knees; another moved behind him and pulled his head back. He heard the 'snick' of a knife leaving its scabbard.

"What of your son?" he choked the words out. "What of your lineage?"

She leapt to her feet, shrieking, "*I have no son*! Because of you *he is dead*! Because of you, my husband's line will die with him!"

Fear vied with rage on Fang-Hua's face. She feared what Wei Lin Chen would do if he discovered her connection with Su-Chong's dishonor and death. Her husband might still be able to father children, but *she* was too old to bear him another son! He could divorce her and take a young wife, one who could give him many children!

She snarled at Morgan, "My husband's line may die with him, but I say that *you* will die first. And I will pleasure myself with the sounds of your agony!"

She began to curse him in Mandarin and did not hear what he yelled back, but Morgan was certain the men holding him down did. They shifted nervously. He continued to talk, knowing that if he kept repeating himself the old witch would eventually stop ranting long enough to hear him.

She did finally stop, swaying unsteadily on her feet, wiping spittle from her mouth. Morgan kept repeating himself, waiting for his words to sink in.

He saw the very moment when what he'd said penetrated the fog of her rage.

"Wha . . . what did you say?"

Morgan was silent, watching for the crazed light to leave her eyes. She strode over and squatted in front of him.

"What did you say?" she insisted, her words ragged, harsh.

The man behind him released his hold and Morgan took a careful, cleansing breath, cautiously watching her. "I said, there is a child. You have a grandson," Morgan announced.

He had no idea whether the child was a male or a female. His informants had only told him that the *Little Plum Blossom* had been five or six months gone when she had been returned to the bosom of her friends in Denver. Surely she would have had the child by now.

He watched Fang-Hua's eyes dilate and saw a light spark in them. She slowly stood up.

"So. The little whore gave him a child . . ." she walked back to her chair and sank into it. He swallowed as she fixed him with her cold, mad eyes.

Fang-Hua Chen tapped a lacquered nail on the arm of her chair and used a silk cloth to wipe the spit that dribbled from her mouth. Her breath was still ragged from the rage she had flown into.

A grandson! Is it true? She did not trust the messenger who delivered this tidbit, but it was of such import that she dared not ignore it.

She studied Dean Morgan, the man she knew as *Reggie*. Her guards had sat him roughly in a chair while she plotted her next move. Morgan seemed unfazed as he waited. His face was placid, his hands rested on his thighs. He even flicked a bit of lint from his trouser.

"What if I were to believe such an unlikely tale, *Reggie*?" Her voice was silky, seductive. "You say the girl lives in the same house my men watched for weeks—months!—with no sign of her. You expect me to believe she is there now?"

Morgan nodded sagely. "She was *not* there during the period you looked for her, Madam Chen, because she was with Su-Chong. In hiding."

Fang-Hua's expression darkened. "Nothing the police told us and nothing the papers reported suggests such a thing."

"Ah yes. My sources tell me that someone—a certain Pinkerton man—influenced the police to leave out specific details in their reports . . . for the girl's sake. She was taken back to the house shortly after being found in the same apartment as your son."

Fang-Hua leaned on her arm and pondered what he said. "If there *is* a child—I say *if*—how would you recommend I proceed, *Reggie*? What would you suggest I do to, ah, *retrieve* him?"

Morgan nodded again as though to affirm that she was asking the right questions. "I would recommend, Madam, that you allow me to assist you."

Fang-Hua's laughter was guttural, malevolent. "You would like to *assist* me, Reggie? And why would I ever allow you to do so? Why would I even allow you to leave this house alive?

"You *will* tell me where to find my grandson," she ordered.

He raised an eyebrow, uncowed by her command. "Madam, begging your pardon, but I can be invaluable to you. The men you sent to Denver were ineffective. Were they not all Chinese? Denver has many Chinese, but they do not frequent, they do not spy upon, the houses and neighborhoods where whites live. Your men stuck out like sore thumbs!

"You require someone with certain, shall I say, talents? Let me pick my own men and take them to Denver. I will study the girl's moves and routines. It may take time, perhaps even a few months—she will not be anxious to take a newborn out-of-doors in the dead of winter, after all.

"But when we take the girl and the child, it will be quick and unexpected. They will find only *her* dead body. And then I will bring you the child."

Fang-Hua said nothing for many minutes. When she did speak it was not to Morgan. "Take him to the basement and keep him there. I will think on this. *Do not let him out of your sight.*"

"Yes, Madam Chen," the men muttered. Two of them jerked Morgan to his feet.

Weeks after the harvest had been gathered in, the first freeze of autumn descended on the prairie. Then the RiverBend farming community commenced its fall slaughter for winter meat. Just as Fiona had asked Esther and Ava to stay with her and Brian for a week of canning, she now asked them to come and help put up the meat.

The long cold season was coming, and Esther and Ava had already tasted the brutal weather of last year's winter. They looked at the jars of fruits, vegetables, pickles, jams, and jellies lining their kitchen shelves; they imagined crocks of meat, strings of sausages, and perhaps a ham, and quickly agreed to Fiona's offer. They would ride home with Brian and Fiona after church as they had several weeks ago to help with the canning.

Esther hummed to herself as she scrawled a new sign for the shop's door: *Closed Until Friday.* She could not understand why, but the rhythm and pulse of the community called to her. When she and Ava stayed with Fiona and Brian, Esther even found herself daydreaming about living on a farm—and laughed at the absurdity of the idea.

Brian and Fiona's children were grown and married with children of their own, and most farmed nearby. It was not, therefore, uncommon for the McKennie table to be filled—with or without notice—any day of the week, and especially Sunday.

Regardless of how many mouths showed up for supper, Fiona simply had Esther and Ava set more plates while she added more potatoes, another jar of vegetables, and biscuits to the meal. The happiness around those simple meals spoke more deeply to the hunger inside Esther than anything else.

Oh, to belong, she sighed within her heart. *To belong and to be woven into the fabric of a family and a community! Would that I could ever be so rich.*

The ache she felt was tempered by the fact that she and Ava had, over the last months, been accepted here, despite their pasts. Yes, some holdouts remained, but the community in general had hearkened to Pastor Medford's call to receive those whom Christ had forgiven.

Søren and Meg joined them for that Sunday supper, as did a dark-haired, dark-eyed man Esther and Ava did not recognize. The man looked to be in his early twenties.

"Miss Esther, Miss Ava, this is bein' ourn grandson, Connor," Fiona waved at the man who slid onto one of the bench seats at the table.

Connor nodded at Esther and Ava but said nothing to them—or during the meal—except to shrug when Søren asked, "Will you be staying long this time, Connor?"

Esther saw Brian and Fiona exchange a glance. Connor ate quickly, thanked his grandmother for the meal, and excused himself. Later, when she was tossing out the dishwater, Esther saw Connor walking the fields, a dog romping by his side.

"Aye, he is our lost one," Fiona whispered near Esther's shoulder. "Canna find himself here nor wherever his journeys be takin' him. Lord, please t' be helpin' him foind his way!"

Esther shielded her hand against the setting sun and studied the man far out in the fields. Connor's long strides ate up the distance and he was soon lost to view. She wondered how he had become "lost," given how tightly knit his family seemed to be.

She turned to Fiona, but Fiona answered without being asked. "Lost his sweetheart, he did, three years back. He canna seem t' get shut of th' hurt of it so as t' move on."

Esther dropped her chin toward her breast. How well she understood pain and the tenacious hold it had!

Chapter 10

November

The weeks following Shan-Rose's birth were some of the happiest Palmer House had seen. Mei-Xing regained her strength quickly and her baby thrived and grew. So did Joy's baby.

I am the size of a house already, Joy moaned to herself as she discarded yet another blouse. Grant, grinning, watched her try on a fifth shirtwaist that she could not button.

"I rather like the bloom in your figure," he teased.

"You would!" Joy laughed. "You don't have to cart this extra weight around—especially to the trolley each day!"

"Don't I, though?" Grant retorted, his words dripping with sarcasm. He tapped the oxygen machine prescribed by the doctor. While lending him energy he had thought he would never have again, the machine was noisy, heavy, and restrictive to his movement.

"But, Darling, I am so glad for your machine!" Joy turned from the mirror.

"And I am so glad for *your* little burden." He stood behind her and cradled her belly in his hands. Joy leaned her head back upon his shoulder. The baby chose that moment to kick wildly.

"I feel him!" Grant exclaimed. "I'm sure that is a foot pounding against my hand!"

"You should feel it from inside," Joy groaned.

Grant was quiet for a moment. "We should be careful, Joy, don't you think?" Grant's voice had softened.

"Careful?"

"Yes. We should be careful not to complain, my love. This baby is the greatest blessing of our lives. And this machine is giving me the strength to enjoy this blessing. I will not complain about it again. Instead, I will be thankful."

Joy was chastened. "You are right, Grant. I have allowed little complaints to creep in." She squeezed her eyes closed. "O Lord, I thank you right now for the many blessings in our lives. I thank you for this baby and for my husband's continued good health."

"Yes, Lord. We are grateful," Grant prayed. "Thank you. Thank you for providing our daily bread and our daily needs."

Joy finished dressing and combing out her long, blonde hair. When she had braided it and pinned it to her head, Grant placed her cape across her shoulders.

Joy faced him. "Shall I send Billy to fetch you?"

"Give me ten minutes, if you please," Grant answered.

Each morning Billy lugged the heavy tank up the stairs and into the house and Grant and Joy would take breakfast with those in the house as they had before his illness. Afterwards Joy would leave for the shop and Grant would spend the morning assisting Rose.

That morning, like so many weekday mornings, the house was bustling with movement. The girls were readying themselves to leave for their jobs as soon as breakfast was over, and those who kept Palmer House running had already been up and busy for hours.

However, this day was of particular import: Today, Tory (short for Victoria) Washington would open her showroom, *Victoria's House of Fashion*, to the women of Denver. Tory herself had, with Joy's help, escaped from the "Corinth Gentlemen's Club" less than two years ago.

Friends in Denver, eager to help Joy end the trafficking of young women in Corinth, had sent Tory and her ailing friend, Helen, to Philadelphia to be cared for by two elderly, unmarried sisters, Miss Eloise and Miss Eugenia Wright. The Misses Wright, believing they saw innate talent in Tory, had apprenticed her to Monsieur Pierre LeBlanc, an established and fashion-setting designer.

Last April Tory had returned to Denver and, with the backing of the Misses Wright and M. LeBlanc, had sought the right building for the establishment of her own high-fashion dress shop and sewing school. After securing a property, Tory had undertaken to fit up the sewing rooms, dressing rooms, and showroom.

For the safety of Palmer House's residents and the sake of her endeavor's reputation, Tory and her sponsors had decided to keep the relationship between *Victoria's House of Fashion* and Palmer House under wraps. To that end, Tory took up rooms near her shop and she did not often visit Palmer House.

However, Tory understood how desperately the women of Palmer House needed marketable skills in order to make new lives. In fact, her primary goal for returning to Denver was to help the girls of Palmer House in this manner. To that end, Tory had taken on three of the young women of Palmer House to train them in design, sewing, fitting, or sales, as their talents and inclinations indicated. As her business grew, she hoped to be able to take on more workers.

Now, with help from her Palmer House employees and a veteran seamstress brought from Philadelphia, all was ready: Today *Victoria's House of Fashion* would open its doors to the public. Tory's business would have competition in *M. Philipsborn & Co.*, *The Emporium Millinery Co*, *J. C. Bloom & Co.*, and a few small, select shops akin to her own. But Tory brought her fresh knowledge of Philadelphia fashion and her own exquisite taste to the fray, and was confident—and determined—to succeed.

This morning Flora, Alice, and Marion dressed with particular care. Tory had warned them that they would, to no small degree, be scrutinized by the wealthy clientele Tory hoped to draw to her shop. Sara and Corrine had also worked with the girls, training them in manners and service in much the same way Joy had worked with them when she and Grant had opened *Michaels' Fine Furnishings*. The girls were nervous: So much rode on the success of Tory's venture, including their own livelihoods.

Mei-Xing was also readying for her day with Mrs. Palmer. She had finished feeding Shan-Rose and was waiting in the foyer for the car Mrs. Palmer sent each day for her. With a start, she realized she had left her handbag upstairs.

"Jenny!" Mei-Xing caught Jenny in the adjoining library looking for a new book to take to the elderly woman to whom she was a companion. "Jenny, would you mind holding Shan-Rose for just a moment? Just while I fetch my handbag from my room."

Jenny whirled around. "No! I mean, yes! I mind!" Jenny's face reddened and, without further words, she brushed past Mei-Xing and ran up the stairs.

Mei-Xing was stunned by Jenny's response. She crossed into the great room and found Rose already settled at her desk.

"Miss Rose, I hope I don't impose, but would you mind holding Shan-Rose for just a moment?"

Rose agreed. "Of course I want to hold my little granddaughter!" She took the squirming infant from Mei-Xing—and spotted Mei-Xing's crestfallen expression.

"Why, Mei-Xing. What is the matter?"

"I-I'm not sure what happened," Mei-Xing explained. "I asked Jenny if she would hold Shan-Rose for just a moment, but . . . I must have offended her. She said *no* and then ran away."

Rose looked thoughtful. "Well, my dear, I will hold Shan-Rose while you finish getting ready. The car will be here any minute."

Rose spent the afternoon closed in the library, praying. "Father God, many weeks ago I asked you to help me see and understand this hidden problem in our home. I asked you to give me wisdom.

"Now I believe you have revealed it to me. I thought it was only Tabitha, but I fear it is not. Lord, I trust you. I trust you are working right now, preparing hearts for what you would have me do."

She stood, stretched her stiff, aching back, and brushed her skirt where she had knelt. "I will do all you ask of me, Lord. Please help me."

Conversation around the dinner table that evening was animated. The first day of business for *Victoria's House of Fashion* had gone well: Flora, Alice, and Marion spoke with enthusiasm regarding the customers who had visited the shop and answered a myriad of questions from the other young women.

Rose smiled and asked a few questions herself but, as dinner ended, she made an unusual request. "If you will allow me, I wish to speak to just the ladies for a bit. Privately, if you please."

The eyes of the girls around the table sought for some explanation from each other, but found none. They waited, calm and quiet, as Rose dismissed the men.

"Gentlemen, if you would be excused? Mr. Wheatley, would you kindly close the doors to the dining room on your way out?"

Even Joy did not know what Rose would speak of. As Grant left the table, he patted Joy on the shoulder. "I will wait in the kitchen," he whispered.

Grant, with Billy hauling the ever-present tank, exited to the kitchen. Mr. Wheatley closed the door into the great room first and then followed Grant and Billy into the kitchen.

The door to the kitchen swung closed, and the women at the table were alone now. Wide, curious eyes focused on Rose. Her calm, grey eyes smiled back at them.

"When the Lord called Joy to the work in Corinth . . . and when he later called me to join with her, we often confessed to each other and to the Lord how inadequate and how unprepared we were for the task to which he had called us. You must know what conventional lives we had lived until then! You must know how little we understood of the . . . horrors you endured."

Except for Rose's soft-spoken words, silence reigned at the table. She took a deep breath before continuing.

"I have, in the last few months, seen something I did not understand, something that perplexed and concerned me. It came to my attention first when Mei-Xing returned home . . . in a family way."

When Rose mentioned Mei-Xing, most of the women looked her way, but not all. Some averted their eyes.

"When she came home I observed a quiet withdrawal from her in some of you. Just a few of you." The girls' attention returned to Rose.

"Joy, too, is now expecting, and I have seen something of the same reactions. Some of you have grown distant to her. Please do not think I wish to chide you today. No, I do not. I only wish to understand . . . and to help.

"You see, I did not know what to think of it at first, but I believe I grasp it now." She looked about the table, her gaze resting on Jenny just a little longer than the rest—not long enough for anyone but her to notice. Jenny's cheeks warmed when Rose's inspection turned away. Rose's words were even softer when she spoke again.

"I did not realize, in the life you left behind, the life from which Jesus redeemed you, that some of you must have become pregnant."

She said nothing more but watched for the eyes that would skitter away from her assessment. Jenny. *And Edith.*

Joy's mouth formed a very small "o" as the implications of Rose's words sank in. Mei-Xing nodded to herself. Breona, Marit, and others blinked in sad realization.

Rose felt her throat close up and choke her; she had to clear it before she could speak on. "I cannot fathom the great injustices done to you . . . and to your child. I cannot fathom how hard it must be to see a sister in this house prepare for the happy event of a baby's birth when yours was taken from you . . . or you, perhaps, chose to have its life ended."

There. It was plainly said, the horror uncovered.

"I have lost children," Rose whispered. "I can feel your loss." She shifted in her chair, pleading with the Lord to help her, to help *them.*

"I will never stop aching for my little ones," Rose murmured, "a son and two daughters. I know your situation is different from mine: There was no wrong attached to me regarding their loss. Nevertheless, the Bible is clear: There is no wrong, no sin, no weakness, no loss, no devastation from which our God, through Christ, has not freely forgiven us. And when he forgives us, he will also heal our hearts.

She looked around the table, and again, her gaze lingered just an instant longer on Jenny and Edith. Edith's chin was quivering. "If you still carry guilt in your heart regarding this, shall we not pray right now to also surrender that guilt to our heavenly Father? Shall we not ask for his forgiveness and grace to cover it? If you still carry sorrow, shall we not ask for his healing touch?

"About our sins he has said, *As far as the east is from the west, so far hath he removed our transgressions from us.* You may carry guilt close to your heart today, but God has already removed our sins far, far away.

"So shall we give our guilt to him to carry away, too? In the same manner, shall we surrender our pain to the One who suffered so much to redeem us from pain?"

Heads nodded. Tears were falling around the table when Rose led the girls in prayer. As she prayed she quietly stood and, while continuing to pray, made her way around the table, laying a hand on each girl, and mentioning them by name.

When she finished praying around the table she stood beside her own chair. "Some of you, by the grace of God, escaped suffering this grief. However, I imagine you saw it happen to others. I hope you will extend your compassion and love to those in our family who, as they see Mei-Xing with her baby and watch Joy prepare for the birth of her child, find it difficult to be as joyful as the rest of us are."

Again, a few heads nodded, acknowledging the rightness of her words. The mood was sober when Rose dismissed the girls, but then she saw Jenny, her chin bravely firm, reach out and hug Mei-Xing.

Rose also watched as Joy drew Edith into an embrace and whispered a few private words in her ear. Edith bowed her head on Joy's shoulder and wept, much like Tabitha had wept in Rose's arms that morning in August. Joy held Edith and stroked the girl's brown, curly hair as she sobbed away her grief.

Jenny's eyes met Rose's; she offered Rose a wobbly smile. "Thank you," she mouthed.

Rose nodded once. *Lord Jesus, I am so glad that you came to heal the brokenhearted.*

Days later Morgan was dragged into Fang-Hua's presence.

"I have thought on your recommendation, *Reggie*. I accept your offer to assist me." She smiled, tight-lipped.

Morgan sensed something cunning in her manner and felt his way with caution. "You will not be disappointed," he answered. "I am certain I can bring the child to you."

Morgan kept his face expressionless but he was cheering for this opportunity. *I will find the child, you witch, and in return you will let me go my way and leave me alone.* He was already plotting exigencies, various means of protecting himself should she renege on their deal and try to do away with him afterwards.

"Oh, I won't be disappointed, Reggie, *dear Reggie*."

Morgan's jaw clenched. For now he would endure her denigrations but his plans would ensure that all her secrets were exposed—long after he was gone. Her exposure would ensure that she could not come after him again!

Fang-Hua stood and glided her way across the room toward him, the graceful motion of her steps resembling a hooded cobra swaying hypnotically in front of its kill.

"I have made a few minor adjustments to your plan, *Reggie*, to ensure that I will *not* be disappointed. But you will still be in charge, still responsible for obtaining my grandson—and ending all of the— what was it that you called her? *Little Plum Blossom?* Yes. An apt name for a whore. You will be responsible for ending all of the *Little Plum Blossom's* sorrows."

Morgan feigned his acceptance. "I am sure the plan will be greatly enhanced by your additions," he smiled.

Fang-Hua chuckled low in her throat. "It seems we have much in common, Reggie. You tell a lie nearly as well as I do. *Nearly.*"

She flicked her hand at the guards. "Show them in."

Two of Fang-Hua's guards opened the door and summoned an unknown party from the hallway. Four men entered. They were ordinary looking, ordinarily dressed, differing sizes and coloring, all white men. Their eyes scanned the room and settled on Morgan.

Fang-Hua had done a good job of selecting men who would not stand out, who could blend into the white community in Denver. Nevertheless, Morgan could tell they were accomplished killers.

"These men will comprise your team, Reggie. I will provide everything else you need—cars, firearms, money. More than enough money."

She pointed again and one of her guards dropped a canvas bag at Morgan's feet. He unzipped it and pulled it open. It was stuffed with bundles of cash. When Fang-Hua nodded, the guard zipped the bag closed but left it next to Morgan.

"I will expect frequent communications, always in a manner I will dictate, *Reggie*. When you are close to securing the child, you will notify me. I will provide a wet nurse to care for him as you bring him to me."

She seated herself again, regal as the witch-queen Morgan knew her to be. "*Bring my grandson to me, dear Reggie.*"

The implications of failure were lost on no one.

Brian and Fiona welcomed Esther and Ava to their table on many Sundays during the fall. When the girls did not ride home with the McKennies, they often found themselves with the Medfords.

It is as though we are being knit into these families, Esther sighed in happy wonder. She held no false dreams of having a husband or family someday; it was enough for her that she and Ava could earn their keep and be included in the goings-on of the little community via these long-established families.

Esther especially loved the McKennie farm. Brian would take her "choring" after Sunday dinner. The physical labor of the farm grew on her, and she learned to bring her worst dress and change into it, gleefully dirtying her hands and skirts while caring for the animals.

The only disturbance in the happy contentment of these afternoons was when Brian and Fiona's grandson, Connor, made an appearance. Esther might see him walking the fields, a long gun tucked under his arm, always alone except for one of Brian's dogs. Afterwards he would slip through the door near the kitchen, laying a brace of pheasant or duck on Fiona's wooden cutting board.

Apparently he lived part time with Brian and Fiona, helping Brian with the farm. More apparently, he did not approve of his grandparents' association with Esther and Ava, for whenever he was in the presence of the two women he said nothing, but his eyes simmered with displeasure.

Fiona rejected Connor's black moods and disapproving eyes. "Ach," she said and waved her hand in dismissal, "Dinna ye be concernin' yersel's o're him. He's b'lievin' s' hard in th' purity o' *some* women thet he's fergettin' we air *all* sinners in need o' grace."

It was Meg, one Sunday, who filled in what Fiona had not. "When Connor's sweetheart died, I'm thinkin' he set her upon a pedestal," she murmured to Esther. "Erica was as lovely a lass as you could be wishin' fer, but she was not s' perfect as he has convinced himself she was."

Meg turned toward Esther. "You have the look of her, Esther, an' I'm thinkin' it galls him. If he does not mind his heart, though, and finish with th' grieving, he'll find himself old, angry, and alone. Bitterness has a way o' findin' a home in us when we don't let go th' anger and give it t' the Lord."

Esther was not convinced that Connor's grief was his only issue. One evening after Brian brought them home, Ava's observations captured Esther's concerns exactly.

"It gives me chills when Connor looks at me, Esther. He reminds me of one of the men in the Bible who wanted to stone the woman caught in adultery. I look at him and it is as though he is just waiting for an opportunity to hurl a rock at my head."

Esther sucked in her breath. *Yes! That is it,* she fretted. *I don't feel safe around Connor. Not safe at all.*

Chapter 11

Roger Thomas, aka Dean Morgan, sniffed to himself as he stared around the room and its meager furnishings. The sour-faced landlady watched from the door as he examined the bed, the desk, and other furniture.

What a pleasure it must be to live with her, Morgan sneered to himself. The woman held herself rigid, arms folded across her chest, face screwed up in a perpetual scowl. He sauntered to the window and, parting the curtains, glanced out.

Ah yes! The view is every bit as good as I had hoped.

"As I said, I am a writer. I need a quiet, peaceful environment in which to work. I do not go out much and rarely have visitors," he tapped his foot as though considering the room, "but I must have absolute peace and privacy. Tell me about the neighborhood," he suggested.

Morgan knew he could be letting himself in for a river of drivel. It was the nugget floating among the flotsam in the drivel he hoped to glean.

"Hrmph!" His prospective landlady screwed her face up further—if that were possible. "Nothing in the neighborhood is terribly remarkable for the most part. The majority of the families are respectable. As you require, my house and the neighborhood are quiet. You will not be disturbed."

"I prefer to take my meals in my room. You may leave a tray at the door and knock to let me know it is there."

"As you wish, sir."

"Well, the room appears to be what I'm looking for," Morgan drawled. If she thought he was deciding, she might come out with the dirt he waited to hear.

"Forty-five dollars a month, no meals on Sunday; one month's rent in deposit," she replied. "Bedding done on Tuesdays."

"I will not require dinner on Thursdays," he mentioned. "I dine out with colleagues each Thursday evening."

"That will not alter the rate," she snapped.

"Indeed, but I would wish to save you the inconvenience of preparing a meal for me." Morgan feigned an intimate smirk for her, and she, predictably, blushed under it.

Now for the hook, Morgan thought, still smiling. "Madam, I believe you indicated that *the majority* of families in the neighborhood are respectable. What about the remainder of the families? Anyone I should avoid?"

The woman's eyes narrowed and she glanced out the window at the perfect view of Palmer House. "I suggest you steer clear of *that* house, Mr. Thomas."

"Oh? Why is that, madam?"

She leveled a reproachful gaze on him. "I do not abide gossip, mind you, Mr. Thomas. I will only say that the goings-on in that house are not proper. You'd be best to avoid all contact."

"I thank you for your concern for me," he replied, feigning sincerity. "I will take your advice to heart and I will take the room. I will move my bags in this afternoon."

He removed his wallet and paused. "And you are quite sure that I have access to the telephone in the hallway?"

"Yes, provided you keep your calls to five minutes or less."

"And I may park my motorcar in the back?"

"As I do not have a motorcar myself, you may make use of the garage off the alley. It makes no difference to me."

"That is quite gracious of you." He made a show of counting out the bills into the woman's hand.

Cora DeWitt, cutting her eyes out the window again, took the money he handed to her. "I'm sure we shall get on well, Mr. Thomas."

Morgan moved into the room that afternoon. He unpacked his clothes, a well-used typewriter, extra ribbons, carbon paper, pens, and notebooks, making a show of turning the room into a writer's workplace.

He also unpacked a fine new telescope, its stand, and a pair of binoculars.

Morgan had no illusions about Miss DeWitt. He was certain that she would, as soon as an opportunity presented itself, snoop through his things.

To that end, he carried a copy of a large, typewritten manuscript in a locking satchel. He also had the author's first attempts tucked into the satchel. Morgan snickered. The language of the manuscript would rival a doctoral student's dissertation, the subject abstract and highly technical. He doubted Miss DeWitt would linger long over its pages.

However, to demonstrate that he was making daily progress in his work and, thus, allay any suspicions his landlady might entertain, each day Morgan would pound on the typewriter a bit, drag out a few more pages of the manuscript, and add them to his "finished" pile. He would also wad some pages from the manuscript's first draft and toss them into the trash can next to his desk.

But before Morgan ever left the room for more than a few minutes, he would secure whatever he wished to keep secret from her. The telescope, stand, and binoculars would all go into a locked suitcase that he would place high on a shelf in the closet.

Binoculars in hand, Morgan positioned a chair before the window and set himself to the tedious business of studying the movements of Palmer House and its inhabitants. After only an hour he frowned.

Two armed men continually patrolled the house. He knew they were armed professionals because he recognized them for the type of men they were, even from a distance.

Those in the house are on their guard, Morgan observed with a frown. *Possibly they are only taking precautions because they recognize the danger Fang-Hua may present to the child. We must certainly do nothing to heighten or confirm that suspicion. It may take months, but it will be only a matter of time—time without incident—before they relax their defenses. And then . . .*

Morgan observed the house for several hours. He kept a notebook of the comings and goings of the residents of the house and the guards' rounds. Within a week or two he would have a solid record of who lived in the house and each person's schedule— especially the *Little Plum Blossom's.*

Quite late in the afternoon an automobile arrived across the street. Two men stepped out of the car, their heads turning, scanning the area around themselves, even while walking to the house. They and the house's two guards spoke together on the house's front porch for several minutes before the two guards turned the shift over to the new men and drove away.

The changing of the guard, Morgan correctly surmised. Movement down the street from Palmer House caught his eye.

What was this? A man lounged in a motorcar parked on the curb several houses down the block. Morgan hadn't realized anyone was in the automobile until movement caught his eye. The man in the car sat forward, watching the same "changing of the guard" Morgan had just watched.

Someone else was watching the house across the street? Morgan pursed his lips and set himself to monitor both the house and the man in the automobile. Each day it was the same; the man arrived early and left at dark.

Who is he watching? Morgan brooded. *More importantly, why?*

Morgan continued his surveillance for three days but never saw the object of his mission. *The girl must still be recovering from childbirth,* he concluded, *and is not yet leaving the house.* It was Thursday. He pulled up to the room's little desk and prepared his first weekly report to Fang-Hua.

When he finished with the report, Morgan locked the telescope and binoculars in the suitcase and stowed the case in the closet. He put the chair against the wall where it belonged, and took pains to make the desk look messy and used. He slipped down the back stairs, avoiding Miss DeWitt, and left in his motorcar for his weekly "dinner with colleagues."

In actuality, he drove less than three minutes and parked in a garage behind an empty, derelict store. From there he walked half a block down the alley behind Acorn Street. He entered a bungalow with peeling green paint through its back door.

When he and the men Fang-Hua assigned to him had arrived in Denver, Morgan had selected this shabby, non-descript house for his crew only a few minutes from Palmer House. The hideout needed to be close, but not close enough for anyone in Palmer House or the neighborhood around the house to connect it with snatching Mei-Xing's child. It also needed to be in an area of town where neighbors tended to mind their own business.

Morgan was more concerned, and rightfully so, over the possibility that *he* might be noticed or recognized rather than Fang-Hua's men. After all, it had only been a year since Morgan and Su-Chong had escaped jail in Denver. For months, Morgan's face had appeared in Denver papers.

Morgan, adept at disguise, had altered his appearance when he took on the identity of Roger Thomas, but he was nothing if not excessively cautious. For this reason, Morgan had one of Fang-Hua's men, a thug who went by the name of Barnes, rent the rundown bungalow on Acorn Street. It was Barnes, not Morgan, who paid the rent and who ordered the telephone be installed. Morgan was careful to ensure that nothing in the hideaway could be tied back to him.

The prune-faced Miss DeWitt was the only person in Denver, other than Fang-Hua's crew, who had interacted with Morgan. She would be easily disposed of at the right time and, given her charming manner, it might be weeks before she was missed.

Fang-Hua's men were to keep themselves in readiness for Morgan's call to action. However, with little to occupy their days other than waiting, Morgan was concerned that the men would grow bored and discontent with inactivity. Boredom could lead to imprudent behavior leading to detection and defeat.

That is not my problem, he glowered. *I warned Fang-Hua that snatching this child might take months, depending on whenever the Little Plum Blossom began taking the child with her when she left the house.* It was one more reason he had kept himself unassociated with the address on Acorn Street.

So, on the third evening after renting the room from Miss DeWitt, Morgan made his way to the crew's house to submit his report to Fang-Hua. His message consisted of a few lines he would speak over a trunk call to an individual named Clemmins who would, in turn, pass it on. While he waited for an operator to put his long-distance call through to Clemmins, Barnes pulled up a chair to listen.

"Go in the kitchen," Morgan growled.

Barnes shook his head. "Nope. Madam Chen set up two parts to her communications. You call and report. I listen and report afterwards that *your* report is on the up-and-up."

Morgan stared at Barnes and silently hurled curses at Fang-Hua. Finally he shrugged. "Makes no difference to me."

When the operator reported that his party was on the line, Morgan said, "Is this Clemmins?"

"Clemmins here."

"The chess game is progressing slowly. My opponent guards his castle with two knights at all times. He has not yet moved the queen, but it is early in the game. That is all."

Clemmins muttered, "Thank you. Good bye," and hung up. Morgan replaced the telephone's receiver.

Barnes nodded. "Now my turn."

Morgan listened as Barnes spoke to the operator and waited for a call to be placed to a Mrs. Gooding.

When the connection was made, Barnes asked, "Mom? Yeah, it's Charles. We're fine. How are you? Any word from Aunt Kate?"

He waited a moment. "All right. Yes. I'll call again next week. Bye."

Barnes turned to Morgan. "No instructions from Madam Chen."

Morgan prepared to leave. "If nothing changes, I'll be back the same time next week."

Morgan frowned as he drove back to his room in Miss DeWitt's house. The fact that Fang-Hua Chen didn't have her men watching him day and night was concerning. Or maybe no one was watching him that he *knew* of?

She is confident that she can find me anytime, no matter where I run, he warned himself, *so even if I do this one, last thing for her, will she keep her word? Will she let me go my way or am I as disposable as Mei-Xing?*

He knew Fang-Hua better than that. *I must have my plans in place and be ready when things go awry.* Already his mind was at work, piecing together his contingency plan. He would carefully gather money from caches he had established two years ago, preparing for a quick escape should the need arise.

Morgan knew he could trust no one other than himself.

Monday morning of his third week of observation, Morgan watched the usual motorcar pull up to the house across the street. This time, however, two guards escorted Mei-Xing Li down the walk from the house to the car. Mei-Xing carried a bundle that could only be an infant.

Morgan's heart quickened when he saw her. *At last!*

Behind the little procession trotted a small woman with black hair. She had a large cloth bag slung about her shoulder. When she reached the motorcar, she unslung the bag and handed it into the back seat.

That week Morgan reported, "My opponent has moved his queen. He keeps her well-guarded, of course, but he cannot do so forever."

It snowed the Saturday before Thanksgiving, a cold, wet snow that froze overnight and iced the roads and tracks in and around RiverBend. A freezing rain followed all Sunday morning and no one was taken by surprise when attendance at church was quite low.

Esther and Ava were frozen to the bone by the time they walked back to their little home at the back of the shop. They spent the afternoon and evening huddled by their stove, sipping soup or tea, and catching up on mending and alterations.

By Tuesday morning a warm wind had erased the snow and ice, and temperatures had eased higher. Esther was waiting on a customer, helping her choose a hat to match the dress she had purchased.

"When you have selected the style of hat you prefer," Esther explained, "we will add the same trim to the hat's brim as is on your dress. Then your outfit will be uniquely yours."

The bell over the door jangled. Esther did not immediately glance up; her customer was comparing two hats before making her selection. Ava, knowing that Esther was busy, came from the back of the shop to help the new customer.

"Oh! Mr. McKennie. What a surprise." Ava's smile was tentative—his presence was indeed a surprise. While Connor had been present at another Sunday dinner two weeks past, his behavior toward his grandmother's guests had been uniformly taciturn. He had certainly never expressed any curiosity about Esther and Ava's dress shop.

Esther glanced away from her customer; she, too, was surprised to see Connor. He had yet to speak two kind words to either her or Ava.

Without acknowledging Ava's greeting, Connor stared around the shop. He frowned and studied the display of laces, buttons, beaded trims, rickrack, and piping. Ava drew near him but waited for him to speak.

"This is how you make your living?" he demanded.

Ava was confused and stuttered, "Well, yes. We accessorize dresses and hats and perform alterations."

Connor grunted and turned his attention to the racks of ready-made dresses. He pulled one from the rack and looked it over. "So you add the trimming? Yourselves?"

"Of course. Who do you think would do it?" Ava sounded miffed; she was growing impatient.

He didn't respond, but he hung the dress back on the rack. Without turning his eyes to Ava he said, "My grandmother sent me to invite you to Thanksgiving dinner. She would have asked you herself on Sunday but the weather was bad, if you recall."

"Oh. I'm sure we would be delighted to come. When—"

"I'm to drive in tomorrow afternoon and bring you back."

"I see. How lo—"

"We'll bring you back Sunday morning in time for church."

"Do you always interrupt?" Ava was beyond irritated.

"Not always." He moved toward the door.

"And can we expect to be graced with your presence at Thanksgiving dinner?"

He shrugged. "That's likely."

"I'm surprised you won't be at your parents' for Thanksgiving."

"We'll all be meeting at Søren and Meg's Thanksgiving Day. My parents, too." he mumbled.

Esther had kept one ear trained on the exchange between Ava and Connor while assisting her customer. The woman decided on the hat she wished to buy and Esther was writing a receipt when Connor opened the door on his way out.

By way of goodbye, he threw over his shoulder, "I'll see you tomorrow about three o'clock."

"Well!" Ava's vexation was boiling over.

Their customer, a matronly woman, chuckled. "Mark the day, ladies. You've heard more words today from Connor McKennie than many a folk around here have heard in years."

"D'ye remember our Thanksgiving at th' lodge?" Breona and Marit were polishing the few silver items Palmer House possessed for the Thanksgiving feast on the morrow. Breona's question held all the beauty and wonder that memory evoked.

"Oh, yes!" Marit stopped polishing and recalled their first Thanksgiving in Corinth—their first and last in the lovely old lodge before it burned.

Joy had envisioned the lodge as a mountain retreat that would attract wealthy city guests longing for peace and quiet. The guests were to provide the income she, Breona, and Marit needed to survive in Corinth. Then, God willing, they would find a way to help the girls ensnared in the two "gentlemen's clubs" located in the tiny town.

To that end, Joy had sent for many of the fine furnishings stored in her warehouse in Omaha—the furnishings she and Grant had planned to use to open a new business. Mr. Wheatley and Billy, Grant and Joy's former employees, had tagged along with the furnishings and had been with them ever since.

Joy had requested the best of what she had in storage be brought to Corinth, and Marit, having never been far from her dairy community, had been overwhelmed when she had seen the men unloading the heavy dining tables and chairs and the ornate china cabinet and sideboard.

She had been in raptures when she unpacked the boxes containing the elegant silver tea service, china place settings, and crystal stemware.

Thanksgiving Day had been the loveliest holiday Breona or Marit had ever known—two tables set with an overabundance of candles in gleaming candelabras, a fine dinner served on the finest china, and the company of new, dear friends.

But all those beautiful things had been lost when the lodge burned. Tomorrow's Thanksgiving dinner would still be served on their best dishes, but those "best dishes" would be mismatched and the table linens cleverly patched here and there.

No, they would likely never have as elegant a Thanksgiving celebration again. Both women chuckled as they looked over their meager silver selection, dinged, dented, and tarnished.

"'Twas grand," Breona breathed. "'Twas t' grandest we're loik t' see in ourn lifetimes, I'm thinkin'."

"It vas the most beautiful I've ever seen," Marit agreed.

"Boot, we be havin' much more than silver now, eh?" Breona grinned, "An' I wouldna be changin' onythin', 'cept t' have Flinty here."

Marit nodded. The mention of their dear friend, now gone, still stung.

"Such riches we be havin' canna be bought," Breona added.

"Ja, you are right," Marit smiled.

Connor delivered Esther and Ava to Brian and Fiona's as promised and then disappeared. Esther found herself hoping he would remain absent during the holiday.

It is hard to relax when he is around, Esther sighed, *when it feels as though he is continually watching us, hoping to catch us doing something wrong.*

Thanksgiving morning dawned, and Esther and Ava were caught up in Fiona's demanding schedule. The two girls peeled a mountain of potatoes and apples and grated bowls of spices while Fiona mashed the potatoes and rolled out crusts for pies.

"How many will be eating dinner at Søren and Meg's?" Esther asked.

"Ach! Thirty-five 'twas bein' th' last count," Fiona replied—as though thirty-five at dinner was an everyday occurrence!

"Thirty-five!" Ava gasped. "Where will they all sit?"

"Dinna ye be worryin' 'bout that," Fiona laughed. "Meg will be havin' it well in hand."

Esther and Ava had not visited Søren and Meg's house before. As they bundled up and piled into the wagon for the ride over, Brian mentioned that Søren and Meg lived in what was the Thoresen brothers' first house, built on Jan Thoresen's homestead, "Boot wi' additions," he added.

Additions, indeed! Esther marveled. She could see where the original house had been substantially expanded: The combined dining room and living room of the farmhouse was at least thirty feet in length. Two long rows of tables extended from the dining room's wall to the end of the living room.

Three of Søren and Meg's four children and their families were already present. Brian, Fiona, Esther, Ava, Connor's parents, and Martha Combs (née McKennie) and her family raised their numbers to thirty-six.

Other buggies and wagons hailed them and drove past Søren and Meg's house on their way to Karl Thoresen's home just across the field.

"We only try to get the entire family together in the summertime," Meg explained to Esther. "We help each other harvest and hold bonfire sing-alongs—like tonight, but without the bonfire."

"A sing-along? Tonight?" Ava clapped her hands, thrilled at the prospect.

"Aye. Around six o'clock the crowd over at Karl's house will come here. The men will break down the tables and we will gather in here and fill this room with singing!" Meg's cheeks bloomed with color and her beautiful auburn hair, only a little faded through the years, made her appear far younger than her mid-forties age.

Esther and Ava found the number of women involved in preparing the feast—all crowded into the kitchen and talking at once—to be intimidating. As the women shooed the children out-of-doors, Esther and Ava slipped through the door that led to the combined dining room and living room. They believed themselves alone until someone cleared his throat.

There in the corner sat Connor.

He stared at them, his dark eyes unwelcoming. Esther and Ava, pretending that the atmosphere in the room wasn't distinctly chilly, occupied themselves by studying the small collection of framed family portraits hanging on the walls.

"Look here, Ava!" Esther pointed to a photograph.

Ava looked closely at the image Esther pointed to, a couple and their young daughter. Her mouth curved in delight.

"It's Miss Rose!" she laughed. "And that must be Miss Joy!"

"Yes, quite a while ago," Esther added. "That must be Rose's husband. I heard he died not long ago. What a handsome man he was!"

They finished looking over the photographs and wandered toward one of the windows. Out of it they could see a knot of men standing near the barn, chatting and laughing, while children gamboled around them. Esther finally selected a chair by the window and sat down. Ava joined her.

They said nothing and did not look toward Connor.

"I was somewhat surprised by your shop," Connor said, breaking the uncomfortable silence.

Esther didn't know what he was implying. "Oh? I'm sorry; I don't take your meaning. In what way were you surprised?"

He shrugged. "Guess I thought the clothing would be . . . gaudier."

Esther blinked, not believing what he was insinuating. "Gaudier. As in what exactly?"

Connor didn't flinch from her question. "As in your former vocation."

"I am happy you were disappointed," Esther responded, her face heating. "But apparently you are not the gentleman your grandfather is. He would not have taken such effort to make your point."

"Because I don't ignore and dance around the obvious division your coming here has created in this community?" His jaw was set, his challenge was unmistakable.

"Division. I see," Esther grated. "So, unlike your grandparents, you're not of the forgiving type."

"Forgiving? I don't feel the need to forgive you. I just don't happen to believe people really change their stripes. I'm just wondering how long your attempt to earn an honest living will last. How long before you turn back to a more familiar occupation or until you corrupt one of our young men or women."

Ava's mouth hung open, but Esther, nearly blind with rage, stood up. "So you're waiting for us to set up *a bordello* in the back room of our shop, is that it? Why? Why would you think such a horrid thing? Is it because you would like to be one of our first customers?"

He blanched. "That is a filthy thing to say."

"Filthy? You have no room to talk, Connor McKennie," Esther spat. "You've just accused us of planning to start a whorehouse in RiverBend! After all the kindness the people here have shown us? You must think us monsters!"

Her expression darkened. "Oh, believe me, I know your type. You practice your 'religion' of redeeming grace within the walls of a church building but as soon as you walk outside, you condemn anyone whose past—forgiven or not—has not lived up to your standards. For you, there is *no* redemption for a fallen woman."

She glared at him, even as her chin began to quiver. "Do you think every 'fallen' woman had a choice in the matter? Well, while some of them did, many others did not, Mr. McKennie. Not every little girl grew up with a father and mother who cherished and protected her. Not every little girl—"

Esther's control abandoned her. She stammered, "Not-not ev-every li-li—" but could not finish. Her face collapsed and she broke down into sobs. Whirling about, she pushed through the front door and ran down the slope toward the road that led over the creek. Back toward Brian and Fiona's farm. Back toward the safety of their little shop in town. Anywhere but here!

Connor McKennie stared after her, his scowl dark and foreboding. "Good riddance," he muttered.

"You are a bigoted, ignorant fool, Connor McKennie." Ava was not usually outspoken, but defense of her friend ripped away her normal reserve. "You think you know so much? You think your *precious Erica* was pure as the driven snow, her virtue the only ruler by which every woman is to be measured?"

"Don't you dare speak her name," Connor shouted. "Don't you defile her name with your filthy mouth!"

Ava glared at him, shaking with shame and pain. "Tell me, Mr. McKennie. Did the father of your precious Erica sell her to a bordello at age twelve? Because that's what Esther's father did. He sold her, like a man sells a cow. Her own father. Sold her into slavery. What would you have thought of your *darling* Erica, had her father done the same?"

Ava felt she was going to throw up. She gagged and started to stumble. Connor instinctively reached out a hand to steady her, but she pushed it off.

"Don't you touch me, you hypocrite!" Ava ran through the door and, as fast as she could follow, trailed after the lone figure now far down the road.

Connor was left alone in the living room, and the emptiness in his heart, the emptiness he was so accustomed to, was displaced by something else, something unfamiliar. He ran a hand through his hair and found he was shaking.

Could what Ava said be true? Could a father ever sell his own daughter . . . like that?

The revulsion he felt made him shudder: Revulsion at the images Ava's words carved into his imagination.

Revulsion at a father scorning his most sacred duty.

Revulsion at the horror of a child defiled.

But above all, revulsion at his own cruelty.

Connor was still standing there, trapped between loathing and regret, when Fiona came looking for Esther and Ava. "We were hearin' bad-tempered words, Connor, and on Thanksgiving! For shame! What—why, where air they bein'?"

She rounded on him. When he didn't answer but turned his head away, she demanded, "Oh, Connor McKennie, what have ye done? Where are Miss Esther and Miss Ava?"

He looked at his grandmother's feet, unwilling to meet her eyes. "I believe *Esther* and *Ava* have walked home," he stated. "We had something of a . . . disagreement."

Fiona stared at him. "I see." And perhaps she saw more than he thought she did, for after many moments, she folded her arms.

"Connor, ye air m' grandson, an' I love ye. Ye air knowin' I do," she whispered. "Boot ye've bin pinin' for your sweetheart long enow. I'm fearin' ye hev allowed th' sorrow t' be twistin' yer heart awry from th' Lord an' his ways."

Nodding to herself, she sighed and added, "I canna allow ye t' harm two lasses already wounded s' badly."

He met her eyes then and her disappointment was plain. "Take yersel' off, Connor. 'Tis a meetin' wi' God ye b' needin'. An' I'll b' thankin' ye not t' darken ourn door till ye be seein' yersel' as much a sinner in need o' grace as onyone else."

He flushed, slowly nodded, and let himself out the same door Esther and Ava had just used.

Chapter 12

Thanksgiving had been ruined for Esther and Ava, something they refused to talk about, even with Fiona. Instead the girls both pursed their lips and set themselves at their work—with the exception of one mournful comment by Ava. "I had so looked forward to the sing-along."

Esther hugged her friend and they did not speak of it again. They both prayed and did their best to put Connor McKennie from their minds. They were grateful when December started well for their shop.

Esther had talked Ava into risking their small savings, maintaining that Christmas would boost their sales. And so they had spent—*invested*, Esther insisted on calling it—all the money they had on new stock for the holidays.

The girls were excited the morning Jeremy Bailey delivered a crate just arrived on the train. It could have been Christmas morning for them, as thrilled as the little shop owners were. They spent the morning unpacking and arranging what they hoped was an artful display of tempting but affordable gifts for women: Handbags, gloves, tasteful pieces of costume jewelry, handkerchiefs, and small bottles of cologne.

They were pausing for lunch when Ava heard a soft knock at the back door. She wiped her hands on her apron and opened it but saw no one. Instead, a pair of pheasants, freshly killed, lay on the back step.

Ava stared at the brilliant green of the pheasants' feathers and called to her friend. "Esther."

"Who is it?" Esther bustled to the back door; Ava stepped aside so Esther could see for herself.

"Oh." They didn't say the words aloud; the peace offering spoke on its own, and neither of them doubted who had left it.

"I must say," Ava huffed, "in the past we have both received flowers and candy from clients who behaved as utter louts, but never . . . *dead birds*."

"It is not as though this fixes anything," Esther muttered. Every word Connor McKennie had hurled at her still haunted her; every day was a struggle to press on with the harsh condemnation ringing in her ears.

"Well, I don't intend to leave this bounty on the step one more minute." Ava, ever practical, lifted the birds by their curled feet. "I plan to eat well tonight!"

"Yes," Esther replied, distracted. She scanned up and down the alley and, seeing no one, closed the door.

Christmas would fall on a Sunday this year. At Palmer House preparations for the holy day grew to fever pitch.

Ten days prior to December 25, Marit set to the Christmas baking with fierce and joyous abandon, conscripting help from every resident of Palmer House. Any soul who dared wander through the kitchen was subject to Marit's command!

Mr. Wheatley found himself grating nutmeg, ginger, and cinnamon; Marion chopped mountains of walnuts, almonds, and candied fruits; Jenny whipped butter and cream until her arms ached, handing off the bowls to Flora or Alice to take over her chore, only to be tasked with sifting flour.

As the days passed, the upper shelves in the pantry filled with cakes, pies, and cookies, and the lower shelves groaned under fruitcakes soaking in pungent, spicy brine.

Evenings were passed decorating the house with evergreens, colorful bows, and strings of cranberries—and singing. The girls of Palmer House sang sacred songs and hymns; they joined in carols; they lifted their voices to sing praises to God for the birth of the Savior.

As the residents of Palmer House twined boughs through the banisters that ran up the staircase and as they bedecked the windows with greenery, they rejoiced that this Christmas would be so different from their last.

The year before, they had been mourning Mei-Xing's abduction, unable to generate enthusiasm for a Christmas celebration. And just days before Christmas they had located Esther and her girls— trapped in Cal Judd's "high-class" bordello. Christmas Eve had not been spent in festivities; it had been spent fasting and praying for the success of O'Dell and Marshal Pounder's men to snatch the women from Judd's hands and spirit them out of Denver.

Now the family at Palmer House decorated, wrapped little gifts in secret, sang beloved carols from their hearts, and breathed silent prayers of thanksgiving that *this* Christmas would be peaceful and joy-filled.

And while they prepared for their Christmas festivities they prepared for visitors!

Gretl would be coming home on Christmas Eve from her position as head cook for a wealthy family in Boulder. She would spend a precious four days at Palmer House.

Joy's cousin Arnie and his family would arrive from Omaha two days before Christmas and stay a week and a half.

Arnie's sister Uli and her family would not arrive until the day after Christmas but would stay until Friday. Uli's husband David was a pastor in Corinth; he and his family would celebrate Christmas Day with their church before taking the narrow-gauge train down the mountain to Denver.

Friends would swell their ranks, too: Martha Palmer would join them for Christmas Eve and Christmas Day as would Pastor Carmichael, Minister Liáng, and Bao Shin Xang. Only Mr. O'Dell had declined their invitation.

Esther and Ava were thrilled when, two weeks into December, Brian and Fiona asked them to spend Christmas week with them. The girls would close the shop the afternoon of Christmas Eve and not reopen until the following Saturday!

Fiona made a point of informing them that Connor would not be present during their visit. Esther tried to keep the young man from her thoughts, but he had left two further offerings on their back step: A small turkey and a dozen fresh eggs, probably from his father's farm.

Actions speak louder than words, Esther grumbled, *except when it comes to apologies.*

What hurt her most was that Connor had taken no time to know her or Ava! He had not inquired into the saving work God had done in either of them. Even now as he, presumably, was rethinking his judgment of them, he had made no effort to apologize for the ugly things he had said.

With effort, Esther again put Connor from her mind. Instead, she was grateful that their December sales were proving to be good.

Lord, we will not have to beg for help this winter, she rejoiced, taking stock of their food supply and little cash box. *Perhaps we can be a blessing to someone else, because we shall have enough and some over!*

For many a farmer dragged his feet through the door of their shop that month, each man hoping to buy a special Christmas gift for wife or sweetheart. Ava, in particular, became so adept at helping their male customers find what they were looking for, that her fame spread by word of mouth.

The bell over the door would jingle and a weather-hardened man, hat in hand, would self-consciously inquire, "Would Miss Ava be available?"

Esther was thrilled for Ava's newfound popularity. Esther had always been the leader; Ava, the follower, had always been eclipsed by Esther's charm and beauty. Here in RiverBend, however, Esther's exceptional comeliness tended to terrify and tongue-tie male customers whereas Ava's plainer looks and her ability to suggest just the right gift made her more approachable.

As their December sales came to a close, Esther could not help but notice how Ava had bloomed. *Why, she is more confident and cheerful than she has been since . . .*

Esther had a sudden recollection of the afternoon Cal Judd had announced that he was taking over their small but exclusive bordello. Ava had cursed Cal to his face, and he had, with no hesitation, punched her with his closed fist, knocking her to the floor—shattering her nose and her confidence with the same blow.

Lord, please heal our hearts from the dark days we brought on ourselves through our stubborn self-will, Esther prayed in humble gratitude. *Let me never again turn from your grace and mercy.*

And please hide us in the cleft of the Rock—hide us forever from Cal, I beg of you, my Jesus!

Christmas Eve arrived and found Palmer House aglow with light and bursting with laughter and good cheer. Martha Palmer, ensconced in the best chair in the great room, beamed her pleasure. Family and friends sang carols and indulged in the many treats Marit had stored up in the pantry. Little Will ran from person to person, doted upon and spoiled to his heart's content.

Liáng stared across the festivities, his heart feasting on Mei-Xing and her child. It seemed to him that, since Shan-Rose was born, Mei-Xing's countenance was always bathed in joyous serenity.

O Lord, she is beautiful in so many ways, he mused. *And what a great desire burns in my heart for her! What shall I do, my Father, seeing I am now poor and unsuitable for her?*

The girl glanced around the room, a gentle smile lighting her eyes for each person. When her eyes reached Liáng, her smile widened and Liáng's heart swelled. He bent his head once and, clearing his throat, looked down. When he raised his face, Mei-Xing had turned back to Breona.

Rose Thoresen's slender figure glided to his side and paused. Liáng was quick to turn his eyes from Mei-Xing and pray no one had discerned his thoughts.

Mrs. Thoresen, however, looked from him to Mei-Xing and back. She whispered, her words only for them, "Mei-Xing does not yet realize."

Liáng flushed and shook his head. "I beg your pardon, madam. I do not take your meaning."

"Minister Liáng."

He was forced to face her. Rose smiled into his eyes. "My daughter Mei-Xing does not yet realize that she loves you."

Liáng paled at her words. *Mei-Xing loves me? That cannot be!* He again cleared his throat. *Was he that transparent?*

Liáng shook his head. "She-she cannot know her heart or mind yet, Mrs. Thoresen; she is but a girl."

"Sadly, she is not, sir," Rose returned, her words firm. "Like the others, she had her girlhood taken from her. She can never go back to it, especially now that she is a mother."

Rose threaded her arm through Liáng's and steered him—ever-so-gently—into a more private corner of the great room. "Minister Liáng, did you know that twenty years separated me from my late husband Jan? And yet, it did not seem to matter. We grew to be dear friends the year that I grieved the loss of my first husband and our children.

"I learned so much from Jan, from his faith and godly life. We became friends in the Lord before other . . . feelings grew between us. In fact . . ."

Here Rose turned and faced Liáng again. "In fact, I did not recognize the depth of our friendship, the dearness of our fellowship, until he proposed to me. We had a very happy marriage, Mr. Liáng, a truly blessed union. So much of whom I am in the Lord—so much of my emotional maturity—I owe to my husband's exemplary walk with Christ."

She cast her eyes to where Mei-Xing and Breona were seated. The two girls were giggling, their heads close to each other over the baby, and their laughter reached Liáng and Rose across the room. Mei-Xing noticed Rose watching her and she blew Rose a little kiss.

Rose thought her heart would melt. *Thank you, Lord, for the many sources of comfort and joy you have brought to me in my later years!*

She patted Liáng on the arm. "Be a little patient, dear friend. But also be hopeful."

Cal Judd was in a foul mood, and it did not take much to put him in one these days. Today he was waiting for his lawyers to visit—the same paid lackeys who had promised that he would be released in six months or less from the dank hellhole he'd sat in for nearly a year now.

Nearly a year! While I have paid them a small fortune to grease the skids for me! he groused to himself.

When the keys jangled in the door to the cellblock, Cal listened carefully. *Yes.* He recognized the footsteps of his two attorneys, Claypool and Nixon, walking down the row of cells: Claypool, the older partner, had a tendency to shuffle; Nixon's shorter stride and small feet tapped a staccato on the stone floor. Judd stood up, facing the bars of his cell.

"Mr. Judd, we have good news," Claypool said by way of greeting. Nixon deferred to his partner and waited without words for Judd to respond.

"Do tell."

"You will be released next Monday morning."

"It's about time."

"Yes. It took longer than we expected. We had to, er, *renegotiate* due to recent personnel changes at City Hall, but we have been successful."

Judd nodded. "And the other matter?"

Claypool gestured to Nixon, who swallowed to mask his nerves. "Still no sign of the young lady, er, in question. And after the Pinkerton agent returned to his home office in Chicago, we lost track of him."

Judd scowled. *So O'Dell has stayed clear of Denver. Smart of him. But Esther could not have disappeared without a trace!*

He folded his arms across his chest. *I am surrounded by incompetence,* he seethed.

With a great effort, he calmed himself. *I need only apply the right amount of pressure in the appropriate manner, and the information I require will rise to the surface*, he told himself.

"Obviously I will have to take charge of the investigation myself as soon as I am out of here. I see your methods aren't up to the task."

"With respect, Mr. Judd, we are attorneys, not detectives," Nixon protested.

"And yet you suffered no scruples when you accepted my money for your efforts."

Nixon shifted on his feet and slanted his eyes toward Claypool. "I am certain we would be happy to consider a partial refund, Mr. Judd, under the circumstances."

Judd stared through the bars at the little man. "Very well, gentlemen. Thank you for personally bringing the news of my release."

Judd wasn't as disturbed as he had allowed his bumbling attorneys to believe. *No, I never put all my apples in one basket.* Judd pursed his lips and plotted his next moves—*come next Monday and my release from this stinking hole.*

Cal's lieutenant, Brady Forbes, had managed the *Silver Spurs* and Cal's other business interests during his incarceration. If the reports were accurate, Forbes was doing a credible job. He pondered again what Forbes had reported to him back in June.

"Just as you asked, Boss, we let one of the doves, a girl named Edith, go to that church downtown you put us onto. Sure enough, she did not come back, but we followed her easy enough—straight to a fancy house, 'bout two miles away. Lots of young women living there, Boss, including our little dove. We're keeping tabs on her, just as you ordered."

Forbes gave him regular surveillance reports on the "fancy house," and Judd was certain that he'd located those who, along with O'Dell, had conspired to interfere in his business dealings—those who, along with O'Dell, had spirited Esther and several of his other girls out of Denver.

Esther! No matter how long since he had last seen her, Judd desired her with an intensity that enraged him.

Esther! No matter how far away she ran, Judd was hell-bent on finding her.

He clenched his teeth as memories of Esther's beauty engulfed him: her midnight blue eyes inflaming him; her lovely face and body igniting in him a fiery need to possess—*and to punish.*

I only need to apply the right pressure and, soon enough, little Edith will fly the coop—leading me straight to Esther.

Dear, sweet Esther! My traitorous little trollop. I told you I would find you.

Chapter 13

January 1911

When the happy Christmas season came to a close, winter was no longer novel or festive: It was just cold, tedious, and inconvenient.

Joy began leaving Blackie home to keep Grant company, and Rose again prayed over the rate at which the coal bin emptied. Grant, who now kept the books for her, realized how little money they actually had and insisted on extreme economies.

"I am so grateful for your help, Grant," Rose told him—as she generally did a few times a week. "I am appreciative of your leadership in the finances."

Grant's laugh was short and wry. "What you mean is you appreciate that *I* am the one announcing to the girls that we are tamping the furnace lower and *I* am the one ordering that no one is to add coal or wood to the fireplaces after eight o'clock in the evening!"

Giggling, Rose nodded. "Oh, yes! Ever so grateful! Because *you* enforce such distasteful rules, they mumble bad things under their breath about *you* rather than about *me*."

"A fine Christian woman you are!" Grant muttered, pulling his mouth down into grave lines. "And I had thought so much better of you, you know. My own mother-in-law! Taking advantage of a poor, sick man."

Rose laughed aloud. "You are a terrible actor, Grant Michaels! Quite terrible."

Then she studied him, abruptly serious. "I don't believe your color is at its best today, Grant. How are you feeling?"

Grant shrugged. "The oxygen machine is not, perhaps, helping quite as much as it did when I started using it, but I feel all right while I am sitting." He reached down to pat Blackie who was curled around the legs of his chair.

"Perhaps you should talk to the doctor? Maybe he can recommend a change to the machine's settings?"

"I will tend to it, Mother, so please don't concern Joy over my health."

It was not a request. Rose understood and nodded her acquiescence. "As you wish, Grant."

The Denver Post duly reported Cal Judd's release in Monday's morning paper. By Wednesday, Pastor Carmichael had telephoned with an alarming report.

"The women in our church who minister to the doves on the street have heard a rumor, and I felt I should call you with all speed. The rumor is that Cal Judd is looking for a runaway from the *Silver Spurs*—a girl named Edith—and he has offered a sum of money to whoever locates her."

"We have waited too long to send her away," Rose sighed as she hung up the telephone. She called Edith to the parlor that evening.

"Edith, my dear, for your own safety and the safety of this house, we must send you on from here."

Edith gulped. "But wh-where will I go?"

Rose took her hand and stroked it. "You will be going to friends in another town. It is a small town; you will need to make some adjustments, but we have sent other girls there. Our friends and the town folk will help you. We just cannot afford for Cal Judd to ever find you or trace you back to this house."

Rose had already placed a trunk call to RiverBend to Pastor Jacob Medford and his wife, Vera. They, with help from Brian and Fiona McKennie and Rose's stepson and his wife, Søren and Meg Thoresen, had taken in Esther and four other young women the previous Christmas. Because Cal Judd considered Esther his special property, Palmer House's involvement in her escape had become quite dangerous.

Sara and Corrine helped Edith pack her meager belongings. "We're sorry you cannot stay here longer and we will miss you," they commiserated, "but we would rather know that you will be safe and cared for."

Early in the morning a brave Edith said her goodbyes. Rose embraced her at the door. One of Samuel Gresham's men had been tasked with driving Edith to the station and putting her on the train to RiverBend.

Morgan observed as the black automobile pulled up to the curb. It was the same automobile that transported Mei-Xing to her work each day. However, only one man, the driver, disembarked, instead of the usual two men.

The car is early, and this is a departure from their routine,
Morgan noted eagerly. He sat up straight and paid close attention.
The guard strode up the walk and returned—escorting not Mei-Xing,
but one of the other young women, a girl with brown, curly hair.

The guard carried a carpet bag. He opened the back door for the
girl, put the bag on the seat next to her, walked around the car, got
into the driver's seat, and drove them away.

Then, for the first time, Morgan saw the other "watcher" start
his automobile's motor. A few seconds later, he followed after the
black car.

Morgan stayed seated, deep in thought, for a quarter hour.
Someone had watched Palmer House for several weeks—at the least.
Morgan really couldn't say for how long, because the sentinel had
been in place when Morgan rented his room.

Someone has been watching, he mused, *but not for Mei-Xing,*
and Morgan was no closer to knowing *who* or *why* than the first day
he'd noticed the other watcher.

All he knew was that the other observer did not return.

Edith stepped off the train in RiverBend and gawked about her, a
bit dismayed. As scenic as someone might describe the small town
and the prairie beyond it *in springtime*, the dull, drab January
afternoon did nothing to recommend either the town or its
surroundings.

Edith lingered on the siding, waiting, but no one greeted her or
seemed to be looking for her. She stared at the sooty remains of the
last snowfall running in a muddy stream down the center of the
town.

Three men began unloading crates from a boxcar onto the
platform. Edith clutched her small bag and, with a sigh, turned
toward the tiny train office.

"Kin I help ya, miss?"

Edith jumped. The voice came from behind her and she whirled
around.

"Sorry, miss. Didn't mean t' startle ya none. Jeremy Bailey, at
yer service. I run this station."

Edith eyed the lanky forty-something man, and he eyed her back,
openly curious.

"Yes," she squeaked, "I-I am looking for Pastor Jacob
Medford?"

"Sure thing. Heered he got called out early this mornin', though. Old Mister Haase passed."

He turned and pointed down the muddy street. "You kin walk to th' parsonage, if y' like. Straight down this street, turn right at th' end. You'll see th' church 'bout a mile ahead. Pastor and Missus Medford live in the house next t' th' church."

Edith nodded her thanks, but the man was staring at her shoes.

"What is it?" Edith managed to ask without squeaking.

"Weeeell . . . I was jest thinkin' how there ain't no boardwalk out t' th' church and all. Mighty muddy b'tween town an' there."

Edith followed his gaze to her shoes. Her only pair of shoes. "I see." She sighed and wondered what she should do. The wind gusting down the street had a bite to it.

"Would ya happen t' be friends with Missus Rose Thoresen?" the man inquired.

Edith's attention jumped back to his face. "Why do you ask?" She hadn't planned to snap at him, but since she'd heard the report that Cal Judd was looking for *her*, her nerves were quite frazzled.

Jeremy nodded and acted as though he hadn't heard the suspicious edge to her question. "I was jest a kid when Miss Rose come here on th' train. Mighty fine Christian woman, Miss Rose is."

He looked at the freight piled on the siding and back to Edith. "Miss, if you care t' wait, I will drive ya t' th' church. I jest need t' check in th' freight first."

Edith shivered. She was disinclined to trust the man. He must have sensed her reluctance.

"Mebbe you could wait in Miss Esther's store?" He pointed down the street. "Be a mite warmer there."

At the name "Esther," Edith brightened. "Esther? Did she, er, also know Miss Rose?"

"Oh, yes, ma'am, she surely did," Jeremy smiled, glad to see some glimmer of trust in the girl's eyes. "You kin ask her 'bout me, if you like."

The boardwalk led all the way to the little dress shop, and Edith was glad: The man had been right about the mud! The town's street was not paved, and its soggy surface was cut and deeply rutted from wagon traffic. Thick mud pooled in the ruts.

A bell jingled as Edith stepped inside the shop. Two women were inside, both of them sitting before a small wood-burning stove with sewing in their laps.

One of the women put aside her sewing and stood up, greeting Edith with a smile. "Good afternoon. May I help you?"

Edith thought she had never seen a lovelier woman. Her eyes were a deep violet-blue, the bones of her face forming a delicate, perfect heart. The woman was dressed in a simple but pretty dress, her hair also simply done.

Edith knew from her description that the woman was Esther— but she was no longer the sophisticated, high-priced courtesan the girls at Palmer House had painted Cal Judd's woman to be.

"M-my name is Edith. I have just arrived on the train," Edith gulped. "From Denver . . . from Palmer House."

At the mention of Palmer House, the other woman stood and they both approached Edith, compassion in their eyes. The first woman held out her hand. "Of course. Edith, I'm Esther. You are welcome here. Will you sit a while?"

"And I am Ava," the brown-haired woman chirped. "Would you like a cup of tea?"

With no more than those simple words, Edith felt safe for the first moment since boarding the train.

The tailor finished fitting Cal Judd's suit coat and murmured, "I will have your new suits delivered in a week, Mr. Judd. And if I may say, sir, you cut a fine figure."

Cal had lost a few pounds in jail and he knew it looked good on him. He preened before the mirror. "A week, you say? Very good."

A week or so will give me time to reassert my control over the Silver Spurs and my other interests while making plans to retrieve Esther.

Judd calculated how many men he would take to the farming town where Edith had disembarked from the train, and he plotted how he would take Esther from those who were harboring her there.

"Forbes. That town where you said the girl got off the train?"

"Yeah? Place called RiverBend."

"Tomorrow I want you to get a map and mark the roads into that hick town." Judd splashed a little cologne on his face. "In the meantime, I'll be looking over my properties. From what I've seen so far, it looks like you've done a good job, and a good job deserves a reward."

Judd pulled a thick roll of bills from his pocket and peeled off several. "Take the night off. Have a good time."

"Thanks, Boss! Appreciate it." Forbes grinned as he contemplated his night of debauchery.

As Edith became acquainted with Esther and Ava the afternoon she arrived, the two older girls had assured her that Jeremy Bailey was "a sweet, kind man who wouldn't hurt a fly." On those recommendations, Edith had allowed the stationmaster to drive her in his freight wagon down the street and out onto the prairie, delivering her (with un-muddied shoes) to the Medford's little parsonage.

Edith found a home and a family in the Medfords that day. Before long, Jacob and Vera were treating her as a granddaughter. Edith loved the Medfords, but she missed Palmer House and the fellowship she had with the other girls—girls who had been through what she had suffered and, therefore, understood.

Because of their similar pasts, Edith felt a kinship with Esther and Ava. The two young women helped fill the loss that Edith was feeling, so Edith often made her way to their shop.

Esther and Ava, a few years older than Edith, were already versed in the ways of RiverBend; they helped the younger girl to adjust to the community and begin to learn new skills.

Ava assigned small sewing projects to Edith, projects that she took home to finish. Vera Medford, herself an accomplished seamstress, tutored Edith and helped her complete her sewing tasks.

Edith soon became a daily visitor to the shop, a curly-haired little sister upon whom Esther and Ava loved to dote. For all three of them, RiverBend became a refuge from the world that had damaged them so deeply.

Chapter 14

Cal drew deeply on his cigar and then sucked down another swallow of bourbon. The plan Forbes had proposed was not elegant, but it would work: He, Forbes, and two other men would take the train to the next sizable town just east of RiverBend. They would disembark, pick up the two automobiles Forbes would arrange for, and drive back toward RiverBend.

On the outskirts of the town, Forbes would take one of the motorcars into town alone and reconnoiter, finding out where Esther was. When Forbes returned with that information, Cal and his men would follow him back into town in the second car.

After that, Judd did not much care. He and his crew carried firepower, and the town boasted of nothing more than a token, in-name-only policeman and a few shopkeepers or farmers, all too backwards to possibly fend off Judd and his men.

Besides, Cal wanted—*no, he longed*—to take Esther in a show of force. He lusted to feel the terror his coming would cause Esther and her friends. He would, with no compunction, destroy those who stood in his way. She would know the fear of his coming for her before he possessed her.

Before I make her suffer. Before I disfigure her. Before I kill her.

Cal wanted that part to be *slow*. His eyes grew glassy as he fantasized over what he would do to her.

Later, when he had finished with Esther, he and his men would drive back to the town where they'd gotten off the train. They would ditch the cars, clean up, and board a train headed on in to Omaha. Cal would put them all up at a fancy hotel, and they would have a good time celebrating before heading back to Denver.

It would be easy.

It would be amusing.

And it would be so satisfying.

Two weeks into January, Joy began to "nest." Grant found her pulling their cottage apart in a frenzy of cleaning and reorganization. Blackie had crawled to safety under the bed and refused to come out.

"Are we expecting guests?" he puzzled aloud.

"Only a permanent one," Joy retorted, not pausing in her labors.

"Ah!" He watched her determined activity, still mystified.

Later he confided in Rose, "Joy is near the end of her pregnancy, but she is buzzing about our little house with more energy than she has had in months. I don't understand."

Rose nodded. "You are right—Joy is near term, and the baby will be coming soon. This spate of liveliness is not uncommon. She is preparing for the baby, making sure everything is in order for him or her."

"So I shouldn't be worried?"

"Not at all. It will run its course." Rose tapped her chin. "Is Sarah prepared to assume management of the store while Joy is home with the baby?"

"More than ready, I would say," Grant answered. "And more than capable."

"I am glad! I know Joy would not be able to rest properly if the store were not in capable hands."

Jeremy Bailey pored over a stack of paperwork at the desk in the freight office, glad of the warm fire in the nearby pot-bellied stove. He glanced up as Connor McKennie sauntered through the door.

"Connor." Jeremy nodded to him.

"Jeremy." Connor stared around the office but his gaze didn't seem to take in much. His hunting piece rested under one arm; a game bag dangled from his other hand.

"Have any luck?" Jeremy jutted his chin at the bag. He and Connor had not been close since Connor's sweetheart, Erica, had passed and Connor had withdrawn from friends and family. Jeremy was puzzled by the surprise visit.

"Yeah. Couple of grouse. Thought I'd drop them off . . ." Connor jerked his head in the direction of Esther and Ava's store but didn't finish his sentence. He cleared his throat. "Thing is, I was wondering if you, that is . . . I mean, how well do you know those . . . those women—"

"Are you askin' how well do I know Miss Esther and Miss Ava?"

Connor shrugged and nodded.

"Seems to me that what I know is the same as what you know, Connor." Jeremy's stare grew chilly. "They share an unsavory past that they don't deny or excuse. They have publicly repented and come to Christ. Now they are a-livin' and a-growin' in their faith as best they can. Seems to me that we should believe what the Bible teaches: *if any man*—or woman, for that matter—*be in Christ, he is a new creature: old things are passed away; behold, all things are become new.*"

"But what about—" Connor struggled to articulate his thoughts.

"Seems to me we should *mind our own business* and let God do his work." Jeremy's normally curving smile turned down into a hard line.

Connor sighed. "Easier said than done."

"Easy enough if you stop judgin' them—and stop behavin' like the jackass I heard you made o' yourself on Thanksgiving," was Jeremy's retort.

Connor's head jerked up. "You—how'd you hear about that?"

"A whole kitchen full o' Thoresen and McKennie women heard you an' Miss Esther. It's all over town. And it's a sad shame, I'm thinkin'. These girls, Esther, Ava, and Edith, are alone in the world, but they are a-workin' hard to make their own way as decent folk. They've earned a mite o' respect here in RiverBend. *You*, Connor McKennie, don't have a right to hold over them what is covered by the blood of Christ. *You* are not their judge."

Connor sank into a chair and dropped the game bag on the floor. "I don't understand why this is so hard for me. I don't know how to accept them."

But Jeremy wasn't looking at Connor any more; he was frowning through the window as two sleek, black automobiles eased their way down the street. He stood up and pulled the curtain aside.

"Connor. We got trouble."

Esther pulled a bolt of trim from the rack and hummed to herself, measuring off the four yards she would need for Mrs. Mullins' dress.

What a lovely color this is, she smiled to herself.

The bell on the door jingled and she glanced up.

A man entered the store. He was a stranger, but his unfamiliarity was not what put her on her guard. No, with a visceral twist of her stomach, she recognized him for what he was—*that kind of man*—dangerous, brutal, and in her shop for no good purpose.

She said nothing, but began backing up even as she watched him swagger toward the dresses, eating up the space between himself and the counter, each step taking him closer to cutting off her escape through the back.

Esther's pulse quickened. *Ava and Edith are in the back—*

The bell jingled again and three other men sauntered through it. Esther flicked her eyes toward them. Even as she did, the first man lunged between her and her escape route. He reached into his pocket and drew a pistol.

Someone chuckled and Esther froze. She recognized the laugh, and she was certain that her heart had seized up, so tightly did her chest contract.

Cal.

"Good morning, my dear," he murmured. He gestured and a man behind him turned over the sign on the door so that it read "Closed." The man then pulled the shade closed.

Esther recognized the distinctive click of the door's lock. She shuddered. *O dear Lord!* she moaned within herself. *Why? Why did you allow Cal to find us?*

"Still haven't learned your manners, have you?" Cal drawled. "I said *good morning*. Now come here, kiss me, and say 'good morning.'"

Esther couldn't move. The man behind her nudged her in the back and, with faltering steps, she moved forward.

Cal took her chin in his hand and forced her to look at him. He had lost the pounds that high living had added to him: His ruddy jaw was lean and sharp, his cheeks hollow, his eyes glittering. *A predator's face.*

"Say *good morning, Cal.*"

Esther stared at him, her expression bleak.

"No."

If I die under his hand, at least I will not die under his thumb, Esther vowed to herself.

The fingers holding her chin squeezed until Esther's eyes watered. Then Cal wrapped his arms about her and pulled her close to him, pressing his lips on her lips, and grinding his mouth against hers until she felt her lower lip splitting and her teeth scoring the tender flesh inside her mouth.

Then Esther did something audacious, something she would never have dared before. She took Cal's lower lip between her teeth. And bit—a*s hard as she could.*

His yelp of astonished pain was followed by a thunderclap upon her ear. Cal had slapped the side of her head with his open palm, and for many seconds Esther could not hear for the ringing throb in her head.

Cal gripped her wrists and cursed her. "You seem to have grown even more rebellious in spirit this last year, Esther," he growled, a dribble of blood coursing over his lip. "We'll see how long that lasts."

"You will never take me back there," Esther hissed. "I will never be your whore again!"

She struggled against Cal's thick fingers on her wrists, but they squeezed like vises. She felt the skin on her wrists bruising as he tightened and twisted his grip.

"Oh, but I'm not taking you back to Denver, my dear," Cal snarled. "Your treacherous heart would not be a good influence on the other girls."

He laughed. "Don't you remember what I promised you when you turned on me? I think my exact words were, *When I find you and I finish with you, little children will run screaming from the sight of your face.* Well, here we are and I assure you—when I finish with you, no man will ever even *dream* you were once beautiful."

He slapped Esther's cheek and she saw points of light all around her. Through the haze, she wondered if Ava and Edith had escaped out the back and were finding help.

Yet, even as Cal pulled back his hand to strike her again, Esther began praying that her friends would *not* find help. In an instant of clarity, Esther realized that she did not want Ava, Edith, or any of RiverBend's citizenry dying for her sake. They had been too good, too kind. She did not want them or their families to suffer.

And suffer they would. Cal's men were armed and brutal—the simple farmers of RiverBend would be no match for Cal and his men's practiced ruthlessness.

"I promised you that no matter how far you went or where you hid, I would find you, my sweet Esther. Now you will pay for your disloyalty."

He slapped Esther again; this time Esther's head snapped back, violently. Cal chuckled. "I've waited more than a year to see you suffer. I even bought a new knife, a sweet little blade, special for the occasion. I will enjoy this mightily."

"No, sir. No, you will not."

Esther could not see much; her eyes were swelling shut and blood ran from above one eye, marring her sight. But she recognized the voice coming from behind Cal.

Of all people . . . it was Connor McKennie.

"Forbes." Cal spat the one-word command from between his teeth.

The man who had entered the store first leveled his pistol—

A blast rocked the store and, through vision blurred by blood and smoke, Esther watched the man Cal had called Forbes clutch at his middle. The gun he held toppled from his hand and his body slid to the floor.

Another gun roared from a different direction. Esther did not see Cal's man nearest the front door fall, but she heard Cal curse and shout an order.

Cal's arm snaked about Esther. He turned and held her body between him and the threat. His last man slid behind Cal. Esther heard the man cock a handgun.

Through the fog, Esther could make out two shapes behind the counter of her little shop. One of them had to be Connor. He pointed a smoking rifle in their direction, even as he slowly sidled out from behind the counter. The other man-sized shape gripped what Esther surmised from the blast to be a shotgun. The weapon was raised and aimed at Cal.

At her.

"We don't cotton to men who disrespect women," the faceless voice behind the shotgun called, "and we have no tolerance for those who prey upon them."

Jeremy Bailey.

Esther wanted to wipe the blood from her eyes, but Cal's arm clutched her closer, pinning both of her arms to her side. She twisted her head and managed to swipe her bloody eye across his sleeve.

She could see a little better now. Jeremy, his expression utterly still, stared past Esther as though she were not there: He had eyes only for Cal.

As for Connor, he was looking right at her. Directly at her. Into her eyes. And then down. And up to her again. And down. He raised one brow as if asking a question.

Esther's frenzied thoughts could not grasp his meaning. Again Connor looked down. He dropped his chin the tiniest bit.

He wants me to drop to the floor, Esther realized in horror. She almost panicked.

When? When would I do such a thing?

Cal chuckled. "You two dirt farmers don't need to concern yourself over this little whore, do you? Why, she's not even a good whore," His words mocked Esther.

He grinned, reveling in his old confidence. "Now here's what I think. I think you should do the wise thing. The prudent thing," he suggested, employing a reasonable tone.

"You just back off, easy like, and we'll be on our way. We won't cause your little town any further disturbance. No need for you to get riled up or . . . *hurt* over a filthy, used-up slut."

Esther flinched at the slur but she continued to stare at Connor. Connor's jaw worked as he digested Cal's words. Again, Connor stared into Esther's eyes. As though he were disagreeing with Cal, Connor shook his head, "no," just once.

"Why, I do b'lieve you are mistaken, mister," Jeremy drawled, managing to sound surprised. "I don't know what you *think* you know, but Miss Esther here is a respected maiden lady in this town."

Cal hooted. "Maiden lady? Really? 'Cause in Denver I can tell you she used to fetch a *very* pretty penny for her, shall we say, *unmaidenly services*." He scoffed. "I'm sure even you backwards clod busters relish a good romp in the hay, am I right?"

Esther felt as though she had been stripped naked in front of Connor and Jeremy. She moaned in shame.

O God, I cannot bear this!

Connor's mouth pinched tighter—yet he was not looking at her, but at Cal . . . and Esther was, in that moment, afraid for Connor.

Jeremy drawled again. "Weeeell, we aren't *just* farmers out here, y'know. Seems we also have a few herd animals. Cattle, goats, maybe a few sheep."

Jeremy's voice was low and patient, almost patronizing. "And the prairie out here? Out beyond the town in the distance? Turns out, the prairie is home to all kinda predators—wolves, coyotes, foxes. Even a big cat once in a while. And y'know what we do when a predator comes after one of our lambs or calves?"

Cal didn't answer, but Esther swallowed, her throat suddenly dry.

Jeremy, his gun never wavering, always pointed at Cal—*at her*—added softly, "Why, we shoot that wolf. We shoot it dead. That's what we do."

Esther could feel tension rising in Cal's arms and in his chest; she knew he was wound as tight as a spring, ready to be loosed, ready to pounce.

Cal snarled, "This is my last warning, farmer. Back off and we'll be on our way—otherwise your little *maiden lady* gets hurt."

"I still don't think you understand, mister," Jeremy answered, his words soft. "Y'see, if we wouldn't hesitate to shoot a wolf in defense of a lamb, what d'ya think we would do when something *or someone* threatens a woman our God says is made in his very image?"

Cal cursed. He was accustomed to men jumping to obey him; he could not abide being thwarted or beaten. Jeremy's refusal to back down was goading Cal's anger, and Esther knew his temper well.

Then Jeremy growled, all softness gone, the menace unmistakable. "Mark m'words, mister. You will not take Miss Esther. If you try, we *will* kill you."

Esther swallowed again. *Sweet, kind Jeremy Bailey?* Her insides turned to water.

Jeremy raised his voice. "I give you to th' count-a five to let her go and get t' runnin'." His words rang with cold certainty.

From alongside his rifle, Connor's eyes bored into Esther's.

The count of five!

Esther blinked and then nodded.

Connor smiled in acknowledgement, but it was not a pleasant smile.

Jeremy counted. "One . . . Two . . . Three . . . Four . . .

"Five."

Esther lifted her feet and went limp in Cal's arms, sliding halfway to the floor.

Connor's rifle had never moved off Cal. The boom of his gun's report shattered the windows behind Cal.

Cal's remaining accomplice raised a revolver and fired at Jeremy just as Jeremy side-stepped to the right and loosed the second barrel of his shotgun.

Esther scrabbled on her hands and knees to the rack of dresses and burrowed inside. The dresses covered her, hid her. As she squeezed against the rack's post she heard nothing but her own sobs through the deafening concussion of gun blasts.

O God, I trusted you!

She could not hear the store's front door burst open, the lock breaking and jams splintering, or hear men stream into her store. She could not hear the alarmed voices and shouted questions or Jeremy's calm reassurances in answer. She could hear only her own keening voice from far away as she rocked back and forth, sobbing.

Then, inexplicably, Esther calmed. A solemn Presence surrounded her where she knelt within the shelter of inexpensive, off-the-rack dresses, a Presence that comforted her and whispered,

Do not be afraid. I am with you.

Esther blinked. Again the Voice sighed,

Do not be afraid. I am with you.

Esther's world began to right itself. When a slow, gentle hand drew the dresses apart, she did not shrink back. The hand brushed her shoulder and, tentatively, rested there.

"Miss Esther."

It was Connor's voice, sounding quite far away.

"You are safe now, Miss Esther."

"Yes . . ." Esther murmured.

Do not be afraid. I am with you.

Connor offered his hand. She placed hers in his and he drew her out from the rack and the dresses that had hidden her. She managed a shuddering breath as he steadied her.

Connor tried to lead Esther away, but she saw the bodies lying on the floor—the floor of her shop!—and froze.

"Cal . . ."

"He won't bother you again, Miss Esther," Connor muttered. His eyes shifted involuntarily toward the floor a few feet from them.

Esther's mouth opened a little as she stared at what remained of Cal Judd, the man who had hunted and terrorized her.

Do not be afraid. I am with you.

The words that had assured her moments ago sank down into her soul and she drew another cleansing breath. *Yes, Jesus. Thank you.*

Connor was shaking his head. "I am so sorry, Miss Esther; I had no idea—" He broke off, regret written in lines around his mouth. "I am so sorry."

Esther's mouth opened a little and she realized, *Miss Esther! Connor called me 'Miss Esther!'*

"I forgive you, Connor," she whispered.

Then Ava was reaching for her, weeping over her. Edith was behind her, sobbing. Jeremy, unharmed but grave, watched from a few feet away.

"Oh, Esther! What has he done to you?" Edith moaned.

Rivulets of blood, some dry and some fresh, ran from Esther's brow to her chin. Her face was a mass of purpling welts. A great stupor was creeping into Esther's bones, but as Ava and Edith wrapped tender arms about her, Esther could still hear that Voice, wooing her, strengthening her.

Do not be afraid. I am with you.

෨ ❀ ෬

Chapter 15

Breona called Rose from the dinner table to the telephone in the great room near Rose's desk. "Miss Rose! 'Tis Pastor Medford a-callin' from RiverBend!"

Alarm sprang to Rose's heart. Edith had only been gone a few weeks—and Cal Judd had been released from prison about as long.

She listened, astonished and then astounded, as Jacob shouted over the tinny connection all the details of Cal Judd's attempt to take Esther—and his subsequent defeat and demise at the hands of Jeremy Bailey and Connor McKennie. When the long telephone call ended, Rose stood still, the wonderful implications of Jacob's news soaking into her heart.

"O Lord, how I thank you for this deliverance," she breathed. "And, Father, I pray you have mercy on these men who must now face you and your righteous judgments." Rose trembled, remembering the many heinous crimes for which she knew God would call them to account.

Straightening her shoulders, she walked into the dining room to rejoin the house for dinner, a faint smile playing about her mouth. Many pairs of questioning eyes turned toward her.

Taking her seat she looked around the table. "I have received news . . . momentous news."

Rose did not want to repeat the ugly details of the event; after a moment's reflection she announced quietly, "Cal Judd and his men somehow tracked Edith to RiverBend."

No one at the table moved or spoke.

"They found Esther and were trying to take her away, but friends of ours defended her." Rose rested her face in her hand, her relief evident. "Esther was hurt a bit, but Pastor Medford assures me she will be fine. And, he tells me, Cal Judd . . . is dead."

Those at the table sighed, as though they had been holding their breath together.

"Oh, Mama! Oh, thank you, Lord!" Joy's praise was taken up by the others, followed by a babble of questions.

Rose quelled the questions with an upraised palm. "I know finishing dinner may be difficult, but I would prefer not to discuss the, er, unpleasant details at the table. Right now, I am simply overwhelmed with relief and gratitude."

Breona, her black eyes snapping, called, "'Tis writin' Tabitha this verra night we mus' be doin'! Won't she be rejoicin' an' dancin' on a cloud? Thank ye, Lord!"

"And Mr. O'Dell!" Grant added. "We must let him know right away."

"Yes," Rose answered, smiling larger. "Cal Judd will never pose a threat to us again. And Mr. O'Dell need not be concerned about visiting us here in Denver!"

That night as Joy and Grant prepared for bed, Grant touched Joy's face. "My dear, I would like Mr. O'Dell to come visit as soon as possible. How do you feel about that?"

Joy studied Grant. He had not complained, but she could tell he was not doing as well as he had been when they first acquired the oxygen apparatus.

Does he want to say goodbye to his friend? O Lord, he thinks I do not see, but I know he is struggling. Father, please give us more time, she prayed, even as she fought to keep her face serene. *Please give Grant time with his son or daughter, Lord! I am calling on you!*

"Of course, Grant."

"Thank you. I will write him tomorrow, first thing."

Grant wrote to his friend O'Dell in the morning but did not send the letter until the next day. With the short note he wanted to enclose a clipping from the Denver Post. The headline read, JUDD KILLED IN SHOOTOUT.

Grant had to shake his head at the paper's sensationalized report, but he admitted that the story read well. What his letter lacked in enthusiastic detail, the article amply provided!

However, he had not been allowed to cut up the paper until it had been read many times by all in the house. Moreover, Mr. Wheatley had walked several blocks to buy two more copies of the paper so that Breona could cut and send the article to Tabitha and paste the other in a scrapbook.

When the two letters left the house that morning, their two writers anticipated the great relief the letters' recipients would feel upon reading them.

Esther and Ava studied Esther's reflection in the mirror. Her heart-shaped face was a tender, mottled blue and purple. One eye was swollen shut. A line of stitches sewn closed by the community's doctor testified to the split Cal's hand had opened just under her eyebrow.

"It looks worse today than yesterday," Esther muttered.

It had been four days since . . . Esther did not like to put a descriptive name to *That Day*.

"Remember when Cal broke my nose?" Ava stood behind Esther, her hands on her friend's shoulders, peering into the mirror with her.

"How can I forget? You looked like a raccoon for weeks." Ava's eyes had been ringed with bright fuchsia and magenta—bruising that pooled below her eyes, darkening to an ugly purple before fading to sickly yellow.

"My nose has not been the same since." It was true; Ava's nose listed to the side.

"I'm grateful he did not break my nose," Esther admitted, "but I will bear a scar to remind me of him."

Cal's blatant attempt to take Esther by force had produced an uproar that reached all the way to Denver where Cal's reputation was already known. Soon after, Esther and Ava's shop had seen a marked increase in traffic. Strangers—reporters and law men from Denver—had descended on RiverBend and its citizens, asking questions, taking photographs—and prying.

The reporters, to their chagrin, found that the little town's inhabitants were remarkably close-mouthed when interviewed. Later, when the journalists compared notes, they found that *not one* individual in RiverBend had been able to provide information on Esther and Ava's backgrounds.

Furthermore, not one citizen could conjure a clue as to why Cal Judd—a complete stranger in RiverBend—had appeared one day in their town, intent on harming one of their innocent young women!

The reporters departed RiverBend in disgust, certain they had been stonewalled.

Esther had declined to meet with the reporters—or anyone from RiverBend for that matter. She had hidden herself and her damaged face in the back of the shop, refusing to come out.

Ava, with help from Edith, had handled all the shop's business and the many questions and curious eyes. Only the doctor, Pastor Medford, and Fiona had gained access to Esther, and Esther had cried her swollen eyes upon Fiona's plump, grandmotherly shoulders until she exhausted her tears.

Between dodging the reporters, the people of RiverBend had visited the shop. Yes, they were curious to see the spot where the four men had been gunned down—not an everyday event, after all— but Ava didn't know how to convey to Esther the many expressions of sympathy and indignation that their RiverBend neighbors had poured into her ears. She let the hot meals and homemade pies and cakes with which they filled Esther and Ava's cupboards speak their own messages of kindness.

"I won't be able to show myself for quite a while still."

"No." Ava shook her head, agreeing with Esther. She straightened as the shop's bell jingled the arrival of a customer—or another inquisitive local.

"Pastor Medford!"

Esther heard Ava greet Jacob Medford. He had been by every day to visit and pray with Ava and Esther. He had been a pillar of strength to both of them in the aftermath of *That Day*.

"Esther? May Pastor Medford come back to visit with you?"

"Yes, of course." Esther turned from the mirror.

She set herself to brew him a cup of his favorite tea, something of a routine for them now, while he conveyed greetings and little bits of news from Vera.

"Esther, tomorrow is Sunday," he said, taking the cup she offered him.

"Yes." Esther nodded but said nothing more.

"You have been keeping yourself hidden these past four days. Vera and I understand and do not fault you in the least. This has been a difficult time for you."

Esther glanced up. "Thank you."

Jacob smiled and nodded. "We have a suggestion, however."

When Esther looked toward him again, he continued. "Vera and I were praying this morning. It has been hard for you and Ava to become part of this community. The circumstances of your, er, move to RiverBend has made life here difficult for you sometimes. And then . . . this happened."

Alarm shot through Esther. "Are you asking us to leave?" Her heart was pounding.

"Not at all. The opposite, in fact."

Esther could breathe again.

How did this place become so dear to me? she wondered. *When did my soul grow roots down into this little town?*

"We feel you should come to church tomorrow."

"What?" His statement jerked Esther from her thoughts. "No."

But Jacob persisted. "Miss Esther, this is a very tightly knit community. We are loyal to each other. Do you want to be part of that? Do you desire an enduring place in this community?"

Esther's eyes were brimming when she answered. "Yes, I do. More than anything."

"Then come to church tomorrow. Vera and I believe the Lord spoke something to us, but it will require that you bare your pain to your neighbors. Can you do that?"

Esther swallowed and thought on it. "Yes."

The next morning Esther and Ava readied themselves for church. Esther played with her hair, arranging it so that curls draped the sides of her face and hung low over her brow. Staring into the mirror, she huffed in frustration.

"Nothing will hide those bruises, Esther," Ava murmured. "If you ask me, trying to hide them only draws more attention to them."

Esther had come to the same conclusion: The hairstyle she had labored over was fussy by RiverBend standards and looked nothing like the simple Esther folks here knew.

She pulled all the pins from her hair, brushed the blonde tresses back from her face, placed a comb on each side, and let the curls hang naturally.

"There." She looked like herself again—herself beat black, blue, and purple.

Their breaths created puffs of steam in the frosty January air as they walked to the edge of town. The quaint old building where the church met was a mile farther. As they walked, they passed or encountered others going the same way.

"Good morning, Miss Ava. Good morning, Miss Esther," was called or murmured several times.

Miss Ava. Miss Esther.

Esther heard Connor's voice speaking the same words. She gulped and fought the tears that pricked her eyes.

Lord, please help me to not fall apart this morning!

Families and neighbors gathered in informal knots in the churchyard waiting for the bell to call them to worship. Again, soft greetings called to them, and Esther and Ava bravely bent their heads in return.

A grizzled old farmer and his wife nodded as Esther and Ava passed by. Then the man was holding out his hand.

As Esther took his, the farmer cleared his throat. "Glad t' see yer doin' ok, miss."

Esther nodded. "Thank you."

Another family waited at her elbow. She reached her hand toward the one held out to her.

"Jest wanted t' say . . . we don't abide with anyone hurtin' one o' our own," the weather-worn gent growled. "Made me plumb mad t' hear it, it did. We're mighty grateful ya didn't come t' harm." His wife smiled and squeezed Esther's arm.

One of our own?

The man peered at Esther's bruised face. "Shooo-ee! Them's some fine 'uns! Don't fret none 'bout thet color, though. It'll go quick. Why, my mule kicked me in th' face once, and my face were a shiny purple fer three weeks!"

Another couple had drawn near. The woman whispered in Esther's ear, "We bin prayin' fer ya. Don't lose yer courage now, hear?"

Esther sobbed once and nodded; it took all she had not to break down. The woman patted her gently before she and her husband moved off.

The rest of the morning blurred for Esther. Looking back, she could recall no details of the service except one moment that etched itself in her memory. She and Ava were standing in the dim light of the church's small vestibule, searching for open seats.

"Miss Esther?" Connor McKennie appeared beside her. He took her hand. For a moment he struggled to find the words he wanted to say, and they both stood there, mute.

Finally, he whispered, "I didn't understand." He hesitated again before adding, "You are a brave woman. I . . . I'm proud of you."

With that and a nod, he went to join his family.

O'Dell gaped at the copy of the Denver Post Parsons had just slapped on his desk. He grabbed it up and raced through the headline article.

What? Judd had found Esther! Had died trying to take her from RiverBend!

"Put your eyeballs back in your head, O'Dell," Parsons growled. "Judd has gone to his reward, and I gotta say, it couldn't have happened to a nicer guy."

O'Dell didn't answer; he didn't trust himself to speak just yet.

Thank you, Lord! No more worry about Judd's revenge; no more looking over my shoulder! And no more avoiding Denver for fear of leading Judd straight to Palmer House!

Thank you, Lord, for sparing Esther and the other girls! Thank you for . . . removing this threat forever.

Midmorning, days later, O'Dell slit open an envelope. A clipping of the same Denver Post article he had already read fell out onto his desk. O'Dell plucked a letter from the envelope—it was just a note, really—and scanned it twice.

"Boss?" O'Dell stood in Parson's office doorway. "I'm taking a week off." He already had his derby in one hand, his cane in the other.

"What in blazes? O'Dell, you won't earn a week off for another two years!"

"Sorry. It's family business."

Parson's expression darkened further. "You don't have a family."

O'Dell grinned and flipped the bowler neatly onto his head. "Yes I do, and it's in Denver. See you in a week." Out of habit, he patted his breast pocket for a cigar—empty!—and laughed at himself.

He strode down the hall toward the door, his thoughts fixed on those dear to him: Liáng and Bao; Mei-Xing and the baby daughter he'd not yet met; Rose and Breona; Billy, Marit, and Will; Mr. Wheatley; Grant and Joy and the baby soon to be born.

I'll be on the afternoon train. The people I love are asking for me and I can, at last, go to them. Thank you, Lord!

Chapter 16

Joy woke in the night. She lay quiet but alert, listening to Grant's steady snoring and the sound of the machine that helped him.

What is it that awakened me?

She listened but heard nothing out of the ordinary. She closed her eyes and began to drift back to sleep only to abruptly waken again. She glanced at the clock near their bed.

It is still the middle of the night! Maybe a glass of warm milk will soothe me, she decided.

She scooted until she reached the edge of the bed and dangled her feet over the side. When they touched the floor, she rolled and was able to sit up.

I can scarcely get out of this bed! she grumbled. *And where are my slippers?* She looked down but could not see past her distended belly. Turning this way and that, she glimpsed the elusive slippers and, with her toes, dragged them toward the bed where she could sit and, by touch alone, maneuver her feet into them.

Joy gasped as a stream of warmth gushed from between her legs and puddled on and around her slippers.

"Oh, my!" When she stood up, more fluid trickled down her legs.

"I am having a baby," she whispered in amazement.

She waddled to a cupboard and found clean towels and a fresh nightgown. With a little effort, she did a credible of job of sopping up the fluid and changing into the clean gown.

"What are you doing?" Grant's whisper startled a shriek from Joy.

"You scared me!" Then she laughed; she giggled like a girl. "I'm having a baby, I think."

"It's about time." Grant started to get out of bed. "I haven't been able to sleep this past month worrying and wishing this were over." He turned up the gaslight and grinned across the bed.

"Grant Michaels! You take that back, right now! Just five minutes ago you were snoring so loudly you didn't even know I'd gotten up, let alone mopped up the floor and changed my gown."

He kept grinning but then Joy's demeanor went still and she frowned.

"Has it started?" he asked. "What can I do?"

"I-I don't know. Nothing just yet, I think." She stayed quiet for a few seconds longer. "That one is over. If I understand correctly, when the pains get close together, that's when we should call the doctor."

"*Close together?* What does 'close together' mean? How many minutes apart is *close together?*"

"Oh, Grant!" Joy laughed and set the kettle on the stove. "I'm sure it will be a while. I'll just make myself some chamomile tea. And I'll make you a pot of coffee."

At daybreak Grant opened their cottage door and picked up a handful of pebbles, stopping to catch his breath afterwards. One at a time he tossed the gravel stones against the window of Billy and Marit's little house, not far from theirs.

After six or seven pebbles pinged off the glass, Marit looked through and spied Grant. Seconds later she opened their door.

"Vat is it? It is Miss Joy's time?"

Grant was relieved to see Marit; Joy had taken to their bed half an hour ago. "Yes. Would you send Billy to fetch Joy's mother?"

He did not have to wait long. Rose, who looked as though she had thrown on her clothes while racing down the stairs, bustled into their cottage; Breona was fast on her heels.

Grant was more than ready for Billy to help him into the house when he came—Grant did not want to hear any more of the groans Joy tried so hard to smother. He collapsed at the kitchen table and began to pray.

No one disturbed him; the girls came and went, mindful of his presence, and breakfast preparations went ahead. Marit placed a cup of coffee near his elbow. The aroma pulled him from his prayers and he sipped it with gratitude but soon returned to lifting his wife before the Lord.

O Father, after all this time, you have blessed us with a child. I know you are with Joy right now, strengthening her and giving her hope. Hope! Lord, if our child is a daughter, Hope would be a perfect name. But, you know that if the baby is a son . . .

He prayed on, pausing to finish the cup of coffee gone cold and to greet Dr. Murphy as Mr. Wheatley showed him through the house and out the back door toward the cottage.

"Well, you'll have a fine son or daughter before long, I expect," the doctor assured him. "Joy is from strong stock and will not have difficulty birthing this child."

About that time O'Dell passed under the scrutiny of Gresham's men and rang the doorbell to Palmer House. Mr. Wheatley, his hair more disheveled than ever, shuffled to the door and welcomed him inside.

"Mr. O'Dell, you are a sight for sore eyes," the old man wheezed. "Got us quite a commotion today, too."

"Oh?" O'Dell frowned.

"Miss Joy's havin' her baby right now. Doctor Murphy went back there to their house 'bout an hour ago."

O'Dell's stomach lurched at the thought of Joy laboring to birth a child. "And Mr. Grant?"

"Why, he's been in the kitchen all morning, just praying."

"If you think it all right, I would like to join him."

"Mr. O'Dell, you've come!" Grant had never seen a more welcome sight. He struggled to stand and held out a welcoming hand.

O'Dell's eyes were sharp, and he did not like the way his friend looked. He was thinner than the last time he had seen him. Thinner and . . . too pale. He did not miss the slight tinge of blue about Grant's mouth . . . or the odd-looking cup he held . . . or the hose that led from the cup to a tank of some kind topped by gadgets.

O'Dell hid his dismay. *This is what Joy would not tell me when I was here last,* he realized. He shook hands with Grant and took the chair offered to him.

"Mr. Wheatley tells me you are about to become a father," O'Dell smiled.

"Thanks be to the Lord!" Grant grinned. He breathed from the cup he held in his hand and added, "The doctor just came. I hope it does not take much longer."

It was past lunchtime when Breona bounded into the kitchen. "Mr. Grant! Coom! Coom, ye mus' be coomin' now!"

If possible, Grant paled further. "Is she all right? The baby?"

"Ye jes' be coomin' now," was all Breona would say, but she was grinning and, spying O'Dell, she winked.

O'Dell knew then that all was well with Joy and the child. "Need some help with that contraption?"

"Yes, I would be obliged." Grant caught O'Dell watching him and saw the questions he had not spoken. "I would like to talk to you later," he said quietly.

O'Dell, while also managing his cane, rolled the tank to the back door, down the steps, and along the brick walkway to Grant and Joy's cottage. Grant followed him, breathing from the cup.

When they reached the cottage door, O'Dell felt he should not go inside and intrude on such a hallowed moment, but it was obvious that Grant was in no condition to haul the machine inside on his own.

"I apologize," Grant whispered, "but could you help me inside?"

O'Dell took a deep breath. He hauled the tank through the doorway ahead of Grant. O'Dell peered down a short passage and saw Rose Thoresen, her face glowing, standing beside a bed that was around the corner.

"Mr. O'Dell! I am so delighted to see you! Thank you for helping Grant."

He wheeled the tank close to the bed and then backed away toward the door, wondering what happiness awaited his friend Grant beyond that corner.

O'Dell stepped outside and closed the door behind him. Then he heard the squall of a newborn through the door and he went still with wonder.

Joy is a mother!

With Rose's help, Grant maneuvered himself and the breathing apparatus so that he could perch on the edge of the bed. The doctor was packing his bag and Joy was sitting up, a small blanketed bundle in the curve of her arm.

The bundle squawked and squalled; Joy and her mother both laughed.

Grant stared at the blanketed baby and then scanned Joy's face; she appeared exhausted and elated at the same time. "Are you all right, my darling?"

"Right as rain," Joy answered, her smile growing.

With awkward movements, she lifted the bundle and held it toward him. Grant sucked in a breath and took the now jiggling bundle. Joy lifted a corner of the blanket away and he stared into the *very* red face of a crying newborn.

"Meet our son, Grant. We have a son!"

"We have a son . . ." He was going to weep; he did not know how he could prevent it. The moment was too full of wonder.

The baby stilled and looked straight at him. Grant had heard that newborns could not see, but the baby seemed to be aware or listening. His eyes were a deep, dark blue, almost black.

Peeling the blanket back a little more, Grant saw wisps of light brown curls. "You are perfect, my son," Grant whispered. His voice caught and Joy brought her hand up and clasped his.

O'Dell returned to the house where everyone there had already received the news from Breona that Joy and Grant had a baby boy. Marit, as exuberant as O'Dell had ever seen her, set about making him a late lunch.

While O'Dell waited, little Will clambered up his leg and into his lap to tug on his mustache. O'Dell studied Will's clear eyes and happy, toothy smile and was more content than he could remember.

Mr. Wheatley had already eaten his lunch, but he sat with O'Dell as Marit served him, and Breona joined them, taking Will from O'Dell's lap so he could eat—and eat he did with an appetite.

"Sure an' 'tis good t' be seein' yer face again," Breona sighed. "You've heard th' news 'bout Cal Judd?"

"Aye, that I have," O'Dell answered, copying her accent perfectly.

She smacked him playfully on the arm. "We canna help boot rejoice. Th' weight o' th' worl', 'tis lifted from our heads."

"And from mine," O'Dell replied. "I came as soon as I received Grant's letter."

The doctor entered from the back door just then. "All is well with Mrs. Michaels and I will be on my way," he said, full of cheer. He waved Mr. Wheatley back into his chair. "No, I will see myself out, thank you."

After the doctor's footsteps echoed down the long hallway, O'Dell spoke again. "I have missed this house and this family and I have missed many happy times. I hope you will indulge me and just allow me to spend my day here? I hope to speak more with Grant later and, of course, I have not seen Mei-Xing's baby."

"Tosh! Ye are knowin' yer welcome onytime," Breona assured him.

"Care for a game of checkers after lunch?" Mr. Wheatley asked. He raised both brows hopefully.

"That, my friend," O'Dell nodded sagely, "is jest what th' doctor ordered, I'm thinkin'."

Mr. Wheatley slapped his leg. Even Marit chuckled.

It is so good to be here, Lord, O'Dell prayed silently. *I am grateful that you have blessed Joy and Grant with a child. Thank you for letting me be here to rejoice with them.*

Joy stared at the baby in her arms, half blind from the tears that seemed to flow every time she looked at him.

Look how beautiful he is, Lord! she rejoiced. She took inventory again: The haze of light brown, curling hair on his head was from Grant; the pursed, rosebud mouth was from her. The tiny thumb jammed in his mouth—almost from birth!—was all his own. While he sucked his thumb, the fingers of his dimpled hand curved around his cheek, cupping his face in the most endearing manner.

Grant peeked over her shoulder. "How amazing he is! Perfect in every way." They stared at the sleeping child, unaware of how much time was passing. It did not matter. They would treasure these precious hours all their lives.

"What will we name him, Grant?" Joy peered into Grant's face, treasuring, too, the happiness she saw there.

Grant squeezed her hand. "I have a name in mind that I wish us to give him, Joy, but only if you agree and approve." Gently, Grant shared his request with Joy.

Against her will, Joy's eyes began to droop. Rose swaddled the baby and tucked him into the bassinette near the bed. Then she went to fetch Billy to help Grant into the house.

Rose returned with Billy and determined to stay with Joy, even though Grant could see how weary she had become. He left Joy and the baby sleeping in the cottage and Rose nodding in the chair next to the bed.

I will ask Breona to come sit with Joy so Rose can go upstairs and take a nap, Grant thought as he and Billy made their way to the back door of Palmer House. *And I hope Mr. O'Dell has not left yet.*

He had not, of course.

After Grant sent Breona to spell Rose, he invited O'Dell to join him in the parlor where they could speak privately. O'Dell wheeled the tank into the room for Grant.

"Congratulations, Grant," O'Dell murmured when the apparatus was situated and Grant was seated. Grant breathed deeply from the machine before answering.

"Thank you. We never expected such a blessing." Grant was quiet, unsure how to proceed.

O'Dell, however, never one to stand upon niceties, had questions and wanted answers.

"I consider us good friends, Grant, but I have to say I was shocked to see . . . *that*, whatever it is, and you looking so poorly. You want to tell me what is going on?"

Grant sighed and drummed his fingers on the arm of the chair. "The fact is, Mr. O'Dell . . . I am dying."

O'Dell sat so still for so long that Grant became nervous and, on his own, kept talking. "The influenza last winter. Most of us in the house came down with it, you know. And then afterwards, Flinty . . ."

O'Dell nodded, mourning Flinty, missing his jokes and his tall tales, missing his wonderful, joyous spirit.

"What happened to you?"

Grant cleared his throat. "The doctor tells us that the influenza virus went into my heart and damaged it. It is not working well . . . and, well, it is getting worse." Between sentences, Grant breathed from the cup he placed over his mouth and nose. "Eventually, it will not work at all."

O'Dell studied Grant, again taking in his unnatural pallor. "That machine. What does it do for you?"

"It feeds me oxygen so I breathe better. For now."

O'Dell placed his hand over his eyes, listening, grieving. "Why didn't someone tell me?"

Grant shrugged. "What could you have done, Mr. O'Dell? You have already done more for us than anyone could have—standing with Joy and Rose against Morgan, reuniting me with Joy, bringing home Mei-Xing. You have been a faithful friend to all of us these past few years."

"But what does the doctor say? How long . . ."

Grant shook his head. "He doesn't know, but I can feel that the oxygen is not helping as much as it did a few months ago when we first got it."

"Can't they do *anything* to fix this? Slow it down?"

Grant shook his head again. "No."

"Grant . . . what can I do?" O'Dell felt helpless, and he struggled against the hopelessness of the situation. He thought of the child, just born, who would be losing his father before he really knew him.

Joy will be losing Grant all over again . . . O'Dell mourned. *No wonder she could not speak of it when I was here last. O Father!*

Grant leaned toward O'Dell. "Do you wish to help? You are my closest friend, Edmund O'Dell. Will you help me?"

O'Dell looked up, dreading what was coming. "Of course, Grant. Whatever it is."

O'Dell did not stay longer that day. He returned to his hotel to think on what Grant had requested and to pray.

What Grant asks of me . . . is too much, Lord, and yet he is already counting on me.

He opened his Bible and spent the evening doing nothing but seeking God, seeking answers to questions that seemed to have no answers.

O God, please help Grant and Joy. Please help me, he prayed again.

Chapter 17

(Journal Entry, January 19, 1911)

I am a grandmother! Grant and Joy's son was born yesterday at midday—a healthy, plump baby, as beautiful as can be. O Lord, thank you for this great blessing!

O'Dell checked in at the Denver Pinkerton office the following day and returned to Palmer House that afternoon, a few hours before dinner. Palmer House was returning to its normal routine after the excitement over the birth of Joy and Grant's baby: Mr. Wheatley saw him in, Rose and Grant greeted him from where they were working together at Rose's desk, and Breona fetched him tea and a plate of Marit's gingersnaps. O'Dell sat down, looked about himself at the familiar sights, and sighed in satisfaction.

He was delighted when Rose mentioned that she had also invited Liáng, Bao, and Carmichael to dine with them that evening. Liáng and Bao arrived early, and O'Dell was amazed at how healthy Bao was looking.

An animated hour of fellowship passed far too quickly—Liáng and Bao filled O'Dell with details of their ministry to the Chinese community of Denver. Before O'Dell realized how much time had flown by, the young ladies of the house began coming home from their labors.

O'Dell enjoyed watching Rose welcome each girl as she came through the door. He greeted the girls he already knew as they passed into the great room; Rose introduced him to several young women he had not met.

"I am sorry to have missed Tabitha's departure," he admitted to Rose. "Nursing school!"

"We are so proud of her, Mr. O'Dell," Rose smiled. "She will return for a month in June, but I know she will be so changed by then."

Mei-Xing stepped into the great room accompanied by two of Gresham's men; she was carrying the baby O'Dell had not yet seen. O'Dell eagerly stood up to welcome her, but Liáng—in a move quite uncharacteristic of himself—pushed ahead of O'Dell to help Mei-Xing with her coat and ask how her day had gone. Mei-Xing, occupied by Liáng's helpful ministrations, had not yet noticed O'Dell.

O'Dell turned to Rose, cocking a disgruntled eyebrow—and was astounded as she, her grey eyes brimming with merriment, slowly and deliberately winked at him! O'Dell shot a glance at Bao who covered a smirking mouth with his hand and shrugged.

What?

O'Dell folded his arms and stepped back to eye Liáng with Mei-Xing.

Well!

That was when Mei-Xing noticed him. She placed the baby in Liáng's arms and flew to O'Dell. With no self-consciousness, she grasped his outstretched hands.

"Mr. O'Dell! I was so hoping you would be here this evening!" Her eyes sparkled; like Bao, her health was markedly improved but, even more, she was lit with a glow from within.

"I can see that motherhood agrees with you, Mei-Xing," he grinned in return.

"Oh! But you haven't seen Shan-Rose yet!" Liáng had followed Mei-Xing, and he offered the bundle back to her. Mei-Xing took the baby and O'Dell stared down into a tiny, chubby, perfect replica of Mei-Xing. The infant's skin was as smooth as porcelain; her eyes were closed in sleep. As he studied the baby, her tiny mouth moved as though suckling.

O'Dell shook his head in admiration. "She looks so much like you, Mei-Xing."

Mei-Xing gazed on the baby with love and O'Dell, a mite overcome, had to glance away. He noticed that Liáng, too, was watching Mei-Xing with her baby. O'Dell did not mistake the desire written on Liáng's face.

O'Dell glanced again at Mei-Xing and then back to Liáng. Mei-Xing received Liáng's attentions with the gratitude of friendship, but she seemed oblivious to the deeper feelings that others could easily see.

Even though you still must win her, I envy you, my friend, O'Dell thought while studying Liáng.

Minutes later, Isaac Carmichael arrived and O'Dell was soon engaged in a lively conversation with him.

"How long will you be here?" Carmichael asked. "We have not seen you since you brought Mei-Xing home. You have been sorely missed."

"I will stay at least a week—that is, I told Parsons a week, but I may find some odd jobs at the Denver office that will allow me to stretch the time a bit longer. Now that Cal Judd is no longer a threat, I hope to visit Denver more often."

"Wonderful! Say, would you care to join Bao, Liáng, and myself for Bible study tomorrow morning? We spend at least an hour studying God's word together and then praying before starting on our rounds. We would feel honored to have you join us."

O'Dell was the one who felt honored. He sorely missed the hours Liáng had spent sharing from the Scriptures with O'Dell, Bao, and Miss Greenbow back in the little house in Seattle—nearly a year ago now.

"I confess, I have been floundering some in my study of the Bible. When you see me tomorrow, you will see a man very hungry and thirsty for spiritual nourishment."

"Then it is settled. We will see you tomorrow at eight o'clock. We look forward to our fellowship with you!"

The evening O'Dell spent at Palmer House was everything he could have wanted. The food and conversation around the table refreshed his heart. Of course, Flinty was gone, Tabitha was away, Joy could not join them so soon after childbirth, and Grant took his dinner with Joy, but the rest of the "family" at Palmer House was present.

Carmichael led them in the blessing. Then the girls talked of the ordinary events of their day, and O'Dell soaked up their cheerful laughter and easy banter. Carmichael and Liáng mentioned a few needs in the church and shared a recent salvation experience.

How do I live without this vitality, this joyful interchange? O'Dell wondered. *How bland and empty my life is away from here!*

After dinner, the girls began cleaning up from the meal and changing to less formal dress to enjoy an evening of relaxation and company in the great room. O'Dell set aside his coat and helped Mr. Wheatley lay in firewood for the great room fireplaces.

"We keep the place a mite chilly in the winter time," the old man confessed. His hair stood on end as he ran a gnarled hand through it. "Mr. Grant has t' keep us on short shrift t' pay the bills, so we turn the furnace down and heat the great room with its fireplaces."

O'Dell hadn't realized it until then, but the house *was* cold, with the exception of the great room and nearby dining room. His mind, ever analytical, began to wonder how Rose and Grant managed the many expenses of the house.

I will certainly pray over this, he determined. *What else do I have need of to spend my money on? This is my family, after all.*

As he and Mr. Wheatley built up the fires in the great room's two fireplaces, those in the house began to gather and find their usual places. Some of the young ladies had books; others had mending or other handwork. With the doors to the room closed, the room soon took on a cheery glow.

Mei-Xing appeared with Shan-Rose. Once she was settled in the much warmer room, she uncovered the wriggling child. Now five months old, Shan-Rose sat upon Mei-Xing's lap and gazed around the room with bright eyes.

O'Dell noticed that wherever Mei-Xing was, Liáng hovered close by, watching for a need he could fill. Shan-Rose caught sight of Liáng and laughed, reaching out her hands to him. Receiving permission from Mei-Xing, Liáng picked the tiny girl up and carried her around the room, bouncing her enough to make her gurgle and squeal.

What would that be like? O'Dell wondered. *What would having a child recognize me and reach for me be like?*

"We have decided on a name for our son," Grant announced. Days had passed; Joy was joining them at the dinner table for the first time since giving birth.

It was the first time O'Dell had seen Joy since the previous April when he had found and brought Mei-Xing home. O'Dell saw that motherhood had rounded Joy where she had once been as slim as a sapling. Joy glanced often into the bassinet that was near her chair, every part of her seeming to glow with contentment.

This night would also be O'Dell's last in Denver; Parsons had sent him a terse summons: *Party's over. New case.*

"All of you know that I have no family remaining on my side," Grant continued. "During the two dark years after my ship went down, while I was searching for home and my memories, I counted only one man my friend."

He nodded at O'Dell. "If not for you, Mr. O'Dell, Joy and I might never have been reunited—and this child of ours would not have been born."

Grant breathed from the machine and everyone waited until he was ready to continue, but O'Dell was already feeling his shirt collar tightening, choking him. He did not enjoy being the object of attention.

"Our dear friend, Edmund O'Dell, is here with us as we make this important announcement. In honor of this friendship, our son will be called Edmund. His middle name will be Joy's maiden name, Thoresen. Our son is Edmund Thoresen Michaels."

The table burst into happy applause and voices tried out the child's name, calling him "Baby Edmund" and "Little Ed." Mr. Wheatley and Liáng, on either side of O'Dell, pounded him on the back.

O'Dell couldn't breathe.

Joy seemed as uncomfortable as he felt. She smiled at him, but it was a weak smile.

You, like I, cannot but view this as an unwelcome harbinger, O'Dell thought, *and you resist it, as do I.*

As soon as he could excuse himself, O'Dell bolted out the front door. Gresham's guard examined him with wary eyes. O'Dell ran his hand through his hair and went down the porch steps two at a time, testing the limits of his touchy hip. He walked around the side of the house where he hoped to find a bit of privacy.

He patted his breast pocket absently, but stopped when he realized what he'd been reaching for. "Lord," he whispered. "I am overwhelmed."

"Who goes there?" It was the second guard.

"O'Dell," he croaked. "Just getting some air."

The man didn't answer but continued on his rounds. Then O'Dell noticed another figure in the dark coming toward him.

"Ed?" It was Carmichael.

"Yeah; I'm here."

Carmichael sidled up to him and they stood together in the shadows, both of them silent for a long while. "It is quite an honor to have a child named after you," Carmichael finally murmured.

When O'Dell didn't respond, Carmichael added, "It must also be something of a burden to the man who loves the child's mother."

O'Dell stirred uneasily. *How does he know this? Is it visible, even after all my efforts to surrender it, to give it to God? Can others see it?*

"I have never been anything but a friend to Joy." O'Dell's voice was rough. "She is a married woman, the wife of my good friend, and I do not entertain thoughts otherwise."

"No, your comportment is and has been exemplary." Carmichael sighed. "I just wanted you to know that I understand . . . and I will be here as a friend for you . . . and for Grant and Joy . . . when things . . . change."

In the dark, O'Dell bowed and shook his head. *No, Lord! Please help Grant! Please sustain and keep him!*

When Carmichael and O'Dell reentered the house, Bao and Mr. Wheatley were engaged in a rather intense game of checkers and Rose was reading aloud to a small knot of the girls.

Grant and Joy were seated together on a comfortable sofa, staring at the baby in Joy's arms. Breona leaned over the back of the sofa laughing and cooing at the baby.

"Mr. O'Dell!" Grant motioned him over. "Would you like to hold Edmund?"

A panic rose up in O'Dell—the idea completely unnerved him. *No! What if I drop this precious newborn?* "Uh, perhaps when he is a bit older?"

Joy glanced up, and O'Dell saw that she understood his sudden anxiety. "Don't worry. If you sit in that chair, I will place him in your lap. You can hardly drop him if he is in your lap—he is too young to wriggle out of your grasp."

With reluctance, O'Dell settled himself in the chair and Joy brought the baby to him. The infant was wide awake, blinking deep blue eyes like a wise old man. O'Dell gently touched the wisp of a curl on the babe's head. "Just like Grant's hair?"

"Yes," Joy laughed with pleasure.

O'Dell stared into the child's face. "Hello, little Edmund," O'Dell heard himself say. "I'm your uncle Ed."

Chapter 18

(Journal Entry, January 26, 1911)

*Grant and Joy have named their son Edmund, after our dear Mr.
O'Dell. This honor speaks of the great friendship between Grant and
Mr. O'Dell—and, truthfully, of Mr. O'Dell's friendship to us all.*

*I am happy for this precious man. I remember how hardened by
the world he was when I first met him in Corinth—how skeptical,
disillusioned, and cold the difficulties of his work had made him.
Lord, you have done a great work in his heart!*

*And work you have given us in Denver is progressing, too. Each
week Pastor Carmichael, Minister Liáng, and Bao minister to those
they meet on the streets of Denver—some snared by alcohol, others
simply homeless or impoverished. Some of our more spiritually
mature girls now join them in the evenings, speaking words of hope
to the women who walk the streets.*

*Breona and Sara are growing so much through this work!
Watching their passion to bring Jesus to hopeless women gladdens
my heart. I am confident that we shall see many of them come to
Jesus and be restored.*

*The threat that Cal Judd posed is gone, and Mr. Gresham's
guards have observed no threat toward Mei-Xing's child in these
many months. Now I begin to hope that we will see happy days
ahead for us here at Palmer House.*

Lord, if only I were not so concerned for Grant's health.

O'Dell felt the pull to return to Denver keenly and found the
means to revisit the city again mid-March. Spending his time
between Palmer House and the cramped quarters Carmichael, Liáng,
and Bao shared, O'Dell felt that he had "come home."

When O'Dell held baby Edmund again, he could not believe how
much he had grown and filled out. Edmund was wide awake,
looking around, attempting to track faces, and sometimes
succeeding.

O'Dell was amazed. "He has your eyes, Joy," he breathed.

"My father's eyes," Joy laughed. "I was certain his eyes would
be hazel, like Grant's, but see? They certainly have the look of a
Thoresen." She laughed again with pride and confidence.

She is so happy, O'Dell realized. *Happy and fulfilled.*

He studied Edmund again. The dark blue of his eyes had brightened until they were nearly the same startling blue as Joy's eyes.

"Hey, little Edmund," O'Dell whispered, "It's Uncle Ed." The infant, hearing his voice, turned his head and fastened his blue eyes on him. O'Dell's heart flipped over when the baby flashed him a toothless smile. As quickly as it appeared, it was gone.

"Did you see that?" O'Dell was stunned. He had no idea a baby could smile at two months.

"Did he smile at you?" Joy asked, delighted. "He began doing that a week or so ago. If you talk to him, he will coo."

"I certainly will *not* be cooing to a baby," O'Dell growled. At O'Dell's gruff words, baby Edmund's face scrunched up in concern.

"Hey! Hey, everything is all right," O'Dell murmured. "I wasn't talking to *you*." Edmund seemed fascinated with O'Dell and appeared to be listening to him.

O'Dell leaned closer and Edmund smiled again. O'Dell realized he was grinning back like an idiot. "I have to leave tomorrow and go back to work, little Ed, but I'll be back soon. You wait and see."

Yer a complete and utter fool, O'Dell, a mocking voice whispered.

He sighed. *Perhaps I am,* he mused, *but if I am a fool, at least I am a happy one. I will choose happy over shrewd and miserable any day.*

It was Thursday, time for Morgan to call in his weekly report. He left the house and walked to his destination rather than start the motorcar. His legs cried with relief as he ate up the blocks between his room in Miss DeWitt's house and the rundown bungalow where Fang-Hua's thugs awaited him. The fact was, Morgan was in a rotten mood.

I have been confined to that blasted room for months, he raged, *doing the work of a peon because I can trust no one else to do it.*

When he arrived at the house on Acorn Street, it was clear that the men were in as surly a mood as he. Morgan glowered at each of them as he placed the requisite call to Clemmins and waited for the operator to call him back.

"Nothing to report. The queen and pawn are well guarded and never leave the castle with less than two knights in attendance," Morgan growled. "Nothing yet has changed."

He hung up and Barnes, who had listened in as usual, placed his call to Mrs. Gooding. Morgan idly leaned against the wall and picked at the crease in his immaculate trouser legs while he waited for Barnes to report "No instructions from Madam Chen." Instead, Barnes turned pale and handed the phone to Morgan.

"It's her," he breathed, eyes wide.

Her? *Fang-Hua!* She had come to the mysterious "Mrs. Gooding's" location to speak to him? Morgan gathered himself and lifted the receiver to his ear.

"Reggie, are you there, dear?" Fang-Hua's disembodied voice floated over the wires to him and Morgan's throat closed up. He had to swallow twice before he could answer.

"Yes. I am here."

"Oh, Reggie," she breathed. "I am growing . . . concerned. You promised me so much, if you recall, but five long months have passed. Can you sense my disappointment?"

What Morgan sensed was a noose tightening about his neck.

He fixed a wary eye on Barnes, waved him back several feet, and nonchalantly slipped his hand into his coat pocket. Morgan placed no confidence in Barnes; he was well aware that Fang-Hua, given her mercurial temperament, might easily order Barnes to dispose of Morgan. The cold steel of the revolver in his pocket was reassuring.

Morgan's eyes never left the other man. "Madam Chen, the weather in Denver is still contrary to our purposes. No mother takes her infant child out in winter weather. If you recall our conversations, I expressed my concern on this point, and I did suggest that the *ideal opportunity* to fulfill our mission would arrive with spring weather. I assure you: I have had our objective under continual surveillance, and warmer weather is very close now."

Fang-Hua was silent on the other end for so long that Morgan feared she had hung up. He kept Barnes in view, *just in case*. At last, however, Fang-Hua spoke, her words chilling him.

"Dear, dear Reggie. I have never known you to be, shall we say, unresourceful. Perhaps the *ideal opportunity* is less than expedient in this situation. I do count on you for a certain measure of ingenuity, *of initiative*, after all. Please think on that, dear Reggie, and on . . . other eventualities should the cleverness I ascribe to you prove to be . . . misplaced."

Blast the witch! Blast her to— Morgan cursed. His eyes flicked back to Barnes.

Morgan calmed himself and replied, forcing himself to speak words that were oily and ingratiating. "Do not fret yourself, madam. I will secure your grandchild as promised; in fact, I suggest that now is the time to secure the services of a wet nurse. You may send her along as soon has she has been hired."

Another long pause followed before, "Very well, Reggie. I expect to hear news of your success soon, then."

A loud clack in Morgan's ear signaled that Fang-Hua had hung up. Morgan replaced the receiver and again leaned against the wall.

I am running out of time.

He dredged up the idea he had turned over in his mind many times, ill-advised as it might be: *On any weekday, we could ambush Mei-Xing on her way from the house to the car.*

He arrived at the same conclusion he had each previous time: Against four guards (the night shift did not leave until Mei-Xing was safely away) and in broad daylight, too, the odds were decidedly against them. Even if they somehow managed to pull it off, getting the child clear of Denver before the law caught up to them would be difficult.

A second approach seemed too far-fetched: *Given enough men and the element of surprise, we could take Palmer House at night, kill everyone in the house except the child, burn the house to the ground, and be gone before anyone was the wiser.*

He always returned to the same conclusion. *Be patient. The right opportunity will present itself. It is only a matter of time.*

But an abundance of time was what Morgan did not have.

"Oh! What wonderful news! Tabitha has done well on her exams and will be allowed to come home for a week between terms!" Rose looked up from the letter she was reading to share the news with Grant and Joy. "It is a reward only granted the top students!"

Grant sat behind Rose's little desk, adding recent expenses to the house's ledger; Joy nursed Edmund from the comfort of her favorite overstuffed great room chair.

"When will she come? We will all be so glad to see her," Joy said with enthusiasm.

"Her train will arrive this Friday, April seventh! We must arrange to be there to greet her."

"Yes, certainly. What an unexpected blessing!"

That evening, Rose shared the news. Mei-Xing offered to ask one of Gresham's men to drive the welcoming party to Union Station to fetch her; Rose and Breona were the most available to meet her on a weekday and planned to do so.

Friday arrived, and so did Tabitha. Everyone who had not seen her for six months observed a calm assurance in her manner. She carried herself with this newfound confidence, still her old, sometimes passionate self, but with less of the stormy toss-and-turn of emotions.

Tabitha was allowed to stay only a week, but she effortlessly entered into the routines of the house again, assisting Breona with the housekeeping duties and doting on the babies and Will. The rigorous training nursing students underwent had strengthened her physically and mentally. She was a breath of fresh air and a whirlwind of energy and goodwill rolled into one.

"I like this new, mature Tabitha," Rose whispered to her the next morning.

Tabitha blushed. "I love the school, Miss Rose. I am learning so much!"

"You will make a fine nurse," Rose enthused. "Why, anyone can see it!"

She caressed Tabitha's face. "Flinty would be so proud. I can just hear him telling you: *That's th' ticket, Red! Yer jist what th' doctor ordered, I'm thinkin'!*"

Morgan addressed Barnes and the men around the table in the hideaway house's kitchen. He had finished his latest telephone report to Clemmins.

"The weather is beginning to improve," Morgan said. "I think we can expect to see the child being taken out of doors soon. We have been quite careful; the guards have not had even a whiff of me watching the house.

"*But,*" he punctuated his words and drilled a look of emphasis into each man's eyes as he spoke, "when you receive my call, you may have mere minutes to act. If you are not vigilant and ready, we will miss our opportunity—and trust me, we will have only one such opportunity.

"The men guarding Mei-Xing and the baby are professionals. Do not underestimate the situation or the opposition. If you do not move quickly and decisively, *you will fail.*"

Barnes squirmed under Morgan's lecture. "I think we all get the idea. No need to rub it in like we ain't never done this before."

The other men muttered in agreement, but not one met Morgan's icy gaze or spoke loud enough to be heard. Their dark expressions told Morgan that they resented his calling the shots.

"You don't care for my precautions. You feel I am overstating the obvious," Morgan snarled, "But I will remind you: *If you botch this*, you will not answer to me; you will answer to Madam Chen."

No one made a sound as Morgan finished. He stood up and left through the back without a parting word.

Chapter 19

April

"I am the most blessed grandmother in the world," Rose declared. In one arm Edmund slept soundly; in the other arm Shan-Rose wriggled and reached for baby Edmund's face.

"Let me take Shan-Rose before she wakes up little Edmund." Mei-Xing laughed and raised her chubby girl into the air. Shan-Rose giggled in delight.

After an absence of more than two-months, Joy had returned to the shop that morning. She would see to the inventory and gauge how Sarah was faring as the interim store manager.

"Are you sure it is all right to leave Edmund with you? If all is well at the store, I hope to be back early this afternoon, Mama," she had told Rose.

"Don't worry about a thing," Rose had laughed. "I am greedy to have this baby boy all to myself for hours today!"

Now Mei-Xing was echoing Joy's question. "Are you sure I can leave Shan-Rose with you, too?" Mei-Xing asked yet again. Two of Mrs. Palmer's maids had come down with colds, and Mrs. Palmer had called suggesting that Mei-Xing not come to work today, "just to be on the safe side."

Instead, Rose had insisted that Mei-Xing leave Shan-Rose with her so that Mei-Xing could attend Mrs. Palmer as usual.

"Just as sure as I was when you asked five minutes ago," Rose chuckled. "I thought I would take them both out in the pram for some fresh air."

Mei-Xing peered out the great room windows. "But the sky looks rather gloomy, don't you think?"

"Goodness; it is spring, you know! And even with snow still hanging about, the almanac calls for sunshine midday," Rose laughed.

"I daresay the air will do them good." These words came from Tabitha. "Breona and I will certainly take advantage of the nice weather to do all the marketing."

"Yes, indeed. My poor bones have had no sunshine for weeks now, and these children will love an outing. Mr. Rawley and Mr. Hicks will accompany us, so do not worry, my dear. Grandma Rose will bundle her babies up and we will all enjoy a brisk walk."

Gresham, on hearing that Mei-Xing would be going to work but leaving her baby home, had added Hicks to the day's roster: Betts would escort Mei-Xing to work and remain on watch; Hicks and Rawley would stand guard over the child.

"All right then. I know Shan-Rose will enjoy the fresh air." Mei-Xing slipped on gloves and her long coat. When she nodded at Betts, he escorted her to the waiting automobile and drove her to work.

Rose had a delightful—but busy—morning with the babies. After lunch, while she readied the pram, she studied the sky. The sun was boring its way through the grey gloom and sparkling off snowy drifts.

I am more than ready for spring. Perhaps I will just bring along my journal, she decided. *If, as the almanac predicts, the skies clear and the temperature warms a bit, we will stop in the park and I will sit on a bench and catch up on my entries.*

She picked up her Bible and the little book bound in wine-colored leather and put them in the corner of the pram.

Grant had just settled on a couch in the parlor for a nap when Rose wheeled the ornate buggy—another gift from Martha Palmer—out the front door. Hicks and Rawley, one in front and one behind her, lifted the pram as if it were made of cotton balls, carried it down the steps, and set it on the walkway.

Rose took hold of the buggy handle and strode down the walk. The two guards followed not far behind her, scanning for danger in all directions. A park Rose particularly enjoyed was about four blocks away. It was planted with beautiful pine trees and had several park benches along a meandering path. Rose relished a slow, winding stroll through the trees.

Before she set off, Rose checked on the babies. She heard Shan-Rose gurgling to herself and Rose smiled down at her. Shan-Rose beamed back, two tiny teeth peeping from between her lips. Edmund stared at the sky, his little forehead puckered, fascinated by the lights and trees overhead.

Satisfied, Rose hummed to herself as she pushed the buggy ahead of her. When she reached the gate to Palmer House, she turned right, toward the park.

Snow still covered most yards and mounded more deeply in the shadows of trees and houses, but the sidewalk was dry. Rose breathed in the crisp air and walked on. Hicks and Rawley, ever vigilant, followed close behind.

Morgan leapt from his chair, tipping it over in his haste. He grabbed up the binoculars and stared at the little procession coming out of the gate to Palmer House.

Finally! Not Mei-Xing . . . but certainly her child!

He hesitated only a few seconds. Fang-Hua would not get everything she wanted today—the child, yes, but not Mei-Xing. However, once the child was gone, wouldn't those who watched over it relax their guard over its mother? He noted the two men who trailed after the woman pushing the baby buggy.

Only two guards. Barnes and his crew will take them by surprise and finish them and the woman, leaving no witnesses. After we have delivered the child to Fang-Hua, she can order her men to lie in wait for the Little Plum Blossom. They will be able to finish the task— after I have already gone.

He unlocked and opened the door to his room, tiptoed down the stairs, and used the telephone hanging on the wall. Just as discreetly, he went in search of Miss DeWitt.

I am sorry, my dear, he mocked her in his thoughts. *You have outlived your usefulness.*

But Miss DeWitt was not to be found. Morgan called to her, and the empty house echoed back. Morgan mentally thumbed through Miss DeWitt's activities and realized the woman was at her club meeting and would not return for at least two hours.

He stood in the woman's kitchen pondering the ramifications of leaving this loose end undone. And yet, he could not afford to wait for her—the deed would be done within the hour. Morgan needed to send Mei-Xing's child on its way to Fang-Hua immediately and, by nightfall, *he* needed to be as far from both Denver and Fang-Hua's clutches as he could possibly be.

Morgan returned to his room. Throwing a suitcase onto the bed, he tossed into it only what he needed for the journey ahead.

Once at the park, Rose slowed her pace and did what the path encouraged: She wandered along as it wended through the trees, thoroughly relishing the pine-scented air. Hicks and Rawley followed at a judicious distance.

The almanac had been right—the overcast sky burned away as the sun rose toward its zenith. Near the boundary of the park Rose found a bench in the sunshine and sat with her face turned toward the bright warmth.

O Lord, she worshipped. *What a day to be alive! What great blessings you have given me in my latter years! I am so content.*

She stood and checked on the babies. Both were tightly swaddled, and over them Rose had tucked the heavy, white afghan Mrs. Palmer had given Shan-Rose. She made sure it was tucked around them. Edmund's head was covered in a baby-blue knit cap; Shan-Rose wore a matching pearl-pink knit hat. They had succumbed to the gentle sway of the buggy and were sleeping. Their heads were just touching, their chubby faces barely visible.

Rose retrieved her Bible and journal from under the afghan. She returned to the bench and began writing in her journal.

(Journal Entry, April 12, 1911)

Father God, it has been a year since Mei-Xing came home, and life here in Denver has taken on a rhythm and a cadence that I have missed. The happy years with Jan were, in the most part, predictable, perhaps even boring by someone else's measure, but not to me, Lord. No, when I think back, those years were filled with contentment and peace, something for which my soul has been sorely longing.

It seems that from the time Jan passed and I joined Joy in this endeavor, she and I have moved from crisis to crisis—until now. Thank you, Father, for bringing us into this place of rest, even as we continue to labor for you. Thank you for the blessing of these two grandchildren.

I know hard times will come our way again. It is the way of life upon this earth, until we reach you in eternity. But right here, in this moment, I thank you. I thank you for contentment and rest from our enemies.

Thank you, too, for allowing Tabitha to come home to us. We have missed her so.

She wrote on until she had finished journaling her thoughts and prayers. Then she laid aside her journal and picked up her Bible. Soon she was engrossed in a passage in Romans.

A while later Rose shivered. With a start, she realized how much time had passed. The sky had again clouded over and temperatures were dropping. In fact, the air was filling with a fine snow.

"Time to go home, my baby chicks!" she whispered. Hurrying, she picked up both books and folded them under the afghan. She saw Hicks standing watch not far away and nodded to him.

A moment later she was pushing the buggy out of the park and onto the sidewalk. Hicks and Rawley followed close behind. Beautifully trimmed hedges bordered the park here. Their glossy green leaves sparkled as snow floated from the sky onto their branches.

Rose hummed as she walked and she lifted her face to the fine snow falling around them. She did not notice a motorcar as it glided alongside the curb behind them.

A sharp report echoed against the snowy hedges. Rose flinched and snapped out of her reverie. Another shot! And another! She jerked around to see Hicks crumple to the sidewalk. Again! Rawley, his gun drawn, facing the threat, sank onto the snowy grass. Crimson stained the snow where he fell.

Rose could not comprehend what was happening even as three men rushed from the motor car toward her—toward the pram! She grabbed hold of the handle and ran, pushing it ahead of her. But before she had gone many steps, rough hands seized her.

No! The babies!

Rose fought with all the strength she had, clawing and screaming, until the man grappling with her threw her to the ground. Even then, Rose grabbed at his trouser leg and held on—until the full force of his boot landed on the side of her head and she fell backwards, the back of her head striking the stone walkway.

She could not breathe; the fall had stunned her, knocking the air from her lungs. She managed to turn her head and catch a glimpse of two men carrying the buggy in much the same manner Hicks and Rawley had toted it down the porch steps of Palmer House.

Hicks! Rawley! Save the babies! But the two men did not stir.

"No! Please, no!" Rose pushed herself to sitting to plead with those taking the pram but she had little air to voice her pleas. Her cries were not much more than choked whispers.

The men reached their automobile and dropped the buggy near the curb. One man reached inside and then paused. He shouted something to the others and beckoned them toward the pram.

They peered inside and seemed to be arguing. One of the men bent over the buggy. When he stood, his motions awkward, he held a bundle swathed in the thick afghan.

"No!" Rose's shriek resounded in the air.

The man holding the blanketed bundle, his mouth moving, gestured with his chin to one of his companions and then toward Rose. His companion, a short man, nodded and strode toward her. From his pocket he yanked a gun.

Rose saw the ugly, snub-nosed weapon in his hand. She jerked her eyes to the man's face. His visage glistened with adrenaline and a wild resolve.

He raised the weapon and pointed it at Rose's breast.

"Do you know how very much God loves you?" Rose's words were softly spoken. Her eyes locked onto his as the determination burning in them gave way to uncertainty.

His arm wavered. Lowered.

A shout from the car reached them, but Rose did not look away. It was the man who, frowning, closed his eyes to block her out. Lifted his arm. Aimed.

Rose whispered, "Lord Jesu—"

Fired.

The man ran back to the others and they piled into the waiting car.

"Did you take care of her?"

"Yeah. She's done fer." The short man frowned as he tried to shake the effect of the dead woman's words on him. He was still frowning as they sped away.

Morgan glided down the alley and through the back door of the house with the peeling green paint. Fang-Hua's men were gone, but Morgan was not alone in the house. A timid young woman sat at the kitchen table.

"You are the wet nurse Madam Chen sent?" Morgan inquired.

"Yes, sir." She licked her lips and looked down, clearly nervous. "But I am a little confused, sir. I was told that I would be nursing an infant but . . . I have been here five days and . . . I see preparations for a child, but no baby, and the men here will not answer any of my questions."

Morgan smiled. "What is your name?"

"Agnes, sir."

"Well, Agnes, please do not fret yourself. We are, er, *recovering* Madam Chen's grandchild at this very moment, and you are playing an important part in the child's recovery. I'm certain Madam Chen will be pleased with your service. In fact, I expect the baby to arrive shortly."

"You do?" She was relieved, quite happy at the news.

"Yes. Will you be ready to care for the child?"

"Oh, yes, sir! I-I am quite looking forward to it."

"Then do not be anxious," Morgan replied. He looked around. "We will be leaving for Seattle shortly after the baby arrives. I suggest you pack your things and the child's and be ready to go as soon as the men arrive."

"Yes, sir." The woman went into one of the house's bedrooms and Morgan heard her shuffling about.

Was that a cry? Are my babies crying?

Rose blinked snow from her lashes and summoned her waning strength. Somehow she pushed to her knees. She struggled to standing and swayed. Blood streamed from her coat sleeve onto the snow at her feet.

The world spun and darkened as she tried to walk. Hicks and Rawley lay where she'd seen them fall. Staggering but resolute, Rose lurched toward the pram—it listed toward the curb, dangerously near to rolling into the gutter.

Clutching the buggy's edge, Rose peered inside. Even as her knees gave way and the encroaching darkness took her, she knew what she had seen.

Shan-Rose slept on, unaware of the horror that had swirled about her. *But baby Edmund was gone.*

Rose lay unmoving, her eyes staring at the molten sky above her. She could sense the cold seeping into her bones and the warmth of her life flowing out.

Her eyelids fluttered and closed. Tiny flakes of snow fell toward her and came to rest on her cheeks, her nose, her forehead, her mouth.

Chapter 20

"Banks! Stop! What is that?" At Mason Carpenter's shouted order, his chauffeur stomped on the brake and turned his head in the direction his excited employer pointed. Before the vehicle came to a complete stop, Carpenter leapt from the door.

He raced to the form of a woman lying on the curb, a fancy baby buggy near her. Farther up the sidewalk lay two men, unmoving. "Banks. Check those men."

Carpenter stifled an oath at the sight of so much blood and knelt beside the woman. He could plainly see the shredded hole in the coat from which the blood seeped. He ripped the bowtie from his neck and tied it about the woman's arm, coat and all, twisting the stem of his pipe in the knot and cinching it as securely as he could.

"Banks!"

"Yessir!"

"Those men?"

"I-I am certain they are dead, sir."

Carpenter shook his head and looked down at the woman again. Her breathing was ragged and slow. "Go to the nearest telephone and call for the police and an ambulance. Come straight back."

Banks ran to the car, the urgency of the moment obvious when he did not even acknowledge the order he'd been given.

Carpenter bent over the woman. "Madam! Madam! Can you hear me?" The woman did not respond, but Carpenter was startled when a mewling rose from the pram.

"Hang it all!" He dared not loose his hold on the tourniquet he'd fashioned about the woman's arm. The fussing cry climbed to a full-fledged howl, and Carpenter grew frantic. He turned back to the woman and realized her eyes had opened partway.

"She . . . cold . . ." the woman mouthed.

Carpenter leaned over her. "I cannot turn loose of this tourniquet," he answered. "You will bleed to death."

The woman's grey eyes came into calm focus and, as he watched, her mouth firmed up. "Where?"

Carpenter was confused but then understood. He stroked her arm. "Here."

The woman lifted her other hand and tried to place it on the knot. He guided her fingers to it. "Can you hold it? For just a minute? Then I will see to the baby."

He saw her grit her teeth and grasp his pipe where it was twisted in the knot. "Go," she ordered.

The baby was crying so abjectly now that the pram rocked and shook. Carpenter leaned over the child. She stopped wailing to stare at him, large tears sliding down both sides of her face.

Carpenter knew at once that the child was a girl—the pink cap and lacy swaddling blanket announced that, after all—but her features were a surprise. They were distinctly Asian.

"Blanket . . ." the woman on the ground groaned.

"There's no blanket other than this thin lacy thing." Carpenter wasn't a father, but he was no fool. The baby had to be freezing. He sighed, unbuttoned his heavy coat, and—so awkwardly!—lifted the child and tucked her to his chest.

Carpenter turned and saw that the woman's hand had slipped from the knot and she had passed out. Muttering under his breath, he knelt in the snow and re-tightened the tourniquet. He stayed kneeling there, with one hand holding the now-quiet baby inside his coat and the other hand on the knot, until the police arrived.

Even as the ambulance took the unconscious woman away and the police busied themselves with the two bodies nearby, he held the child against his chest. Banks approached, silently awaiting orders.

Carpenter sighed. "To the hospital, I suppose." He pointed to the buggy. "What can you do about that contraption?"

"I may be able to strap it onto the back."

"Do it, then, as quickly as you can."

Mason Carpenter waited a long time—on a *very* uncomfortable chair, he grumbled—for word of the woman he had found. The baby awoke and poked her head out of his coat. Mason had no earthly idea what to do with her, so they stared at each other. The infant studied him with serious, sober eyes. He studied the child in return, unable to gauge her age because of her dainty size and his own ignorance of children.

Mason had been waiting more than an hour when he realized that a great many people were flooding into the ward's waiting room. The size and composition of the group might not lead a disinterested observer to believe that they were together, but he soon realized that, indeed, they were. Among them were a tiny black-haired woman wringing red, work-worn hands; an elderly gent whose white hair stood straight up; a young couple with a toddler; and a fiery, determined redhead.

Close behind them strode three burly gents with grim expressions. Carpenter decided on sight he would not like to meet such men in a dark alley. All the newcomers were clamoring at the nurses for news of a Rose Thoresen, but the red-haired woman was most outspoken. Carpenter listened in as a doctor appeared and informed them of the woman's condition.

"Mrs. Thoresen has lost quite a lot of blood, but I believe she will survive her wound," he announced in a low voice. "However, the bullet broke her arm before exiting."

At the word "bullet" the doctor's audience gasped. One of them turned to stifle a sob and her eyes locked on to Carpenter. It was the red-haired woman.

Her eyes widened. "That is *not* your baby!" she shouted. She ran across the room and tried to pull the infant from Carpenter's coat.

"Well, I daresay she is not *your* baby," he growled in return. He stood and refused to relinquish the child to a stranger.

Before the red-haired woman could say anything further, the three rough-looking men converged on him. One of them placed a calming hand on the redhead's arm and addressed Carpenter.

"My name is Samuel Gresham. You are . . . ?"

"Mason Carpenter."

"Mr. Carpenter, can you tell me how you came to have that child?"

"Certainly. I saw a woman lying on the curb, a pram nearby. I had my driver pull over. The woman was bleeding. I then gave my driver orders to ring for the police and an ambulance. In the meantime, I tried to stop the bleeding and keep the baby warm."

The little woman with bright black eyes sprang between the men and demanded, "And where ist th' other babe bein'? Th' little man babe?"

Carpenter was confused. "What do you mean? There was only one baby."

A dread silence descended on the group.

Nearly two hours had passed. The nurses had allowed Breona and Tabitha assume some care of Rose. Breona leaned Rose forward and, with infinite care, draped a warmed blanket about her shoulders. "There now, Miss Rose. Now be takin' a sip o' th' tea."

Rose lay back, weak and unmoving in her hospital bed. She did not respond. She stared straight ahead. Her head and her arm ached with a fierce throbbing; her stomach pitched uneasily if Breona even jostled her.

Father God, how am I to ever tell Joy? she prayed. *How will she ever forgive me?*

Rose's left arm was bandaged and strapped to a board so she would not move it. Breona wrapped Rose's other hand about a warm mug and lifted it to her mouth. "Sip. Sip, Miss Rose." Tabitha had loaded the tea with sugar to combat the shock Rose was in.

Gresham had dispatched his men to fetch Joy from *Michaels' Fine Furnishings*. He had called the man on duty at Martha Palmer's house and ordered him to bring Mei-Xing to the hospital at once.

He did not call Palmer House where Grant waited by the telephone for news of Rose. Tabitha warned him off. "We don't know what this news will do to his heart," she advised him. "He is home alone right now."

A phalanx of police officers now swarmed the hospital lobby, the ward, and Rose's room. Gresham was dealing with them at the moment, but Chief Groves wanted to speak with the only witness to the crime.

"Time is of the essence, Mr. Gresham," Groves insisted. "The sooner we interview Mrs. Thoresen, the sooner we may recover that baby."

Gresham tipped his head toward the door; Breona nodded and led Groves into Rose's room. Gresham, relieved of Chief Groves for a moment, went out into the lobby and found a nurse. "Show me to the telephone," he demanded. Tabitha, sadness etched on her brow, followed him.

The nurse pointed. "It is here."

Gresham dialed up the operator. "Put me through to the Chicago office of the Pinkerton Detective Agency. And hurry."

He hung up to wait for the call back. Tabitha stared at him and did not move away. "Mr. O'Dell?"

Gresham nodded. A few minutes later the phone rang and he snatched up the receiver.

"This is Gresham in Denver. I need to get an urgent message to O'Dell." He listened to a voice on the other end. "No, I *don't* know where he is! He works for *you*, not me!"

The voice said something and Gresham replied. "Give me Parsons, then." He was connected and explained the situation as best he could.

"Look Parsons, we both know O'Dell is the best man for the job. I don't care what else he is working on—as soon as he knows that his best friend's child—*his namesake*—has been kidnapped, he will be on his way here, regardless of what you say."

Gresham listened for a few seconds. "Right, then. Wire me when to expect him. We'll meet his train."

The door to the ward slammed open. Joy, frantic and disheveled, burst into the waiting room. "Mama! Mama, where are you?" She caught sight of Breona. "Where is Edmund? Where is Mama?"

Breona ran to Joy and caught her arm. "Miss Rose is here, Miss Joy, boot wait. Wait, jist a minute, please."

"No! No, don't tell me anything bad, please, Breona!" Joy begged. "Please tell me Mama is all right?"

"Aye, she will be, she will be," Breona soothed.

"Take me to her, then!" Joy demanded.

Breona took a deep breath. "Coom wi' me," she ordered. She dragged an unwilling Joy into a nearby storage room, the only private place she could think of, and closed the door.

"Why are we in here?" Joy's eyes filled with dread. Breona gripped Joy's arms so hard that Joy flinched. "What have you not told me?"

"Miss Joy, th' man what was findin' your mama . . . he . . ." Breona's teeth were chattering. "He found Shan-Rose, Miss Joy. She wast in th' pram."

"And Edmund?" Joy demanded. "Where is my son?"

Breona's chin and mouth quivered. "He wasn't in th' pram, Miss Joy. Someone took him."

Joy's shrieks pierced the closed door and echoed through the hospital floor. Carpenter, still possessed of the baby girl but finally understanding that someone had taken a second infant, gripped the child he now held on his knee more tightly.

He watched the red-haired girl weep silently in the corner. The others who had arrived with her turned their faces away and hid their tears.

In her room down the hall, Rose heard Joy's shrieks. *O Lord! O Lord!* she moaned. *Hold us now in your strong arms!*

Fang-Hua's four thugs tromped into the house. Barnes carried a something wrapped in a heavy, lace-edged blanket and offered it to Morgan. Sniffing in disdain, he gestured for the man to place the blanketed object on the table. He leaned forward to look, holding himself aloof, away from the distasteful smells of a baby.

The sleeping infant was smaller than he'd expected but, given his mother's tiny stature, perhaps the baby's size was unremarkable? A pale blue knit hat covered his whole head; the rest of his body was hidden in the thick white blanket.

Something bothered Morgan. He knew next to nothing about babies but . . .

Shouldn't Mei-Xing's baby, at six or seven months old, be larger? he asked himself. *This one appears to be . . . too small, too young. Still a newborn?*

Something else bothered him.

This baby does not have the look of an Asian.

With tentative fingers, Morgan pulled back the corners of the thick outer blanket. As he did, a small red-bound book dropped onto the table. He slid it aside. Inside the thick outer wrap the baby was swaddled in a thinner blanket the same pale blue as the hat.

The men stood by, awaiting his next order, and Morgan was about to demand details of them, when the baby stretched, arching his little body and struggling to free his arms of the swaddling blanket. Blinking, the baby awoke.

Two brilliantly blue eyes stared up at Morgan.

He recoiled, stunned.

Not Mei-Xing's child! his mind screamed.

He whipped the knit cap from the baby's head. Soft whorls of honey-brown hair curled across the top of the babe's head.

Morgan's mouth fell open. He paced around the room in an effort to control his rising panic.

I am a dead man! We had one chance to ambush them and take the child by surprise! We will not have another! I am a dead man!

He stopped. "Whose child is this?" he roared.

The four men looked at each other. One of them stuttered, "We did just as you instructed. Killed the two bodyguards and the woman and took the baby."

Morgan rounded on the man, his eyes cold, penetrating, infuriated. The thug who'd spoken, although much larger than Morgan, quailed before Morgan's rage.

"This is *not* Fang-Hua's grandchild," Morgan screamed.

The men shifted, uneasy and worried. They well understood that it was not just Morgan's life hanging in the balance. Each of them knew Fang-Hua tolerated no failures and suffered no excuses. Barnes and the man who had spoken exchanged wary glances.

Barnes mumbled, "Y'see, there were *two* babies in the buggy—one with a pink hat and one with a blue—a girl and a boy. You said the child was a boy. We took the boy."

Morgan stepped back and placed a hand to his mouth. *Two babies! What—?*

He had said "grandson" so many times to secure Fang-Hua's cooperation, that he had half begun believing it himself! The odds had been fifty-fifty after all . . . but *two babies*?

He again leaned over the infant squirming on the table. The infant's eyes, such a striking color, stared up at the ceiling, looked around, and drooped closed again in sleep.

Did Mei-Xing give birth to a girl? If she did, then we took the wrong child! Morgan's mind was racing. *This baby is certainly not Mei-Xing and Su-Chong's brat—but if we took the wrong child, whose baby is this?*

At the same moment, a niggling voice in Morgan's head interrupted. *You have seen those eyes before.*

Morgan shivered. *What does it matter? I am a dead man!*

He paced the room again, his excellent mind running through the data, organizing facts and options. Then he stopped.

I have seen those eyes? Whose eyes indeed?

Mei-Xing swept into the hospital with her guard on her heels. She spotted Tabitha and ran to her.

"Where is Shan-Rose?" Mei-Xing was nearly frantic.

"She is fine—there. She is there." Tabitha pointed at Mason Carpenter. She glared at the man who still refused to give up the child to anyone but her mother.

Carpenter smiled. He had grown used to being on the receiving end of the redhead's accusing looks and barbs. In fact, as his appraising gaze swept over the woman again, he admitted that he was beginning to enjoy her attention!

Shan-Rose also spied Mei-Xing and bounced up and down on Carpenter's lap, babbling happy syllables. As Mei-Xing approached, Shan-Rose strained against Carpenter's arms.

"Are you the mother?" he asked. It was obvious from how Shan-Rose was reaching for the woman that she was.

"Yes." She took Shan-Rose from Carpenter and buried her face in the baby's neck, nuzzling her. Her relief was palpable.

"She is a lovely child," Carpenter remarked. "I am ill-suited to care for a baby, but she has been delightful."

He paused and drew a breath. "I'm sorry for this terrible occasion, but I assure you that your child is fine—although I believe she does require a dry nappie."

Mei-Xing, who was still unclear as to all that had occurred, studied him. "Thank you for your assistance to our family, sir."

"Mason Carpenter, at your service. I happened to be driving by shortly after . . . and found Mrs. Thoresen and your child."

Mei-Xing turned to Tabitha. "Miss Rose? Is she all right? What happened?"

Tabitha, keeping one suspicious eye on Carpenter, briefly explained.

"Edmund is gone?" Mei-Xing's voice rose in horror.

Chapter 21

You have seen those eyes before.

Morgan frowned and chewed on the thought. He reached back into his memories. Just then the baby fussed and stretched again, at last pulling free of the blanket's swaddle. Now exposed to the cool air in the house's kitchen, the infant began to wail. Within seconds he was red-faced, screaming, and trembling in every limb. The four thugs shifted uncomfortably and backed away.

"Cowards!" Morgan muttered. Irritated, he strode to the table and stared at the baby once more. Tears leaked down the babe's face. Morgan awkwardly pulled the thick outer blanket over the infant.

The baby shuddered and ceased crying. He stared up at Morgan, blinked his cornflower-blue eyes, and sucked his mouth into a tiny pout.

Morgan swallowed as the realization unfolded. *Joy Thoresen Michaels.* He could see her in the infant's face. As clear as day.

He stepped back. *Joy Michaels has a baby?* His mind raced to register the new fact and determine its benefits to his present crisis.

None! his panic screamed. *We have the wrong baby and Fang-Hua's grandchild is female, not male. No possible scenario will satisfy her—and she will not rest until she has watched me die—as painfully as possible.*

His survival instincts kicked in. *If you want to live, you will run,* they dictated. Morgan accepted his only option and paced again, knowing from experience the magnitude of Fang-Hua's reach. It would not be easy to escape her grasp—or foolproof—but he had planned for such an event.

As he mentally listed his next steps, he sneered. *Joy Thoresen Michaels! All my bad luck began with her! I had a perfectly regulated, perfectly satisfying life until she—*

He seethed and turned a merciless eye toward the child.

So. Before I run I will kill the child. I will leave its body where the police will be sure to find it. I might even write a note with Joy Michaels' name on it and leave it for them.

He imagined Joy receiving the news; he visualized her mourning over her baby's body. He pictured her grief and he laughed aloud. He knew he sounded crazed; the men in the kitchen shuffled their feet and looked at each other, concerned.

No. Too easy. She deserves something better!

He sucked in a breath as another idea swirled and formed. He stopped his pacing, astounded with the audacity of his new thoughts.

Joy Thoresen Michaels.

Edmund O'Dell.

Su-Chong Chen.

And now Fang-Hua Chen.

His enemies. The very ones who had interfered in his life and destroyed his livelihood. He had spent months in Denver's jail scheming and plotting suitable revenge on them—only to be handed the most imaginative and fitting payback conceivable—and all when he had least expected it!

Of course, Su-Chong was already dead, but how *appropriate* would it be for Fang-Hua to suffer in her son's place?

As he formulated his plan, he smirked. The strategy was brilliant. Even, perhaps, *inspired*. Not only would he have his retribution, but this plan would ease his escape and safeguard his future.

This will be my greatest coup ever, he gloated.

Within a few seconds he had resolved on his course. He called for the wet nurse.

"Yes, sir?" The woman, although nervous, slanted her eyes toward the bundle on the table.

"Take the baby into the other room and get ready to leave." The woman hurried to obey him. She smiled as she picked up the baby and carried him into the room she had been sleeping in.

Morgan turned to the four men, calm and in control. "Obviously we have a problem," he announced, "but all is not lost. I will devise our next move and call Madam Chen this evening. In the meantime, we should dispose of the guns you used in the abduction. We cannot risk them being found on any of us if we are stopped. Let me have them."

Barnes and another man reached into their pockets and produced revolvers. As they handed them over, Morgan inquired, "How many shots did you fire?"

"Four," the short one answered. He seemed distracted and would not meet Morgan's eyes.

"Only one," Barnes smiled.

You are a touch proud of killing your assigned guard with just one shot, Morgan observed to himself.

"Excellent work," he grinned. He nodded his approval for good measure and Barnes winked at his men as though to applaud his marksmanship.

Two bullets left in this gun and five in this one, Morgan told himself. He set both revolvers on the counter, the one with five bullets closest to him.

He opened a drawer, retrieved a folded map, and placed it in the center of the table. He unfolded the map and used the small book that had been under the blanket to anchor a corner of the map. "Sit down, all of you. We need to devise a route for the next phase of the plan."

As Fang-Hua's thugs pulled out chairs and seated themselves at the table, Morgan picked up the revolver closest to him with his right hand and the other with his left.

He shot each man in turn, pausing only to thumb the hammer back between shots. His last target, Barnes, had scrambled to his feet and Morgan had to fire twice before winging him. He dropped the first gun and switched to the second, finishing him.

Blue smoke clouded the kitchen. *One bullet left.* Morgan laughed aloud.

He walked toward the wet nurse's room holding the gun before him. She was cowering behind the bed, the baby cradled in her arms.

"Get up," Morgan ordered. "Do you want to die or live?"

The woman shook uncontrollably but she stuttered, "Live. *Please!*"

Morgan nodded. "Then listen carefully. This child—" he waved the gun at the baby "—is *not* Fang-Hua's grandchild. Those idiots stole the wrong baby. Tell me, my dear, how do you think Fang-Hua will respond to that news?"

The woman did not answer, but she shook more.

"Well? What do you suppose she will do to those of us who fail her?"

"Sh-sh-she will kill us?"

"Very good, Agnes. It is Agnes, isn't it? I'm glad you have no illusions with regard to Fang-Hua's forgiving nature! So here is my proposition to you. We will leave here. Today. Just the three of us—a happy little family, eh?"

"Yes, sir," Agnes managed to choke out.

"We will go far away. You will take care of the child and I will manage all the details. Sound good?"

"Y-yes, sir."

Morgan stepped closer to the woman and she cringed. "I should give you fair warning: Just in case you are entertaining ideas of, say, going to the police? Remember this: From this moment on, you are as guilty of kidnapping as I am. You can either live a long, happy life with this little one as your own or you can live out your miserable life in a nasty, stinking prison. It's your choice."

He gestured for her to go into the kitchen. As she passed him he added, "Oh, and Agnes. If I ever suspect that you intend to leave me, I will save the citizens a lot of expense and just kill you myself."

Sobbing and clutching Edmund to her breast, the woman stumbled down the hall to the kitchen.

"Sit down." Morgan drew one of the kitchen chairs toward her with the toe of his shoe. A bloody body propped against the chair's legs slid to the floor. Morgan gestured with his chin and the shaking woman sank onto the chair.

Morgan shoved another of the thugs' bodies, freeing one more chair. He pulled plain paper and a fountain pen from a drawer and seated himself at the table.

Before he could write, the baby began fussing. Agnes discreetly bared a breast and began feeding the child. She drew the baby's swaddling blanket up to cover herself, but Morgan could hear the suckling sounds as the infant tried to eat. The baby fussed, pulled away, and latched on again.

Agnes, her head bowed, whispered, "I don't have much milk for him today, but in a few days it will come in again. He will be all right; I will give him a little in a bottle when he is done trying to nurse."

Morgan frowned as he processed what she was saying. "How is it, exactly, Agnes, that you came to be wet nurse to this child at just the right time? Wouldn't you have needed to *have* a baby in order to nurse another's?"

She blanched. "I did . . . have a baby."

"Oh? And what happened?"

I cannot wait to see how Fang-Hua managed this, he snarled inside.

The woman swallowed. "M-my husband worked for the Chens. About four months ago there was a terrible accident and he . . . died. The Chens were very good to me, especially Madam Chen."

I'll bet, Morgan snickered to himself. He could tell Agnes was struggling to place credence in Fang-Hua's generosity.

"Since I was expecting and had nowhere to go, they . . . they took care of me. They even gave me a little house to live in. I had my baby a month later. He was a healthy baby . . ."

"Was?" Morgan had a good idea where her tale was going.

"He died in his sleep just two weeks ago." Tears trickled down her face. "Madam Chen was so . . . kind. She told me that her grandson would need a wet nurse, that I could stay with him and raise him as if he were my own! She sent me here . . ."

"How very convenient," Morgan sneered.

"Wha-what do you mean?"

"Oh, the timing, my dear, the timing! You see, we've been planning to snatch her grandson for how long? Longer than *four months*. And I told Madam Chen we were ready for the wet nurse *three weeks ago*. See if you can figure it out."

Morgan's sneer had turned to a snarl, and Agnes shrank before him. Shrank and stared stupidly at him as she began comprehend his meaning.

"You . . . you cannot mean . . . that would mean . . ." her words trailed off and her eyes widened in horror.

Morgan leaned toward her. "It is exactly what I mean. You are mistaken if you think that viper knows the meaning of kindness," he scoffed.

"She looked for a woman who would be producing milk and found you. What happened to your husband? Your baby? She planned those."

He turned toward the table to write the message. "And if you think she would have allowed a white woman to raise her grandson for long . . ." He took up his pen, "Let's just say that your employment would have been terminated in similar fashion not long after you returned to Seattle with the baby."

Morgan knew Agnes was in a state of shock. *All the better,* he decided. *She has no one left to turn to and no alternative other than to go with me.*

He turned his mind to the message he was about to write. The wording was *so* important. It needed just the right touch. He sighed with delight and began.

To the police:

The men whose bodies you find here were recently in the employ of one Fang-Hua Chen of Seattle, Washington.

Morgan added her full address for clarity and snickered.

Madam Chen ordered that her men perform the following crimes: a) Abduct the infant child of one Mei-Xing Li from the address below, b) Dispatch (kill) Miss Li and her bodyguards, and c) Bring the child to her.

Morgan wrote out the address of Palmer House.

The father of Miss Li's child is Su-Chong Chen, the late son of Fang-Hua Chen, making Madam Chen the child's paternal grandmother.

He added a short list of details that would point decisively to Fang-Hua, including Clemmins' and Mrs. Gooding's telephone numbers. He hesitated and then wrote the last line.

Sorry about taking the wrong child, O'Dell.

He stared at the words and smiled, his satisfaction full. *Should I sign my name? What I would give to see Joy Michaels and that blasted Pinkerton man when they see my name! Oh, it is rich!*

Morgan was certain his own part on the plot would come out—Fang-Hua would not hesitate to implicate him as soon as the police confronted her with incontrovertible evidence of her guilt. And, after all, Morgan wanted to be *sure* that Joy Thoresen knew who it was who had *mistakenly* taken her child. Most of all, he wanted to be positively certain that she knew exactly why he was *keeping* the child.

O'Dell will spend the rest of his miserable life trying to find the child, Morgan speculated. *Everlasting payback for all the trouble he has caused me.*

Oh, revenge was sweet! Morgan laughed aloud. It was perfect: Three priceless repayments with a single blow.

He decided to compromise on the name—it would not confuse O'Dell long, but the code would add another degree to Morgan's pleasure. With a flourish he signed the letter with his initials. His real initials.

Sorry about taking the wrong child, O'Dell.

R.S.

Compliments of Regis St. John! Morgan chuckled. Of course the initials *should* have read *R.St.J.* but Morgan didn't want to make it *too* easy for O'Dell.

He left the message on the table and composed a second but much shorter note containing only the address of the house they were sitting in and the words, *You really should visit!.* He placed that note in an envelope and addressed it to Edmund O'Dell, care of the Denver Pinkerton office, the word Urgent scrawled on the back.

"Come, my dear." He pulled Agnes to her feet. "Let us pack all the baby's necessities and be gone from here."

He glanced at the counter where he had laid the small book that had fallen from the baby's blanket. He picked it up and opened it.

A journal? He frowned and searched for a name on the flyleaf.

Rose Thoresen. Joy Michaels' mother? So his men had killed Joy Michaels' mother? Could this day get any better? He gloated over the pain her mother's death would cause Joy Michaels.

He skimmed two or three of the journal entries. *Total religious hogwash!* He sneered and tossed the book back onto the counter. Then he thought differently. He picked it up again. *Perhaps it is something to peruse later. I might find some useful information— between the ridiculous prayers and absurd hallelujahs.*

He laughed and turned to the back and read the last entry, written just today, paging one at a time to earlier entries. He stopped and read, his mouth agape.

January 26, 1911. Grant and Joy have named their son Edmund, after our dear Mr. O'Dell. This honor speaks of the great friendship between Grant and Mr. O'Dell—and, truthfully, of Mr. O'Dell's friendship to us all.

This is proof that the child belongs to Joy Michaels, Morgan marveled, *and is named for the Pinkerton man. What a priceless memento!*

His wiser instincts warned him to destroy the book: *If this journal is found in your possession, it will prove categorically that you were involved in the shootings and baby snatching.*

But the irony of the moment was too delicious, too satisfying for him to abandon the book just yet. He thought for a moment before going out to the motorcar. He unscrewed a panel in the car's trunk, slid the book inside, and replaced the panel.

Then Morgan filled his wallet from the bag of money Barnes kept in the hall closet—*courtesy of Fang-Hua,* Morgan guffawed—before stuffing the bag into the car's trunk with his and Agnes' cases.

Morgan had made other financial preparations for such an opportunity as this, but the extra cash he had just acquired would not be wasted. After all, he had to buy himself a new start, a new life. In a year or so, if all went well, he would reach out to reclaim the other monies and investments stashed here and there.

Agnes brought a great many things for the child to the car and placed them on the rear seat where she could reach them. Twenty minutes later he, Agnes, and the child—*the portrait of a common, law-abiding family*—were driving sedately south, out of Denver.

Morgan stopped the car only once on the way out of town—to drop the letter in a mail receptacle. He whistled a lively tune as they pulled away from the letter box.

"Agnes, I've been thinking. I think that instead of us being married, you should be my brother's widowed wife," he informed her. "Yes! A much better fit."

Over the next miles he rehearsed her on their new identities. "And what would you like to name the baby?"

She was startled. "I can name him?"

"Yes, indeed. His last name will be the same as ours, of course, but do pick something pleasing for the child."

"Michael, I think," she offered. "Michael Andrew."

"I like it," Morgan smirked, struck by the irony of the child's new first name being nearly the same as the child's real last name.

"So. Have you ever been to New Orleans? No? Well, I understand that it's a grand town—particularly since I haven't lived there before. I think we will feel right at home there."

He was still whistling as they cleared the county line.

Chapter 22

"Sir, what shall I do with the, er, contraption?" It had been quite an eventful day, and Mason was glad to finally be home. Banks had opened the door to Mason's automobile for him to step out.

"What? Oh! Is it still strapped to the back?"

"Yessir."

Mason thought for a moment. "After you have put the car away, please call the hospital and see if we can get an address for Mrs. Thoresen. Tomorrow we'll deliver the buggy to them."

"Very good, sir."

When O'Dell received the urgent summons to telephone Parsons, he was interviewing a family in a missing persons case in Kansas City.

"Give me Parsons. It's O'Dell, calling him back." He hung up and waited for Parsons to call him at the number he'd left. Five minutes later the telephone rang. He grabbed it off the wall.

"O'Dell."

He listened to Parson's garbled account with growing horror. "Call Gresham back for me, will you? Tell him I'm on my way."

O'Dell listened. "Tamberline is here. He can take over."

He listened a moment more and cut off his boss in mid-sentence. "I'm sorry, Parsons, but I'm done here. I'm heading to Denver. Fire me if you need to."

He left the receiver dangling and raced for his hotel, praying that he had not missed the late afternoon train. Long hours later he arrived in Denver and grabbed a cab from the station to Palmer House. It was after eleven o'clock at night, going on twelve hours since the kidnapping.

One of Gresham's stone-faced guards recognized him and nodded as he mounted the front porch. Inside, weary faces stared at him as he let himself in the front door: Tabitha, Billy, Mr. Wheatley, Grant.

"Mr. O'Dell." Grant Michaels spoke to him from an overstuffed chair in the great room. O'Dell had seen Grant only weeks earlier. The oxygen gauges hummed from the tank nearby, but Grant had shriveled. His skin was grey, his eyes sunken.

"Grant." O'Dell was fearful for his friend. He pulled up an ottoman and sat in front of him. "You don't look at all well."

"Know. Struggling. Please help. Help us. Again. Find Edmund!" The effort to speak exhausted Grant; between words he clamped the rubber cup over his face and strained to breathe.

O'Dell placed a calming hand on Grant's knee. "I will do all I can, but I must have your word, Grant. Listen to me; I'm serious."

Grant nodded, too worn to look up.

"You know that I will do my very best, but you must promise to *trust in God.* You must promise to rest in his peace and not tax your body further. *Your wife and son need you*, Grant. You must care for yourself so that you may care for them. Now, will you give me your word?"

Grant, still breathing heavily, nodded.

O'Dell got up and turned. Joy stood in the doorway to the dining room, watching him, watching Grant. Her eyes were swollen from weeping and her body drooped with exhaustion; O'Dell knew she had to have heard what he said to her husband.

"Joy. I'm so sorry. I came as fast as I could. How is your mother?" He asked about Rose to distract Joy's attention from Grant, if only for a moment.

"Mama's arm is broken and she has lost a lot of blood. It will take time for her to recover from it. They insist she stay in the hospital for a few days. Breona is with her." Her eyes were still on Grant even as she sobbed, once. "We are both glad you are here, Mr. O'Dell. Please . . . please bring Edmund home!"

O'Dell roughened his voice. "You heard what I told Grant. I will do my best, but first off, we *must* pray and ask the Lord for his help and guidance. *Trust in the Lord with all your heart; lean not on your own understanding.*"

"Yes," Joy whispered. "We have set our hearts to lean on him. No matter what."

O'Dell reached for Joy's hand and led her to Grant. "Then let's pray right now."

O'Dell spent a restless night in one of the overstuffed chairs in the great room of Palmer House. Early in the morning he called ahead and left to meet with Chief Groves in his office. He was surprised but glad to see Marshal Pounder and Samuel Gresham also waiting for him, even though the expressions that greeted him were grim.

"I'm sorry about Hicks and Rawley, Sam." O'Dell had known both of Gresham's men personally; Gresham looked as though he had not slept.

"Thank you. They were good men. They had to have been ambushed, taken completely by surprise, for this to happen," was all Gresham could manage.

At Gresham's signal, Groves began to brief O'Dell on the few facts they had gathered. "Mrs. Thoresen provided a good description of the man who shot her," Groves reported, "and told us she saw two other men with him, although her descriptions of them are only superficial. A fourth man was likely driving, but she did not see him. That is the extent of what we have learned."

"The thing is," Pounder interrupted, "the outing to the park was not planned in advance. Miss Li and Mrs. Michaels only decided to leave their children in Mrs. Thoresen's care that morning. Because the almanac predicted sunny weather midday, Mrs. Thoresen decided *that morning* to walk the babies in the park."

"You are saying that the outing was not planned in advance but *the attack* was." O'Dell grasped the implications quickly. "If that is so, someone had to have been watching the house at the exact moment Mrs. Thoresen left. Whoever that was had the attack planned with men ready and waiting."

"Yes." The other men nodded their agreement.

"But why take Grant and Joy Michaels' baby?" O'Dell fretted. "All along, we've been concerned for Mei-Xing's child, not theirs! The Michaels have no real assets—if it were kidnapping for money, the kidnappers would most certainly have picked a richer target."

"We haven't figured out a motive either, Ed," Gresham cut in. "It doesn't make sense. The only thing we know is that Palmer House had to have been under surveillance to pull this off, so Groves' men have already been through the neighborhood, searching for lookout posts and questioning residents to see if they have seen anything unusual."

"We haven't uncovered anything so far," Groves admitted. "This morning we requested the newspapers to ask for anyone who has noticed anything to come forward, but . . ."

O'Dell frowned. "Well, *someone* knows something. I will head over to the Pinkerton office to wrangle some extra sets of eyes. The office has someone in temporary command—I figure I can bully him into doing whatever I want."

He turned to Gresham. "Sam, you want to come along?" O'Dell and Gresham left the chief's office and hailed a cab to take them to the Pinkerton office.

As it turned out, the temporary chief of the Denver Pinkerton office, Ettisie, suffered from a mild case of awe regarding O'Dell and his reputation; he was willing to bend over backwards to accommodate him. O'Dell asked him immediately for as many men as he could spare to re-canvass the neighborhoods around Palmer House.

"Say, Mr. O'Dell, we've got a letter for you, came this morning." Ettisie offered an envelope to him. O'Dell had little attention to spare for distractions and waved it away, but Ettisie insisted, "Well, it says 'Urgent' on the back of it."

O'Dell took it from the man's hand and slid it into his breast pocket, determined not to be sidetracked by anything trivial. But as he opened his mouth to say something, a sharp caution pressed on his spirit. He paused and felt for the letter again.

The envelope bore no return address. *Odd.* Tearing it open, he scanned the three lines penned in a fine hand and frowned. The note contained only the address, no salutation, no signature, and the odd phrase, *You really should visit!* He turned the sheet over. Nothing. He looked again at the single word, "Urgent," scrawled almost like an afterthought on the back flap of the envelope.

Then he studied the postmark. Late yesterday, here in Denver. *Late yesterday.*

"Gresham! We need to go." Grabbing up his hat and cane and not waiting to see if Gresham was following, O'Dell hobbled for the curb to hail a cab. Gresham caught up with him just as O'Dell was opening the door of the cab.

"What is it?"

"I'm not sure." O'Dell shouted the address to the cab. Then he showed Gresham the note.

He and Gresham stared at the neglected bungalow just down from where O'Dell had asked the cab to stop. The fact that the address had led them to within blocks of Palmer House was not lost on either O'Dell or Gresham.

"Drive around the block," O'Dell ordered. "Go slow past that green house there." As they rolled by the house, he and Gresham studied it: The yard was uncared for; the house unremarkable.

Then the driver, following O'Dell's instructions, turned the corner. When O'Dell spotted the alley he called out, "Stop here and wait for us."

He handed the cabbie a large note before he and Gresham slipped out of the cab and started down the alley. No one seemed to pay them any mind. A dog barked from one of the yards along the alley but left off of its own accord after O'Dell and Gresham had passed by.

When they reached the house with the peeling green paint, they stayed out of sight behind its falling-down garage, watching, looking for signs of activity within the house.

"Awfully quiet," Gresham observed.

O'Dell nodded and pointed to tire tracks in front of the garage. "Still pretty fresh."

They waited longer.

"I'm going to have a look," O'Dell said after watching for ten minutes. He made no attempt to be stealthy; he just hobbled to the back of the house and up the short steps to a door. He listened, turned to Gresham, and shook his head. Then he tried the door handle. The door swung wide and O'Dell stood there, listening.

As he stepped into a small washroom, he could sense the emptiness of the place. Aware of a presence behind him, he turned. Gresham nodded from the doorway. O'Dell removed his revolver from his coat pocket and gestured with his chin. The two of them gingerly went forward.

They did not have to go far. Four bodies sprawled on the kitchen floor. The blood pooled on the kitchen's cracked linoleum had dried, leaving no doubt that all four men were dead.

Gresham and O'Dell exchanged worried looks but said nothing. Gresham gestured that he would search through the remaining rooms and O'Dell nodded. He squatted awkwardly and studied each man's face. One of the men matched Rose Thoresen's description.

When he stood up, he noticed the paper on the table. He picked it up and began to read, his stunned alarm growing with each line.

To the police:

The men whose bodies you find here were recently in the employ of one Fang-Hua Chen of Seattle, Washington.

Madam Chen ordered that her men perform the following crimes: a) Abduct the infant child of one Mei-Xing Li from the address below, b) Dispatch (kill) Miss Li and her bodyguards, and c) Bring the child to her.

The father of Miss Li's child is Su-Chong Chen, the late son of Fang-Hua Chen, making Madam Chen the child's paternal grandmother.

O'Dell scanned through a few unknown names and details, racing to the end of the letter.

Sorry about taking the wrong child, O'Dell.

R.S.

With rising horror, O'Dell reread the last line. *The wrong child? Whoever had taken Grant and Joy's son had taken the wrong child? But what did that mean for little Edmund?*

Cora DeWitt twisted her hanky around her wet fingers, and her stomach twisted along with the damp fabric. Her eyes darted around the room again. Quite apparently, her tenant had packed and vacated the premises, hastily throwing only a few things into a bag, leaving the room in a state of chaos.

The breakfast and lunch trays Cora had left for the nice-looking man who called himself Roger Thomas had sat untouched outside his door. Since she had not seen or heard her renter move about since she left for her club meeting yesterday morning, she had used her key to enter.

Her first concern when she entered had been the rent that was nearly due. Then she had grimaced in smug satisfaction.

Fortunately, I required a month's rent as deposit! Her hard mouth had turned up on one side. *If I acquire a new tenant quickly, I will actually be ahead by forty-five dollars!*

Her concern over the rent had quickly dissipated, however, as Miss DeWitt had observed, not what was missing, but *what her tenant had left behind*: A chair had been placed before the window, and between the chair and the window sat a mechanism on a tripod she readily recognized—a telescope.

That was when Miss DeWitt's hands had begun to sweat and her stomach clench.

The morning papers were trumpeting the news of a heinous crime—two men shot and killed yesterday only blocks from her house, right down the street in this decent neighborhood, *on the very sidewalks she herself walked!* Not only had the two men been shot, but also a grandmother walking her two infant grandchildren!

Miss DeWitt recognized the woman's name: Rose Thoresen. The papers proclaimed that Mrs. Thoresen would survive, but the shootings were not the worst of the news. No, the worst of it was that whoever had shot Mrs. Thoresen and the two men had also kidnapped the infant son of Grant and Joy Michaels.

Cora scowled. She bore a grievous offense against Mrs. Thoresen and her daughter, Joy Michaels. They had brought soiled women into the house across the street—*directly* across the street—from her home! They had brought those soiled women to live in Cora's own neighborhood!

Palmer House they call it, she sneered to herself, *after old Martha Palmer!* Cora bore an even deeper grudge toward Martha Palmer. The old woman had set Cora down, thoroughly mortifying her, in front of a score of her friends!

For more than a year Cora DeWitt had nursed her grudges against Mrs. Thoresen, Mr. and Mrs. Michaels, and Martha Palmer. How she had looked for an opportunity to pay them back for their affronts!

But . . . to take a child? The distress and revulsion she felt at such a crime overshadowed every other feeling.

She swallowed and slumped into the chair sitting before the window. She sighted along the barrel of the telescope. From where she sat she had a perfect view of Palmer House, its front entrance, and its walkway to the street. With a telescope one could monitor every coming and going in great detail.

Without question, the man who called himself Roger Thomas had spied upon Palmer House and upon the people who lived there. He had sat in this same chair yesterday and watched Mrs. Thoresen, guarded by two men, wheel a pram down the sidewalk and toward the park . . . just before someone murdered them and took one of the babies that had been in Mrs. Thoresen's care.

Well, why on earth would Mrs. Thoresen require guards? Cora fretted. *That is just an example of the sort of sordid activity I have been against since she and the others set foot in that house!*

Cora DeWitt shuddered. *But if I hide this information and the police find out I did so, will I not be guilty of aiding in murder and kidnapping?* The idea that she might be swept up in such disreputable actions alarmed her even more than the distressing alternative!

She swallowed again. Against her preferred inclinations, Cora knew she must come forward with what she knew. Scowling, she stood and trod reluctantly down the stairs to her front door.

Banks stopped the automobile near the front gate and Mason studied the imposing house with interest. He hadn't been able to figure out the relationships among those of the concerned horde that had descended upon the hospital yesterday, so he was more than a little intrigued.

As Banks unstrapped the buggy from the back of the automobile, Mason stepped out. "I will take it, Banks," he directed.

"Very good, sir."

Mason wheeled the "contraption" down the long walk to the house's front porch—only to be confronted by two powerful-looking, no-nonsense men.

"Please state your business," one growled.

Mason looked from one to the other, realizing that they were cut from the same cloth as the man who had identified himself as Gresham. "My name is Mason Carpenter. I am, uh, returning this baby buggy."

"You're the man what found Miss Rose yesterday and called the cops?"

"Yes, that's me."

"We'll take the buggy for you."

Mason's curiosity had only increased. "Um, is it possible for me to see one of the young ladies I met yesterday? I believe her name is Tabitha."

The two guards glanced at each other. One of them pointed to the walk where Carpenter was standing. "You stand right there—and don't move. I'll ask."

The other man folded his arms across his chest and stared at Carpenter. Mason put his hands into his pockets and rocked back on his heels—a sure sign that he was nervous.

What in the world am I doing? he quizzed himself, half turning toward the front gate.

You want to see if that red-haired woman sets your heart on fire as much as she did yesterday, a voice whispered back to him.

Mason had all but decided to trot back down the walk to his waiting automobile when the front door to the house opened and she was standing there. Glaring at him.

Mason grinned and her frown faltered a little.

"You wanted to see me?"

He was mesmerized! "Yes. How is Mrs. Thoresen faring? And the little one? Shan-Rose?"

She hadn't asked him up onto the porch or into the house; Mason was still standing on the walkway and Tabitha was still standing in the doorway. The two guards looked from one to the other and Tabitha sighed.

"Would you care to come in, Mr. Carpenter?" Her words dripped with reluctance.

"Thank you! I would, indeed." He skipped up the steps and into the foyer, looking around, inquisitive and intrigued. The two guards placed the buggy on the floor in the entryway.

"By the way," he mentioned as Tabitha led the way to a large room warmed by two fireplaces, "Mrs. Thoresen's Bible is in the buggy. It looks well used—I'm sure she will be happy to have it back."

He took the seat that Tabitha gestured to, although it was plain that she was merely going through the motions of cordiality.

"Thank you, Mr. Carpenter," she responded, "and I wish to express the gratitude of everyone at Palmer House for your quick thinking yesterday. Mrs. Thoresen is resting in hospital; she will not be released for a few days."

"And Shan-Rose?"

Tabitha glared at him again, and Mason almost chuckled. She had not yet forgiven him for refusing to hand the baby over to her!

"Shan-Rose is well, thank God. And thanks to you . . . I guess."

Carpenter looked around again, puzzled. "You called this place Palmer House? What sort of place is this?"

When he walked down the steps toward his car thirty minutes later, Mason Carpenter's head was spinning. Tabitha, as thorny as a rose and obviously trying to fend him off, had employed few niceties in the history and description of the house and those who lived there—herself included.

Carpenter had difficulties focusing when she described the current tragedy with which they were coping—the kidnapping of the infant boy.

At least Carpenter now understood why the crowd at the hospital had been so diverse but so united in their concern for Mrs. Thoresen and the missing child. However, Tabitha's recitation had been almost more than he could take in and nearly more than he could stomach.

Mason understood her intent. She had done her best to put him off and discourage the attentions he wished to pay her.

Tabitha! He bowed his head as he marched, unseeing, toward the front gate. *Lord, it breaks my heart that this lovely woman has been so misused.*

Carpenter had insisted on returning the pram himself because he wanted to see this woman again, wanted to see if the fiery spirit she'd demonstrated at the hospital beckoned to him as it had yesterday.

Carpenter's brow plunged into a stern line as he pondered all she had—with no holds barred and no self-pity—recited to him in the space of half an hour. He turned her words over in his thoughts—the horrors she had glibly rattled off while his mouth hung farther and farther open.

Could he see beyond those cold, cold facts?

Because he had the answer he had sought today: The moment Tabitha had appeared in that doorway, glowering like a thundercloud, he'd known—here was a woman he could love.

Now what, Lord? he demanded.

Chapter 23

Groves' officers swarmed over the house on Acorn Street while O'Dell showed Groves and Pounder the letter he had received containing the house's address.

"We came in through the back and found those four," O'Dell gestured toward the bodies in the kitchen, "and this letter."

Groves and Pounder perused the letter written, presumably, by the same person who had shot the four men lying dead on the kitchen floor. "This letter clearly implicates Madam Chen in a plot to kidnap Mei-Xing Li's baby—but they took the wrong child?"

"That's what it says," O'Dell answered through gritted teeth. *Why?* he reasoned to himself. *Why take Edmund and not Shan-Rose?*

"*R.S.* Any idea who that might be?"

"Not at the moment," but O'Dell's mind was in overdrive, racing for a name to fit the initials.

"You shouldn't have investigated this without us, you know," Groves chastened O'Dell and Gresham, his expression grave. "You, O'Dell, have a history with this Chen woman. At trial, her lawyers could speculate that you had a hand in all this, that you killed these men and wrote this letter, even. Might throw the evidence this letter provides into doubt."

O'Dell bristled. "These men have been dead at least a day—a trained monkey can see that. I was in Kansas City yesterday and only came into Denver on the train near midnight last night. I can prove that. Besides, see those names and telephone numbers? If telephone calls from this house and telephone calls from Madam Chen can be tied to those numbers, they will prove her involvement."

Pounder added, "We need to get to this Clemmins fellow and the person on the other end of the second number quick. If we clamp down on them, before Madam Chen does, then we'll have their corroborating statements."

"I agree," O'Dell answered. "In fact, knowing how Madam Chen works, if you don't get to these folks first, by the time you do, Madam Chen will have disposed of them—permanently. She won't risk them remaining loyal to her, regardless of how much she is willing to pay them."

Groves, Pounder, O'Dell, and Gresham formulated their plans; Pounder left immediately to contact colleagues in Washington State.

"We have a lot to think over," Groves remarked, "a lot of possibilities."

"Less than we think, is my opinion," O'Dell answered. "If we answer one question, I believe we will have the key to all of this."

"What question?" Gresham and Groves both stared at O'Dell.

O'Dell lost no time explaining where his thoughts had taken him. "This one question: *Who would leave such a provocative letter?* The last line of the letter, *Sorry about taking the wrong child, O'Dell*—is personal. It's a taunt. Toward whom? Obviously, toward *me*. And the same individual who wrote this letter cared enough to send me an urgent note containing the address of this house. Why? So I could discover these men and this letter—and receive this personal jibe."

O'Dell raised a finger. "So I ask you: Who knows me well enough and whose ego needs this type of vindictive stroking to send me such a provoking message? If we answer that, we have our man."

Groves stroked his chin, thinking. "You handle a lot of missing persons cases, O'Dell, some of them kidnappings, like this one. You could have enemies you aren't aware of."

"Somehow, I think this is more personal than my work with the Pinkerton Agency—and something tickling the back of my mind tells me that I should recognize these initials, *R.S.*" O'Dell's mouth dropped down into a scowling frown. "I should *know* who wrote this letter and took Edmund, and, by God's grace, I *will* figure it out."

With Grove's permission, O'Dell copied the words of the letter into his pocket notebook, taking care to copy them exactly. "Sam, I'm going back to Palmer House to check in with the Pinkerton men canvassing the neighborhood."

"I'll come with you."

Joy lay next to Grant and listened to the even cadence of the tank as it fed precious oxygen to her husband. He was sleeping, his body and mind exhausted. Joy wished she were sleeping, too—blissfully reprieved from the pain and worry attending Edmund's absence.

She wrapped her arms about herself, curled into a ball, and tried to shut out the fearful fantasies that were playing havoc in her imagination, but she could not. Edmund's little face floated before her closed eyes and her breasts, swollen with milk, let down in response, soaking her bodice and sleeves.

Joy gritted her teeth against the discomfort. *He must be so hungry!* she mourned. *Are they feeding him or is he crying in hunger? Is he warm? Are they tending him well or are they letting him cry without comforting him? He must be so frightened!*

The terrible possibilities tortured her soul until she gasped and broke down. And then she was in Grant's arms, and he was holding her, crushing her to his chest. He had pulled off the breathing mask, and Joy could hear that he was short of breath, but he held her with all the strength he had.

"Don't, Joy," he whispered between shallow gasps. "Don't allow the evil one to fill your heart and wound you with his evil thoughts. Wherever Edmund is, our Father sees him."

Joy burrowed into Grant's warmth, sobbing into the comfort she found there. Slowly she released the thoughts and relaxed, exhaustion taking over. Grant slipped the mask back over his mouth and they slept, folded in each other's arms.

O'Dell and Gresham passed under the scrutiny of two of Gresham's guards and let themselves into Palmer House. Mr. Wheatley and Tabitha were the only ones in the great room.

"Where is everyone today?" O'Dell inquired.

"Joy and Grant have gone to their cottage to rest," Tabitha informed them. "Pastor Carmichael and Minister Liáng were here earlier; they have gone to the hospital to see Miss Rose. Most of the girls have gone to work except Mei-Xing. She and Shan-Rose are upstairs. Billy and Marit are in the kitchen."

Tabitha looked as worn as O'Dell felt. "Oh, Mr. O'Dell, I am so concerned about Grant!"

"I must agree," O'Dell commiserated. "You probably understand his condition better than we do . . . is there not anything that can be done?"

She hesitated. "Only that he should take care not to overtax his heart either emotionally or physically."

O'Dell nodded. "More easily said than done, under the circumstances. What is the report on Mrs. Thoresen?"

"Breona telephoned to say that Miss Rose slept well last night, with the help of a sleeping powder. She will be coming home in two or three days, if she has recovered enough by then."

"Well, I have men going door-to-door throughout the neighborhood," O'Dell told her, "and I have asked them to report to me here, if that is all right."

"Of course it is! I will ask Marit if she would make some sandwiches and coffee and have them ready when they are needed."

"I could use something to eat," Gresham realized, patting his empty belly.

The front door to Palmer House opened and one of the guards put his head into the great room. "Begging your pardon, sir, miss. A neighbor woman is at the door. Claims to have something to say to the police. She won't talk to your Pinkerton men."

"Show her in," O'Dell ordered. "She will talk to me." The iron in his words sent a chill down Tabitha's back.

"Yessir."

The guard returned immediately with a thin, sour-faced spinster who eyed O'Dell with distaste. "I already told that *man* that I would only speak with the police," she insisted.

"You are?" O'Dell fixed the woman with a cold stare.

"I, ah, I am Miss Cora DeWitt. And who are you?"

O'Dell recognized the name. Grant had told him of the bitter woman and her vigorous attempts to rally the neighborhood against Palmer House when they had first moved in. He had described to O'Dell how Miss DeWitt and her friends had picketed *Michaels' Fine Furnishings*—costing them days of income.

O'Dell's face hardened. "Edmund O'Dell, Pinkerton agent. Chief Groves has assigned the canvassing of this neighborhood to me." O'Dell stared, unflinching, at the woman.

She seemed to wilt under his stony gaze. "Oh! Well I, um, wanted to report . . . a concern to the police."

"You will report it to me," O'Dell answered, never taking his eyes from the woman's face.

Miss DeWitt looked as though she wished she had not come forward. Her gaze cast about the room, taking in the homey, humble décor, while her mouth tightened and her hands fidgeted with a worn hanky.

"I am waiting."

Miss DeWitt stared at the floor and began to mumble. O'Dell had to strain to hear her.

"Speak up!" he barked.

She jumped. "Oh dear! I-I, what I said was, I rented a room in November to a gentleman—that is, he *said* he was a gentleman—but-but, he has left without notice, and I find that I am concerned . . ."

O'Dell grasped her by the arm. "Show me the room."

Miss DeWitt found herself being propelled through the door and across the street to her own home. Within minutes, she was trying hard to catch her breath as O'Dell stared around the room that Roger Thomas had vacated.

Gresham stood at O'Dell's shoulder looking through the window toward Palmer House. "He's been watching the house. Since November."

"Yes. But who?"

O'Dell took Miss DeWitt into her own drawing room and questioned her for more than an hour. By the time he was finished, she had to retire to her bed to rest her nerves, and O'Dell had a man's physical description that did him little good. Other things she mentioned, though, resonated with O'Dell.

He seemed like such a gentleman! His clothes were impeccable—always pressed and never a speck of lint. Why, I never saw him other than immaculately dressed and his grooming perfect. And so well-spoken! Obviously, very intelligent.

Something in those descriptive phrases nagged at O'Dell's memory. That and *R.S.*

R.S.?

Chapter 24

The individuals gathered in the great room of Palmer House three days later gave their whole attention to O'Dell, Chief Groves, and Marshal Pounder as they talked through what they knew regarding baby Edmund's kidnapping.

Breona and Mei-Xing sat side-by-side and arm-in-arm on one of the threadbare sofas, Shan-Rose curled upon Mei-Xing's lap. Liáng, standing with Carmichael and Bao on the edge of the assembled party, hovered close by Mei-Xing.

Grant and Joy sat together; Joy, O'Dell observed, did not let Grant out of her sight. Her eyes, though hollow from lack of sleep, were continually on him, seeing to his needs. Every so often, O'Dell saw her gaze slide to Shan-Rose. The aching on her countenance pierced his heart.

Rose leaned her head upon the back of her chair. She was suffering from recurring headaches in addition to the pain her arm caused her. Tabitha attended her needs.

Lord God, Rose prayed through the blinding headache, *you are the only strength we have. We lean on you.*

We lean on you.

We lean on you.

We lean on you.

O'Dell had selected those who should attend this meeting, but those he had summoned did not yet know the purpose of the meeting. They had not yet heard the audacious and hazardous plan O'Dell, Groves, and Pounder had devised—and those attending did not know the role each of them would be asked to play in that plan.

"Lord," O'Dell whispered, "Your word tells us, *Except the Lord build the house, they labour in vain that build it.* If you are not in these plans, we cannot hope to succeed. Help us, O God, I am asking in the mighty name of Jesus."

Then O'Dell stood and addressed the room. "Here are the facts as we understand them and as the evidence seems to indicate," he began. "First, we know that a man rented a room across the street from this house in November. From November until the day that Edmund was taken, *more than four months,* he watched this house using a telescope and a pair of binoculars.

"Secondly, we know that the kidnappers were organized; they were prepared and ready to attack Mrs. Thoresen and the guards even though the outing to the park was not planned in advance. This leads us to believe that the man spying on Palmer House alerted the kidnappers, telling them that Mrs. Thoresen and the children were vulnerable, as soon as they left Palmer House."

Chief Groves took up the narrative. "The telephone company has checked with its switchboard operators, and they have testimony to prove this theory: A telephone call did originate from Miss DeWitt's telephone to the house on Acorn Street prior to the attack."

He nodded at O'Dell, who continued. "The third fact we know is that, the day after the kidnapping, the Pinkerton office here in Denver received an urgent note for me through the mail. The note contained the address of the house on Acorn Street. The person who wrote that note certainly wanted me to go to the house and find the second letter.

"The second letter tells us that Su-Chong's mother, Fang-Hua Chen, financed a plan to kidnap Shan-Rose—not baby Edmund. For reasons unknown, the kidnappers took Edmund rather than Shan-Rose. The letter tells us this was *a mistake*."

O'Dell had to stop; a sob had escaped from Joy, a sound so broken that he choked and could not continue. Mei-Xing stared straight ahead, her relief for herself and Shan-Rose warring with her grief and sense of guilt for Joy and Grant's loss.

Pounder cleared his throat and stepped in to take over for O'Dell. "We do not understand why the kidnappers took Edmund instead of Shan-Rose, but the letter tells us that the kidnappers had been instructed to do away with Mei-Xing as well.

"We can speculate that the stringent efforts taken to protect Mei-Xing and Shan-Rose from the very beginning were effective in preventing an earlier attack. The kidnappers, having watched for an opportunity for months, may have been under tremendous pressure to produce results. They may have elected to take advantage of this opportunity—the first time Shan-Rose had been taken outside for a walk—even though it meant, er, *failing* at their other objective, er, regarding Mei-Xing."

O'Dell was able to continue. "Since the letter identifies two co-conspirators, Marshal Pounder reached out to law enforcement in Washington State with their names. U.S. marshals in Washington have apprehended two people, a man named Clemmins and a woman named Gooding.

"When Clemmins and Mrs. Gooding were shown the letter implicating Madam Chen and themselves, they were terrified to give evidence—terrified that Madam Chen would find a way to silence them permanently. The Pinkertons, as a personal favor to me and with the permission of the U.S. marshals, have hidden Clemmins and Gooding away. In return, we now have their sworn testimonies that Fang-Hua Chen was behind the entire scheme."

"You said the letter indicated that Mei-Xing was one of the kidnappers' objectives." Rose's words were quiet but clear, although her eyes were pressed closed and her brows furled in pain. "Does that mean we should still be concerned for her well-being?"

O'Dell exchanged a glance with Liáng and then replied, "Yes, I think that is a fair assumption. We should not become lax on that point."

Rose nodded. "Then, with regards to her safety, I have an additional concern."

The room stilled and waited for Rose to go on. "When I took the children to the park, I also took my journal and my Bible with me. I tucked both of them under the afghan that covered the babies. A few days ago . . . when Mr. Carpenter brought the pram back home, my journal was not in it. My Bible was, but not my journal. I . . . I am concerned that whoever took Edmund also took my journal, whether by accident or by intention."

"Your journal. What was written in it?"

Rose sighed and, with difficulty, sat up straighter. "A record of our journey, beginning just after the lodge in Corinth burned. I am afraid my journal contains many personal details and insights."

O'Dell thought for several moments. "I don't know that it puts Mei-Xing in more danger than she is already in, but I can understand how troubling it may be to know that whoever has the book is privy to your personal thoughts."

O'Dell returned to his briefing, "In conclusion, we still do not know why the kidnappers took Edmund instead of Shan-Rose, only that the letter left in the house on Acorn Street clearly tells us it was a mistake. More importantly, we do not know *who* took him and where he is at present."

"I believe I may know why they took Edmund." Mei-Xing's lovely face was a sad mask of realization.

Liáng was nodding, speculation in his expression. "Will you tell us what you mean, please, Mei-Xing?"

She nodded once. "Yes. Most of you do not, perhaps, understand Chinese tradition or know the Chen family personally, as I do. In traditional Chinese culture a girl child is negligible; a boy child is desirable."

She hugged Shan-Rose as if to dispel such a notion. "Wei Lin Chen is a very traditional Chinese man. Fang-Hua only gave her husband one son, Su-Chong. A grandson would be invaluable to them. A granddaughter? Hardly worth mentioning."

She turned to Joy, compassion and sorrow now crumpling her face. "The kidnappers may have been told that my child was a boy, you see. Miss Rose said she saw them standing over the pram, confused. I am so sorry, Joy! I believe they may have taken Edmund only because he is a boy! I am so sorry! Please forgive me!"

Mei-Xing broke down entirely. Shan-Rose, seeing her mother distraught, screwed up her face and howled.

As confusion and tearful commiseration took hold of the room, Joy walked to Mei-Xing and knelt by her feet. She and Mei-Xing wept together, their cheeks touching, while Shan-Rose's shrieks rose and added to the general chaos.

Liáng reached out his arms to the child, and she leaned toward him, sobbing. He picked her up and took her out of the room, whispering comforting words as he departed.

"Mei-Xing, my sister," Joy whispered through her tears, "I do not blame you. I do not fault you. There is nothing to forgive. Please."

But it was still many minutes before O'Dell felt he should continue.

"We do not know who wrote the letters, but we believe it was the same man who rented the room from Miss DeWitt. She has been able to positively state that none of the dead men was the man who rented her room.

"So, what do we know of this mystery man? Very little. We have a description and we have his initials: *R.S.* I am convinced that he expected me to recognize those initials but, I am sorry to say, I do not as of yet."

His face became stern and the group stirred, nervously waiting. "I want to say this in front of all of you, because it needs to be said: If anyone is to blame for the death of two good men, the attack on Mrs. Thoresen, and Edmund's abduction, it is I. Why? Because *I know better* than to leave an enemy such as Fang-Hua Chen to her own devices. *I know* that one should never let sleeping dogs lie.

"However, because we were worn and weary when we finally found and brought Mei-Xing home and because she needed to heal and desired only peace, I disregarded my own true instincts. I allowed myself to be persuaded away from them."

He turned to Mei-Xing. "Mei-Xing, I should have insisted, even against your wishes, that we seek out Fang-Hua and make her accountable for her many crimes. It is the only way to truly be safe from her."

O'Dell addressed the entire room: "My lapse in judgment is to blame.

"That brings us to the real reason for this meeting. Our primary objective is to recover Edmund. As far as we know, only *Fang-Hua Chen* knows who this mystery man is and only *she can tell us*. If we find *him*, we hope and pray to also find Edmund.

"And so, we can no longer wait passively here in Denver. Now we must take this battle to our enemy." His voice rose and strengthened with conviction. "We must go to Seattle immediately, and we must attack Fang Hua where she lives."

Chapter 25

Toward the end of the discussion, when most of the questions had been answered and the objections overruled, a silence descended on the room.

At last Rose Thoresen spoke. "Mr. O'Dell, what you have proposed is most difficult and, as you say, dangerous. However, I believe I speak for each of us, that we would give our lives to return Edmund to us."

With Tabitha's help, she stood up. "I must retire now, but I promise to do my part. You may count on me. And I will pray, diligently, for those who are going into the battle."

Joy and Grant rose from their seats. Grant leaned upon Joy's arm and his voice shook. "I admit that I do not like the part I have been assigned." He paused to breathe from the machine. "But I accept my limitations and I accept my role."

Joy looked at the floor. "But I am faced with an impossible decision! Do I stay with my husband who needs me? Or do I go to look for our son who will need me when we find him?"

She began to weep again. "Would that I could be in two places, but I cannot! O God, please lead me!"

"You will go, Joy," Grant decided quietly. "I am in God's hands; you will go and do your part." She nodded and clung to him, crying into his shirt.

The others looked at each other and began to rise, all except Mei-Xing. "We will do as you ask," they answered, one by one.

Mei-Xing stared at O'Dell. "Is there no other way?"

"No."

Liáng reached for Mei-Xing. "You will never be alone. We will be with you—*I* will be with you. And the Lord our God will be with you. He will give you the strength you need."

She slowly nodded. "Yes." She took his hand and stood to her feet. "Then I must go."

"Mr. O'Dell." Martha Palmer had to touch his arm before he realized she was there was speaking to him. Mr. Wheatley had admitted her to the house some time before, but O'Dell had been too preoccupied over the details of the plan to notice.

"Mrs. Palmer."

She looked up at him in that curious, sideways manner her body forced on her. "I understand you are taking them to Seattle. To confront *that woman*."

O'Dell nodded, but slowly. "I wouldn't miss hunting her out for the world but, of course, our primary objective is to regain little Edmund."

She grasped his arm and he steadied her. "Please take this." She held a thick wallet in her hand. "I wish to pay all the expenses of the trip—No, no, Mr. O'Dell. I want no distractions to interfere with your efforts."

The hand clutching his arm tightened. "We spoke once of letting sleeping dogs lie, my dear boy."

O'Dell gritted his teeth. "I believe I said I wasn't in favor of it."

If they had planned a move against Fang-Hua Chen in the first place, baby Edmund wouldn't be missing today! He could not get past the sting of that conviction.

Martha answered, "Yes, I believe we were agreed on that point. But now that *this dog* is no longer sleeping?"

"You mean now that *this dragon* is no longer sleeping?" He chuckled without humor. "We have overused the metaphor, Mrs. Palmer. It no longer amuses me."

Martha's voice sank to a whisper. "But if I weren't a Christian, Mr. O'Dell, I would charge you with slaying this dragon, not just uncovering her evil actions."

O'Dell's mouth hardened. "The old O'Dell would be happy to oblige you, madam, but the new O'Dell? I confess that I am struggling. Minister Liáng and Pastor Carmichael have . . . preached me quite a storm on this matter. The new O'Dell must not seek revenge. He must allow God and the law of the land the opportunity to work."

He leaned closer. "But this much I will tell you: When we step onto that train tomorrow, *we will be going to war*. We will do all that is necessary to bring baby Edmund home—even if it means these two clans and their armies clash over this. Please pray for us, for much is at stake, even many lives."

His voice dropped. "And yet, with the proof we have against Fang-Hua, I am confident that she will not escape justice. No, she will not escape."

The party that boarded the train to Seattle was subdued. Their group consisted of twelve adults and one child: Chief Groves, Marshal Pounder, Edmund O'Dell, Samuel Gresham and three of his men, Bao, Minister Liáng, Joy, Breona, and Mei-Xing, who clutched Shan-Rose with an intensity that bespoke her fears.

Those remaining behind had their assigned tasks. Rose, with help from Mr. Wheatley, was to stay near the telephone, continue to guide the house, and pray. Grant, because of his declining health, would remain behind with her. "I can pray," he gasped. "I do not need breath to pray from my heart."

Tabitha's decision was most surprising. "I have informed the dean of my school that I cannot return this term," she announced quietly. "This family emergency requires that I remain at home for the time being. She was understanding of the situation and has promised to hold my spot open for me."

Tabitha would take Breona's place as housekeeper. No one mentioned it, but all understood that she would be watching Grant's health in Joy's absence.

Gresham's remaining men, Morrow, Jeffers, and Goldstein, would remain at Palmer House, even sleeping there, until the party returned from Seattle.

On the train as it climbed toward the Montana border before turning west, Joy, Breona, and Mei-Xing shared facing seats. O'Dell was seated across the aisle from them and observed how, with calm and composed demeanors that belied the dangers ahead, the three women spoke together in soft tones, often grasping hands and bowing their heads to pray.

O'Dell had many times admired Joy Michaels' grit and determination. But today he could not help but to also notice the sadness that seeped through her steadfast manner.

Lord, he prayed for her, *I know my prayers are awkward, but my friend needs you. She has suffered so much! I am asking you to help us find her and Grant's baby. I give myself to you in this task; please use me in any way you choose.*

Gresham's men, Betts, Cluney, and Donaldson, had but a single task: protect Mei-Xing and Shan-Rose. To that end, Betts and Donaldson occupied the first and last seats in their car, each facing the opposite door. Cluney sat in the middle of the car to back them up. No one entered the car who did not first pass under their scrutiny.

O'Dell knew they were armed—as were Gresham, Groves, and Pounder. *As am I,* he added.

Gresham had his head together with Groves and Pounder nearer the front of the car. Bao and Liáng—when he was seated—occupied the seats opposite O'Dell, just across the aisle from the women.

O'Dell was not the only one who noticed that Liáng stayed close by Mei-Xing, often foreseeing and taking care of her needs before she spoke. O'Dell and Joy exchanged a knowing look and Joy, studying Liáng as he asked something of Mei-Xing, nodded, approving what she observed.

Perhaps something good and beautiful can come of all this, O'Dell mused. *Perhaps Mei-Xing will at last find happiness and peace.*

They disembarked at the King Street Station under a drizzling sky. Liáng hailed two cabs to transport them to the hotel he had recommended—a fine, modern establishment they could afford, given Martha Palmer's gift.

The gloomy afternoon had slipped into early evening by the time they registered. Mei-Xing confessed that she was weary, so the group said goodnight with the intention of meeting for breakfast in the morning.

Early the following day, Liáng arranged for a small, private dining room where they could prepare for and pray over their plans without interruption. By eight o'clock they had all gathered to eat.

For two hours after breakfast they discussed the day and each person's role. When their plans were complete, Liáng led them in prayer. O'Dell knew that Groves, Pounder, Gresham, and his men were uncomfortable and out of their elements with the whole "praying thing."

Lord, it wasn't that long ago that I was like them—unbelieving, cynical, and blind to my own ignorance, O'Dell prayed. *Open their eyes to see you! As you revealed yourself to me, I am asking that you reveal yourself to them.*

They finished praying and looked to Liáng. It was his task to set their plans in motion. All of them knew; all of them understood: *Once begun, there would be no going back.*

As Liáng requested, their dining room had a telephone. Liáng dialed a number and waited as it rang. "Mr. Li? Good morning; it is Yaochuan Min Liáng calling." He listened. "Yes, thank you, I am doing well in my Denver pastorate! I thank you for asking. I have returned to Seattle on important business."

Liáng listened further and then spoke. "My friend, I have something of great consequence to discuss with you. May I see you this afternoon?"

He listened. "I appreciate your taking time out of your busy schedule for me. If convenient, may I meet with both you and Mrs. Li?" A moment later he added, "Yes, your home would be best. Two o'clock? Thank you."

He hung up and turned to the rest. "Two o'clock."

Everyone nodded; Mei-Xing appeared ill to O'Dell; Breona clasped her hand.

Please help Mei-Xing to be strong, Lord, O'Dell prayed.

Gresham and Cluney left to rent three motorcars for the next few days. Not long after lunch, O'Dell and Liáng divided their party into three groups for the three cars: O'Dell, Liáng, and Bao went into one; Joy, Breona, Donaldson, Chief Groves, and Marshal Pounder into the second; Mei-Xing, Shan-Rose, Gresham, Betts, and Cluney into the third.

The three automobiles sped through a fine, misting rain toward the Li home. O'Dell parked in front of the house. The other two cars drove past him, turned right at the corner, and drove all the way around the block. Both cars parked along the curb, just before the corner, facing the street on which the Li family lived. They would only need to turn the corner to park behind O'Dell's motorcar.

Betts got out of his assigned vehicle, walked to the corner, and crossed the street—standing in nearly the same place Liáng had first seen Bao. From there, Betts had a view of the Lis' front door and of the two motorcars parked across the street facing him. He pulled his hat down against the damp weather and sat on a nearby bench to await a signal from Liáng or O'Dell.

Liáng and O'Dell, both of them somber, rang the bell to the Li home. A servant showed them into a living room where a warming fire burned. After only a few minutes, Mr. and Mrs. Li joined them.

"Minister Liáng! How we have missed you!" Mei-Xing's father bowed, greeting them formally. Then he and Liáng embraced.

O'Dell recognized in Mr. Li the same kind and gentle eyes that he knew in Mei-Xing. As Mrs. Li greeted them and Liáng introduced O'Dell, he saw that Mei-Xing's mother, Ting-Xiu, had once been every bit as lovely as Mei-Xing—indeed, she was still a strikingly beautiful woman.

Jinhai Li gestured to some chairs near the fire. "Please. Sit down and warm yourselves."

They sat down. "You said you had business of great consequence?" Jinhai asked. "I confess, you have puzzled me, my friend. What can be of great consequence between us?"

Liáng gathered himself and began. From the moment he began to speak, he knew, he could not take back his words.

"My friends, we have difficult things to speak of this day, things that will try your very souls," Liáng said in a quiet voice. "I know you have both come to love the Lord Jesus with all your hearts, but what we will tell you will pain you greatly.

"Before we begin, I must ask you: Are you willing to submit the situation of which I will speak to the Lord? Are you willing to pray with us right now and trust that God will see us through it?"

"You are frightening me, Minister Liáng," Ting-Xiu whispered. "What can be as fearsome as you describe?"

Liáng nodded. "It is not my intent to frighten you, madam; nevertheless, shall we commit this time to God before we go further? Let us bring our chairs close together and join hands."

"Our God, you are Lord of the universe and Lord of us," Liáng prayed. "Help us this day to uncover what has been covered and bring what has been hidden into the light. Help us this day to submit to your word even as we speak of difficult, painful things. Be with us, O Lord! Give us your grace, I ask in the name of Jesus."

Without pausing, Liáng began, "Mr. and Mrs. Li, my friend, Mr. O'Dell, is employed by the Pinkerton Agency. He is a detective."

Jinhai and his wife stared at O'Dell. "A detective!" Jinhai expostulated.

Liáng continued. "He has a . . . story to relate to you. Please hear him."

O'Dell nodded to the couple. "Yes, I am a detective with the Pinkertons. I specialize in finding lost people, often those who have been kidnapped. A while ago I helped on a difficult case. It ended in a small mountain town not far from the city of Denver in Colorado.

"Young women had been kidnapped and placed in two large houses there. These houses were frequented by men who . . . pay for services." O'Dell looked into Jinhai's eyes and willed him to understand what he was saying.

That he did was evident—Jinhai stiffened and his face grew grim. Beside him, Mrs. Li looked confused, but only for a moment before she paled.

"Do you both understand the kind of house of which I speak?"

Mr. and Mrs. Li nodded, but Mrs. Li would not look at him.

"As I said, these young women were kidnapped. They were held prisoner and forced . . . to do things."

"Please," Ting-Xiu whispered to her husband. "I do not wish to hear this. Please excuse me."

She had started to rise when Liáng placed a gentle hand on her arm. "I am sorry, dear woman, but it is important that you remain." He stared at Jinhai who reluctantly agreed and asked Ting-Xiu to be patient. She reseated herself but kept her eyes on the floor.

O'Dell took up his tale again. *How* to tell Mei-Xing's father and mother that she was alive and what had happened to her had been the most difficult part of their preparations; however, no matter how the words came out of his mouth, O'Dell knew the facts would stun and hurt her parents grievously.

"Mr. and Mrs. Li, we rescued close to twenty young women from these houses." He took a deep breath. "One of those women was your daughter, Mei-Xing."

Neither of her parents moved.

"No," Jinhai breathed. "No, you are wrong. Our daughter is dead."

Ting-Xiu trembled and swayed on her chair; Liáng reached out a steadying arm but she shoved him away, and slid closer to her husband, a sob escaping her.

Liáng nodded to O'Dell who stepped to the window and swept aside the curtains. Across the street Betts raised his arm in acknowledgement and signaled to the cars parked just around the corner.

One of the cars rounded the corner and parked behind Liáng and O'Dell's vehicle. A minute later Mei-Xing, supported by Betts and Cluney started up the walk toward the steps to the Lis' imposing front door.

Ting-Xiu, clinging to Jinhai's arm cried, "Husband! Make them stop! They are speaking horrible lies! Make them leave!" She buried her face in his side, weeping.

But Jinhai stared into Liáng's eyes, unwilling to see confirmation there but finding it nonetheless. Neither Liáng nor O'Dell said anything further for the moment.

In the background, the doorbell sounded and a servant went to open the door. The servant's shriek of shock and incredulity pierced the doors of the room they were in.

"How can this be?" Jinhai whispered over the wails of his wife, still staring into Liáng's face.

The door to the room opened. Jinhai stood up as a young woman entered followed by two large men.

"Father." Mei-Xing's voice cracked.

Jinhai walked toward her. Stared.

"Mei-Xing?"

She bowed. When she unbent, she whispered, "Yes, Father."

He touched her face as Ting-Xiu stumbled toward them. O'Dell and the other men in the room turned away from the intimacy of the scene as Mei-Xing and her parents reached for each other and, finally, embraced.

Chapter 26

More than thirty minutes had elapsed before Mrs. Li was composed enough for O'Dell to continue. Liáng brought Mr. and Mrs. Li back to the sofa and gave his chair to Mei-Xing. Her parents continued staring at Mei-Xing as though she might vanish.

"Mr. and Mrs. Li," O'Dell gently recalled them, "I must tell you that there is more to talk of."

Liáng, hovering near Mei-Xing's chair, nodded. "We have broken the surface now, but more remains to be said. I must ask you again, are you willing to give the pain of these things to the Lord? Will you resist the temptation to seek retribution? Will you submit your own vengeance to the Lord's care?"

"How can it be worse than this?" Jinhai protested, looking from Liáng to O'Dell, until he remembered O'Dell's story. "Wait—you said . . . you said the young women had been kidnapped . . ."

He looked at Mei-Xing. "You? You were kidnapped?" He looked from Liáng back to Mei-Xing. "You were in the . . . house in the town he spoke of?"

Mei-Xing bowed her head once but did not break down. She answered his question with one of her own. "Father, did you ever ask yourself why I broke my engagement to Su-Chong Chen?"

Jinhai slowly moved his head back and forth, not believing the connection she was implying. Ting-Xiu still stared at Mei-Xing in disbelief.

Mei-Xing took a deep breath. "Quite by accident, I discovered that the Chen family is involved in many . . . dishonorable business dealings, things you would never approve of, Father."

"What things?" Jinhai demanded.

O'Dell answered for Mei-Xing, sparing her the discomfort of saying the words. "The Chens are involved in drugs. Extortion. Gambling. Prostitution. Their many laundries, eateries, and import shops are legitimate businesses serving as fronts for these activities. As Minister Liáng introduced me, I am a detective. I have investigated these allegations for myself and found them to be true."

Jinhai blinked and looked away. Mei-Xing took up the narrative.

"I discovered that Su-Chong participated in these . . . illegal things, Father. I wanted to tell you! Oh, how I wanted to tell you, Father, but I was afraid . . . because Wei Lin is your close friend. I was afraid at first that you would not believe me."

She looked down at her hands. "Later I was afraid because men who work for them told me . . . they said they would hurt you and Mother if I spoke of these things to you, so I did not dare tell you!"

Jinhai sat stock-still, staring fixedly at the floor.

"Do you remember . . ." here Mei-Xing began to cry. "Do you remember how Su-Chong left and no one knew where he had gone? Do you remember how Madam Chen blamed me and how her behavior toward me in public caused you so much shame?"

Liáng handed Mei-Xing his handkerchief and patted her gently on the shoulder. Mei-Xing glanced at him, grateful.

"I did not know," Ting-Xiu moaned. "We-we-we treated you terribly! *I* treated you terribly!"

Mei-Xing nodded. "I know," she whispered. "And life became unbearable for all of us."

She wiped her eyes. "A man I considered a trustworthy friend offered me a way to remove the shame of my existence. He said that he knew a good Chinese couple living in Denver who had no family. They would take me in, he said, and treat me as a daughter.

"I wrote a note saying I had gone away to remove your shame. This man I thought was a friend put me on the train to Denver, but when I got there . . . when I got there . . ." She could not finish.

"When she arrived," O'Dell interjected, "She found that her friend had lied. Men were waiting for her and she was taken by force to the little mountain town I spoke of, to the houses there."

"Who is this *friend*?" Jinhai's voice grew in wrath. "*I will kill him!*"

"You will kill him?" Liáng asked, raising his voice over Jinhai's. "Did you not just commit your retribution to the Lord God, who is *the Righteous Judge*?" Liáng pointed his finger. "And are you without fault in all of this?"

Jinhai's mouth opened as he realized how much his treatment of Mei-Xing had contributed to her decision to run away.

"There is still more to tell, I am afraid," Liáng added, "but I will tell you something I told Mei-Xing. This 'friend' who betrayed her, has repented of his deeds and turned to Jesus the Savior. This man, *who was an enemy*, is now a brother in Christ. Can you receive this, Jinhai?"

Jinhai swallowed. "I-I do not know! There is more? I cannot take this! It is too much!"

Liáng's tone changed; it hardened. *"Jinhai Li!* You are a *Christian* man! You must act like one and not sink into self-pity. *Think of what your daughter has been through!* She and your wife look to you to lead them in this situation."

Jinhai bowed his head and then sat up straight. "You are right, Minister Liáng. I am sorry. I am sorry, daughter. I . . . I will pray to forgive this man, whoever he is."

O'Dell waited until Liáng nodded for him to continue. "Mei-Xing escaped from the house of ill-repute. Dear friends of ours welcomed Mei-Xing into their home and hid her there. They shared the good news of Jesus with her. Then they moved from the little mountain town to a house in Denver, and there Mei-Xing lived for many months, happy and content."

O'Dell shook his head. "Did you see newspaper reports two years ago when Su-Chong Chen was arrested?"

Startled, Jinhai and Ting-Xiu glanced at each other and nodded.

"When Su-Chong was arrested two years ago, he *saw* Mei-Xing. He, too, had been told she was dead, you see—just as you had. But when he saw Mei-Xing with his own eyes, he then knew that her death had been a lie."

"And did you read the newspapers when he escaped from jail months later?"

Again Mei-Xing's parents nodded.

"When he escaped from jail he went looking for her because he was still enamored of her. He searched for her until he found her in the home of our friends in Denver. He kidnapped her from her happy home. He kept her hidden, a prisoner, for six months."

Ting-Xiu began crying fresh tears. Jinhai put an arm about her but he was overwhelmed himself.

"Father. Mother." Mei-Xing waited until they faced her. "Mr. O'Dell is the one who found me. I would have died if he had not found me. I was locked in a room, and Su-Chong had died on the other side of the locked door with the key to my room around his neck.

"Father? Mother?" This would be the most difficult for Mei-Xing, but she did not want it coming from someone else.

"When Mr. O'Dell found me, I was carrying Su-Chong's child."

Jinhai did not look at her but he slowly nodded his head, acknowledging what she said. His wife blinked as if in a stupor and then she focused on Mei-Xing.

"I have a grandchild?"

Mei-Xing glimpsed hope on her mother's face for the first time since she had entered their house. "Yes," she whispered. "A granddaughter. She is nearly seven months old."

Her mother's hopeful expression deepened. "*Perhaps*, perhaps we can say that you and Su-Chong married during that time—no one will know any different! And, and will not Fang-Hua be pleased to know her son left a child? Will that not ease their shame a little?"

"No! That will *never* be!" Mei-Xing's voice rose to a shout. "Fang-Hua will *never* see my child!"

"No, she will not," Liáng agreed. He squeezed her shoulder and Mei-Xing calmed under his assurance.

"Thank you," she whispered.

She turned again to her parents. "Who do you think was behind the plan to send me to a *whorehouse* in Colorado?"

Jinhai struggled to understand. "Are you saying . . . *Fang-Hua* planned to send you there?"

"Yes. Yes, she did. She hated me for rejecting her son and blamed me for his leaving his home and family."

"I-I, but I cannot believe my friend Wei Lin had anything to do with this!"

Ting-Xiu agreed. "The Chens are our oldest, dearest friends!"

O'Dell stepped in again. "Mr. and Mrs. Li, we don't believe Wei Lin knows of the evil done to Mei-Xing, but we have proof that Fang-Hua planned and orchestrated it."

"What proof?" Jinhai demanded, still struggling to accept Fang-Hua's role as fact.

"Two things," O'Dell answered. "The first proof is a witness we can call right now. The second proof, we will show you . . . when we finish telling you all."

"More? There is more?" Jinhai lifted his hand to his head, overcome, and quite beside himself.

"There is, but let us first call our witness." O'Dell signaled from the window. A minute later, another knock sounded on the door.

A wide-eyed servant showed Bao into the room. Bao was healthier and not as hopeless looking as he had been when he had asked Mei-Xing's forgiveness nearly a year ago. He bowed to Mei-Xing's parents.

"Bao!" Jinhai exclaimed. "Where have you been? You uncle and aunt have been searching for you for more than a year! We had nearly given up hope for you."

"Mr. Li, I have been in hiding," he murmured.

"Hiding? Hiding from what? From whom?"

"From my uncle's wife, Fang-Hua Chen. She wants me dead because I can expose her deeds. Our deeds."

In simple terms, Bao detailed his role in sending Mei-Xing to Denver. He left nothing out and did not attempt to minimize his own culpability. He explained the rewards Fang-Hua had promised him. He described how, later, Fang-Hua instructed Bao to break her son from the jail in Denver and bring him back to Seattle. He repeated how Su-Chong had killed his mother's men and escaped.

Jinhai Li clenched his teeth and glared at Bao; it was clear to all that he was struggling with rage, but he held himself in check. Bao understood and soldiered on.

"Soon after all this, my wife and infant son died in childbirth. My conscience told me it was fitting punishment for what I had done to Mei-Xing." Here Bao's voice at last gave out and he sobbed. "I was so sorry for my many sins. I wanted to tell you Mei-Xing was alive, but I could not find the courage. You saw me that day . . ." he pointed through the window, "standing across the street. You sent Minister Liáng to speak to me. He came and told me of Jesus."

Liáng interjected, "You should know, my friends, that because what Bao told me was so extraordinary, I could not believe him. I went to Colorado myself to discover the truth. I found the house in Denver where Mei-Xing lived with her friends—but after he escaped from jail, Su-Chong had gone looking for Mei-Xing. By the time I arrived, he had already taken her and hidden her from us.

"It was many months more before Mr. O'Dell found her and brought her home. Then I again went to Colorado—to meet her and see if she was all right."

Jinhai and his wife stared at the floor, silent and still. Liáng and O'Dell had been in the Li home now two hours.

Mei-Xing stirred. "I need to look after Shan-Rose," she murmured. Accompanied by her two guards, she started to leave.

"Mei-Xing!" Jinhai stood. "Is your baby here? May we see her? Our granddaughter?"

O'Dell answered. "Perhaps not yet. We have more to tell."

Jinhai sank to his chair. "There is more?"

As Mei-Xing and her guards left, O'Dell picked up the thread of the tale. "It will pain you to hear this. After Mei-Xing was recovered and brought back to her friends in Denver, Minister Liáng hoped she would come home to you. You must understand how much she has been through and why she chose to let you continue to think her dead."

He looked at Mei-Xing's parents. "Do you understand?"

Jinhai met O'Dell's questioning eyes. "She did not want us to be ashamed?"

"That was certainly part of it," O'Dell acknowledged.

"What other part would there be?"

"She was afraid Fang-Hua would come after her child."

O'Dell could see the doubt shadowing Jinhai's eyes. He pressed on. "It has now been close to a year since Su-Chong died and Mei-Xing was rescued and returned to her friends in Denver. Her baby is almost seven months old. She has been constantly guarded against such an attack since Shan-Rose's birth. Why do you suppose that she has now changed her mind and returned to you?"

O'Dell's words hung suspended between himself and Jinhai. Jinhai Li forced himself to face the truth about his friends, the Chens, particularly Wei Lin's wife, Fang-Hua.

"Something has happened?" Jinhai breathed.

O'Dell nodded. "Yes. Something terrible has happened. Men hired by Fang-Hua killed two of the men guarding Shan-Rose and attempted to abduct her. Instead, they mistakenly took another baby, the child of a woman dear to Mei-Xing's heart—the same woman who hid Mei-Xing when she escaped from the brothel where she was imprisoned."

Jinhai and O'Dell stared into each other's eyes for a long time, each taking the measure of the other.

"You say you have other proof of Fang-Hua's guilt?" Jinhai insisted.

O'Dell removed an envelope from his breast pocket. "This is an exact copy of a letter written by one of the men hired by Fang-Hua—the leader, we believe. He wrote it after discovering they had kidnapped the wrong child. Knowing they would not have another chance to take Mei-Xing's baby by surprise, this man shot and killed the other four men hired by Fang-Hua. Then he wrote this letter. Please read it."

Jinhai received the folded sheet of paper. He opened it and, with Ting-Xiu looking over his shoulder, read

To the police:

The men whose bodies you find here were recently in the employ of one Fang-Hua Chen of Seattle, Washington.

Fang-Hua's full address was written next.

Madam Chen ordered that these men perform the following crimes: a) Abduct the infant child of one Mei-Xing Li, b) Dispatch (kill) Miss Li and her bodyguards, and c) Bring the child to her. This is Miss Li's place of residence.

A Denver address unfamiliar to Jinhai was printed below.

The father of Miss Li's child is Su-Chong Chen, the late son of Fang-Hua Chen, making Madam Chen the child's paternal grandmother.

Someone had scrawled notes and names and numbers, details that Jinhai skipped over. As he scanned the last line Jinhai thought he would be ill.

Sorry about taking the wrong child, O'Dell.
R. S.

"Who is this "R.S." and what of the child he stole?" Jinhai's voice shook.

"We don't know who he is and we have had no luck finding the baby, a two-month-old boy," O'Dell admitted.

"He knows *you*, though! He named you in this letter!"

O'Dell sighed. "I know, but I have not been able to decipher the initials."

Jinhai stirred and groaned. "The mother of this baby helped Mei-Xing escape from *that place*, the house in the mountain town outside Denver?"

O'Dell nodded once without comment.

Jinhai hung his head. "We owe this woman a great debt. A very great debt."

His wife agreed. "It should have been our grandchild he took, not her baby. She is suffering her baby's loss because of this mistake."

Ting-Xiu spoke directly to O'Dell; her eyes burning and resolute. "Here and now, we renounce our friendship with the Chens. Whatever you ask of us, we will do."

She stared hard at Jinhai. "*Whatever* they ask of us."

Chapter 27

When Wei Lin Chen heard from his receptionist that the caller was his old friend, Jinhai Li, he picked up the telephone receiver. "My friend," he greeted him. "It has been too long."

I have not seen you since Su-Chong died, he thought.

"It has, and I have missed you, too, my friend," Jinhai Li returned. He was nervous and off balance. Only yesterday his entire world had been turned upside down. Today he felt anything but friendship toward the man on the other end of the line.

"Is all well with you?" Wei Lin asked. "You sound . . . different."

Jinhai sighed. "Wei Lin, may I ask a very great favor?"

Wei Lin sat back, surprised. "Of course. Whatever you ask."

"I need to speak to you, my friend, in person. May I ask that you come to my home this afternoon? I would not ask, but it is indeed important."

Wei Lin frowned. "It sounds serious."

"I assure you, it is. Please say you will come."

Wei Lin looked at his schedule. "What time? I will cancel my appointments to be there."

"Four o'clock."

"I will come," he reassured Jinhai.

"I, ah, I must ask one more thing, Wei Lin. It is vital."

Wei Lin paused before answering. "Yes?"

"I must have your word . . . that you will tell no one you are meeting with me."

The frown on Wei Lin's face deepened. "I must say I am becoming concerned, Jinhai." Wei Lin heard a few whispered voices in the background and then Jinhai spoke again.

"Have no fear for yourself, my friend. Please, bring your bodyguards. I will feed them a fine meal while we speak. There is no danger to you."

Somewhat reassured, Wei Lin relaxed. "I will be there. I will tell Fang-Hua I will be late for dinner." He heard only silence on the other end for a moment. "Jinhai? Are you there?"

"Yes. Yes, I am here." He sighed. "Wei Lin, when I asked that you tell no one you are meeting with me, I particularly meant Fang-Hua. You must promise me that you will not tell Fang-Hua that you are meeting with me."

Wei Lin's chin dropped to his chest. After close to thirty years of marriage, he well knew his wife's nature and reputation. *What has she done now that my friend must speak to me of her behind her back?* he wondered. It was his turn to sigh.

"As you wish, Jinhai. I will see you at four o'clock."

A soaking rain was falling when Wei Lin and his two bodyguards stood before the door to the Li home. The time was exactly four o'clock. The maid who opened the door bowed low and motioned them in.

Jinhai himself greeted Wei Lin in the foyer. "Thank you for coming. This servant will show your bodyguards to the kitchen. My cook has prepared something special for them."

The two men guarding Wei Lin looked to him for direction. "Go. I will be fine," Wei Lin instructed them. He followed Jinhai into their drawing room.

Several men stood waiting for them. Jinhai introduced them one at a time.

"Wei Lin, may I present Mr. Edmund O'Dell, Mr. Samuel Gresham, and our former pastor, Yaochuan Min Liáng. These other two gentlemen are Police Chief Groves and U.S. Marshal Pounder, both of the city of Denver."

Wei Lin cut Jinhai a dark look. "Why would a police chief and a marshal from another state be here? What is going on?"

Jinhai bowed again. "Wei Lin, for the sake of our families and what is about to be said, the officers have agreed to leave the room."

Chief Groves and Marshal Pounder both nodded to Wei Lin and left the room.

When the door closed behind them, Jinhai spoke again. "We have things to tell you, Wei Lin, important things. I-I cannot do it myself. I have asked my friends to help me."

They were, perhaps, not as kind to Wei Lin as they had been to Jinhai. Without preparation, O'Dell opened a side door to the room and Bao entered.

"Uncle." Bao could scarcely utter the word. He bowed and straightened and stood before his mother's brother.

"Bao! Where have you been all this time? Your aunt and I have been looking ev—"

"I know my aunt has been looking for me, Uncle." Bao had interrupted his uncle, an unconscionable breach of etiquette.

Wei Lin frowned and growled. "If you knew she was looking for you, why have you not come home? Where have you been all this time?"

"Repenting of my sins," Bao answered. He held up his hand as Wei Lin started to inject another question. "Uncle, please forgive my second instance of rude behavior, but I must speak."

Wei Lin looked about the room. "Do these men know what you are to tell me?"

Bao inclined his head.

"Go on then."

"My aunt has not been looking for me, Uncle. She has been *hunting* me. You see, over the last few years she and I have conspired to do many terrible things—horrific and illegal acts that shame me, shame you, and shame our family. However, after my wife died in childbirth, I refused to do Fang-Hua's bidding any longer."

Wei Lin's face flooded with anger. "Of what acts do you speak? And if, as you say, they shame our family, why do you speak of them to my friend and to strangers?"

"Forgive me, Uncle, but these things involve Mr. Li. You see, the first service I performed for Fang-Hua was to punish Mei-Xing for rejecting your son." In short, concise sentences, Bao repeated what he had told Jinhai. Mei-Xing's father wept behind his hand as he heard it again.

"This is outrageous nonsense, Bao!" Wei Lin roared, standing to his feet and shaking his finger in Bao's face. "Mei-Xing has been dead these three years!" He turned to Jinhai. "My friend, you do not believe these lies, do you? I apologize for the gross misconduct of my nephew. I will punish him, I promise!"

"No, Mr. Chen. You will not punish him."

Slowly, Wei Lin turned *toward the voice of a dead woman.*

Mei-Xing walked past Wei Lin and stood next to Bao. "I am not dead, and Bao is not lying, Mr. Chen."

When the telling of it all was over, Wei Lin stared straight ahead. He did not speak or move. He sat motionless for a long while, until O'Dell would give him no more time.

"Mr. Chen."

Wei Lin woke from his stupor. "Yes, Mr. O'Dell?"

"To save Mei-Xing and the Li family the further grief of a public spectacle, we have decided not to openly accuse Fang-Hua of Mei-Xing's abduction and enslavement. Nor will we reveal that Fang-Hua had a part in breaking Su-Chong from the jail in Denver.

"However, Chief Groves and Marshal Pounder have already been in close communication with Seattle police regarding the death of the two men who guarded Mei-Xing and her child and the subsequent abduction of Mr. and Mrs. Michaels' baby.

"Groves and Pounder have shown the evidence to the police. Fang-Hua will be arrested for planning and financing the kidnapping and the two murders."

"When?"

"Tomorrow. Late morning. We wished you to know and be prepared."

The morrow was a Sunday; neither Wei Lin nor Fang-Hua would have a reason to be away from home before noon.

Wei Lin nodded, and remained thoughtful.

"Mr. Chen, our highest objective is to recover the missing child. We will ask for Fang-Hua's assistance toward that end. When we do, we hope that you will encourage her to cooperate."

As O'Dell spoke, Liáng stirred to a tiny, insistent jangling in the back of his mind. A moment later he realized that Samuel Gresham was staring at him. Communicating without words.

A warning?

Liáng stared back. He gave an almost imperceptible nod of his head and searched out Jinhai. His friend, too, seemed concerned. A frown creased his brow.

Wei Lin shook himself. "Jinhai, your home must be overflowing with a party this size." The line was delivered so effortlessly that Liáng would not have recognized it for what it was—if the Holy Spirit had not, only seconds before, aroused him to danger.

Jinhai was not a man of guile so, before he could speak, Liáng answered, his manner quite matter-of-fact. "We have not troubled Mr. and Mrs. Li with housing us; we have rooms at the Washington Arms."

"Ah. A fine hotel. I know you are comfortable there," Wei Lin murmured.

A short while later as Wei Lin took his leave, Jinhai found Liáng. "I must talk to you."

"I think I know what you will say. Let us gather the others so we may all hear your words, shall we?"

Mei-Xing excused herself from the room as Liáng and Gresham called the men together. "Mr. Li has something to say to us," Liáng murmured.

"Please, I hope you will attempt to understand what I say and how important it is," Jinhai began. "I realized as I watched Wei Lin take in our news that we have made a mistake."

He had everyone's attention. "Even though I have considered Wei Lin a dear friend for many years, nothing in our culture is more important than *family*. And just because Wei Lin did not participate in Fang-Hua's despicable crimes toward Mei-Xing, I realized *too late* that we should not have believed that he is incapable of similar actions where his family's reputation is concerned."

Jinhai sought Liáng's face. "Do you follow what I am saying?"

Liáng grew grim. "Yes. He may not care *for Fang-Hua's sake* that she will be arrested tomorrow, *but he will care for his family's honor*."

O'Dell and Gresham quickly caught on. Gresham cleared his throat. "A tactical error," he muttered. "I saw the wheels going around in that guy's mind, and even though he has a good poker face, I realized right then that we can't trust him."

O'Dell spoke up. "I ask all of you to remember—bringing Fang-Hua to justice is, for us, only a means to an end, and that end is the recovery of baby Edmund. For that reason, we must ensure that nothing prevents us from confronting her tomorrow!"

"You are saying that Wei Lin will try to finish what Fang-Hua started," Groves charged. "That Mei-Xing and Bao are still in danger—and so is the evidence we have gathered?"

"That is it exactly," Liáng agreed. "If the witnesses and evidence disappear, the case against Fang-Hua goes away—as will the public stain on Wei Lin's family name."

"Then he will strike quickly," Jinhai breathed. "He must. Before Fang-Hua is arrested tomorrow. Not even our friendship will stop him from acting to protect his family honor."

He looked around the room. "We must keep Mei-Xing, her child, and Bao here in my home. We can defend them here. I have men I trust, men who are loyal only to me."

O'Dell looked from Gresham to Groves and Pounder. "Agreed. But we do so secretly. We must allow Wei Lin to believe they have returned to the hotel. And then we must prepare and be ready for the attack."

He directed his next words to Groves and Pounder. "Can we involve the Seattle police? Can we request that they provide some of their men to stand with us at the hotel?"

"Leave it to me," Groves replied. He asked Jinhai for the location of a telephone and went into his library to use it.

Joy and Breona—and Shan-Rose—were waiting outside in one of the motorcars. Gresham and Pounder rushed outside to escort Joy and Breona into the house. Mei-Xing noted the change in their manner and hurried into the room again.

"What has happened?" she cried. "What is going on?"

Liáng took her aside. He sat her down and took her hands before telling her their concerns. "We have made a mistake in trusting Wei Lin with the knowledge of his wife's actions. To protect his family's honor, we believe he will try to . . . finish what Fang-Hua began, try to eliminate Bao, you, and . . . Shan-Rose. You will all be staying here tonight where you will be safe."

"Shan-Rose!" Mei-Xing flew up in a panic, but Liáng caught her by the arm.

"They have gone to get her, Mei-Xing. Wait one minute and you will see."

Mei-Xing pressed herself against the window and watched as Pounder, Gresham, and Gresham's crew escorted Joy and Breona up the walk to the front door. The men were on high alert: Their eyes swept around and they kept their hands inside their pockets where Mei-Xing knew they carried their guns.

Pounder had Joy by the elbow and was setting a pace she was pressed to keep; Gresham walked beside Breona with his hand on the small of her back, urging her on. Breona clutched Shan-Rose in her arms. No female bear would guard her cub with more determination than what Mei-Xing saw in Breona expression at that moment.

Seconds later, they burst through the door and spilled into the foyer. Liáng and Jinhai waved them into the living room.

Mei-Xing ran to Breona who still held Shan-Rose in a possessive grip. Joy hovered close by.

"Sure, an' she is just foine, Mei-Xing," Breona reassured her. "Sleeping loik a baby, eh?"

"Thank you, Breona. I know you would have defended her with your life!" The tears that stood in Mei-Xing's eyes mirrored the ones in Breona's.

"Aye, that I would," she said, her words heard only by Mei-Xing. Breona relinquished the baby to Mei-Xing who collapsed into a chair, breathing in the sweet scent of her child.

Jinhai slowly approached Mei-Xing. "Is that . . . your little one?"

Liáng stepped nearer the chair and Jinhai recognized his protective posture. Jinhai blinked and bowed in submission. "I am not Wei Lin Chen. I would never harm my own grandchild. May I at least see her?"

Mei-Xing looked to Liáng for his opinion. "Of course," he murmured, but he was not replying to Jinhai; he was reassuring Mei-Xing. She climbed to her feet again and lifted the corner of the blanket from Shan-Rose's face.

Jinhai peered down at the sleeping child. Her hand was fisted and pressed against her face, both cheeks rosy and plump. Tears stood in Jinhai's eyes. "My beautiful granddaughter!" he exclaimed. "Thank you, my God, for restoring our daughter and granddaughter to us!"

Liáng and Mei-Xing exchanged an inscrutable look. They said nothing.

As evening drew on, the Li house hummed with activity. Jinhai barked terse orders into the telephone and, thirty minutes later, a dozen of his trusted men arrived and surrounded the house. Some concealed themselves in the shrubbery; others took up posts in the shadows by the doors. All were armed.

Jinhai called his household staff together. Most had been with the Li family during Mei-Xing's childhood and had grieved with Jinhai and Ting-Xiu over their daughter's purported suicide.

To say that the family's servants had been stunned to see Mei-Xing the day before would be an understatement. The anger that visibly grew in their ranks as Jinhai described Fang-Hua Chen's actions toward Mei-Xing was all the assurance O'Dell and Gresham needed to leave the house principally in Jinhai's hands.

They instructed Liáng, Bao, and two of Gresham's men to remain close to Joy, Breona, Mei-Xing, and Shan-Rose at all times. Before O'Dell, Chief Groves, Marshal Pounder, Gresham, and his remaining man left for the hotel, O'Dell called Joy aside.

"I promised Grant I would not leave your side, Joy, but I feel I should be at the hotel tonight to stand against Wei Lin's men."

"I know; he told me," she whispered, "but I agree with you. Go; we are well protected here."

The pain on her face was etching permanent lines around her eyes. It was as though she were aging as O'Dell watched.

O'Dell, breathing a prayer for her, nodded and turned away to join Groves at the door.

Jinhai, Ting-Xiu, and those of the Denver party remaining in the Li home sequestered themselves together in the living room. Conversation was sparse. When dinner was served, most of them picked at the food.

Mei-Xing kept close to Joy and Breona, and Liáng was never more than a few feet away. Gresham's men, Betts and Cluney, stood guard outside the living room door. One of them would step into the room every so often and look around; the other prowled the first floor, checking the locks on the doors and windows.

Ting-Xiu, with Mei-Xing and Liáng hovering over her, held Shan-Rose, weeping and then laughing as the baby awoke and smiled.

As the evening wore on, Liáng gathered them together to intercede for the battle to come. "Everlasting Father," Liáng prayed. "Of whom shall we be afraid? Though a host encamps against us, of one thing we are confident: The Lord is our Light and our very great Salvation."

A Seattle detective and six officers joined O'Dell and the remaining Denver complement at the hotel. The detective was dressed in a plain tweed suit, but his officers wore the blue serge uniforms of the Seattle police: brass buttons up the front, belted at the waist, and a seven-pointed star above the left breast. The crests on their dome-shaped hats identified each officer's rank.

The combined force met in one of the hotel rooms to plan for the attack they were certain would come before morning. The Seattle detective, Martin Wolsey, suggested that they mix the six officers and the Denver party together and place them in three rooms—the room Mei-Xing had slept in, the adjoining room that Breona and Joy had shared, and the room across the hall. They agreed that Mei-Xing's room would likely be the primary target.

Groves, Gresham, Wolsey, and one officer took Mei-Xing's room. Wolsey sent O'Dell, Pounder, and two police officers to the adjoining room. Donaldson and the three remaining officers took up their posts in the room across the hall.

"I relish the opportunity to catch the Chens red-handed in anything," Wolsey confessed with unsuppressed satisfaction, "and I fully intend to be present when Madam Chen is arrested tomorrow."

"But first, we must survive this night. I suggest we make up the beds to look as though they are being slept in. I further suggest we place ourselves in the darkest corners of our rooms and have two men on watch at all times."

With determined expressions, O'Dell, Groves, and Pounder followed Wolsey's instructions. When O'Dell, Pounder, and the two officers settled in the room adjoining Mei-Xing's, O'Dell fell into a chair in the corner. He was weary and his hip ached abominably from overuse. Pounder and one of the officers would take the first watch and would waken O'Dell and the other officer halfway through the night.

"Breona."

Breona was nodding next to Joy, nearly asleep in a comfortable sofa near the fire. She awoke with a start. "Whist?"

Mei-Xing handed a yawning Shan-Rose to her. "I . . . would you and Joy take Shan-Rose upstairs to bed? I must speak to my father."

"Of course." She nudged Joy and the two of them dragged their feet up the stairs. Cluney followed them and stayed until he heard the snap of the lock on their side of the door.

"Father, may I speak with you?"

Jinhai turned toward Mei-Xing. She could see the sadness that engulfed him. "Yes, daughter. Of course." Ting-Xiu had gone up to bed an hour ago, but he had not been able to think of sleep.

Mei-Xing looked for—and found—Liáng's watchful presence not far away.

Why, how have I come to depend on him so? she marveled within herself. *And he is always . . . with me.* Pushing those thoughts aside for later consideration, she faced the task ahead.

"Father, I must tell you something."

Jinhai's countenance sank further and Mei-Xing faltered, but only for a moment.

"I am sorry that we have brought such turmoil to your home," she began. "I am sorry if what I wish to say will grieve you more."

Jinhai touched her arm. "No. Do not be sorry. My heart is rejoicing that you are alive. I am only mourning my blindness and my insensitivity. I know the Lord will heal my heart."

They examined each other then, looking for—and finding—acceptance and forgiveness.

"You were thanking God earlier for bringing me back, for bringing you a granddaughter, but—"

Jinhai took her hand. "I think I know what you wish to say. You will not be staying, will you? You will go back to Denver, to the life you have there?"

"Yes, Father."

"Minister Liáng told us that you did not even want us to know you are alive. Do you wish us to pretend that you are still . . ." He did not finish his sentence.

Mei-Xing thought for a minute. "I don't know yet. I don't know how to handle all the things coming to light. It may be that these things will be public knowledge soon regardless of what we decide. Certainly the servants will talk and news will get out. Could we pray about it?"

"Yes! Yes. We will pray."

"But you are right about the other. I will be going back to Denver when this is all over."

Jinhai nodded.

"I had an idea, though . . . I have the sense that it will upset you. I will only say that it would be my express wish if you could find it in your heart to follow this idea."

Her father looked up, waiting.

"It is that you have no son, no one to carry on our name and your business." Hesitating, and then pressing through, Mei-Xing spoke what was in her heart.

Jinhai said nothing at first, but his expression became forbidding.

"No." It was his only response.

"I understand," Mei-Xing whispered. "It is almost unthinkable. But . . . I think you will reflect on it more. If it is right, I know the Lord himself will show it to you. Good night, Father."

Chapter 28

O'Dell had been on watch for an hour when his ears caught the sound—the lightest metal-on-metal scratching at the door to their room. He used his cane to prod Pounder awake, who jostled the officer dozing next to him.

They had been wrong about the direction of the attack, but it did not matter—they were ready. Three men clothed all in black entered the room, intent on the covered figures in the beds. They did not sense O'Dell, Pounder, or the two officers until it was too late.

The four of them fell on the intruders, pounding them with clubs; O'Dell used the heavy end of his cane to good advantage. A gun went off, harming no one, but O'Dell's ears rang from its discharge.

Someone turned on the lights, revealing three figures prostrate on the floor. Then the two officers were running for the door connecting them to the next room—that was when O'Dell realized that both rooms had been attacked simultaneously.

"Hold them here," Pounder yelled over his shoulder.

O'Dell, using his cane for what it was intended, steadied himself and trained his revolver on the groaning intruders while Pounder followed the officers into the room next door.

The wall between the rooms shook as bodies crashed into it. O'Dell's eyes did not leave the three men he guarded, but he followed the fight with his ears as it grew more violent until—a gunshot. Another. Then silence.

He heard Wolsey. "Get 'em up." More voices shouted in the room; O'Dell recognized Groves and one of the policemen.

Pounder stepped back into the room. "We've got them."

"How many?"

"There were four. Only three now."

O'Dell heard screams and shouts and footsteps pounding the outside corridor. "Guess we've disturbed the other guests."

He grinned and Pounder grinned back.

The sun was lighting the sky by the time the police had hauled the six thugs and one body away. Not one of the attackers—all Chinese—had spoken a word in response to the questions put to them. It was Wolsey who pointed to a small tattoo on the back of each neck.

"Chen," O'Dell heard him mutter.

Wolsey gathered O'Dell, Pounder, Groves, Gresham, and the rest of the defenders together. "Wei Lin will have used a lookout to report back to him. By now he will know his men have failed. He will likely be told that Mei-Xing and Bao were not here. You should warn Jinhai."

Gresham used the hotel telephone to ring Jinhai's house. The sleepy servant who answered rushed to get Jinhai from his bed.

"It is all right," Jinhai replied. "I could not sleep. I will alert my men; please come as quickly as you can."

Wolsey and his officers went to assure the hotel management that the danger was past and that the police had the situation in hand. O'Dell, Groves, Pounder, Gresham, and Donaldson piled into a single car and drove with all speed toward the Li residence.

When they arrived, Jinhai's soldiers were no longer hidden. They openly walked the perimeter of the Li house, an unconcealed warning to any who might think of breaching the home.

Jinhai met the returning men in the foyer. "Come. I have ordered coffee, tea, and food." He led them into the living room. Liáng and Bao were already waiting for them; it was obvious that they, too, had not slept much.

Wiping the fatigue from their faces, O'Dell and Pounder recounted the attack on their room.

Groves and Gresham picked up and finished the account. "We heard the scuffle start in the room next door just as four men broke through our door. We had them beaten, but they would not give up until their leader lay dead on the floor."

"So!" Jinhai stood and paced. "We have thwarted Wei Lin and now he is running out of time and options." He turned to Liáng. "I have been praying and studying all night on how Wei Lin would act and how to counter him. And then something Mei-Xing asked of me began to work in my heart and the Lord has been wrestling with me all these hours. I believe he has given me his direction."

He turned to Liáng. "Minister Liáng, you led me to Christ and you helped Ting-Xiu and me find peace after losing Mei-Xing. I value your friendship and your counsel." In a few sentences, Jinhai explained what two things he had prayed and struggled over through the night.

Liáng could scarcely believe what he heard. "You are sure?" Liáng's heart was pounding.

Jinhai nodded. "I believe they are the Lord's answers, both to stymie Wei Lin . . . and to heal my family."

He tipped his head a little to the side and Liáng recognized the gesture immediately. *Just like Mei-Xing,* Liáng marveled.

"My friend, Yaochuan Min Liáng," Jinhai asked formally, "You love my daughter, do you not?"

Shan-Rose, Joy, and Breona were still sleeping when Mei-Xing awoke. She dressed and wandered through the halls of her parents' home. While all things about the house were familiar, they also seemed strange and foreign to her now.

As the sun was rising she slipped down the back staircase to the ground floor and out the back door. Heavily armed men watched her as she paused at the gate to her father's garden. Lifting the latch, she stepped inside.

The buds on his ornamental plum trees were just opening, enveloping the branches in a haze of delicate pink. Mei-Xing walked among the trees, remembering the evening, three years ago, she had stood here, plum blossoms falling like snow all around her. It was here she had decided to accept Bao's offer of a train ticket to Denver.

I never wished to return here to my father's house, Mei-Xing pondered. *I was afraid to revisit those painful days, yet here I am.*

She turned her eyes toward heaven and smiled. *My heart is hidden in you, Lord Jesus,* she whispered. *You have healed my pain and you have made me whole again. Thank you.*

At peace, Mei-Xing returned to the house and wandered through the kitchen where the servants were already busy preparing a large breakfast. Mei-Xing was starting up the front stairs when Liáng appeared.

"Mei-Xing, I would speak with you." Liáng extended his hand to her. Mei-Xing automatically took his outstretched hand but she was off balance, unsure of the boldness of his words and actions.

He grasped her fingers and gently tugged her into the Lis' library. He closed the door behind them. They were alone in the room, facing each other.

"Mei-Xing, this morning your father and I will face Wei Lin and Fang-Hua together. With honor and in God's power, we will defeat them both." He stared at her lovely face; he stared into her dark eyes. Liáng took a deep breath.

Then he poured his heart before her.

Joy had not slept soundly. She sensed the household stirring and, with a start, realized the sun was lightening the curtains of the room in which she, Breona, and Mei-Xing slept. When she saw that Mei-Xing was gone, Joy dressed as quickly as she could, hoping that someone would have news of last night.

Did Wei Lin send men to the hotel as Jinhai and Liáng were sure he would? Are my friends, O'Dell and the others, safe?

She was relieved to find the men of their party gathered in the living room. They stood in small knots, speaking in low voices. She spied O'Dell. He was hunched over in a chair, rubbing the side of his thigh. Joy ran to him.

"Is all well?" Joy demanded. "Did they come?"

"Yes, they came. Seven men, all Chen. Wolsey shot one of them, but the rest have been arrested. We came back as soon as it was over."

Joy glanced around the room again. "What is happening? Where is Minister Liáng?"

"Ah! Liáng." O'Dell was exhausted but a ghost of a smile lit his tired eyes. "He is fine. He is . . . preparing for the battle this morning."

Joy knelt on the carpet next to O'Dell's chair. "Will you go with them to face Fang-Hua this morning?"

He nodded. "Yes, but . . ."

"What is it?" Joy was alarmed by his reticence.

"We know Wei Lin is running out of time and options. He knows the police are coming to arrest Fang-Hua this morning and that we will be there to confront her. I don't trust the man—he may be counting on this house being vulnerable while we are gone."

O'Dell sighed. "I promised Grant I would not leave you vulnerable."

"But Mr. Li has the house protected, doesn't he? You left last night and all was well here, wasn't it?" Joy searched his face. "Besides, I want to go with you. I want to be there when you ask her where Edmund is. He may even be there, in her house!"

"You cannot go, Joy."

"But—"

"No. *I will not permit it.*" O'Dell's expression turned to stone. "Even with Wolsey and the police with us, we will be walking into Chen territory and will be surrounded by his men. And I am concerned, Joy. Cornered animals strike unpredictably, and Wei Lin is cornered."

He sighed again and scrubbed his eyes. "That is why I am considering staying here. Just in case, while the others are gone . . ."

Joy reached her hand to his and touched him. "But you *must* go this morning, dear friend. You really must. That woman may have Edmund! Please! Go and *make her tell you what she has done with my baby boy!*"

She was at the end of herself, and O'Dell could not stand the desperation he heard in Joy's words and witnessed in her weary eyes.

Lord, he begged, *what if Fang-Hua doesn't know where baby Edmund is any more than we do? Ah, God! Then what do I tell Joy? What will I tell Grant?*

"Grant would want you to go!" Joy sobbed. "We will be safe here. Just, please . . . *I beg of you,* find Edmund for us!"

O'Dell sensed a small nudge in his spirit. He nodded a grudging response. "All right. I will go."

Joy went back upstairs to calm herself and do a more adequate job of her toilet. She found Breona, bleary-eyed, bouncing Shan-Rose on her knee. The baby was fussy and cantankerous.

"Air ye knowin' where Mei-Xing is bein'?" Breona was almost as cranky as Shan-Rose.

"I didn't see her downstairs. Just let me comb and braid my hair and I will see if I can find her."

But she did not need to look for Mei-Xing; the girl opened the door just then and peeked in. "Oh! You are all awake!"

"Aye. And this wee one is bein' that hungry," Breona growled.

Joy studied Mei-Xing. Something about her was a little off. Her cheeks were too pink and—

As though Mei-Xing sensed Joy's scrutiny, she blushed more deeply, but she covered it by cooing at Shan-Rose and getting herself settled to nurse.

Joy eyed Mei-Xing while she finished fixing her hair and began straightening the room. As she spread the covers on her bed, she stole another glance. *Mei-Xing was still blushing! And biting the inside of her cheek!*

Something was certainly up.

Two hours later Wolsey and five officers arrived at the Li home. Wolsey and three officers drove a regular police motorcar; the other two policemen stepped from a vehicle that looked part wagon, part motorcar—a conveyance designed to hold and transport prisoners.

Ting-Xiu had arranged for a late breakfast to be served in the living room as the men laid their final plans. O'Dell, who had once studied the Chen estate, provided insight into the guards and protections they would encounter as they drove through the front gate.

"I knew Wei Lin's business dealings had to be dirty just from watching the Chen house," he stated. "It's built and guarded like a fortress."

Jinhai nodded. "I had not thought of it like that, but you are right." He shivered as he recalled how he and Ting-Xiu had called on the Chens to console them on the death of their son. He would never forget the covert malevolence of Fang-Hua's response.

Joy and Breona sat across the room as men made their arrangements, not hearing the details, but praying for them. Mei-Xing and her mother sat near them; Ting-Xiu played with Shan-Rose, but Mei-Xing seemed distracted, Joy thought.

In addition to Wolsey and the five policemen, O'Dell, Jinhai, Liáng, Bao, Groves, and Pounder would attend the arrest of Fang-Hua. Both Groves and Pounder wore their uniforms. Gresham and his men would remain at the Li home to supplement the guard set by Jinhai.

At the end of the hour, Wolsey scanned the room. "Are we agreed on all the details? Is everyone clear on their jobs?"

He received nods and affirming murmurs in response. "All right. We should get going."

"Wait. We would like to pray first." It was Jinhai speaking, but a small chorus of agreement answered him.

Wolsey and the officers hung back but, with a gesture of his hand, Liáng gathered them into the circle forming in front of the fireplace. He even looked toward the women at the other end of the living room. Joy, Breona, and Mei-Xing joined them.

"Heavenly Father, above all things, we have come to Seattle to find and return little Edmund to his mother and father. We know that Fang-Hua Chen orchestrated his abduction. So we ask, our Lord, that you go before us to prepare the way. We ask that you uncover what is hidden and put to naught the plans that oppose you.

"We also ask for your safety and protection. Thank you for watching over us last night; we are grateful for your many blessings. Let your will be done this day, we ask in Jesus' name."

"Amen," a dozen voices agreed.

"Yes, Lord, amen," Joy breathed.

O God, I know you see my baby right now. You are watching over him. Please comfort him and comfort us! I will not let my heart be afraid. I know you are caring for him.

Wolsey's motorcar, with Pounder and Groves seated inside, was followed by the paddy wagon and Jinhai's automobile. The three vehicles rolled to a stop in front of the impressive gate to Wei Lin's home. Two Chen guards with stony expressions stood between the cars and the gate. A third guard came to the window.

Wolsey rolled it down and pointed to the badge pinned to his suit coat. "Detective Martin Wolsey to see Wei Lin Chen. He is expecting us."

The guard said nothing, but he gestured with his chin. The gate swung open. Wolsey rolled up his window and drove on. The two other vehicles followed him up the long, curving drive to the imposing house.

As the motorcars emptied, armed men stepped from the shadows. O'Dell felt the hair on his arms and the back of his neck prickle and, not for the first time, he wondered: *Would Wei Lin dare to attack policemen in the conduct of their duty?*

If he did, it would be a massacre.

Wolsey, his officers, Pounder, Groves, and those from Jinhai's car walked up the large porch to the Chen's front door. Wolsey rang the bell. At his word, three of his uniformed officers turned and faced the menacing Chen guards, folded their arms across their chests, and remained there, blocking the doorway, as the rest of their party entered the house.

A servant told them to wait in the foyer while she announced them, but Wolsey ignored her instructions. He set off behind her, and the rest of the group followed.

The servant, seeing that they were right behind her, became agitated; she half-ran to the end of a corridor and burst through the door, babbling as she entered. Wolsey and the others stepped into a breakfast room.

That Wei Lin had not told Fang-Hua of her impending arrest was obvious. The woman, dressed in an elaborate silk gown, paused stock-still, a corner of toast halfway to her mouth.

"What is this?" she hissed.

Two guards who had been standing inconspicuously in a corner took a few steps forward. Wolsey pointed at both of them. "Do not interfere in police business, boys. My men will not hesitate to shoot you."

Wolsey and his party knew their roles. His two officers faced the guards and drew their weapons, keeping them trained on the nervous guards.

Wolsey took a step forward. As did Bao Shin Xang.

Fang-Hua's eyes bulged and she sputtered a curse word. Her head whipped toward Wei Lin, but he had not moved, nor had he shown surprise. Fang-Hua's eyes narrowed.

So! This traitor has come home and has, perhaps, betrayed me to my husband. No matter.

She composed herself by slowly and meticulously wiping her fingers on a napkin and then smoothing the folds of her gown. She ignored Bao and addressed Wolsey.

"May I ask who you are and why you do not properly introduce yourself rather than behaving as impolite ruffians?"

Wolsey smiled and chuckled. "Detective Martin Wolsey, at your service, madam. Here to serve an arrest warrant on you."

Fang-Hua froze. She shifted her eyes toward Wei Lin. His face still reflected no emotion.

Reggie must have been caught, she reasoned, her breath coming in shallow gasps, *and he has turned on me!*

"You will be booked into custody, Mrs. Chen, but before you are, we will read the charges and, if you care to make a statement, you may do so."

Wolsey tugged a notebook from his inside breast pocket. "Let's see. *First degree murder—two counts. Attempted murder—one count. Kidnapping—one count.* That should do it for now."

Fang-Hua caught herself before she spoke. *Kidnapping? If Reggie had been caught, it would only be attempted kidnapping. He must have the child!*

She calmed herself by picking at the tablecloth as though the detective's words had not been directed toward her. "I beg your pardon," she scoffed, "but would you kindly explain how I could have been involved in such sordid activities? My comings and goings are well known. And witnessed."

Wolsey's smile grew. "We have evidence that you planned and financed the abduction of the child of Mei-Xing Li. Your co-conspirators, however, made a mistake. They took the wrong child, the baby son of a friend. Miss Li's daughter was found unharmed."

"Daughter?" Fang-Hua jumped to her feet. "That little whore had a son, not a daughter! *He told me*—" she closed her mouth on the words and sat down, grinding her teeth.

O'Dell was spellbound by the evil coldness of the woman in front of him. Her voice was familiar to him from his own encounter with her and her thugs, and he listened, mesmerized—until her words sank in.

"So you *did* believe Mei-Xing's baby to be a boy!" he declared. "You sent your thugs to take a baby *boy*!" He turned to Wolsey. "*That* is why they took the wrong baby—the two infants were in the same buggy, and they were sent for a *boy*!"

O'Dell could tell Jinhai was stunned, but Wolsey nodded thoughtfully. "That makes sense. Chinese put more stock in boys."

Wolsey turned back to Fang-Hua. "You sent them to steal your own grandson and kill his mother—only, as it turns out, you don't have a grandson." He laughed. "I guess the joke is on you." He took handcuffs from his pocket, but O'Dell shouldered his way toward him.

"Wait. What she just said—*He told me*, she said!" O'Dell rounded on Fang-Hua. "The leader of your conspiracy sent us written evidence that you hired him to kidnap Mei-Xing's baby. He wrote that letter after he shot four men—your little band of thugs.

"He also gave us a man named Clemmins, a woman named Mrs. Gooding, and their phone numbers. The police have already arrested them and they have confessed."

O'Dell's eyes met Fang-Hua's. "The man who wrote the letter signed it with the initials *R.S.* Who is *R.S.*?"

"I'm sure I don't know what you are talking about." Fang-Hua waved her hand dismissively.

O'Dell became quiet, but his face turned down into menacing lines. He crossed to the table where Fang-Hua sat and she drew back, alarmed.

"I am a Pinkerton man, Mrs. Chen. My job is to find missing kids. Kidnapped kids. I have a lot of experience with my work."

He leaned in closer to Fang-Hua's face. "One thing I know? I know that kidnappers are *almost always* caught. And when they are? If the kid is dead, the law hangs the kidnappers—and their co-conspirators hang right along with them."

Fang-Hua shrank before O'Dell's growing rage.

"If we don't find that child, I will see that *you* hang, Madam Chen, and *I will watch when they drop you through that trap door and the rope snaps your neck*," he snarled. "But before that? I will give interviews to every reporter I know, making sure that the precious name of Chen is smeared in every newspaper across the country.

"Your only hope is if we find that baby alive. Now, *R.S.* Who is he?"

"Say nothing more, Fang-Hua. Say nothing at all."

Wei Lin had, at last, come to life. His eyes, simmering with disdain, swept over the men in the room—Wolsey, his officers, Jinhai, Liáng, Bao, Groves, Pounder, and O'Dell.

They came to rest on Bao. "You! My own sister's son. After I gave you every opportunity, you betrayed your own family. You know what the penalty will be. You cannot run far enough to escape your shame—*or the wrath of my hand!*"

"He does not need to run."

Jinhai faced Wei Lin. In a voice that resounded through the room he announced, "I proclaim here today, before these witnesses, that I am adopting Bao Shin Xang as my son and heir."

Wei Lin's expression hardened; Fang-Hua's mouth opened just a little. Bao himself gaped and stared at Mei-Xing's father as though he were mad.

Well done, my friend, well done, Liáng cheered in silence. He could not stop the smile that crept to his lips.

"He is my sister's son," Wei Lin growled, "and no relation to you!"

"But he will be. From this moment on, Bao Shin Xang will be known as Bao Shin Li. And anyone—" he turned in a wide circle to include Wei Lin and his restless thugs and repeated the word with emphasis "—*anyone* who attacks or slanders Bao Shin Li attacks *me* and the might of all I own and those I command." Jinhai's threat was unequivocal.

"Moreover, my protection extends over my daughter Mei-Xing and my granddaughter, Shan-Rose."

"*My granddaughter!*" Fang-Hua screeched. "My son's child!"

Jinhai rounded on Liáng. "What say you of my daughter and her child, Yaochuan Min Liáng?"

"They are mine," Liáng responded in a clear voice. "The child is mine! She will bear my name: She is Shan-Rose Liáng!" A triumph surged through Liáng's breast—a possessive, protective love that enfolded both Mei-Xing and Shan-Rose.

"You hear this man? *He* is Shan-Rose's father." Jinhai turned to Wei Lin and Fang-Hua and added, his voice cold, "Your son is dead. *He has no offspring.*"

A garbled curse burst from Fang-Hua. Lacquered nails bared, she lunged toward Liáng. Wolsey and Jinhai reacted quickly, but it was Wei Lin who caught Fang-Hua by her wrist and twisted it until she shrieked—shrieked and turned her grasping talons on him.

The crack of Wei Lin's open palm connecting with her cheek silenced the room.

He released her wrist and she dropped to the floor, her silk skirts pooling around her.

Wei Lin picked up a linen napkin and dabbed at the blood dripping from his cheek. He motioned to Wolsey.

"You came for her. Take her."

He jerked his head for his guards. They formed around him and, without a backwards glance, Wei Lin Chen stalked from the room.

Wolsey and his officer grabbed at Fang-Hua but they could not fasten the handcuffs as she struggled and screamed curses. Chief Groves and Marshal Pounder helped subdue her until the manacles locked. Wolsey sent one of his men to fetch the other officers.

While they waited, O'Dell leaned near Fang-Hua's face. Her features were distorted and spittle dribbled from her chin.

"Tell me who *R.S.* is!" he demanded.

"Never," she gasped. "But I assure you, he will soon die."

"Tell us where he took the child!"

"Even if I knew, I would not tell you!"

She burst into crazed laughter, and they carried her, kicking and writhing, from the room. O'Dell could only stand there thinking, *She does not know where baby Edmund is! What will I tell Joy?*

O'Dell, Jinhai, and the others who had confronted Fang-Hua were now alone in the Chen's dining chamber. It appeared that none of Wei Lin or Fang-Hua's servants remained to show them out.

From the shadowed doorway a timid voice whispered, "Sir? Sir, I can tell you what you wish to know."

Bao blinked. "Will you come forward so we can see you? We are alone, I believe. No one will hear you."

A small woman, likely a servant, crept into the room.

"Your name is Qiong, isn't it? You are my wife Ling-Ling's cousin?"

The woman nodded. "Yes, Bao. For Ling-Ling's sake, I will tell that man who *R.S.* is." She pointed to O'Dell.

O'Dell slowly turned to her. "You know him?"

"Oh, yes, sir. Fang-Hua called him *Reggie*, sir. Her men brought him here and she had him locked in the basement—very hush-hush—until she sent him away to get her grandson."

O'Dell stared at her and then at Bao. "*R.S.* stands for Regis St. John—*Morgan.* Morgan has Edmund?"

How could I have been so blind! O'Dell raged. *I believed he had fled far from Fang-Hua's clutches!*

He asked the woman, "If this *Reggie* were to bring Mei-Xing's baby here, what preparations were made for caring for the child?"

Qiong drew closer. "It is known that Madam Chen sent a woman to Denver to be wet nurse to the child. The woman had recently lost her own baby."

"We found no evidence of a woman at the house Fang-Hua's men were in. The men were all dead, but we found no woman."

O'Dell was talking to himself, grasping at possibilities. "Why would he take Joy's son away? As part of a disguise? Or out of simple spite? Where would Morgan take this woman and Edmund if he dared not come back here?"

The woman, thinking O'Dell was asking her for answers, shook her head. "I do not know, sir, but he hid himself from Fang-Hua once before, and she hunted him and found him. I am sure that now he will run as far as he can to never be found by her again."

As O'Dell heard her words, his heart sank.

Chapter 29

O'Dell was silent on the drive back to the Li residence.

It all made sense now—the urgent note *to him* with the Acorn Street address; the letter left at the house; the snide, insincere apology made *to him*—*Sorry to have taken the wrong child, O'Dell*—and the enigmatic signature *he* should have recognized: *R.S.*

Morgan.

I was right. He was laughing at us, taunting us, and especially Joy. How is it that at every juncture Morgan has plagued Joy's life? O'Dell deliberated. *The fire in Omaha was designed to run her out of town. Burning down the lodge was supposed to drive her from Corinth. Morgan was behind both these heartbreaks.*

O'Dell could still recall every detail of the night the lodge in Corinth burned.

That night in the plaza, Joy managed, in one blow, to uncloak Morgan's crooked dealings, destroy his ill-gotten wealth, and send him to jail. And I was right there helping her to thwart him. Morgan would have taken that personally.

O'Dell's mind wandered back to that scene, the torches lighting Corinth's little town square, and Joy, her hair hanging loose about her shoulders, passionate but eloquent, her every word tearing down the false empire Morgan had built.

How Morgan must hate Joy, O'Dell realized. *And now he has abducted Edmund. Did Morgan know that he had taken Joy's baby when he found that his men did not have Mei-Xing's child?*

Rose's words in Palmer House's great room the night before they left for Seattle came back to him: *I have a concern . . . I am afraid my journal contains many personal details.* O'Dell had to face the possibility that if Morgan were in possession of Rose Thoresen's journal and had read it, he would know, with certainty, who Edmund was.

When the cars returned to the Li residence, Joy was standing in the doorway, watching for them. O'Dell dragged himself up the walk behind Jinhai and Liáng, loathe to burst the fragile bubble of hope to which she clung.

This is not the first time you have had to deliver bad news to a parent, he told himself, but it did not help, because this was not any parent—*this was Joy.*

Without looking her in the face, he took her elbow and steered her into Jinhai's library. He could feel her trembling as he seated her. He forced himself to keep his tone level and impersonal. If he did not envelop himself in detached professionalism, he feared he would shatter with her.

"Joy. The police have arrested Fang-Hua; she is in custody right now. When we confronted her with the proof that she initiated and financed Edmund's abduction, she refused to provide information about the man whom she hired to do so. In a fit of rage she admitted to hiring him, but would not give us his name." O'Dell paused. "I demanded that she tell us where Edmund is. Her answer was, *Even if I knew, I would not tell you.*"

O'Dell finally looked at her. "The truth is, Joy, I can spot a lie when I hear it, and . . . I don't think she was lying. I don't believe she knows where Edmund is."

Joy was shaking all over now, shock taking hold. O'Dell recognized it. He stepped to the door and called a servant to him. "Mrs. Michaels requires hot tea immediately. Please add several spoons of sugar. Hurry."

He turned back to Joy and gripped her hand, hating to give her even worse news. "After they took Fang-Hua away, one of the servants, a cousin to Bao's wife, approached us. She was able to tell us whose initials were *R.S.*"

Joy's eyes were glassy when they lifted to his. "Whose?"

"Regis St. John—Morgan's real name. Morgan took Edmund."

It was, as O'Dell had feared, too much for her. She pitched forward, unconscious. O'Dell caught her before she slid to the floor and then he called for help. Breona and Bao were first to respond. Jinhai was right behind them.

"Please call a doctor," O'Dell rasped.

The doctor arrived after Breona and Mei-Xing had put Joy to bed. He said she was, understandably, under a great deal of stress, and he recommended complete rest. Breona stayed with her while she slept.

Downstairs, the atmosphere in the Lis' living room had changed—the tension of impending danger was gone—but disappointment clung to those in the room: They knew now who had taken baby Edmund, and even O'Dell had little hope of successfully tracking him.

It's been a week now. He has a week's lead over us. O'Dell thought about Morgan traveling with a woman who would be nursing Edmund. Like a family.

Finding them would be like trying to find a pebble in a rockslide.

Mei-Xing and Liáng sat together but apart from the others, talking privately. Mei-Xing's mother and father joined them.

"Will you marry in Denver?" Jinhai asked. Ting-Xiu waited with sad eyes for their response.

"We will," Liáng answered. "But we hope you will come and be part of it. You are Mei-Xing's parents, after all, and Shan-Rose's grandparents. You will always be welcome with us—" he broke into a rueful laugh.

"What is it?" Ting-Xiu asked, concerned.

"It is only that at present I share a small two-bedroom house with two other men, although I assume Bao will not be returning to Denver with us?"

"No. He will stay here. I will have my attorneys draw up the adoption papers this very week and will begin training him in my business. And now that Bao does not have to fear for his life, he can reclaim what is his in his own right—his house and possessions."

"Ah! Then I now share a small house with only *one* other man." Liáng laughed but turned to Mei-Xing, his serious eyes finding hers.

"I had not intended to ask you to marry me—I would not have dared to ask you—before I had a home for you and Shan-Rose. Are you willing to wait a while until I can adequately provide for you?"

Ting-Xiu tugged at Jinhai's sleeve and he placed his hand on hers, patting it. "Mei-Xing will have a generous dowry when she marries, my dear friend, and Ting-Xiu and I wish to buy you a home as a wedding gift. More than that, we will help finance the ministry you have given yourself to."

Jinhai and Ting-Xiu both stood and bowed low to Liáng. "We owe you our lives, Yaochuan Min Liáng. It was you who led us to the Savior and you who reunited us with our daughter and granddaughter. We could not be prouder to call you our son-in-law, nor could we be more pleased that you will be Shan-Rose's father."

O'Dell entered the Lis' living room and saw that Inspector Wolsey had come to report on Fang-Hua's booking. He, Jinhai, Gresham, and Bao were talking near the fire.

"Wei Lin has no options left," O'Dell heard Wolsey saying. "The court will air all the filthy things his wife has done—and we will use the occasion to delve into every aspect of Wei Lin Chen's businesses. We have been waiting a long time for just such an opportunity!"

"I fear you underestimate him," Jinhai murmured. "I sincerely doubt you will have such an opportunity."

O'Dell drew near to hear what Jinhai was saying.

"Why, what do you mean?" Wolsey was indignant. Gresham frowned but said nothing.

The crease between Bao's eyes also came together as he pondered Jinhai's enigmatic words. "Mr. Li, what do you think Wei Lin will do? He cannot hope to prevent Fang-Hua from going to trial or keep the trial from the public eye. The newspapers will sensationalize her crimes. It will destroy the Chen family name. I cannot see how Wei Lin will deal with the shame."

"Bao, I ask you to think as Wei Lin. He has an option left that will spare his family all you describe."

Wolsey looked from Jinhai to Bao and, finally, to O'Dell. "I don't get it. What is he saying?"

The glimmer of an idea crept into O'Dell's mind, a thought terrible in its cold-blooded practicality. "Jinhai. We must do something!"

But Jinhai shrugged. "And what would you have us do, Mr. O'Dell?" It was as though Jinhai's eyes shuttered and closed as they watched, leaving his face expressionless.

Gresham and Wolsey were still searching, trying to understand. Bao blinked with uncertainty as his mind reached the same conclusion O'Dell had come to.

"Mr. Li! Will he—"

"Let us speak no more of it, my son," Jinhai interjected. He placed an arm around Bao's shoulders. "I assure you, we can do nothing to change what will happen."

A servant interrupted them. "Begging your pardon, sir. There is a telephone call for Mr. O'Dell."

"Who is it, please?"

"A Mrs. Thoresen, sir."

O'Dell's heart twisted. "I'm coming."

He excused himself and found the call waiting for him in Jinhai's library. "Hello?"

"Mr. O'Dell."

He could hear the pain and stress in those two words. "I'm here, Mrs. Thoresen! Is it Grant?"

"Yes." She sobbed once and then caught herself. "Please bring Joy home. He is asking for her. There isn't much time."

O'Dell thought of Joy, upstairs in an exhausted sleep. "We will take the next available train."

"Thank you. Oh, Mr. O'Dell! Is there any news of Edmund? I so want to be able to tell Grant . . ."

O'Dell bowed his head. "I'm sorry, no. Fang-Hua has been arrested, but . . . but she does not know where Edmund is."

The silence on the other end of the line lingered until O'Dell broke it. "Please tell Grant I am bringing Joy to him. Tell him he must hold on."

Gresham's man, Jeffers, was waiting for them outside Union Station when O'Dell, Joy, and Breona returned to Denver. The doctor had given O'Dell a few more sleeping pills, and he had insisted Joy take one after boarding the train in Seattle.

"Sleep, Joy," O'Dell whispered. "So that you are stronger when we reach Denver."

And she *had* slept. The wheels of the train had hummed over the rails, the hours had ticked by, and Joy had slept on in the seat across from O'Dell, curled upon the hard bench, her head cradled in Breona's lap.

When she finally awoke, O'Dell could see her gather herself for what was ahead. Before they reached the station, the three of them put their heads close together and prayed.

O'Dell asked Jeffers only one thing before they slipped into the motorcar. "He is holding on, Mr. O'Dell," Jeffers replied, but he wasted no time sliding behind the car's wheel.

Morrow, standing on the front porch, opened the door for them. "Please go straight back, Mrs. Michaels," he directed.

O'Dell took Joy by the arm and walked her through the house, out the back, and to the cottage she shared with Grant. She was trembling as they reached the door.

"Courage," he whispered.

She nodded. He opened the door for her.

He followed her inside, hoping for a word with Grant, hoping it was not as bad as Rose had intimated, hoping there was still time. Rose looked up and saw them; she sprang forward and embraced Joy.

O'Dell stayed in the cottage's tiny vestibule where he could see the corner of the bed as he had after Joy had given birth. Down at the end of the bed, O'Dell observed Tabitha. She was worn, but still strong. She nodded to him and then looked away.

Joy sank to her knees next to the bed, and O'Dell could only see her feet and the skirt of her dress from where he waited. He could hear the breathing machine. He could also hear—and it broke his heart—Grant's loud, labored gasps.

Rose came toward him. He opened his arms to her and she sank into them, clinging to him, sobbing. He held her tight and found himself stroking the back of her head, his own tears streaming down his face.

The better part of an hour elapsed. Rose remained in O'Dell's comforting arms. They waited.

Then the machine went silent. O'Dell could no longer hear Grant's gasping. The room was filled with only a very loud silence.

Tabitha's hand crept to her face and she covered her eyes.

Rose straightened and squared her shoulders. "I must go to Joy now, Mr. O'Dell."

"Yes."

Oh, Grant! O'Dell mourned. *I wanted to say goodbye.*

"Thank you," Rose murmured. She left the shelter of his arms and went to her daughter.

O'Dell returned to his hotel that afternoon and put through a trunk call to Chicago. When the operator rang him back, he heard the voice of his boss over the line.

"O'Dell?"

"I'm here." O'Dell paused only a moment. He was taking a step that would forever alter his life, but he had promises to keep.

"Parsons, is the offer to head the Denver office still on the table?"

Chapter 30

The cell door clanged shut and Fang-Hua took stock of the squalid surroundings. She had sat for days in a Seattle jail before being transferred to this women's facility to await trial. She had yet to see her lawyer—a delay that enraged her.

It is Wei Lin's doing, she fumed. *He thinks to frustrate me by keeping my attorney from me? You cannot do so forever, my husband!*

While she was being moved, she had received notice that her attorney would visit the next day. Now she stood in the middle of a cell whose stone walls seeped moisture and reeked of mildew.

I will not allow this hellhole to degrade me, she swore. *And I will not be here long. My lawyer will come tomorrow and he will see that I am released.*

She knew, however, that she would not be returning to her husband's house. In her vain, racing thoughts she mocked Wei Lin. *I have plenty of money, dear husband—more than you know, you fool! I will build a new life—and an empire that will rival yours.*

But when her thoughts turned toward Dean Morgan, her blood boiled. *I will spend my entire fortune, if needed, to hunt you down and watch you die,* she vowed. *I rue the day I trusted you to bring my grandson to me.*

It occurred to her again that she had no grandson—only a worthless granddaughter—and it surprised her to find that she still wanted the child, the only tangible piece of her son remaining on earth.

So! What need have I of a husband or a grandson? I will find a way to procure my granddaughter, Fang-Hua plotted, *and I will raise her as my own; I will rear her and mold her into my image. She will assume control of my empire when I am gone.*

The novel idea pleased her and she began to think on it and how she would use her fortune to first crush the Chen family and then take control of all Wei Lin's interests.

The day drew on toward dinner time. The barred door at the end of the cellblock opened. The women in the other cells stood to attention.

Fang-Hua sneered. *They cannot force me to follow such lock-step rules that mark prisoners as less than human. I am above such things.*

One by one, the guards opened cell doors up and down the line—all except Fang-Hua's cell door. The women prisoners stepped out of their cells and filed down the hallway and out the end of the cellblock. The door at the end clanged shut after them.

Fang-Hua had paid scant attention to what the guards were doing other than to observe to herself, *Surely the warden knows that I am not to associate with such trash or eat their common food!*

She was now alone in the cellblock yet no one arrived to deliver a meal to her. *Fine,* she fumed, and again began plotting her next steps once her lawyer achieved her release.

When the door at the end of the cellblock opened again, Fang-Hua heard two sets of footsteps pad toward her cell. *Good! They are bringing my dinner. Or perhaps my lawyer is finally here,* she rejoiced.

Instead, two burly guards stood in front of her cell, one medium height, the other tall.

Fang-Hua glanced at them and then at their faces—their hard, implacable faces. They each held a short club.

"Hey, there, Madam Chen. I'm Bob. This here's Charley," the tall one said, smiling. "Wei Lin Chen sends his greetings." His glittering eyes and cruelly twisted mouth were not lost on Fang-Hua, who sputtered into an uncertain silence.

The guard fitted a key into her cell door and turned it. A moment later both guards were inside her cell. Fang-Hua backed up against the cell's wall.

She had nowhere else to go.

The shorter guard thumped his truncheon on his open palm. "Wei Lin asked us to deliver a message. He was very specific, your husband was," he grinned. "He said to tell you that he would no longer allow your behavior to sully his family's honor."

The man screwed up his face and, in a mocking imitation of Wei Lin, quoted, "*My dear Fang-Hua, a trial, no matter the outcome, can only serve to sully the Chen name. I will not permit this dishonor to touch my family.*" The man laughed. "He said you would understand."

"Yep. So his instructions to us were *very* specific," the tall one repeated. "He said we were to, what, Charley?"

"Make our little session *very* long, Bob," Charley giggled, anxious to begin.

"That's right! And make it *very* painful?" Bob snickered.

"Oh, Bob! You're a card! Yes, *very* painful. But don't forget—it is also to be *very* permanent."

"Why, Charley! I would never forget that!"

Fang-Hua opened her mouth to protest when the first blows landed on her. Her shrieks and screams for help echoed without answer against the damp stone walls of her cell.

෧ ✳ ෧

Chapter 31

The trees above their heads rustled in a warm breeze; new-green leaves and a scattering of clouds shaded the mourners gathered near the freshly dug grave. Next to the grave, a simple coffin rested upon a stanchion. Joy stood before the mourners, as tall and with as much decorum as she could muster.

"My husband, Grant Michaels, faithfully served his Savior all the years that I knew him. I don't believe I have ever known a man as devoted to the Lord and his family as he was, unless it was my father, Jan Thoresen.

"To lose Grant . . . *again*, will pain me the rest of my days on this earth, but . . . but you may be surprised to hear that it will not pain me as much as it did four years ago when his ship went down at sea.

"I confess to you that the woman I was when I lost Grant the first time is not the woman I am today. My faith in my heavenly Father has changed in these last years. Grant and I both grew in our faith and, although our love for each other was deep and abiding, our love for our God was greater, as it should be."

She paused and looked off in the distance as though remembering something. "I should say, too, that I have had a good example of how to deal with loss and suffering. I have watched my mother bear with dignity her own grief and loneliness. She has set her heart to live a life of service to the Lord and to others. How can I not but follow her example?"

Joy swallowed and waited until her voice was hers to control again.

"My mother has, several times in the past two years, mentioned something I thought rather curious. She has alluded to her "prairie heritage." I didn't understand her—I didn't realize what it meant. I think now I do.

"Some thirty years ago, during the darkest time in her life, she came west, searching for solace. In a tiny country church out on the prairie, she found Jesus and made him her Lord and Savior, and she found consolation in a simple farming life lived for God.

"Farmers may seem plain and unsophisticated, but the hardships of the prairie require honest work, spines of steel, and faith that cannot be shaken. This is the heritage she found out on the prairie, *this faith that cannot be shaken*, and this is the heritage she and my father passed to me as I was growing up and the heritage I hope to pass on.

"We are here to say goodbye to my beloved husband and to testify how he lived for Christ. We will see him again in the Resurrection. I am confident in this and look forward to That Day. His testimony will live on in all of us—and in our son.

"Which is why, while we are here together, I will also speak of our little boy. My arms long to hold him. I have wept until I have no tears left. I tell you, my heart is broken, but I will also proclaim to you that *my faith is not.*

"Where is Edmund? Where is our baby? I ask this question every hour of every day.

"I do not believe he is . . . dead, but I could be wrong. If I am wrong, then *I know* with certainty that he has merely gone home to join his papa, ahead of the rest of us. I say *home*, because life upon this earth is not our real home, you know. Here we are merely sojourners and pilgrims. We are merely passing through.

"But because I sense in my heart that Edmund *is* alive, I will not forget to pray for him. I have set my heart to remember him in prayer daily and to believe that, even though he is apart from me, *God will make himself known to Edmund* and, on That Day, the day when we see Jesus face-to-face and every injustice is revealed and recompensed, we will see each other again and all this grief will vanish away.

"I spoke a moment ago about my prairie heritage—the enduring faith my papa and mama lived as an example for me. It is because of their faith that I have such hope for Edmund even though he is, today, lost to us.

"You see, what is lost to us is not—*is not*—lost to God! I remember Papa saying this very thing: *In God, the lost are found.* Our Lord sees the entire world—and nothing in all of his creation is hidden to him! I am comforted to know that wherever Edmund is, *God is there with him.*

"How do I feel about the man who took our son? I confess that I am tempted to hate him and to curse him, but . . . I cannot call myself a Christian if I do.

"And so, here and now, I declare that I forgive Dean Morgan for every wrong he has done me. I leave his life and our vindication in God's hands. I believe that the just and righteous God I serve *will make all things right in the end.*

"I will not hate and I will not be afraid; I will not allow my mind's eye to wound me with fearful imaginings. And I will not lose hope.

"This is how I stand before you today; this is how I will live: with faith that cannot be shaken. From now until I draw my last breath, I will believe that, if I cannot hold Edmund in *my* arms, my heavenly Father will hold him in *his* arms—until he brings us all safely home to himself.

"Like my papa, I declare, *that in God, the lost are found.*"

A ripple of *amens* followed Joy as she stepped toward the grave. Tears washing her face, she kissed her hand and placed it on the coffin, letting it linger. Then she straightened and, composing her face, she turned away.

Edmund O'Dell was next to walk to and stand beside the coffin. As he did so, he was remembering the most remarkable conversation of his life.

My friend, I don't have many months left to me—No, no. Why do you deny this? It serves no good purpose. Nothing can be done to help me, and death comes to us all in due time, doesn't it? My departure will be my entrance into eternal joy, and I am glad beyond measure that you, too, have received the Savior's gift. Someday you and I will meet again, in the glorious presence of God the Father and his Son!

Now, because I am dying, Edmund O'Dell, my dearest friend, I must talk plainly: I know you once had feelings for Joy. Please do not protest. I knew this the first time I saw you look at her—while you still thought her a widow.

I do not mention this in condemnation! Rather, I say this to one of the most honorable men I have had the privilege of knowing. I have never feared you, Mr. O'Dell, because I know your worthy heart, just as I know that Joy's heart belongs to me. No, you did not dishonor me, and I say this to your credit, realizing the struggle you endured.

Why did I write and ask you to come to Denver? Before it is too late, I wish you to make me a solemn promise. I wish you to promise me that when I am gone you will watch over Joy and our son. In time, if it is God's will and when Joy's grief allows her to love again, I hope you will marry her and raise my son—my son to whom I gave your name.

I cannot think of any man I would wish to be a father to my son besides you! I say, "if it is God's will," because he will lead and guide you in this. I am content that, if you pray and follow his direction, all will be well.

I am asking a difficult thing of you, my friend, I know—but it is so strong in my heart, and I sense death closing in on me. I cannot let what time I have left slip away without speaking to you and asking for your sincere word.

Will you give me your word on this?

O'Dell, too, rested his hand on the casket for a moment. "I will miss you, Grant, and I will miss your example of godly manhood. As long as I live, I will not stop searching for Edmund. When I find him, I will cherish him as my own. I will not relinquish my promises to you."

The End

Postscript

Peter Granger—AKA Dean Morgan, formerly Shelby Franklin, formerly a dozen or so men including Regis St. John—settled back in the easy chair of his new home and sighed with contentment.

His house, perhaps a mile from the fabled Garden District, boasted nothing extraordinary when compared to the Italianate, Colonial, or Greek Revival beauties of St. Charles Avenue, but it still had character—the kind of character that marked him as a man of wealth and means.

The bag of money Fang-Hua had "contributed" had paid for the house, and he still had sufficient cash in reserve, more than enough to establish him in his new life. Peter Granger, his widowed sister, Alicia, and her son Michael would do well in New Orleans.

I don't know why I didn't come here sooner, Granger/Morgan mused. *The hospitality of this town suits me.*

He was already forming valuable friendships and connections—but not, this time, to embezzle from. No, here in New Orleans with the leg-up his cash assets afforded him, Peter Granger would build a perfectly respectable and permanent life. Here Joy Thoresen Michaels would not interfere; here the Pinkertons would never find him.

Granger had discreetly sought and found a man whose artistry for forged documents passed even his discerning eye. Granger had paid a small fortune for false birth certificates for himself, Alicia, and Michael, and a death certificate for his late "brother," Alicia's "husband" and Michael's "father."

As extra insurance, Granger had planned to eliminate the forger, but the man had not stayed in business this long without honing his own instincts. He had sent a messenger to Granger to deliver Granger's finished birth certificate and this neatly penned message:

Send the remainder of the payment with this boy. He has no knowledge of our arrangement or where I am; I am watching him and will contact him for delivery when I know you are not following him. When I receive the money, I will be leaving town and will send your remaining documents to you by mail—once I am confident that you pose no threat to me and mine.

Granger had no choice but to do as the forger instructed, but he smiled thinking about it: The forger was as much a professional as he was. Granger could admire him for that.

His thoughts returned to Joy Michaels and the Pinkerton man, O'Dell. *No, they will not find us here,* he was certain.

And here, from a safe distance, he had smiled and gloated over the Denver and Seattle newspapers Alicia had purchased for him from a vendor in town. Even weeks and months later, the news was quite titillating.

Granger's eyes glittered with satisfaction as he reread the articles in the Denver Post: *No Progress in Kidnapping,* but he laughed aloud each time he reexamined the article in the Seattle Daily Times: *Chen Found Dead in Cell.* Fang-Hua dead? Why, it was better than candy on Christmas!

He moved to his desk and, with a pair of sharp scissors, cut both articles from the papers he had carefully kept and read many times. He laid the clippings on the desk and removed a key from his pocket. He inserted the key in the bottom desk drawer and drew out a small book bound in wine-colored leather.

He had read every entry in the journal twice, some three times. He thought the book a unique perspective from which to view his enemies, Joy Michaels and Edmund O'Dell.

The friendship between Joy's husband and O'Dell puzzled Granger. Their lives seemed incongruous . . . and yet the Michaels had named their son after the Pinkerton man. *Edmund.*

Granger shrugged his shoulders and slipped the clippings into the back of the book, between blank pages. *Pages that will never be filled,* he thought. He knew that by holding on to the book he was taking an unnecessary risk—it was, after all, the only physical evidence tying him to the murders in Denver and the kidnapping of the Michaels' baby—but he had not yet let the book go.

He chewed his lip for a moment. *I've derived all the pleasure I can from its pages,* he admitted, but he was still loath to destroy it as his more practical side insisted he do.

A baby's waking cries interrupted his deliberations. Granger smiled. The little tyke was growing on him, an unexpected benefit to his decision to punish Joy Michaels *ad infinitum.* The boy, at five months, was a happy thing, already attempting to crawl.

"Peter? Brother, I have my hands in bread dough. Would you mind getting Michael from his crib and bringing him to his highchair?"

"I will be right there."

Agnes/Alicia was proving to be a better bargain than he had imagined: She was compliant, content to see to his and the child's needs, and had fully embraced her new identity and station in life.

She was brighter than Granger had given her credit for, too. As Granger had begun redecorating the house, she had learned styles, fabrics, and color schemes, showing herself to be a quick study with passing taste.

Granger climbed the staircase to the nursery. He had allowed Alicia to plan its décor herself—pale blue walls with blue and yellow sprigged paper above the chair rail, a soft blue rug over parquet floors, fluffy curtains, and a walnut rocking chair to match the walnut crib.

He bent over the crib. Michael stopped crying and beamed at him, displaying four tiny teeth and Joy Michaels' brilliant blue eyes.

Granger grinned back. "Hello, little man. Come to Uncle Peter." He lifted the baby up in his arms.

Don't miss the powerful conclusion of
A Prairie Heritage

Book 6:
Lost Are Found

About the Author

Vikki Kestell has more than 20 years of career experience as a writing, instructional design, and communications professional in government, academia, semiconductor manufacturing, health care, and nonprofit organizations. She holds a Ph.D. in Organizational Learning and Instructional Technologies.

An accomplished speaker and teacher, Vikki belongs to Tramway Community Church in Albuquerque, New Mexico, where she has taught adult Sunday school and a Bible study for working women. She and her husband, Conrad Smith, make their home in Albuquerque.

To keep abreast of new book releases, visit her website, http://www.vikkikestell.com/, or find her on Facebook, http://www.facebook.com/TheWritingOfVikkiKestell.

A Prairie Heritage

Prequel: *Land of Dust and Tears* (free Kindle download)
Book 1: *A Rose Blooms Twice*
Book 2: *Wild Heart on the Prairie*
Book 3: *Joy on This Mountain*
Book 4: *The Captive Within*
Book 5: *Stolen*
Book 6: *Lost Are Found*

25131838R00142

Made in the USA
San Bernardino, CA
19 October 2015